"It's almost like you don't hate me anymore," he teased her.

She'd been pretty horrible to him, she supposed. And she'd had her reasons, of course, but he couldn't know that and they weren't his fault. "I never . . . hated you," she tried to explain. "I just thought . . ."

"Thought . . . what?"

She blinked. And was honest. "That you . . . seemed like trouble."

He responded by freeing his fingers from her mittened grip, changing the connection so that he held her hands in his now. And he leaned closer, a lock of dark hair falling over his forehead as he said, "You got that part right then, Candy."

She pulled in her breath.

"Because the truth is, I'm more trouble than you can handle."

And then he kissed her.

By Toni Blake

TONI BLAKE

CHRISTMAS IN DESTINY

A DESTINY NOVEL

AVONBOOKS

An Imprint of HarperCollins*Publishers*

CHRISTMAS IN DESTINY. Copyright © 2016 by Toni Herzog. All rights reserved. Printed in the United States of America. No part of this book may be used or reproduced in any manner whatsoever without written permission except in the case of brief quotations embodied in critical articles and reviews. For information, address HarperCollins Publishers, 195 Broadway, New York, NY 10007.

First Avon Books mass market printing: November 2016

ISBN 978-0-06239259-6

Avon Trademark Reg. U.S. Pat. Off. and in Other Countries, Marca Registrada, Hecho en U.S.A.
Avon, Avon Books, and the Avon logo are trademarks of HarperCollins Publishers.
HarperCollins® is a registered trademark of HarperCollins Publishers.

16 17 18 19 20   QGM   10 9 8 7 6 5 4 3 2 1

*To Blair Herzog, Lindsey Faber, and Jacqueline Daher—
angels in disguise.*

Acknowledgments

Some of these acknowledgements may sound familiar from earlier books, because I habitually turn to the same people for help with my work. After all, if it ain't broke, don't fix it. And when someone helps you repeatedly, they definitely deserve to keep being thanked.

Thank you to Renee Norris, who lent me her insights and suggestions on this project over and over again. I don't think there's a literary problem she can't solve or work around.

Thank you to Lindsey Faber, for feedback and reactions throughout the writing process, every time I needed them, and for reassurance that my vision was clear.

Thank you to Robin Zentmeyer, who, when I said I needed a name for a white cat, immediately said, "Frosty!" And Frosty, the newest Destiny Cat, was born.

Thank you to my publishing team—my agent, Christina Hogrebe; my editor, May Chen; and everyone at

Avon Books—for all you do for me and my work! I'm so grateful for our long association—this book celebrates ten happy years together!

And thank you, last but not least, to my loyal and beloved readers, who I know are happy to be coming back to Destiny for Christmas this year. Wishing you all a lovely, heartwarming holiday!

"Tonight's his crucial night."

Franklin, *It's a Wonderful Life*

Prologue

Snow had just begun to fall as Shane Dalton sprinkled his father's ashes over a stark, lonely little pond on a farm outside Mansfield, Ohio. His father's childhood home, and "a place where I was happy," his dad had said just before his death last month. "And there weren't many of those."

Shane stood looking around the area—thinking about his father's life, and his own. They'd both made a lot of mistakes. And he'd probably make some more—after all, he was only thirty-four.

He'd been born near here, raised here until he was nine—but he'd never been back. Never had a reason to come. And while one part of him thought maybe he should linger a little, take a look around . . . the rest of him thought: Nah, waste of time. A brisk gust of wintry wind sliced through him, confirming the decision.

Next stop: Miami. Fast cars, fast women, and the first Christmas he'd spend not surrounded by Montana snow. He'd never liked Christmas anyway—so a few lights hung up in palm trees would suit him just fine.

There was a job waiting for him. Though he wasn't sure exactly what it was—he had only an address and a phone number. A guy named Donnie V. was going to hook him up—a friend of a friend of a friend. All he knew was the money sounded good. And the fast cars and fast women didn't sound bad, either.

Climbing back behind the wheel of his Chevy pickup, he set the GPS on his cell phone for Miami, ready to start the next leg of his cross-country road trip to a new life. He'd spent a long time heading east, but now it was finally time to turn south.

As he was about to put the truck in Drive, though, he stopped. Thought a minute. Picked the phone back up.

Despite himself, he keyed in the name of the place his father had muttered only a moment before he'd passed away. "Go there after Mansfield," he'd mumbled to Shane. "Something there for you."

"What? What's there for me?"

He hadn't been able to pull any more from his dad on the topic before, seconds later, his father's eyes had closed for the last time. So he'd decided it was the ramblings of a man out of his head on pain medication.

And yet the words had stayed with him. *Something there for you.*

What the hell could that mean?

Hitting the search button, he found that a town by that name actually existed—and lay only a couple hours away. *Well, I'll be damned.*

Kind of out in the middle of nowhere, but when would he ever pass this way again?

So . . . maybe he should make a quick side trip before it got dark. Just to check the place out. See if he could figure out what his dad had been talking about. If it had even meant anything at all.

It wouldn't take long. Then he'd be back on the road to sun and fun and money, three things he'd never had quite enough of.

Phone still in hand, he changed the destination on his GPS once more—to Destiny, Ohio.

"There's a squall in there that's shapin' up into a storm."

Uncle Billy, *It's a Wonderful Life*

One

$\mathcal{F}$unny how a snowy night could change the landscape, the whole feel of a place. Candice Sheridan stood peering out the window into an early December snow that had transformed picturesque Blue Valley Road and the lake on the other side into an unrecognizable and desolate-feeling place. The snow had been falling heavily since this afternoon and didn't appear to be letting up anytime soon. Using her mailbox next to the road as a measuring stick, she concluded there was nearly a foot of wet, heavy snow on the ground already.

The snowplows would come in the morning, and if she needed anything, her neighbors Mick and Jenny Brody were only a phone call away in their cottage up the road. And she had plenty of provisions. But winter nights like this always made her feel lonely. Even the blinking lights on her Christmas tree and strung across the mantel didn't take away the feeling of emptiness that settled inside her.

It was one thing to close yourself off from life by choice—but another to have nature do it for you.

Easing back into the cozy, overstuffed chair next to the fire, she reached for her open laptop—only to find a solid white cat stretched across the keyboard.

"Is this your way of saying I should call it a night, Frosty?"

The cat looked up but didn't answer. He was the sort of cat who always seemed mildly bored with her—except for when she was feeding him, of course. Then he was a regular meowing machine, but the rest of the time, he mostly just lounged around acting like some kind of kitty king.

"Sometimes I wonder why I adopted you," she said, using both hands to remove his lanky body from the computer. She was teasing, of course, but she wouldn't have minded a more affectionate cat.

Amy Whitaker, who ran the bookstore in town, had a habit of taking in stray cats and then finding them homes—even if it meant foisting them off on people who weren't necessarily in the market for a pet. Frosty had lived at the store, Under the Covers, for several months before Candice had finally decided that maybe a kitty would be nice company for a woman like her—a woman who lived and worked alone in a large house in a rural area. "So where's the affection and company?" she chided the cat. He was curling up in front of the fireplace now, and pretty much ignoring her—as usual.

Taking up the laptop, she refocused on her work. She made her living as a technical writer, composing instruction guides and owner's manuals for everything from toys to software programs. Her current project: an instruction and safety manual for a vacuum cleaner set to hit the market in spring.

She still found herself preoccupied by the snowfall, though—or more by the idea of it. Wondering how much there would be, and still thinking about how it could alter one's world so drastically—at least for a little while. So after typing just a few lines, she took Frosty's implied advice and closed the lid on the computer for the night. She moved back to the front bay window and pulled aside the pale sheers to look back out on a sea of white and the dark surface of the lake beyond. She wondered if it would freeze. Normally that didn't happen until after Christmas, but temps were unusually low for December, and winter definitely seemed to be blowing into the region early and fierce.

Letting out a sigh, she let the thin curtain drop, checked the dying fire in the hearth, and then scratched Frosty's chest as she said, "You were right—calling it a night." And after climbing the old wooden staircase in the stately Victorian home she'd bought a few years ago, she changed into a cozy old red-and-white flannel nightgown. It was definitely a night that called for flannel.

As she pulled up the covers on her four-poster bed, she was heartened to remember that tomorrow the snow would be cleared and life would get back to normal.

And with this much snow—well, it was early in the month yet, but unless a whole lot of melting took place, looked like it would be a white Christmas in Destiny.

Bang. Bang. Bang.

Candice's eyes sprang open as the jarring noise jolted her awake.

Bang. Bang. Bang.

What on earth? She briskly sat up, trying to get her bearings in the dark.

The sound came again. Louder this time. And as she sat there in bed, the room lit only by the deluge of white outside, she realized someone was beating on her door in the middle of the night. Which seemed almost impossible given that the weather outside was more than a little frightful.

Her heart beat rapidly as the relentless banging continued. Even while she dragged herself out of bed and headed toward the stairs, her sleep-addled brain whirled. As a woman who lived alone in an isolated area, she didn't particularly want to answer. But what if it was Jenny or Mick—what if something was wrong with their little boy?

Flipping on the dim porch light, she made out a shadowy male figure and concluded it was indeed Mick. The fact that he was out in this weather, at this hour, filled her with worry. So she flung open the door.

Then gasped. It wasn't Mick.

It wasn't Mick at all.

She didn't know who *this* was—but he looked horribly out of place, and a little bit scary. "Wh-wh- . . ." Words failed her in her fright.

The tall, dark stranger regarded her through piercing blue eyes. "Look, I know it's late, but my pickup spun out and I hit a snowbank around that last bend." His voice was deep and his tone unapologetic as he pointed over his shoulder in the general direction of the road. "Can't get a signal on my cell, so need to use your phone."

Strangers didn't just show up on porches in the middle of the night in Destiny, and she simply stared at him as if he were a ghost standing at her door in the blowing snow. The scary kind, with a lock of dark hair dipping over his forehead, a thick shadowy stubble on his chin, and even a little scar near his right eye. Though she wasn't sure if ghosts bothered to knock.

"Who are you going to call?" she managed to ask. Then blinked repeatedly. It was an unfortunate habit of hers—blinking when she was nervous.

He arched a critical brow as a cold wind blew around them, his expression implying that maybe he thought she was still half-asleep. "A tow truck," he said, enunciating, as if the answer was obvious.

But he was clearly uninformed about something *she* thought obvious. "Have you seen the roads? A tow truck won't come out here when it's like this. I don't know how you got *any* truck out here tonight. And we don't have a tow truck in Destiny anyway."

His eyebrows *both* shot up then, though his voice came out sounding almost matter-of-fact. "Tell me you're kidding."

"I can't."

A heavy sigh left him as he muttered, "Jesus Christ." Since she was pretty sure he wasn't making a Christmas reference, she ignored that and went on. "Someone will have to come from Crestview," she explained. Then blinked and added, "But I'll try to call anyway. Just in case. Wait here."

After which she shut the door on him. And locked it. In a near blizzard. Which didn't exactly feel kind or charitable, but a woman had to protect herself. And as for calling—despite what she'd told him, she'd decided it was worth making sure, worth a try, to get the scary stranger off her porch as efficiently as possible.

She rushed to the phone, looked up the number, and dialed briskly. Then promptly heard a recording on the other end, saying what she already knew: Meffler's Towing was closed due to inclement weather and anyone in need of a tow should call back after the storm. And they were sorry for the inconvenience. "Me too," she whispered to no one, hanging up.

Then she steeled herself and walked back to the front door. Unfortunately, when she opened it, he was still standing there. Looking cold and a little snow-covered since the snow now even blew up under the roof that covered her porch.

She just shook her head. "They're not answering their phones until the snow stops." Only then it occurred to her to ask, "What on earth are you doing out here in a blizzard anyway?"

"Got lost," he said.

And as he shifted his weight from one snow-covered work boot to the other, she noticed for the first time that his coat was too thin for the cold, and she thought of him trudging from around the bend in a foot of wet snow and for some crazy reason wondered if his feet had stayed dry. She also wondered what kind of person was out in the country this late at night in this kind of weather. Escaped convicts and serial killers came to mind.

"Made a wrong turn looking to find a room for the night," he said, "but I'm guessing a motel's gonna be pretty hard to come by here, too." He sounded wearied by the very thought, perhaps understandably.

But she could only nod, sorry—for both of them—to have to deliver the bad news. "The Half Moon Inn is miles away."

As another heavy sigh left him, she began to realize—almost against her will—that underneath all the scary he was also maybe . . . kind of hot. His voice was deep and a little raspy, and that thin coat didn't hide his broad shoulders. There was something visceral about him—she could somehow feel his very maleness. And that was when he narrowed his blue gaze on her and said, "Looks like you're stuck with me then."

Which made her blink. Twice. Oh Lord, surely he wasn't suggesting . . . "You can't stay *here*, if that's what you're thinking." Scary ghost, hot convict—there was a lot going on here, but none of it seemed good. Or safe.

He shifted his weight again, and gave her an exhausted look. And she realized what she'd just said. Which made her feel the need to say more.

"I don't mean to be rude," she told him, "but . . ." But what? No room at the inn for scary guys who show up in the middle of the night?

He met her gaze. "I don't mean to be rude, either, but I don't think either one of us really has a choice." Then murmured under his breath, "Unless you want me to freeze to death in my truck."

Candice gasped slightly, caught off guard by the very idea. "Well, of course I don't want that," she rushed to say. "It's just that . . . I don't know you and . . ." She stopped, still stuck for words, and blinked some more.

The hot, scary guy at the door—who seemed more real and less ghostly every second—looked put out. As if this was *her* fault. Then said, "Maybe you could go get your husband. Maybe you'd feel better if I talked to him instead."

And she flinched, her spine going ramrod straight. The very notion suggested that she should *have* a husband. And that a man would be more reasonable about this. "I'm not married," she informed him snippily.

"Oh." Clearly this surprised him, and he switched his blue gaze from side to side, as if taking in the scope of the house. "I just assumed with a place this big . . ."

Yes, she'd known the home was too large when she'd bought it from Caroline Meeks Lindley after she'd gotten married and moved in with her new husband. But Candice had been in love with the grand old house her whole life and Caroline had made it affordable, wanting a quick sale. Candice had hoped that, as someone who worked at home and spent most of her time there, a roomy place would be nice. As opposed to cavernous, hard to heat, hell to keep clean, and providing a million spots for a cat to hide.

"Well, you assumed wrong," she said smartly. "I live here by myself." *Oh, that's just great—blurt out to the scary convict stranger that you're all alone here; ripe pickings; easy prey.* She finished by blinking several times. And probably looking a little freaked out—because she'd never been skilled at hiding her feelings. Then, operating on pure instinct, she made a move to close the door on him again.

"Look," he said softly, holding up his hands, which lacked gloves despite the blizzard conditions, "believe it or not, I'm not here to rape and pillage. I'd rather not be here at all, trust me. And I get it—woman alone, strange dude on your porch. But I need a place to sleep. And I'll be out of your hair as soon as I can get a tow truck here tomorrow morning."

Candice went silent, feeling a little trapped by the dilemma.

But that was when the stranger, perhaps sensing that, took a step back from her—and the simple gesture made her feel a little less threatened by all that masculinity. "What can I do," he asked her, "to put you at ease? Name it and I will."

Just then, a brush of fur swept past her ankle and Frosty slipped past her, dashing out the door and down into the snow. "Frosty! What on earth?" They both turned, their eyes following the darting cat, but that quickly he'd disappeared in the deep snow. "Oh my God," she murmured, instantly gripped with dread.

"Was that a cat?" he asked, eyes narrowed.

"Yes!" she said, still searching the white yard for her white cat, panic-stricken.

"It went by so fast I wasn't sure. Been trying to escape a long time now?"

She flicked her gaze to the stranger. "No," she answered pointedly. "He's usually perfectly content. I have no idea what's gotten into him—or where he's gone." She let out a ragged breath, full alarm setting in. "He'll freeze to death out there."

"I can relate," the stranger muttered.

She just gave him another look. But then turned her attention back toward poor, dumb Frosty, somewhere out in the snow. "Here, kitty kitty!" she called in a high-pitched voice. "Here, kitty kitty! Come back, kitty kitty! Before you die out there!"

But still Frosty was nowhere to be seen in the snow, even though some of it was a lot more strewn around than before. It was as if her cat had simply vanished in it, that quickly.

And when she next looked back at the stranger on her porch, she realized that . . . maybe she needed to be braver. For Frosty's sake. She didn't know what that crazy cat was thinking, but desperate times called for desperate measures. And since there didn't seem to be any knights in shining armor around, this guy would have to do. "Can you help me look for him?" she asked.

The scary stranger appeared completely astonished by the request, his eyebrows rising dubiously. "Me?"

She nodded.

Yet he seemed doubtful. And suddenly tired. "Look— it's not that I don't want to help, but I, uh, don't know anything about cat rescue. Isn't there a fireman you can call or something?"

Actually, Amy's husband, Logan, was a fireman, and given Amy's penchant for cats, he'd rescued more than a few. And they lived right up the road from Jenny and Mick. Yet Candice felt forced, once more, to state the obvious. "Again—impassible roads, blizzard conditions." She stopped, sighed. "I'll get dressed and get some flashlights and—"

"No—stay inside."

Once more, she flinched, taken aback.

"I'll look for the cat—you stay here. I'm already half-frozen—might as well freeze a little more."

She blinked—this time less from nervousness and more from awkwardness and surprise and even a little unexpected gratitude. "Thank you," she said quietly.

He replied by murmuring to no one in particular, "This night just keeps getting better and better." Then to her, "So how is it exactly that I should lure this run-away cat in?"

Candice thought about it, then said, for the second time in just a few minutes, "Wait here." As if there was anyplace else for him to go. After which she shut the door yet one more time, rushed to the kitchen, yanked a can of cat food from an overhead cabinet, and used the can opener to remove the lid. Hopefully the smell of tuna—Frosty's favorite—would penetrate the night air. She grabbed the promised flashlight from a drawer as well.

Hurrying back to the open front door, where wind and a little snow now swirled into the foyer, she held out the can and flashlight to the stranger. He turned his collar up against the cold, then took both from her, their fingers touching briefly as he mused, seemingly more to himself than to her, "I'd think I was having a nightmare, but this is getting weirder than anything my brain could invent."

She ignored that and said, "His name is Frosty and he's white."

"A white cat, lost in the snow. Just my luck. Yep," he muttered, "stranger than I could make up." And then he ventured down off the porch into the cold, snowy night that seemed to be getting more blustery by the moment.

Despite the cold and her bare feet, Candice stepped out onto the porch, wrapping her arms around herself, peering desperately out over the scene. "Here, kitty kitty," she called, watching as the hot, scary stranger swung the flashlight beam around in the falling snow—appearing to try to follow the cat's path.

"Oh!" she said a long, cold moment later. "Movement! I saw movement!" She pointed in the direction of a tree Frosty had seemed fond of on two previous outings into the yard—which she refused to think of as escapes just now.

The stranger looked toward her, then swung the light to the tree—from which the sound of a faint meow could be heard. "He's in the tree!" she yelled.

"I don't see a thing," her stranger said, even with his flashlight shining right on the cat. Admittedly, Frosty *was* hard to make out.

"I see his eyes," Candice told him. "And I heard a meow. He's over there!"

But when her late-night visitor didn't reply, she sensed he was tired and cold and already weary of cat rescue, and she thought maybe she should do what she'd suggested before—get bundled up, put on snow boots, and come help. "Listen," she shouted, "if you can just keep an eye on him for a few minutes, I'll get dressed and try to coax him down."

"Didn't I say I'd do it and for you to stay where you are?" he called back to her, starting toward the tree himself now. "And besides, I *can't* keep an eye on him because he's freaking invisible."

Yep, definitely no shining armor on this guy, but she supposed she should just appreciate his help and let the rest go. So she switched her focus back to her cat, whose plaintive meows told her he'd realized the error of his ways and was appropriately afraid now, and probably getting frozen, snowy fur. As her impromptu cat rescuer reached the base of the bare, snow-covered tree, she sent up a little prayer for her usually smug kitty and hoped he would trust the guy—even if she still wasn't certain *she* should.

She heard the stranger now saying in a just slightly softer tone, "Hey there, cat—come on down. Got some smelly cat food for ya. And it's a lot warmer and dryer in there than it is out here. If you come down, maybe we'll *both* get to warm up." He held the cat food up toward where Frosty huddled in a furry even if barely visible ball in the crux between two branches just beyond the guy's reach.

She wondered if he knew she could hear him. She wondered what was going to happen after he rescued her cat. Though as much as she loved her silly feline, Frosty suddenly didn't seem as handy as a nice watch-dog would right about now.

A long moment later, after a little more coaxing, the kitty made a move, stepping carefully down into the stranger's arms. And something in her heart expanded. Not only because it meant Frosty was safe. It also touched her on some unexpected level to see the cat do what she'd thought about just a moment ago—trust him. More than she did.

But that doesn't make him a great guy. It doesn't even make him good. Even if it doesn't make him bad, either. He's still perfectly scary. And unknown. She still wished Frosty was more of a protector and less of a wuss.

She watched as the stranger carried her cat, wrapped inside his coat now, toward the porch, trudging through knee-deep snow. Yep, still scary. And darn it—still hot. The worst possible combination.

His dark hair, sprinkled with blowing snow, touched his coat collar, and the stubble on his cheek made him look strong even in the midst of a blizzard as he climbed the front steps.

"Here ya go," he said as he met her on the porch, then handed the now shivering, icy cat off to her. She tried to ignore the strange, awkward closeness involved in the exchange and wondered for the first time if any intimate parts of her showed through her nightgown in the cold, windy conditions. *God, please, no.* The notion made her all the more uncomfortable and nervous, and she blinked twice as she took the cat.

Turning, she rushed in the still-open door, ready to warm up her cat, and herself. She headed straight for a throw on the back of her sofa, wrapping Frosty inside to melt the iciness that had quickly accumulated in his fur. She tried to ignore the fact that her stranger had followed her into the house and that she *felt* him there, behind her—that maleness again, that stark masculinity. Then she lowered cat and blanket to the couch and crossed the room to start building up the fire in the hearth, burned down to just embers now.

"I can do that," he offered.

"I'm already doing it," she told him, looking back, the poker still in her grasp.

"You can quit looking so afraid of me," he said. "I'm not going to beat you to death with that poker, promise." He sounded irritated enough that she felt . . . well, more reassured. That he was telling the truth.

"That's a relief," she said. Still feeling braver. Then realized there was something else she needed to say. "Thank you. For getting my cat."

His voice went matter-of-fact again. "Figure if I hadn't been at your door, he wouldn't have gotten out."

"But if I hadn't stood there arguing with you and had just let you use my phone," she reasoned in return, "he wouldn't have gotten out, either."

The stranger tilted his head, narrowed his gaze on her. "Is that your way of saying I can stay?"

Oh crap—that question again. And as her chest tightened, she spoke to him with full honesty. "I truly don't want to let you freeze to death, but . . . you're still a stranger to me. So what you're asking is . . . a lot. Any woman would feel that way."

He just let out a tired sigh. "Look, lady, I understand that, but I'm so exhausted that your cat could take me out right now. You want to check me out—here's my phone, here's my wallet." He pulled the items from his pockets with both hands and held them out, offering them to her.

And a part of her did want to take them and check him out—but another part of her didn't want to get any closer to him, and somehow to take his worn leather wallet, warm from his body heat, and look inside it, inside his personal world, would feel like exactly that—

getting closer. Even to just take it from his hand, same as she'd taken the cat a minute ago, felt like too much. Too much nearness.

"Lock me in a room. Or tie me to your couch if you want," he went on, sounding all the more worn out. "I just need a little sleep. That's all I'm after here, nothing else."

The man before her now appeared weary . . . and alone.

And it was basic human kindness to give shelter. Especially at Christmastime.

No matter how uncomfortable I am with the idea.

But you have to sleep on the couch. And waking up to you and this situation in the morning already sounds awkward. And please, please don't be an escaped convict.

All of those replies flitted through her brain, but instead she simply said, "Okay. You can stay."

"If you're going to help a man, you want to know something about him, don't you?"

Joseph, *It's a Wonderful Life*

Two

"Good. Thanks," he replied with a short nod.

She nodded, too. And despite having a guest bedroom upstairs, concluded that the couch was indeed a far better idea. He might have saved her cat and he might not have a choice about being here, but he was still a total unknown quantity. So she left the fireplace, saying, "I'll go get a pillow and blankets."

He didn't reply, but shoved his belongings back into his pockets as he crossed the room to take her place by the hearth, holding his hands out to warm them.

Upstairs, she considered putting a robe on over her gown but decided that might seem silly at this point.

Not that she cared. But she was a grown, capable woman—she could act like one.

When she descended the steps and re-entered the living room, a fresh blaze rose around a couple of newly placed logs, so he'd tended the fire while she was gone. He'd shed his coat to reveal a plaid shirt over a dark T-shirt and blue jeans. He stooped next to the hearth now, still looking in at the flames. And Frosty seemed recovered as well—he'd left his blanket and stood eating out of the cat food can that had been absently placed on the coffee table. All was well in this weird-feeling little scene.

She plopped a pillow and blankets on the couch and said, "So what brings you to Destiny?" Some sort of effort to make this feel more normal. And make her seem less uneasy.

He looked up. "A wrong turn, mostly."

"So you won't be staying in town?"

He shook his head. "Nope, just passing through on my way to Miami."

Like the fact that he wasn't going to kill her with the fireplace poker, that too was a relief. "What's in Miami?"

"A job."

She nodded. And thought about asking what kind of job, yet decided not to. She wanted to be cordial, but wasn't looking to become besties, after all.

Though then something made her inquire, "Do you have a name?" Maybe a name would make him seem less intimidating somehow. And she could have found that out on her own by investigating his wallet, but since she hadn't . . .

"Shane Dalton," he told her, rising up. "Do you?"

"Candice Sheridan," she introduced herself.

"Candice," he repeated. "That seems like kind of a fancy name."

She didn't know what to say to that. Fancy for what? Such a small town? A woman in a flannel nightgown? In a big house without a husband? So she said nothing at all.

He narrowed his gaze on her. "Anybody ever call you Candy?"

She shook her head. "No."

"I've always liked the name Candy for a girl," he informed her. Suddenly making small talk.

"I haven't," she replied. And the truth was, in elementary school, people *had* tried to call her Candy, but she'd put a stop to it. Now no one would even consider it. Well, except for this guy. "Too cutesy."

He'd taken a seat on the ottoman in front of her easy chair, started taking off his work boots. "For what?"

"For me," she said. "I like to be taken seriously."

He looked up from loosening the laces, pinning her in place with those blue eyes now illuminated by firelight along with the twinkling of the Christmas tree. "Why's that?"

She thought it another odd question—she was thirty-three years old, an adult, and what grown woman didn't want to be taken seriously?—so she answered with an observation. "You seem like a pretty serious guy yourself, so I'd think you'd understand."

He just shrugged. "If I'm serious, it's more by circumstance than choice. So it's different."

What are your circumstances? Escaped convict came

back to mind. And she was dying to ask in a way, but again thought better of it.

And she could have tried to defend her position—but it was late and she was tired. So she took the high road and instead glanced toward his boots to ask, "Are your feet cold?"

"Yep," he said, pulling the boots off to reveal thick, wooly socks of gray underneath. "But they'll be fine in a few minutes."

"The fire will warm you up," she agreed. Yet then experienced the sudden need to back away, end this. Because why was she asking about his feet being cold? Like she . . . cared or something. There was a fine line between thanking a man for saving your cat and developing too much of an interest in him. Especially a man like this one. So she added, "If you have everything you need, I'm going to turn in. Again."

"I'm fine. And hey—thanks. For letting me stay." His tone was hardly warm and fuzzy—it had come out as stiff as the rest of his conversation. But it was something anyway.

She answered with another nod, then turned toward the stairs and said, "Goodnight."

"'Night, Candy," he replied.

The words stopped her in her tracks, made her dart a look in his direction.

"Sorry," he said. "Guess I couldn't help myself. 'Tis the season." Then he pointed to a handful of candy canes resting on the coffee table, his expression the closest he'd come to a smile.

Candice said nothing more, just turned and went on her way.

Though she noticed as she hit the stairs that Frosty had stayed behind, curled up by the fire now. Traitor.

The clock next to her bed said it was 3:30 A.M. And as she closed and locked her bedroom door, then crawled back under the covers, exhausted from all the excitement, she longed desperately for slumber. But there was a strange, mysterious man in her house, and even as tired as she was, she knew she wouldn't sleep a wink.

Shane had slept like a log. It surprised him, but the fire was warm and the room comfortable. And chasing a crazy lady's cat around in the damn snow had been exhausting. So far, *everything* about Destiny, Ohio had been exhausting. *You better have sent me to this hell-frozen-over town for a reason, Dad.*

He'd given that last odd instruction from his father little thought since it had come. Maybe because there'd been a lot going on. The funeral, the loss. Packing up both their lives. Deciding to move on from the existence he knew in Montana to something entirely new—a new start.

Or maybe he'd *chosen* not to give it much thought. Because it had come out of nowhere. And made no damn sense, no matter how he sliced it. *Something there for you.* What the hell could that mean?

He'd almost wondered if his dad had thought he was someone else when he'd said it, if he'd even drifted into some other place in time, in his life. He'd wondered if it had something to do with his father's youth in Ohio— he'd lived in this state until he was a little older than Shane was now before loading Shane up and heading west.

And the truth was—Shane had probably come here for nothing. Which meant he'd wrecked his damn truck for nothing. And now had to have it hauled out and hope the damage was cosmetic, something that could wait until Miami, until he could get settled enough to take care of it himself. For nothing.

He did body work by trade—his father had taught him. They'd done work out of the garage behind their house until just a few years ago. Not a lot, just on the side. The side of whatever else his dad was into at the time. Shane had enjoyed it, and he'd held down jobs at a few different body shops over the years as well—but he would have liked if he and his dad had made more of a business from it together. His dad's heart just hadn't been in it the way his was.

His dad's heart had been . . . scattered.

Some people hadn't thought much of his father, but Shane knew he'd done the best he could with what he'd been dealt in life. He thought *most* people did the best they could. Whether or not it was good enough for everybody else.

And his dad had always tried to do right by *him*, even when he didn't deserve it. He'd always been trouble, plain and simple, but his dad had loved him anyway. So if he'd sent him here, surely there was a reason. Surely.

Unless his first instinct was right and it had just been a meaningless ramble.

As he lay there, sun shining through the windows, he realized two things: There was a cat curled up asleep near his feet, and the snow had stopped at some point, even leaving behind a bright wintry blue sky.

It made him think of similar bright winter mornings

in faraway Montana. But that reminded him that he'd chosen to leave winter—mornings and otherwise—behind for a warmer existence, and that as soon as the roads were cleared, he could start heading south.

Hearing shuffling from the stairs, he looked up to see his reluctant hostess enter the room through the foyer. She looked like a different person than she had last night—wearing a cozy red sweater with jeans, and her auburn hair appeared far less crazy pulled back into a high, bouncy ponytail. She was actually . . . cute. Whether her "wanting to be taken seriously" attitude matched that or not.

"Morning," she said, glancing in his direction for only a second before pulling back a white sheer curtain to look out the window. She was clearly uncomfortable making eye contact with him and preferred staring out into the snow.

"Morning," he replied. "Any chance a plow came through yet?"

Eyes still focused outside, she bit her lower lip pensively. "No, but maybe soon. In the couple of winters I've lived here, they usually get to us pretty fast. Probably because the police chief used to live up the road and his daughter still does."

"The sooner the better."

"Agreed," she replied. But then surprised him with, "Would you like some breakfast?"

Given that he hadn't eaten since lunch yesterday, it was a welcome offer. "Um, yeah—that'd be good, thanks."

It wasn't so much that Candice wanted to make her stranger breakfast as that she wasn't sure what else to do with him. She wasn't used to having an unwanted overnight guest, and this morning felt as awkward as she'd expected.

"Pancakes?" she asked, noticing that Frosty was curled up on the couch with him. Like they were buddies or something. That cat clearly had no loyalty.

"Pancakes are great," he said. Even if his tone stayed all-business. There was an undeniable hardness about him that kept her on edge, even in moments when it seemed like that should fade. Even when he added, "Um, anything I can do to help?"

She headed for the kitchen without looking back as she said, "Thanks, but no—I've got it." She supposed it was nice of him to offer, but she already felt his presence too much, so she at least preferred having a wall between them for the moment.

Not that it kept her from remembering things she'd noticed about him as she'd passed through the room. He'd lain on the couch looking rumpled and sort of sexy. His hair was messy, his flannel shirt gone to reveal tattoos on both arms, peeking from beneath the sleeves of his T-shirt. And his feet had been bare, too—his socks draped over the fireplace screen to dry.

As she mixed the batter, the griddle heating on the stove, she couldn't help thinking he'd looked far too comfortable in her home—especially with her silly cat practically in a cuddly bromance with him already. She'd be glad when he was gone and things got back to normal around here.

Pouring the first pancakes in neat, precise circles that allowed her to fit four on the griddle, she prayed for the snowplow. Then set her table for two, something she didn't think she'd done since . . . well, since she'd lived here.

She hoped that by the time he came into the kitchen, he'd have his shirt back on over his tee—and his socks on, too, for that matter. She wasn't sure why. But maybe it had to do with the hotness factor. She didn't want to keep noticing that about him. She wanted the hot stranger to keep being more strange than hot.

Then she tried to distract herself with thoughts of her day to come once he was gone. Roads plowed or not, a winter storm made it seem like a day to do what she *usually* did—stay in.

She might wrap presents. She was an early shopper and had most of them already. She'd picked up the candy canes on her coffee table at the General Mercantile in town just yesterday, in fact, intending to use them as package decorations. After that, she'd do some work on the vacuum cleaner manual, and later she should probably shovel her walk and driveway. And maybe, just maybe, she'd spend some time playing with her dumb cat—if she decided he deserved any affection at all after certain particularly egregious transgressions over the past twelve hours.

That was it, another exciting day in the life of Candice Sheridan.

But then again, maybe she'd had more than enough excitement already. Hadn't she told herself she wanted things back to normal?

Placing a tall plate of pancakes in the center of the kitchen table a few minutes later, she hesitantly called to her houseguest that breakfast was ready.

"Looks good," he said, low, walking into the room.

Hair still rumpled. Plaid shirt still off, tattoos visible. On one arm she made out a tribal-looking band that circled his biceps and on the other a sort of star that resembled the points on a compass. He'd at least put his socks on, but unfortunately, she thought something about a man's feet in thick, wintry socks looked invitingly cozy.

As they both dug in, she wished she'd turned on some Christmas music or something, since the silence was killer. Normally, she enjoyed the quiet, but right now it was deafening. So like last night, she felt compelled to make conversation. Even though she didn't have any new topics. "What did you say brought you to Destiny again?"

He swiped a napkin across his mouth and shot a quick glance her way before returning his attention to his food. "I didn't."

"Well, you said a wrong turn," she reminded him. "Where were you trying to go?"

Now he met her gaze a little longer. "Not sure, actually. Truth is . . . my dad died recently, and he said if I was in this area, I should drive through. Not sure why, but . . . just honoring that wish, I guess."

"Sorry about your father," she told him. Her own had been out of her life since she was young, so she didn't have a lot of nice feelings about fathers in general, but she knew some of them could be good ones. It was difficult to imagine *this* guy's father, though. "Where were you coming *from*?"

"Montana," he said. And left it at that. A man of few words.

"You lived there? Or . . . ?"

"Since I was nine. Lived up north of Mansfield before that, but don't remember much about it."

She felt herself squinting, trying to understand this. "So you thought a good time to check out this area was in the middle of a blizzard?"

He shot her a look. Then resumed cutting off a big bite from his stack of pancakes. "I got here *before* the blizzard. Mostly. But then it was too late to do much about it, especially when I lost the signal on my phone. Lotta country roads around here and not many seem to lead anywhere."

She laughed, because she could see why an outsider would think that. Destiny was pretty far from anything like an interstate, pretty far from anything like a city. Then she informed him, "Destiny is usually more hospitable."

"Bad timing, I guess."

She offered a nod in reply—just as a rumble in the distance told her that, *hallelujah*, a snowplow was coming!

They both looked up and he said, "Is that what I think it is?"

"Yes!" she answered, then pretty much dropped her fork and headed to the phone in a cubby just off the kitchen.

Which made her stranger arch one brow, casting a dryly amused expression as she passed. "You in that big a hurry to get rid of me?"

She frankly wondered why that would be a surprise, but just kept walking as she said, "Figured you'd be in a rush to get on your way to Miami." Then she dialed Meffler's, who promised to send a truck within the hour.

They finished eating, then both headed back to the living room, to the windows. The first swath cut by the approaching plow revealed just how deep the snow had gotten. "There must be nearly two feet," Candice mused.

"Damn," her houseguest said. "That fell fast."

She nodded, feeling their collective awe.

"I told the tow truck place to have the driver swing by here to get you first," she explained, "so you don't have to walk back up the road."

"Thanks," he replied, looking a little surprised again, even at that small kindness, making her wonder if not many people had been kind to him—or if she'd really come off as that much of a shrew last night. She feared the latter. But thought she'd had perfectly good reason not to welcome a stranger into her house with open arms. Then he sat down on the couch and started putting his work boots back on, which had dried next to the fire alongside the socks.

By the time a tow truck came, he'd put his shirt and coat back on as well and was heading toward the door. And she, oddly, found herself wishing he had a scarf and gloves—but then remembered he was a big boy and could take care of himself. Except maybe in freakish blizzard conditions.

Before leaving, he stopped, looked over his shoulder. "You, uh, be okay here?"

She bit her lip and peered up at him from beneath lowered eyelids, taken aback by the concern. Her voice came out softer than intended when she assured him, "I'll be fine."

He replied with a short, brisk nod, then said, "Thanks

for letting me stay even though you didn't want to, Candy Cane." Their gazes met once more, and like last night when he'd called her Candy, it was the closest he'd come to a pleasant expression—but still not quite a smile.

"It wasn't personal," she tried to explain. "Well, not exactly anyway." Ugh. Awkward. *Be quiet now.*

But he let her off the hook. "I know. I get it."

"Merry Christmas," she told him, her voice coming out unintentionally soft.

"You too. I'll be celebrating mine in Miami." And as he opened the door, he paused once more, pointing toward the candy canes on the coffee table. "Um—mind if I take one of those for the road?"

"Of course not," she said, bending to pick one up, then walked it over to where he stood. As she handed it to him, their fingers brushed, and she suffered an undeniable awareness. Of his hotness. And that he was leaving.

"I like peppermint," he explained. "And candy canes are my weakness."

Then he shocked the hell out of her by giving her a wink—just before he disappeared out the door, shutting it behind him.

"You worry me . . ."

George Bailey, *It's a Wonderful Life*

Three

When a knock sounded on her door three hours later, Candice flinched and looked up with a start—and so did Frosty, who'd been curled up sleeping by the fire and appeared annoyed by the rude interruption. "Who on earth . . . ?" she murmured as she abandoned the roll of reindeer-covered wrapping paper in her hand and got to her feet. Weeks could pass without a visitor at her house, but apparently an early snowstorm brought people out en masse.

Though at least it wasn't the middle of the night. And she breathed a sigh of relief to see Mick Brody standing on the other side of the door—for real this time—instead of her stranger. Wait, not *her* stranger—*the* stranger. Who was blessedly gone now, off to Miami, never to darken her path again. The whole thing almost seemed like just a bad dream now.

She opened the door with a smile. "Mick—hi."

Her rugged neighbor looked tired, cold. "Make it through the storm okay?"

She kept her smile in place as she shrugged. "More or less."

His dark eyebrows rose in silent question.

"Everything's fine," she assured him. "Cat got out in the midst of it, that's all. And a guy got stuck in the snow and had to spend the night here—but he's gone now and all's well."

He balked. "A guy?"

She gave another shrug. "Yeah, not from around here."

"Jenny thought she saw a tow truck out the window this morning—is that why?"

Candice nodded. "Yep."

Mick narrowed his gaze on her. "You coulda called, you know."

"It was four in the morning," she said sheepishly. "And unless you bought a snowmobile when I wasn't looking, I'm not sure how you could have gotten here anyway."

He tilted his head. "Still coulda called. Just so somebody would know."

"In case he hacked me to pieces in the night?" she asked teasingly.

He squinted a small grin her way and just said, "Next time, hon, call. And in the meantime, I brought the snowblower down to do your walk and driveway. Just did Miss Ellie's and checked on her, too."

As Mick pointed toward their elderly neighbor's place up the way, Candice felt all the more sheepish realizing that he was probably right—she should have let someone know what was happening. But she hated the idea of bothering someone that late. And at the same time, she appreciated that her neighbors looked out for her. She'd only really gotten to know Jenny and Mick since moving here to Blue Valley Road—and they were close friends with her cousin, Tessa, and Amy as well. While she was a few years younger than them all, she'd become a part of their circle the last couple of years and enjoyed the friendships she'd begun forming.

"That's awfully generous, Mick. But you look cold. I hate to ask you to do that while I'm all warm and cozy in here. I'd planned to shovel later."

He was a matter-of-fact guy. "It's two feet of snow, Candice. And I have the blower. Tell you what. Bring me out an occasional cup of hot chocolate and we'll call it even." He ended on a wink, and she agreed it was a good deal. Though better for her than for him.

As promised, in between wrapping presents, she kept an eye on his progress out the window and twice took him hot chocolate. And when the longer-than-average drive and walk were finally cleared of snow, she insisted he come in to warm up for a few minutes by the fire.

He asked after her mother—who lived in in a small house not far from town square, and who she'd checked in with by phone this morning. And she asked after Jenny and their little boy, to which he'd replied, "This storm is actually a blessing in disguise for me. Jenny had this wild plan of getting us—by which I mean me, Dustin, and the cat—all in reindeer antlers for a Christmas card picture today. None of us were very happy about it—well, except maybe Dustin—so I'm good with handling a little snow removal instead and leaving the antlers to the kid and the cat."

She smiled and said, "Well, beware of pointy antlers when you get home."

"Aw, I've got quite a while before that happens," he told her, explaining that he'd be heading into town after leaving here. "Did you hear about the damage?" Looking up from the fire, he raised his eyebrows.

She let her gaze widen. "No. What damage?"

"A few roofs caved in under the weight of the snow."

"You're kidding!"

"Nope, wish I was. The community building, the church, and that vacant building where the butcher used to be. The butcher's building is a shame, but doesn't matter nearly so much as the other two. I hear the damage is pretty bad."

Candice's heart dropped. When you lived someplace your whole life, even the buildings and homes somehow felt like family. She'd been to countless weddings at the lovely old church on the edge of town, and once upon a time had dreamed of getting married there herself someday. And the community building and the church took turns hosting the annual town Christmas party every year. "Where will they hold the party?" she wondered aloud. It was a seasonal tradition complete with a visit from Santa Claus.

Mick shook his head. "Hard to say. And there's Walter and Anita's wedding coming up, too."

Candice flinched, gasped—remembering. "Oh no—poor Anita." Jenny's father, the police chief, was set to marry his longtime love, Anita Garey, on Christmas Eve at the church. The whole town was invited. The couple, both in their early sixties, was an unlikely one—Anita owned the Dew Drop Inn outside town and wore more sparkles than Walter had probably ever seen before she arrived in Destiny some years back. But she'd become a beloved member of the community since then and everyone was excited about the wedding. "What will they do?"

Mick shook his head. "Hard to say, but from what I hear, the plan is to try to get the church cleaned up and repaired by Christmas Eve. The reception was scheduled for the community building, too, so that's one more thing to worry about." Mick looked back into the fire. "A lot to be done, a lot to figure out. That's why I'm heading up there to meet with Logan and Mike and some other guys—start making a plan."

"If there's anything I can do, will you let me know?"

He gave a nod as he pulled his gloves back on, ready to depart. "Think cleanup efforts will start tomorrow and I'm sure anybody who shows up'll be put to work."

Shane stood huddled next to a small space heater in an old cinder block garage on the edge of town, talking to a guy in dirty coveralls named Mo. Mo seemed to be about his age, but lacked a considerable number of teeth and could have easily passed for one of The Three Stooges. If the stooges had ever moved to Mayberry. And if Mayberry had been at the North Pole.

"Did ya a good chunk o' damage there, son," Mo said.

Yeah, Shane had thought so too when he'd seen the

shape of his truck this morning. Turned out there'd been a tree stump under that snow drift he'd hit.

"Took out your radiator and a good bit o' your grille, son, and your right front fender's toast."

"How long will it take to fix?" Shane asked.

"Aw, I'd say quite a while, son," Mo told him. "Made some calls and can place some orders, but supply routes look to be slow after this heap o' Mother Nature."

Shane was tempted to tell Mo he wasn't his son. But instead he let out a sigh and said, "How long's a while?"

"Hard to say, hard to say." Mo shook his head. "We'll do the best we can for ya, son, but I'd say you're lookin' at a couple weeks at least. We can do the mechanical repair here, but then we'll have to send it over to A1 Body in Crestview for the body work."

"I'm guessing you don't have a body shop in Destiny," Shane said low, dry.

"Nope, sure don't. But A1 does quality work. Should I order up them parts for ya?"

"Do I have a choice?" he murmured.

Mo laughed, like something was funny here, making Shane's jaw clench slightly. "Not really, I don't reckon. Not unless you want to rent a truck and trailer over in Crestview and haul it someplace. Or rent a car and leave your truck with us, then come get it when it's ready."

Tempting ideas—though unfortunately Shane couldn't afford either. The little house where he'd nursed his father through lung cancer was on the market in Montana but hadn't sold yet, and his credit card was maxed out on funeral and cremation expenses. Insurance would cover the truck repairs, but beyond that, he only had the money in his wallet, which had been about enough to get him to Miami, factoring in a few nights in a motel until he could start working for Donnie V. and get himself settled. So being stuck in Destiny, Ohio was about the last damn thing he needed.

"Order the parts," he said, "son." Then walked away, out of the old-school small town garage, aptly called Mo's.

Shit. What was he gonna do now? The woman he'd stayed with last night had mentioned some local inn, but that sounded pricy for a man who was broke. And it was past lunchtime now, and he'd spotted a diner on town square when the tow truck had passed through on its way to Mo's, but even a diner meal suddenly sounded like a luxury under the circumstances.

Turning up his collar against the cold, he shoved his hands in his pockets and started walking the short distance back toward the square. He wasn't sure what his plan was, but it seemed like the best move. And if he was going to get any useful advice, or pick up any short-term work, it probably wasn't gonna be from Mo.

As he approached town, he came across an old-style building with rocking chairs and a couple of barrels on a wide wooden porch with an awning. Though much of it was hidden by snow, he could see the wood was a sun-washed gray, and a large plaque with vintage lettering above the door told him it was the General Mercantile. An *Open* sign hung in the window, and it struck Shane that it might be an economical place to grab a snack—some beef jerky or peanuts or something.

The inside of the store was as old-fashioned as the outside with candy jars on the counter and packaged food like he sought sold out of bushel baskets tilted on their sides. Cold drinks filled a cooler to the right, and near that rested a coffeemaker, hot chocolate machine, and a stack of paper cups. Spotting shelves that held mini cereal boxes and packaged donuts, and spying bags of rock salt near the door, he realized he'd just walked into the world's quaintest convenience store.

"Help ya, son?"

The word *son* was much less grating coming from the old dude behind the wooden counter. The hefty man sported worn overalls over a flannel shirt and a thick white mustache. "Looking for a few snacks," Shane said. Then pointed in the general direction of Mo's because he was pretty sure anyone out on a day like this who didn't live here was probably about to get asked more questions than about what he'd come to buy. "Had an accident passing through last night on my way to Miami. Looks like I'm stuck for a while until my truck is repaired."

"Reckon that explains your lack o' gloves and a hat," the old man concluded.

Shane nodded and tried out the local lingo. "Reckon it does."

"Gloves on a rack over there." The old man pointed.

But gloves weren't in Shane's budget at the moment. Right now, even five or ten misspent dollars could come back to haunt him, and he could get by with cold hands for a while. Despite being headed for a much warmer destination, he'd had gloves when he'd left Montana, but he hadn't been able to find them anywhere in his truck last night when it had really counted.

"Thanks, but I'm good." He shifted his gaze from the old fella to the bushel baskets, trying to decide what and how much to buy amid his sudden poverty. It wasn't a completely foreign feeling—his life had held a lot of ups and downs in the money department—but damn, it was one he'd hoped to never feel again.

"You just come from Mo's?" the old man inquired.

Shane nodded. "Yep." And kept his eyes on the baskets. Jerky, peanut butter crackers, cookies, nuts.

"Got a place to stay? I can call up to the Half Moon Inn if ya like. Sure they'd have a room for ya. There's a couple decent motels over in Crestview, too, if that's more your style."

The offer forced Shane's hand, urged him to honesty. "Truth is, I'd sure as hell *like* a room, but I don't have any way to pay. Not for as long as Mo says I'm gonna be here anyway." He shook his head, looked back to the crackers. "This wasn't part of my plan."

"What is it they say? God laughs when we make plans?" Then the old man held out his hand. "Name's Willie Hoskins. But most folks around here call me Grampy."

Being in no position to decline a little hospitality, Shane stepped up to the counter and shook it. "Shane Dalton," he introduced himself, then felt the need to explain a little more. "I'm headed for a new job, but short on cash right now."

"Happens," the man called Grampy acknowledged with a short nod that put Shane at ease. Then he squinted a little as he eyed Shane, like he was thinking pretty hard about something. "What line o' work ya in?"

Good question, actually. "Need a guy who knows his way around cars and parts," Donnie V. had told him on

the phone. "And who'll do whatever I need him to do."
Maybe Shane should have asked for more details, but
he hadn't. Because he needed that fresh start—and the
big money that would come with it. And in addition to
doing body work, Shane had spent most of his teenage
years taking cars apart and putting them back together
again, so whatever this job was, he was qualified.

To the man behind the counter he replied, "Body
work mostly. But I've got a little experience at a lot
of things—little mechanical, little construction, little
electrical."

Grampy gave his aging head a tilt. "You opposed to
some heavy liftin'?"

Shane stood up a bit straighter, opened his eyes a little
wider. Was the man asking for help with something? Or
offering him a job? "Nope," Shane said. "Why do you
ask?"

"We've had us a bit of a catastrophe here in town
with that storm blowin' through last night. Collapsed
the roof on a church up the road a piece, and did the
same at our community buildin'. Worse yet, we've got
us a wedding comin' up on Christmas Eve at the church
with the reception to follow at the community buildin'.
Couldn'ta been worse luck for the happy couple. A
double whammy."

Shane didn't want to be rude, but he still wasn't sure
what the old guy was asking. "That's a shame, but . . .
what's it got to do with me?"

It surprised him when the question turned Willie—or
Grampy—Hoskins' mouth up into a wide grin beneath
his mustache. "I've been known to ramble a bit in my
speech from time to time, so I can appreciate a fella

who gets to the point." Then he looked upward, and just when Shane feared he was about to get some sort of sermon about Heaven, Grampy said, "I got a couple empty rooms above the store. Ain't much—a fold-out couch, a bathroom, and a fridge that worked last time I plugged it in. Used to stay up there on occasion in the wintertime, back before we had decent snow removal, when I didn't want to close the store. It ain't the Hilton, but I'd be willin' to let ya stay as long as ya need. And be grateful if in return you'd be willin' to pitch in on the clean-up efforts in our damaged buildin's." Grampy shifted his weight from one foot to the other. "Whata ya say? Interested?"

Shane didn't think it mattered much whether or not he was interested—the way he saw it, he had no choice. And he didn't believe much in miracles, the Christmas kind or otherwise, but this seemed pretty close.

"It's a deal," Shane said.

Candice's heart broke as she walked into the grand old church to see the damage the next day. Pieces of roofing, plaster, wood, and other debris peeked and poked from beneath the snow that had caused the mess, all lying scattered across the pews and altar. A glance up revealed a blue winter sky dotted with white puffy clouds—it felt surreal seeing a beautiful day from inside the church, bits of broken roof and ceiling hanging down from around the view like stalactites. "This is awful," she murmured.

Jenny Brody stood beside her, taking in the damage, and let out a sigh of agreement.

"How do we begin?" Candice asked softly. The task

of fixing this felt even more overwhelming now that she'd seen it.

"For starters, the guys are going to try to cover the roof with plastic tarps for now until the insurance adjuster arrives. Mick, Lucky, and Duke have taken charge of that part." Lucky Romo was Mick's long-time buddy and Candice's cousin-in-law—a big, burly biker whose wild ways her cousin Tessa had succeeded in taming. His best friend, Duke, lived with Lucky's sister, the beautiful Anna Romo, and together they ran the Half Moon Inn.

"After it's covered, we'll all dive in and start cleaning the place out and see how bad the pews and carpet and pulpit are," Jenny went on. "One step at a time after that, I suppose. The community building should be a little easier. No carpet or upholstery there to be damaged—just the tables and linoleum floors. Mick and the guys are going to cover the roof there, too."

Still, Candice could only shake her head. "How did this even happen? I mean, I know the community building's roof is flat and that snow could weigh it down and collapse it, but this one isn't—at all." It was a typical arched, gabled roof which had—until the night before last—been held up by large beams.

"Mick said they think one of the beams was weak or damaged and gave way."

Candice pulled her eyes from the rubble and looked at Jenny. "How are Anita and your dad dealing with it?"

Jenny sighed and attempted a smile that didn't quite make it to her eyes. "Well, Dad is taking it in stride. He wasn't that excited about a big wedding anyway—it was all for Anita, to make it special for her. So he told her

he'd be happy to marry her in a cornfield or a barn—
that the place didn't matter. But Anita's been planning
this for a long time and wanted it to be perfect. Dad
even suggested they elope, but Anita said the people
here had become her family and it was important to
share this with them. She doesn't want to get married
anyplace but Destiny."

A little more conversation revealed that Jenny and
Mick's son was with Anita today—she'd chosen to play
grandma and take her mind off her wedding troubles
rather than even see what shape the church was in.
Meanwhile, some of the town leaders had gathered at
Dolly's Main Street Café to work out a plan and make
a sign-up list for the various tasks that would need to
be done, while even now people entered the back of the
church and started moving furniture and such out of
the large foyer.

"We're taking anything not damaged to the basement," Rachel Farris-Romo announced when Candice
and Jenny looked up. "To get it out of harm's way."
Rachel was married to another Romo sibling, a cop
named Mike, and had clearly taken charge of some of
the operation. Candice had attended their wedding in
this very church. "Feel free to grab anything not nailed
down, including stuff hanging on the walls."

Together, Candice and Jenny eyed the weekly attendance plaque and a few paintings on a far wall, then
made their way toward them around the back pews
where less debris lay.

"But we have to remember," Jenny said, continuing
their conversation as they went, "it's Christmas. We'll
have to find somewhere else to have the town party,

and despite all this, we have to keep our traditions in place." Then she stopped to look at Candice. "That reminds me, you're still coming to the cookie exchange at Edna's tomorrow, right?"

The truth was, with all the excitement, Candice had nearly forgotten about the invitation to the ladies' party at Edna Farris's farmhouse, one of the many little ways she'd been included by Jenny and Tessa's circle of friends. And part of her thought it would feel pretty frivolous to rush home and start baking cookies right now, but she supposed Jenny was right—they couldn't forsake Christmas altogether.

"Of course," she said. "I'll be there—with sleigh bells on."

Jenny smiled—but then got serious. "And hey, I almost forgot, but Mick told me about your visitor the other night. And that he insisted you call us if anything like that ever happens again. You will, right?"

Candice nodded.

And Jenny leaned closer. "Sounded kinda scary."

"It was," Candice confessed. "*He* was. I mean, sort of. Even though he was at least nice enough to chase down Frosty when he ran out into the snow."

She left out the part about him also being kind of hot. Because that would just make it sound confusing. And it *had been* a little confusing to think he was hot and also be afraid of him. So she was just glad it was over.

She wondered vaguely if her hot stranger had reached Miami by now, but then resolved not to think about him anymore. Or the undeniable awareness she'd experienced in certain moments with him.

Candice removed the large wooden plaque from the wall, and Jenny a religious painting, and they headed back toward the foyer, which led to the basement stairs. They ended up in a line of people, some carrying stuff down, others coming back up for more.

She found it more challenging than anticipated to haul the sizable slab of wood down the steps—she could barely see around it. And when she reached the bottom, she turned a corner—and plowed right into someone.

"Ow!" said a deep voice.

"Oh!" She drew up short, the awkward plaque still in her grasp—then peered across the top of it to see who she'd collided with.

The blue-eyed man on the other side met her gaze, a lock of dark hair dipping over his forehead.

"Oh God," she murmured.

"Nice to see you, too, Candy Cane."

"You look at me as if you didn't know me."

Mary Hatch, *It's a Wonderful Life*

Four

*O*ne dark eyebrow arched upward. "But are you supposed to take God's name in vain in a church?" he asked. "You must hate me even more than I thought."

Candice blinked. Twice.

And Jenny stood at the bottom of the stairs now, too, looking confused. "Um, do you two know each other?"

Candice whispered through gritted teeth in Jenny's direction, as quietly as she could, "Scary stranger." Then glanced back and forth between them, realizing . . . "Do *you* two know each other?"

"Mick introduced us a couple of hours ago," Jenny said. "Shane's going to help out with the cleanup."

Candice darted her eyes back to Shane Dalton overtop the attendance plaque.

"Truck parts on order. Not lookin' good for my green Christmas," he said, answering her unasked question matter-of-factly. Then eyed her critically. "You seem a little shaken up there, Candy—let me take that for you."

And he smoothly lifted the wooden plaque from her arms, his hands brushing over hers as he did, sending yet another brisk flutter of awareness through her when she least expected it. Oh dear. Oh my. Sensation—just from the brief touch—whooshed up into her breasts and down into her panties. This was *so* not what she needed in her life.

"Um, um . . ." she sputtered as Shane Dalton walked away with the plaque, leaning it against a basement wall. She took in his back, his shoulder blades through his T-shirt, his butt through his jeans. All were . . . too pleasing to look at.

"Shane's the guy who wrecked outside your house?" Jenny whispered with wide eyes.

Which Candice returned. "Yes."

"He doesn't *seem* so scary," Jenny said.

Candice lowered her chin. "Easy for you to say. He wasn't at your door in the middle of the night."

"Just maybe a little rough around the edges," Jenny added. "Like Mick was when we first met. And *he* turned out not to be scary."

Now Candice flicked her neighbor a sideways glance. This comparison explained a lot. Jenny thought *all* guys who seemed a little rough were really harmless underneath—because she'd tamed one of them. Just like Tessa had tamed Lucky and Anna had tamed Duke. But it wasn't that simple. Not every tough guy was tamable. She'd found that out the hard way once upon a time. And it had changed her life.

But she chose not to reply because her thoughts would sound paranoid—and they didn't matter anyway. Shane Dalton wouldn't be here long, after all. She tried to shift the conversation in a slightly different direction and also get some practical information. "Do you know where he's staying while he's here? At the inn on Half Moon Hill?"

"No, apparently in the rooms above the General Mercantile—Grampy Hoskins offered them up if he'd help out here."

Candice nodded, absorbing the information. She wished he'd chosen the Half Moon Inn instead—it was farther away, both from town and from her house.

"So he expects to be here until Christmas?"

Jenny shrugged. "I think that part is pretty iffy—dependent on repairs."

Another nod from Candice—as her scary stranger tossed a quick glance her way while passing back by and heading up the stairs. She'd thought maybe he'd stop and say something more. But she was glad he didn't. At least she *thought* she was glad. Her heart beat a little harder in her chest just from his nearness.

And that brought about a decision. "Well, if I'm expected to have a big batch of cookies ready by tomorrow, I should probably go home and start working on them." Then she wiped her hands together to remove any dust and indicate she was done here.

Jenny nodded, smiled. "Okay—see you tomorrow then?" She probably knew Candice's departure was about more than cookies yet was too nice to say it, which suited Candice fine. There were actually upsides to not being in someone's inner, *inner* circle, in someone's deepest confidence.

"Like I said, wearing sleigh bells." Candice finished with a forced smile of her own, then walked up the stairs and out the church doors without seeing Shane Dalton again. Even though a part of her almost wanted to. Because of his back and butt being nice to look at. Or maybe it was the brightness of those blue eyes, the way they contrasted with the darker parts of him—his hair, the rough stubble on his jaw. Or maybe it was that strange feeling she experienced just being around him—that awareness. A certain pull.

Attraction. That's what it was. Plain and simple. Attraction.

Maybe it was easier to admit that to herself now that they weren't alone together in an uncomfortable situation that made her wary, now that people she knew thought he wasn't an awful guy.

That didn't make her any less wary in her heart, though. In fact, the way the touch of his hands on hers stayed with her as she got in her car and began to drive home was . . . downright troubling.

Well, I just have to avoid him while he's here, that's all. Which just meant avoiding the General Mercantile. And the church. And the community building. And finding other ways to help with the efforts that didn't require her being on-site.

And maybe that seemed like a lot of effort to go to, but it would be worth it. Because it would keep her life simpler, something she'd endeavored to do, pretty successfully, ever since the last time she'd had her heart shattered by someone just like him.

Grampy Hoskins stood in his usual spot behind the counter at the General Mercantile. He'd been running the old general store for most of his life, it seemed, standing in this spot so long that the floorboards were worn from it.

The bell above the door tinkled and he looked up to see Anita Garey walk in, bundled in a furry winter jacket and a scarf that glittered. She held the hand of a three-year-old boy, nearly swallowed up by the puffy parka and hat he wore.

"Well, looks like y'all are stayin' warm," Grampy said. "You been out buildin' snowmen, young fella?"

Jenny and Mick Brody's little boy smiled up at him conspiratorially and shook his head. "Nope. Looking for reindeer."

Grampy laughed. He loved Christmastime for just this reason—the light it put in children's eyes and the imaginings it planted in their sweet little heads. "Is that so? Ya find any?"

Dustin shook his head, appearing disappointed. "But Grandma 'Nita says we might find some on the square."

"So we stopped in for some hot chocolate to warm us up on the way," Anita added with a wink. Her small house was located only a few blocks away, close enough to walk to town.

"This time o' year, apt to find 'em about anywhere," Grampy said knowingly. "Could be around any corner." Then he leaned down over the counter as if to confide in the child. "Gotta keep a sharp lookout, though— they try to keep outta sight. But if ya look real hard, ya might just catch a glimpse o' one."

The boy didn't look the least bit surprised by that. "Grandma 'Nita says Santa sends 'em to make sure kids are being good."

Grampy gave a solemn nod. "Your Grandma Anita's a wise woman. So I'm sure you're bein' a good boy, right?"

The child nodded profusely. And then wandered over to a display of Christmas candy.

Anita helped herself to the hot chocolate machine he kept out in cold weather, running two cups, then carrying them to the counter, setting them down to pay. "Add on one of the little chocolate Santas for him, too," she said.

Grampy replied, "Candy's on the house," and told her the price of the hot chocolate. Then gave the boy another glance before looking back at her. "You're real good with him."

She was a woman with sharp features, and who made bold fashion choices. And her shoulder-length hair was currently a very dark red, one of many shades he'd observed on her over time. She still looked like the Destiny transplant she was, even all these years after buying the Dew Drop Inn—but she fit here now, and folks had seen past the boldness and the glitter to the good-hearted woman underneath. "That little one's a light in my life," she said, glancing over at the olive-skinned boy who favored his daddy and was gonna be a lady-killer one day. "Reminds me of my own at that age."

This last part caught Grampy off guard, though. "Didn't know you had any kids, Anita."

And then a stark sadness he hadn't expected passed over her face as she murmured, "I don't usually talk about it—don't even know why that slipped out." She looked down at the counter, fumbling with money, but then raised her eyes back to his. "I lost him—my son."

As a pall fell over the room, Grampy proceeded cautiously. "How did he die?"

But she quickly shook her head. "Oh—no, he didn't die, thank God. It's just that . . . his father took him, ran off with him. When he was just a little boy. We didn't have Amber Alerts and such back then." A tired-sounding sigh came out. "Some days it's still hard for me to believe—but I haven't seen my son since he was little. And I pray for him every day, just hoping life has treated him fair and that his scoundrel father hasn't poisoned his sweet brain."

"Well, that's a downright awful thing, m'dear," Grampy said, reaching out to squeeze her hand. He'd never called Anita by an endearment before—but he'd never seen the woman look the least bit weak or troubled, either. He knew he was witnessing a side shown to precious few.

And as he might have expected, she recovered her usual brave face then and said with a smile, "But life—it does go on. And brings good things to replace those you lost. And Walter, and his family—they make me far happier than I ever thought I'd have the good fortune to be. I'm lucky to be marrying him." Just then, Dustin came running over to Anita, a chocolate Santa covered in foil clutched in his tiny fist. She bent down to scoop him up into her arms. "And lucky to have this rascal to hunt reindeer with!"

The little boy laughed and Grampy could feel the way it filled up the hole he'd just learned about in Anita Garey's heart.

"Real sorry about the situation with the church," he told her.

Another long sigh escaped her. "Me too. Not gonna say everything goes my way all the time, that's for sure," she said on a cynical laugh. "I sure did want my wedding to my Walter to be special, in that pretty church where he's gone all his life, surrounded by the people we both love."

"And it will be," Grampy said. "There's plenty o' time between now and then to get that roof repaired and get the place lookin' nice again. Same thing at the community buildin'. It'll all come together—you just have ya some faith."

She nodded, again looking like the stalwart woman he'd come to know. And now he understood a little better how she'd gotten to be that way. Losses in life could toughen people. He was just glad she'd let Walter soften some of those sharpened edges.

"What I have faith in," she said, "is all the good people of Destiny. I appreciate more than I can say how they're pulling together for Walter and me, trying to make this happen."

"That's what Destiny's all about, Miss Anita," he reminded her. "We're always here for each other. Always have been, always will be."

She lowered the little boy back to the floor, then handed him his cup of cocoa, reminding him it was hot and to be careful. Then she looked back to Grampy. "If you don't mind my saying, sounds like you're speaking from experience, Mr. Hoskins."

The truth was, Grampy didn't go sharing his woes in life much, either. Not so much because he wanted to keep them private as that they'd happened so long ago most people never thought to wonder, or ask, about his past. It didn't hurt his feelings—Destiny was a town filled with folks who had much busier, active lives than his: friends, romance, drama, and lately, some kids of their own, starting that cycle of life over yet again.

So he didn't mind being honest with Anita. Since she'd asked. "Reckon I ain't immune to loss, either, m'dear. Lost my lovin' wife too young—in an auto accident."

Anita tilted her head. "I didn't know that."

He supposed many people didn't. Even as much of a fixture as he was in this town.

"And my own son, our only child," he went on, "moved away after he went off to college. He lives up in Chicago—has a sweet daughter and a strappin' boy, both grown now—but don't see as much of any of 'em as I like. They used to come every summer for a spell— but they don't so much anymore. Life is hectic these days, I know."

Hell, he thought he sounded sad saying it, guessed he *was* sad saying it. He just tried to keep as busy here as he could, tried not to think about it too much. He didn't want to be some sorrowful old man who held other folks responsible for his happiness.

And none of that was the same as what had happened to Anita—but on the other hand, he guessed loss was loss, and loneliness was loneliness, and everybody knew those feelings at some time or another.

Now it was Anita who reached across and did the hand-squeezing. "Next time your boy or grandkids come to town, I'd be honored to meet 'em," she said.

"And I'd be most pleased to introduce you," he replied.

She tilted her head back the other way and said, "Funny—I guess the way people call you Grampy, I just assumed you had a whole passel of grandchildren hidden off somewhere."

He chuckled softly at the assumption. "Not sure how that started up, actually, or even when. But reckon somewhere along the way I musta just somehow appointed myself grandpa to the whole dang town, whether they liked it or not."

"Well, they're all lucky to have you," she said. "*We're* all lucky to have you."

"Come on, Grandma 'Nita," the little boy on the floor next to her pleaded, tugging at her coat, "let's go! I wanna find reindeers!"

Both adults just laughed, and Anita said, "Guess I better get on my way with this one before the reindeer head back to their stables for lunch." She ended by tossing a wink toward Grampy as she and Dustin walked toward the door in their snow boots.

"Sweet woman Chief Tolliver's gettin'," Grampy remarked.

She smiled in parting, and Grampy felt richer for the encounter.

He surely hoped the town would be able to get the two buildings fixed in time for her wedding—she deserved to have exactly what she wanted. And he supposed that spirit of being there for one another was the thing that kept him feeling . . . like he was part of something. Even if he got a little lonely sometimes.

Though that loneliness . . . well, maybe it wasn't something he often admitted to himself. But maybe the older he got, the easier it was to feel it. The easier it was to . . . quit feeling relevant, like he added much to anyone's life.

A few minutes later the door opened again and in walked Shane Dalton. The boy needed a warmer coat for this weather. But Grampy supposed it wasn't his place to say so, especially since he knew the young fella wasn't in a position to run out and buy one.

"What's the news from the church?" he asked.

"Insurance adjuster came this morning and did his part," Shane said. "But they can't find any construction crews to start the repairs until after the holidays. So the plan now is to focus mostly on the church rather than the community building—and to make temporary repairs to the roof, enough to hold until after the New Year. And to try to get everything inside fixed in time for that Christmas Eve wedding."

"My goodness," Grampy remarked. "And how's the work on that goin'?"

Shane ran a hand back through his hair. "Slow so far. The tarps people brought were too small to cover the damn hole in the church roof. So we spent the morning using them at the community building—they worked for that one, and should keep the weather out until the construction guys can come in January. Duke and Lucky are headed over to Crestview now to find bigger ones for the church and we'll deal with that later this afternoon—get it covered over until we can get some plywood up there."

Grampy liked how Shane sounded right now—almost energized about the tasks at hand. It was something he hadn't felt in the fella upon first meeting him. He was the sort it would be easy to assume the worst about—

but Grampy had thought he'd sensed something good underneath the dry exterior, so he'd taken a gamble.

"Care if I grab a hot chocolate to warm me up a little?" Shane asked.

"Not a'tall," Grampy said. "In fact, I'll go ya one better."

Shane looked up, arching one brow in Grampy's direction.

"Since ya got a couple hours to spare, how about I treat ya to lunch at Dolly's and then me and you'll head over to my friend Edna's orchard to get some apples from her root cellar for the store here."

He couldn't read the younger man's expression—he was skilled at hiding his responses. But finally he replied, "I'm not gonna turn down a hot meal." Then he eyed Grampy curiously. "Mind if I ask you something?"

"Shoot," Grampy said.

"Why are you being so nice to me?" He sounded almost suspicious.

And Grampy made a slight face. "A fella can't just be nice?"

Shane looked a little skeptical. "It's just . . . you don't even know me." And true enough—besides offering him a place to stay, Grampy had driven him back to Mo's to get a couple duffel bags of clothes and other things from his truck, and now he was buying his lunch. "In my experience, most people don't go out of their way for people they don't know."

"Maybe I like havin' some company," Grampy said. "Or maybe I'm tryin' to save my old back from carryin' bushels o' apples around in the snow. Or maybe I'm just gettin' old and sappy."

"You don't seem so old. Or sappy. Until right now," Shane said. Then ended with a quick wink Grampy hadn't expected.

And as they walked out the door to lunch, Grampy thought maybe when you boiled it down, the simple reason was . . . sons. His son. Anita's son. This fella was somebody's son. And now he was on his own. And maybe Grampy was missing his boy and hoping that if he ever needed help, someone would give it to him.

"Haven't you got any romance in you?"

Bert, *It's a Wonderful Life*

Five

*B*renda Lee sang a slightly scratchy version of "Rockin' Around the Christmas Tree" over Edna Farris's old record player as the ladies of Destiny sat around her antique dining room table eating tiny ham and turkey sandwiches, potato salad, and tea cookies off plates festooned with holly. Tubs and tins of cookies were stacked on the credenza to one side, ready for the official cookie exchange after lunch.

Candice enjoyed taking part in the chatter, though mostly she just listened. And though the big news of the day was the plan for temporary repairs to the church roof and trying to get the inside ready for the wedding—"which is going to be a race against the clock," Rachel explained—after that, conversation turned lighter.

Candice found out that Sue Ann Simpkins' daughter, Sophie, who was twelve now, was going to be Mary in the middle school nativity play, and the role of Joseph would likely go to one of Adam Becker's twin sons, though neither of them—according to Sue Ann—were all that interested. "They're more into football these days—but Sophie is begging for one of them to be her Joseph so she won't end up with some kid she doesn't like." Sue Ann and Adam had been a couple for so long that Candice was surprised they hadn't gotten married yet. But they were both busy people—he ran a landscaping company and Sue Ann refurbished old homes and worked in real estate as well—and seemed happy in their relationship the way it was.

And there was talk of Jenny and Mick's little boy, who apparently swore he'd seen a reindeer peek out the door of Amy Whitaker's bookstore on town square yesterday. And Rachel and Mike's little girl, it seemed, could speak of nothing but seeing Santa soon. "Apparently she's going to ask him for another cat," Rachel said, looking tired. "Like the enormous one we already have isn't enough. Mike's about to have a cow—one cat is more than enough for him and we're not sure what we're going to do about this Santa/cat business."

"You can adopt Holly. She's a sweetie," Amy said from across the table. They all knew Holly was the current stray living at Under the Covers and waiting for a home.

"I think Shakespeare would probably squash her," Rachel said of their large tabby that everyone knew Mike only just barely managed to put up with.

"If you need a cat," Candice added jokingly, "you can have mine."

"Bite your tongue," Amy said, looking aghast. "Frosty is an amazing cat!"

Of course, Amy thought any cat was amazing. But Candice said, "I'm only kidding—I wouldn't give the big knucklehead away. Even though he escaped out into the blizzard the other night. A white cat—in a blizzard. You see where I'm going with this, right?"

A collective sigh issued from all the cat-owning women around the table. Then Candice's cousin Tessa said, "I was once cat-sitting Mr. Knightley for Amy and he got out. It's how I met Lucky."

Amy's head darted around to cast a glare at her friend. *"What?"*

"Oh crap," Tessa said. "I forgot I never told you about that." She bit her lip. "But it was years ago and Lucky saved the day and all was well." She ended with a smile, silently encouraging Amy to forgive and forget.

"Candice had a handsome rescuer for Frosty the other night, too," Jenny offered up, a tea cookie between her fingers.

And all eyes swung in Candice's direction as Rachel's feisty grandma, Edna, said, "Do tell."

Oh brother. Candice wanted to kill Jenny. The way she'd said it suggested romance. Romance that didn't exist and certainly wasn't going to happen. Handsome or not. Now it was she who cast a glare—at her neighbor—but then she tried to fluff it off. Because fluffing it off was actually the honest thing to do, given her lack of interest in Shane Dalton. "It was no big deal," she said to the room at large, shaking her head. "Just a guy who wrecked his truck in the snow and came looking to use the phone."

"Well, what happened then?" Sue Ann asked.

"Get to the handsome part," Edna prodded.

And Candice told them, "That's really all there is to it. He lured Frosty down from a tree, was towed away the next morning, and that's it."

Unfortunately, Jenny was quick to add, "That's *not* it. He's stuck here until his truck can be repaired, so he's staying above the General Mercantile and helping with the church repairs."

"And still nobody's gettin' to the handsome part," Edna groused, lifting a cup of eggnog to her lips.

"Okay, okay," Jenny said. "He has dark hair, broad shoulders, a strong jawline, and . . ."

"And a nice smile?" Amy suggested.

"Doesn't smile much," Rachel broke in to say. Candice supposed that, as someone who was organizing much of the repair work, it made sense that she'd met him, too. "Kind of an all-business sort of guy. But Jenny's right—he's sexy as hell, and though I'll deny saying this if any of you ever breathe a word, if I weren't a very happily married woman, I'd be all over that."

Candice was swallowing the last bite of a tiny ham and cheese sandwich, then reaching for her own eggnog, when she realized every eye in the room had turned to her again. "What?" she asked.

"You're the only one here who's single," Sue Ann said.

"Except me," Edna pointed out. "But I'm guessin' I'm a mite too senior citizen for him."

"And?" Candice asked, brows raising.

"*You* should go for him," Jenny suggested, her eyes persuasively wide.

Which made Candice's jaw drop. "Me? Oh-ho-ho no."

"Why not?" Amy asked.

"Well, to begin with, he'll only be here for a couple of weeks," she said smartly, reminding them. "Maybe not even until Christmas."

Sue Ann shrugged. "A holiday fling can be nice. Take it from me." She ended with a knowing nod since she and Adam had started dating at Christmastime. But Candice remained aghast because it was two very different things. "You guys want me to . . . just . . . like . . . hook up with a guy I know won't be here in a month?"

The next playful shrug came from Rachel. "I wouldn't have a problem with that. Don't get me wrong—relationships are great. But they don't have to be lifelong to be good ones, and there's nothing wrong with having some fun when a hot guy comes to town for a little while."

"That's not really my style," she informed Rachel, giving her head a quick shake, then said to them all, "And besides, he's not my type."

"You don't like hot guys?" Tessa asked accusingly.

It made her flick a sideways glance toward Jenny, since she'd started all this. "Hello? Scary stranger, remember? Supposed to be careful around scary strangers, call you and Mick if any show up. Does that ring any bells?"

"Wait—what are we missing here?" Amy asked.

Just as Jenny said to Candice, "That was before we met him. Mick thought he seemed okay. Quiet, but willing to work hard, and seemed smart at figuring out the best ways to do things. And obviously Grampy likes him or he wouldn't have offered him a place to stay."

"And," Rachel added, "just to be safe, late yesterday Mike took a glance at his truck at Mo's and ran the plates. No priors, just a few speeding tickets, so no worries there."

Candice only sighed. Blinked. Then looked to Amy and all of them. She really hadn't wanted to get into this, but now she had no choice. "What you're missing is—hot or not, and criminal or not, he still struck me as a little scary when we met, just showing up on my porch in the middle of a blizzard. He had to stay the night and—"

"Oh my," Tessa interjected, a palm to her chest.

But Candice kept going. "And I was uncomfortable the whole time."

"What is it that's so scary about him?" Amy asked.

And Candice tried to think how to explain. "Well, he has a scar near his eye."

Sue Ann swiped her hand down through the air. "Scar, schmar. It adds character. What else?"

Again, Candice thought about it. And finally concluded, "It's difficult to put into words, but he's got a hard vibe about him. It's just his demeanor. He couldn't really explain why he was here in any concrete way, which seemed kind of suspicious. And he just seemed like . . . trouble."

"Look," Tessa said, "I know where you're coming from—if any guy on the planet had trouble written all over him, it was Lucky."

"Mick, too," Jenny added. "But look how they both turned out. Just because a guy seems bad on the surface, that doesn't mean he really is underneath."

"Bad boys can become good men," Tessa added knowingly.

And Rachel added with a wink, "And even if this one can't, he's not here for long, and bad boys can also be a lot of fun."

At this point, Candice felt ganged up on. And just as convinced as before that Shane Dalton had nothing to offer her that she wanted—hot or not. So she spoke her truth. "It's easy for you guys to say that," she pointed out. "You guys all found the love of your lives in your bad-boys-turned-good. But the truth you're forgetting is, sometimes bad boys are just . . . bad."

When everyone went quiet, she knew they were all finally remembering her past. The love of *her* life. Tragic though that was. And now they were just too polite to say it. They'd welcomed her into their circle, but she hadn't ever spilled her guts to any of them about anything, or even confided the smallest secret for that matter, so despite the banter of a moment ago, she supposed this felt too heavy to acknowledge.

A bad boy right down to the leather jacket and motorcycle, Bobby Wayans had broken her heart over and over again. But she'd kept on trying, believing, that she could make him change. In the end—five long, passionate but tumultuous years later—he'd cheated on her with her best friend and disappeared in the night with some cash and jewelry from her dresser.

After an uncomfortable silence, Edna finally spoke up to say, "Well, if you're referrin' to that Wayans boy, he was just a bad seed. You're right, some just are. Once upon a time, I knew a fella who turned out that way myself. So don't let these girls push ya with all their good intentions—you trust your gut, hon."

Just then, the old-fashioned doorbell trilled from

Edna's front porch, and Rachel, being closest, went to answer. A moment later Grampy Hoskins and Shane walked in.

"Lordy, didn't realize I was interruptin' a party," Grampy said, looking uncharacteristically sheepish. "Y'all musta parked around back where I can't see your cars. But at any rate, for those of ya who ain't met him, this here's Shane Dalton. He's helpin' out with our repairs the next couple weeks while he waits for some of his own." Then he looked to Edna. "Come for some apples."

"Key to the root cellar's on the hook by the back door, Willie, and I'll let ya help yourself today," she said with a wink.

The room had gone even more noticeably quiet at their entry, and as Candice drew her gaze away from Shane, she realized every other woman at the cookie exchange was gawking at him like a teenage girl.

This time it was Grampy who broke the awkward silence—by saying to them all, "Don't act like y'all ain't never seen a decent-lookin' fella around here— you've all known *me* your whole dang lives, after all."

Light laughter rang through the room, after which Amy offered up, "It's nice to meet you, Shane, and welcome to Destiny."

Which prompted Sue Ann to add, "It's good of you to help out with the repairs. Are you sure you won't be staying in town awhile?"

But of course he shook his head. "No, just passing through."

"Offer you fellers somethin' sweet to eat?" Edna asked.

"We just come from lunch at Dolly's," Grampy said, patting his ample belly.

"Sure you won't take a slice o' Tessa's pumpkin bread or my gingerbread?"

Shane gave his head a soft shake, murmured a quiet, "No thank you, ma'am," and while still somewhat brusque, it was perhaps the most polite Candice had seen him be.

"You know I love your gingerbread, Edna," Grampy told her, "but I best pass, what with holiday shindigs comin' and all. Gotta keep my girlish figure." He ended with a wink at the girls, who giggled softly.

Edna reached for a plate spread with jagged pieces of red-and-white candy and said, "At least have ya some peppermint bark."

It almost surprised Candice when Shane stepped forward and selected a couple of pieces of it—until he said, "Peppermint's my favorite," and tossed a glance in her direction.

Their eyes met across the room—for some reason she couldn't quite pull hers away—until Grampy started toward the doorway to the kitchen, saying, "We'll just grab that there key and let ourselves out the back," and Shane followed.

Everyone went quiet again, no one breathing even a word until they heard Grampy quietly say, "Here 'tis," and the back door closed soundly behind them.

And then Edna announced, "Yep, that boy's a hot one all right—as you young'uns say." Then she looked directly at Candice. "Forget my advice from before. I'd be open to explorin' that situation if I was you."

"If it wasn't me talking, I'd say you were the prettiest girl in town."

George Bailey, *It's a Wonderful Life*

Six

A path had been cleared to the root cellar through the deep snow, so getting there was easy enough, and the snow had even been removed from the nearly flat-to-the-ground wooden doors. As they opened up the cellar, Shane took a glance around the orchard, spying rows of trees in the distance that looked more like large white mushrooms given the snowfall. And he wondered vaguely what the place looked like in spring, when the apple trees were flowering, or in summer, when they were thick and green and dripping with red fruit.

Following Grampy down narrow steps into a space that was cool but not as cold as he might have expected given the weather, he noticed the descent made the old man move slower than usual and was glad he'd come along to carry the apples up. Grampy knew just where to find the ones he wanted, a bushel each of Red Delicious, Honeycrisp, and Jonathan.

Once they were back in Grampy's old truck, Shane asked, "So what's your deal with Edna?"

Grampy looked over from behind the wheel. "Well, I pay her wholesale prices for the apples and she bills me quarterly."

Shane resisted the urge to roll his eyes. "No, I mean, what's your . . . relationship with her?"

"Oh," the elderly man said, getting it now. "Edna? Well, she's my oldest, dearest friend. I've known her the better part o' forever."

"So, do you two . . . hang out?" He wasn't sure why he was asking—but maybe Grampy had him thinking about what it was like to get old. His own father hadn't made it to sixty-five. And he hadn't really known his grandparents—they were vague, distant memories from before moving to Montana. He just hadn't spent much time with anyone this age—ever.

"Guess you could say we do," Grampy said. "She has me to dinner every couple weeks or so. She makes the best dang apple pie you've ever put to your lips. And as you probably heard, her gingerbread ain't too shabby, either."

"Is she married?" Shane asked.

"Her husband, God rest his soul, passed a long time ago."

Shane took that in, thought a little bit more about people, choices, where you end up in life. Damn, maybe his dad's death had him contemplating shit like that more than he'd acknowledged to himself up to now. The truth was, for better or worse, his dad had been his foundation, the cornerstone of his life. He'd had friends along the way, but they came and went—his father was the only person who'd always been there. And now he was gone.

But that's why you're going to Miami. New start. New people. New life. Better life. Maybe. He hoped so, anyway.

"Reminds me," Grampy said, "don't reckon I know much about you. You got a family—kids or anything? A wife?"

Shane glanced over at the old man, then back out the window as they crossed a stone bridge that led to the main road. The creek beneath flowed fast with melting snow. "Me? Hell no. I'm on my own."

"Guess I shoulda figured—reckon that makes it a lot easier to up and head someplace new." He'd told Grampy about coming from Montana and that his destination was Miami, and that his father had just died.

Shane nodded easily as Grampy inquired further, "Ya got any family a'tall now that your pa's gone?"

Damn, sounded grim saying it, but there wasn't any way to put a good spin on that. So he kept it simple. "Nope."

"No grandfolks? Aunts or uncles? Cousins?"

"Nope."

"Reckon that ain't easy," Grampy said.

And Shane surprised himself by letting out a short laugh and replying, "Guess I don't know yet—still getting used to the idea."

Grampy chuckled gently, too, then changed the subject. "Did I see you makin' eyes at Candice Sheridan over the peppermint bark?"

That earned the old man another sideways look. "Making eyes? No." He might have noticed her, might have thought she looked pretty today—or kind of fresh or something—in a sort of fluffy snow-white sweater and her hair pulled up into another perky ponytail. But he hadn't been making eyes.

"Well, what was it then? 'Cause it looked like makin' eyes to me."

Shane sighed. "I stayed the night at her place when I wrecked my truck. So I know her a little, that's all."

Grampy raised his eyebrows, seeming too interested. "Stayed the night with her, did ya?"

But Shane threw up his hands in defense. "Whoa, whoa, whoa—it's not like that, trust me. The girl kinda hates me, in fact."

"What'd you do to her?" Grampy asked, wearing a sly sort of grin.

"Nothing." He gave his head a short, definitive shake. "But she acted like I was a damn ax murderer for asking to use her phone, and still seems to think I might be one."

Something about this made Grampy laugh a little more. "Candice is a little shy with fellas is all. Or at least that's been my observation. And coming to her door late at night in a blizzard—well, probably made her nervous."

"I *know* I made her nervous. But hell, it was either make her nervous or die in the damn snow." Then he looked back ahead, giving his head a short shake.

And Grampy kept on chuckling, even though Shane didn't know what the hell was so funny. Then he switched the topic again, which suited Shane just fine. "Anybody tell you about the big tree-lightin' ceremony tomorrow night on town square?"

"Yep." In fact, it seemed like almost all people could talk about. He stayed mostly quiet when working with the other guys on the cleanup and roof-covering efforts, but he'd heard all about the enormous tree the town ordered every year through Adam Becker's landscaping company, and that this year they'd had a hell of a time getting it to stand up, and how Logan Whitaker and the rest of the fire department took charge of putting the lights and ornaments on. The ornaments, he'd learned, were made by local schoolkids, but any resident could donate ornaments, too, as long as they were handmade. He'd tried to tune out some of the jabbering about it, but there it was—stuck in his brain.

"You comin' to it?" Grampy asked as they drove back toward town. "Free hot chocolate and music."

"Thanks," Shane said, "but I'll pass."

"Why's that?"

He kept his gaze out the windshield. "Christmas isn't really my thing."

"Christmas is *everybody's* thing."

Shane tossed the older man a glance, thinking that was a hell of a big assumption. "Not really."

"Now, just what do you got against Christmas?" Grampy asked.

They passed by the damaged church then, still waiting for the roof to be covered, and on the opposite side of the road, two teenage boys looked to be constructing a snow fort. "Maybe I, uh, got a lot of coal in my stocking over the years," Shane offered, tossing the old man half a grin.

"Didn't know you could do that," Grampy said, sounding amused.

"Do what?"

"Smile."

Shane sent another sideways glance across the cab of the truck. "Guess it's not something I make a habit of."

Then Grampy got back to the subject. "The tree-lightin' is one o' my favorite things."

"Is that so?" Shane replied absently, more out of courtesy than caring.

"Why, just look at that," Grampy said, motioning out the window at the tall tree as they drove past the square. "It's a grand and glorious sight in our humble little town. And I love me a good Christmas tree. Don't put one up in my own house the last few years, so I think of the town's tree as *my* tree."

Shane threw it back on him. "If you love them so much, why don't you put one up?"

The old man sighed. "Puttin' up trees ain't for the feeble—and guess, much as I hate to admit it, I'm gettin' feebler by the year. Back can't take the work." A moment later, Grampy pulled his truck into the narrow driveway next to the General Mercantile that led to a small lot in back and got it parked. Then looked to Shane. "You really don't like a nice Christmas tree?" He sounded truly perplexed, like he just couldn't fathom that.

But Shane only shook his head. "Not particularly. Like you say, it's a lot of work. Putting it up, taking it down. All for a few lights for a couple of weeks. Don't really get the appeal."

After Grampy killed the engine, they both got out, slammed the old pickup's doors, and started toward the warmth of the Mercantile.

"Tell you what," Grampy said, unlocking the front door, then turning the *Closed* sign to *Open* as they stepped in. "Why don't you come over to my house tomorrow evenin' for supper. I'll set a cottage ham and green beans and potatoes to simmerin' in the slow cooker for us—and that's a good country meal right there. Then we'll go to the tree-lightin' and see if it don't impress ya none."

Shane eyed Grampy Hoskins. "Let me get this straight," he said. "You're bribing me with a home-cooked meal to get me to go to this tree thing."

"Hadn't quite thunk of it that way, but reckon that's about the size of it."

Shane weighed his options and said, "Well hell, I never *could* turn down a good bribe."

The following morning Shane's muscles ached when he woke up to the sun shining in the window covered only by thin curtains he thought had once been yellow but were closer to white now. He pushed back the covers and stood up. Climbing around on a roof with a steep pitch plus sleeping on a lumpy sofa bed with springs that had seen better days was a recipe for soreness. But at least they'd gotten the church roof covered yesterday afternoon.

Going to the fridge, he pulled out some milk, courtesy of Grampy, and poured it over a plastic bowl of cereal with a pull-off lid, also courtesy of Grampy from the store below. A white plastic spoon from the drawer made the meal complete and he stood eating by the window, staring out on a snow-covered Destiny morning in his gray boxer briefs.

He caught sight of a woman in a ponytail walking up the sidewalk and for a second thought it was Candy—or Candice, whatever—but just as quickly realized he was wrong.

So he'd noticed the girl yesterday at Edna Farris's house. Big deal. A guy could think a woman was pretty without being into her. Hell, why would he be into someone who didn't seem to want anything to do with him?

She knows you're trouble. She can tell.

He'd acted to Grampy like the chick was just paranoid, but in fact, Shane couldn't really blame Miss Candy Cane for wanting to keep her distance. He guessed some people could just see the truth about him faster than others.

He didn't understand a lot about life, and it didn't seem to be getting any clearer. He didn't understand what had made him such a rotten kid that his mother hadn't wanted him. He didn't understand why a nice old man was being so kind to somebody who didn't deserve it. And he didn't understand how the hell he'd ended up stuck in this saccharin-sweet little town with only a few sad dollars to his name.

But he was going to at least try to find out the answer to the last one this morning.

Finishing the cereal, he tugged on a pair of jeans with a black T-shirt, and put a warm zip-up hoodie over it. Adding his coat, he headed out the door in back and down the wooden staircase, still slick in spots despite the work he'd done on it with a snow shovel. Thrusting his hands in his pockets to keep them warm, he started up the sidewalk toward town square.

He'd noticed the Destiny National Bank every time he'd walked or ridden past it, but this time he pulled open the door and went inside the old one-story brick building.

Stepping up to a teller's window, where a short, balding man asked what he could do for him today, Shane said, "I'd like to find out if you have a safe deposit box in the name of Shane Dalton. Or Gary Dalton." His father.

The man looked a little surprised, like anyone walking into this bank should know whether or not they have a safe deposit box, but he turned to a computer and started typing. A moment later, he said, "No, afraid not. Any other names you want me to check?"

Shane couldn't think of any. "Don't suppose there's any sort of savings account or anything under one of those names, either."

The man shook his head. "I did a general search, and we don't have any accounts for Dalton at all. Anything else I can help you with?"

Shane shifted his weight from one foot to the other, feeling discouraged. He'd hoped against hope that this might reveal some answers. But maybe this was why he'd waited a couple days to come—knowing that a no would be a letdown. "Any other banks in this town?" he asked.

The man shook his head. "Several in Crestview, but we're the only bank in Destiny."

Damn, this Crestview people referred to seemed to be a metropolis in comparison—but his father hadn't sent him to Crestview; he'd sent him here, to Destiny. So if there was anything waiting for him anywhere, it was in this town, not some other one.

"Thanks anyway," Shane said woodenly, then turned and exited the building.

The church was a short walk away, and Shane was about to start in that direction to see what he could help with next—when he spotted the Destiny Library across the square, next to the police station and community building. On a lark, he headed that way.

He'd already done some Googling on his phone, trying to tie his father's name to Destiny—with no results—but locating a bank of computers in the library, he approached one and took another shot at it. Looking on a big screen was easier, and maybe he'd missed something before.

He was scouring the search results in vain when a middle-aged librarian in a red sweater adorned with tiny Santa Clauses approached him and said he looked perplexed. "Can I help you find something?"

She had a nice smile, a gentle way about her—so he explained same as he had to Miss Candy Cane about his father sending him here with nothing to go on. As well as the additional heap of nothing he'd found so far.

She led him to the library's genealogy section, saying, "I've never heard of a Dalton family in Destiny, but why don't we look in some of the reference guides to be sure."

She did, and he did, too, alongside her—but no go.

The librarian peered up at him. "Could there be any other family names to look under?"

Shane thought about that, felt a little embarrassed, and just said, "No. Not really." *Not really because I don't even know enough about my family for that.* He didn't know his mother's maiden name. He didn't know his father's mother's maiden name. He knew nothing.

He thanked the nice lady for her help and walked out the door feeling at a dead end. Yep, this was why he hadn't been in a rush to start searching out answers. Because he'd feared there wouldn't be any. And it would mean he had indeed come to this godforsaken place for absolutely nothing. "Dad, if you were alive and well right now," he muttered as cold air blasted him in the face, "I'd kick your ass."

He didn't mean that, of course, but hell—this was fucking frustrating.

Just then, his pocket trilled and he realized it was his phone. A surprise because who the hell could be calling him? Though just as quickly, it hit him that he'd given his number to Rachel Romo and Mick Brody to keep in contact about repair work—so he pulled out the phone . . . only to see the name of the one other person on the planet whom he'd recently talked to on it: Donnie V.

Shit.

He punched the button to answer. "Donnie V.," he said in greeting, attempting to sound a little more upbeat about the call than he felt.

"Where the fuck are you, man?" Donnie V. asked in a thick Hispanic accent. "Wasn't you due here by now?"

Damn it. He should have called down to Miami and let the guy know his situation, but he'd actually been busier than expected most of the time since getting stuck here.

He stopped walking, stepped up under the marquee at the Ambassador Theater to get out of the wind. "I've had a setback," he explained. "Been postponed."

"What the fuck postponed you, man?" Donnie V. didn't sound the least bit understanding. In fact, he sounded a lot more like an ass than in previous conversations.

"Had an accident. In a blizzard. Fucked up my truck and waiting on repairs." When the other man said nothing, Shane added, "But I'm still coming. As soon as I can."

Donnie V. let out a long-suffering sigh. No sympathy for blizzards in Miami apparently. "The thing is, man, I need you here, was counting on you. You get that? Carl said you was dependable, but already, I see you letting me down."

Shane's jaw clenched slightly. "Look, this was beyond my control, but I'm dealing with it. It was one hell of a freak snowstorm."

"I don't really give a fuck about no freak snowstorm— it's not my problem. My problem is a shop that needs a knowledgeable parts man. I was told that was you."

"It *is* me," Shane assured him. Even if part of him wanted to tell Donnie V. where he could stick his precious job. But he worked to keep his cool. The job was the endgame here, after all, the whole reason he was traveling across the country in the first place. "I'll do solid work for you. And, uh, speaking of that, you never really told me exactly what the job *is*."

"You know the gig's gonna give you some deep pockets and have you livin' large, so does it really matter?"

Hell. Every damn time he'd asked, he'd been given

this same kind of non-answer. "Just curious," he said now.

Donnie V. surprised him then by laughing and replying, "Let's just say we deal in . . . high-quality auto parts. That good enough?"

Shane let out a sigh, a small knot forming in his gut. "Yep, sure," he heard himself say, even if it came out more stiffly than intended.

Because the truth was that he'd begun to worry the place would turn out to be a garden variety chop shop. Even if for high-end vehicles, since Miami had more than its fair share of those. And maybe that was why he hadn't pressed harder for an answer—he wanted his new start to be a clean one. As clean as a guy like him could have anyway.

And maybe it still *would* be—maybe he'd get there and find a completely aboveboard operation just run by a guy with a bad personality.

And if that was just crazy-ass wishful thinking . . . well, he didn't have to do it forever. He just needed to make some money, get out of the hole his father's illness had left him in. A little cash, plus some more when the house in Montana sold . . . and things would be better.

"So you're still in?" Donnie V. asked him.

"Yeah, I'm in."

"Then when you gonna get your ass down here?"

"As soon as it's physically possible. You won't be sorry you waited for me."

On the other end of the line, Donnie V. stayed quiet a minute—and then finally said, "Listen, dude, because Carl vouched for you, and because I don't trust any of the asswipes already on my payroll to run this place, and because I guess I'm feelin' all generous and shit like fucking Santa Claus, you got until Christmas to get yourself to the Magic City. Got it?"

"Got it."

"And on December 26, the job goes bye-bye." With that, the other man hung up.

Shane shoved his phone in his back pocket, then his hands in his front ones. At last check with Mo, the ETA for repairs was the end of the week. That would leave another week plus change to get the body work done. And hell, as long as they made the damn thing drivable, even if that meant leaving before it was painted, that was all that mattered.

He could get to Miami by Christmas—and he would, come hell or high . . . snow.

"We're going to give the biggest party this town ever saw."

Uncle Billy, *It's a Wonderful Life*

Seven

$\mathcal{S}$ome of the girls gathered at Under the Covers before the tree-lighting ceremony, mainly because it was a good place to keep warm before the festivities started. Candice arrived the same time as Jenny, Mick, and Dustin—and she and Jenny left the two boys with Mick's friends on the square before ducking into the bookstore. Inside, Amy had holiday music playing—currently Elton John was inviting them to step into Christmas.

"Who's this?" Tessa was asking Amy as they walked in. Tessa had just scooped a small pale grayish-white cat—little more than a kitten really—up into her arms from one of the easy chairs in the sitting area near the

door. "Her face looks a little like Brontë's, but fluffier."
Brontë was the cat Amy had pawned off on Tessa years
earlier.

"This is Holly, the new cat I mentioned at the cookie
party," Amy said. "She earned her name by batting at
the fake holly on the coffee table when I first took her
in. And as you can see, she's very sweet." Then she
glanced around the group—Anna Romo and Sue Ann
were there as well—and asked, "Would anyone like a
second cat?"

"*No!*" they all said in unison.

She looked offended. "You guys don't have to gang
up on me."

"Face it," Anna said. "When it comes to friends to
shove stray cats onto, you're tapped out. You need a
new source of unwitting victims."

Amy sighed. "Well, if you guys can think of anyone
who might like a nice kitty, let me know. I'd like for
this one to find a home by Christmas. Just because . . .
you know, it's Christmas. And everyone should have a
home at Christmas."

Just then, Rachel walked in, clipboard in hand. Other
than at the cookie exchange, Candice hadn't seen her
without it since the blizzard and ensuing damage. At
the party, she'd found out that Edna was babysitting
Rachel and Mike's daughter, a pretty little girl named
Farris—Rachel's maiden name—while Rachel helped
spearhead the repair efforts.

"I'm glad you're all here," Jenny announced.
"Because I have great news."

"Well, Destiny could use some of that right about
now," Rachel said, "so spill."

"Mick and I figured out the perfect place to have the annual Christmas party while the church and community building are under repair. Miss Ellie's cottage! And she's already agreed."

Despite her advanced age, their neighbor-in-common had been hosting various Destiny events for as long as Candice could remember. Even if Miss Ellie's daughters, Mary Katherine and Linda Sue, had long since done all the actual work involved. Miss Ellie loved the company, and gatherings at her home were a longstanding and much-beloved town tradition.

"And I know this will be different, being in wintertime and all, but I think with a little creativity, we can make it work!"

"I love it!" Tessa said.

"Me too," Amy agreed. "It's perfect."

Rachel, standing near the door, began nodding, then glancing down at her clipboard. "Now all we need is someone to organize it. I have all the usual volunteers knee-deep in cleanup."

And that was when Candice saw an opportunity and said, "I'll do it."

They all looked toward her, and Rachel said, "You will?"

"It makes sense, really. I'm her nearest neighbor, so it will be easy for me to work on the preparations. And I've . . . meant to get back involved with Destiny activities for a long time, so this is my chance."

Once upon a time, as a younger woman, she'd been more outgoing in the community. Once upon a time before Bobby Wayans had decimated her heart. He'd damaged a big enough part of her that she'd just wanted to keep to herself for a while—and after that, it had simply become . . . habit. A thing that was easier to continue than to change. Lately, though, she'd begun feeling . . . a little lonely, and like maybe her life had become a little too quiet. So it was time to take that part of herself back, once and for all.

And the further truth was—the real opportunity here lay in being able to volunteer, do her part, but in a way that would keep her away from Shane Dalton. He and most people would be busy in town, at the church while she would now be a few miles away, quietly planning a party on her own. There wouldn't be any bumping into him. There wouldn't be any skitters of sensation. There wouldn't be any old memories and fears cropping up about past bad-boy mistakes and not wanting to repeat them. This was the perfect way to keep her distance from him until he was gone, never to darken Destiny's doorstep again.

"It's kind of a big job," Rachel said, "but if you're willing to take it on, that's great."

Candice nodded and said, "I am. I'm excited about it, in fact, and I promise I'll throw a great party."

"And we're here to pitch in," Sue Ann added. "Most of us have planned a few big events, so we can help make sure you've got all your bases covered, and take on some of the tasks."

"And Mick can haul anything big you need from the community building or church basement—like tables, and Grampy's Santa chair," Jenny offered. It was a big, throne-like thing—complete with red velvet upholstery—that spent 364 days of the year in a storage room.

"Great," Candice said with a smile, feeling like this was already starting to come together.

A few minutes later they all bundled back up and headed over to the square, leaving the little stray cat, Holly, behind. It was clear to see Amy felt bad about that as she put out food and water for the kitty, and plugged in a night-light before locking up the store.

Exiting out into the cold caused Candice to shiver and zip her parka all the way up. She and Tessa and Sue Ann made their way to the hot chocolate stand manned by Sue Ann's daughter, Sophie, and a couple of other middle school girls, and as she took a steaming-hot cup between her mittens, she wondered if Shane Dalton had ever gotten any gloves.

Oh God, stop already. Why on earth do you care? He's a big boy and can take care of himself.

"I'm so excited you're planning this party," Tessa said to her.

She met her pretty cousin's gaze. "I know—me too." Tessa knew her well, and though they'd never talked about it, she supposed the whole family was aware of how reserved she'd gotten over the years.

"Oh, there's Adam!" Sue Ann said, pointing—and the trio made their way to Sue Ann's classically handsome boyfriend, who stood with Logan and Mike Romo, coordinating the last few details of lighting the tree.

As the rest of them stood talking, Candice started thinking about the party plans and related tasks. There would be setting up tables at Miss Ellie's and, as Jenny had mentioned, carting things from the church and community building with Mick's help—in addition to the big items like tables and chairs, there would be smaller ones like the hot chocolate and coffee machines. She'd need to confirm with Grampy that he would reprise his usual role as Santa. And confirm with Caroline Lindley that she'd play the piano for caroling—and fortunately Miss Ellie already had a piano. And she'd enlist people to provide cookies and candies and cakes and breads, along with eggnog and some soda. Easy peasy.

And while the snow and cold would provide some unique challenges, she resolved to turn those challenges into blessings—find ways to make the party special *because* of them.

Maybe . . . there could be ice-skating this year, given the venue. Maybe she could hang lights in the trees and shrubbery in Miss Ellie's English garden and they could put the Santa chair in her gazebo, along with a portable heater or two. She was going to make this the best Destiny Christmas party ever.

"Everything set?" Mick asked the other guys as he approached, carrying his son on one hip. "This kid's getting sleepy on me already."

Adam Becker looked around. "We're ready to go—but we were thinking of having Chief Tolliver and Anita do the honors, under the circumstances. Have you seen either of them?"

Mick shook his head. "They're not coming tonight. Walter called earlier. Between running the Dew Drop, pulling Christmas together, and finishing up wedding plans, Anita is strapped for time."

Everyone nodded, and it went without saying that perhaps the woman was also under some *additional* stress, what with wondering if her wedding venue would actually be ready on schedule. No one knew much about

Anita's past, but it seemed like it had held some darkness, and no one begrudged her wanting to experience her dream wedding.

"Guess we'll roll without 'em then," Mike said.

A few minutes later the mayor stepped onto a temporary pedestal near the tree, microphone in hand. Music had been playing—Mariah Carey's "All I Want for Christmas Is You"—but it went silent and the mayor addressed the crowd, thanking everyone for coming.

As he went on, talking about the recent blizzard and how Destiny always pulled together in times of trouble, Candice's eyes fell on Shane Dalton in the crowd. He stood with Grampy Hoskins and Edna across the way. No gloves.

Ugh, why did she have to find him attractive now? Why did she have to think he looked all cuddly and nice to curl up with next to a fireplace? She hadn't felt that way when he'd pretty much barged into her house that first night.

Though she supposed, if she was honest with herself, that she'd felt *something*. She'd just been afraid of him then—in a different way than she was now. And that sort of fear, for her safety, had apparently overridden stark desire. Fear for her heart, it seemed, wasn't doing nearly as good a job.

Just then, Tessa arrived back at her side. "For what it's worth, I agree with Edna."

Feeling caught at something, Candice flicked her gaze hurriedly to her older cousin. "What do you mean?" Even though she already knew good and well what Tessa meant.

It made her uneasy when Tessa hesitated—and when

her reply came out sounding . . . deep. Serious. "When I met Lucky, I was nervous as hell. He scared me to death. I mean, he was in a motorcycle gang, for heaven's sake. But . . . I was so drawn to him that I decided I didn't want to let the opportunity pass me by. No matter what it brought. And I just went for it. It took a lot of courage for me to do that, believe me. But it's the best move I ever made."

Candice took that in. And she thought about just sticking to her story, denying her attraction, claiming she still thought Shane was some sort of dangerous convict type. Really, given how little anyone knew about him—clean license plate check or not—it was a reasonable, practical argument.

Yet Tessa was being so real with her right now, opening up to her—even though Candice didn't often open up to *anyone* . . . but maybe she should. So she answered with honesty. "What if it's *not* the best move I ever make? What if I'm right to be wary? What if he wants nothing to do with me? What if I get hurt?"

Tessa didn't answer instantly—she thought it over. And then she said, "I think my point actually was . . . that it's a risk. Always. And that you have to be okay with whatever happens. But . . . if you never go for it, if you never put yourself out there, if you never take a chance . . . you miss out on life. And I worry for you, Candice. I worry you're missing out on life." Then she stopped, looked down, shook her head. "I'm sorry—I know maybe it's none of my business and I'm being pushy here. But I also know the dating pool is shallow around here and that it's not easy to meet new people when you've lived in the same small town your whole life. And suddenly there's somebody new in town. And I just thought I sensed some sparks between the two of you at Edna's yesterday, and . . ."

"It's all right," Candice assured her. She appreciated her sweet cousin's care and concern. "It's just . . . well, among other issues, he's not staying here. You know? So . . ."

Tessa nodded. "Yeah, I understand why that's an issue—I really do. But even something temporary that's really good can be well worth it. And life is short. That's all I'm saying."

"And to flip the switch," Candice heard the mayor announce then, "here's our own Grampy Hoskins."

Standing in the crowd with everyone else, Grampy looked surprised by the honor as he drew back slightly. Then Edna said, "Go on, Willie," giving him a good-natured nudge, and he ambled toward the platform. Apparently since Anita and Walter weren't on hand, they'd decided on Grampy instead, and the old man looked pleased as punch about it.

"My oh my, what a sweet surprise," he said into the microphone. "I was tellin' young Shane here—" he motioned toward him "—how I see our town square tree like it's my very own, so it's mighty nice to turn the lights on for y'all. Destiny is a special place—nowhere else on this earth I'd rather live. And it's partly about our rollin' hills and our picket fences and our old-fashioned town square here, but mostly it's about the people. And the spirit of community. I thank each and every one of ya for makin' it that way. And even though we got our work cut out for us gettin' these dang repairs done on the church in short order, I know we'll give

Walter and Anita the weddin' they deserve—and I wish you all a real merry Christmas!"

Candice had no idea why her eyes flitted to Shane in that moment when every other was on the big tree in front of them. Well, every other but his—because he was looking right back at her.

Their gazes held as hundreds of twinkling colored lights illuminated the cold night air.

As a collective "Ahhh" echoed from the crowd, and then applause.

As people marveled at the beauty of the tree, and music started up again—the whole crowd breaking into "O Christmas Tree," another town tradition.

Her heart beat too fast in her chest. And though it was impossible, she could have sworn she saw the blue in his eyes even from as far away as he stood.

But then she finally broke the gaze, unable to handle the strange intensity of it for even a second more, and started walking away.

"Where are you going?" Tessa stopped singing to call after her. Despite the pep talk, she was pretty sure her cousin had just missed the whole smoldering stare episode because she'd been watching the tree-lighting like everyone else.

"Bathroom at the café," Candice said over her shoulder, then rushed away, across the square, across the snow, across the street to Dolly's.

The sad truth was, she hadn't dated anyone since Bobby. And five years had passed. Five. It was awful, she knew. And even a little embarrassing if she let herself think about it, let herself wonder if other people noticed.

But it had taken a while to get over the heartbreak. And after that . . . well, it wasn't that she didn't *want* to date. It was like Tessa had said—not much of a dating pool when you lived in a small town surrounded by farms and hillsides. And given that she worked at home and kept to herself a lot—at least until lately—where would she have met anyone?

So she'd grown content to live without romance. Content to just write her instruction manuals and exist on her own. Content to spend time with her mother, Alice, who had also lived without romance since Candice's father had left them when she was young. Content to forge quiet friendships and live a quiet existence.

But did her body feel the same way? Content without romance or passion of any kind?

She'd done pretty well with that until now. She'd seemed to have a pretty low sex drive since that ill-fated love affair.

Except for maybe when she looked at Shane Dalton.

Shake that off already.

He's only here for a couple of weeks, for God's sake. And he's so not your type. If you even have a type. Bobby hadn't been what she thought of as her type either, and that had been her first mistake—to go for the mysterious bad boy.

Dolly's was fairly quiet other than a few folks coming in to warm up with coffee and grab a slice of pie now that the tree was lit. As she exited back out into the night through the café's plate-glass door a few minutes later, cold bit at her nose and the sounds of laughter and more caroling could be heard coming from the square. She pulled up the hood on her parka to ward off the bitter air.

You should go back. Find your friends. Have fun.

But she didn't think she could do what Tessa had suggested—"go for" anything with Shane. There were too many reasons it was a bad idea. If she was meant to explore romance again, it wasn't with him.

And that decision made it easier *not* to go back. To just text Tessa that she was leaving, in case anyone even noticed. And to find her car and go home to her cat. It wasn't a return to being anti-social. She'd just volunteered to plan a big town party, after all. And it was cold out. And she was tired. Going home was okay.

She pulled off one mitten, reached for her phone, then typed the text to her cousin as she crossed the quiet street and walked along the sidewalk approaching the bookstore, bypassing most of the crowd. She'd just hit Send when she collided with someone—hard.

"Oh!" she said and they both drew back.

And—oh God. *Of course* it was Shane Dalton.

He squinted at her. "Is that you in there, Candy Cane?"

Oh. Lord. She'd *had* to put up her hood, hadn't she? "I just can't seem to get away from you," she muttered—not quite realizing she'd said that out loud until he let out a laugh, something she didn't think she'd heard from him before.

"Look, I know I made you uncomfortable on the night of the storm, but damn—you really don't like me, do you?" He didn't sound exactly bothered by the notion—and she felt rather foolish since, indeed, he'd really given her no reason to continue being so rude other than reminding her of her unscrupulous ex-boyfriend. "Did I do something to you I don't know about?" he asked.

"There are plenty of people I don't like, so you're nothing special." Oh crap. That hadn't come out at all like she'd meant it to. She blinked. And felt her usual reaction to him in her panties.

"How's your cat?" he asked.

"My cat?" Why on earth was he asking about her cat? "Fine."

"He plan any more escapes trying to find a friendlier owner?"

She rolled her eyes. "He's perfectly happy with his owner, I assure you."

Shane shrugged. "Seems debatable, but whatever. I'll leave you to your grouchiness."

Her back went rigid, her jaw dropping, as he started to go. "*My* grouchiness? You're not exactly Mr. Bubbly yourself."

Another shrug from him as her words stopped him. "I was dragged here against my will."

"By whom?"

"Grampy Hoskins."

And when she least expected it, the very mention of the old man's name relaxed her attitude. And made her be a little nicer. Everyone loved Grampy. "He has a way of being convincing. And why did you have to be dragged? I mean, it's a nice event. And I'm not sure what you have to do that's any better."

Okay, maybe that last part hadn't been so nice—and now he took on a slightly belligerent look, more like what she was accustomed to from him. "I'm happy to help out with repairs and stuff while I'm here, but Christmas isn't my thing." He gave his head a short, dismissive shake.

Christmas "wasn't his thing"? She frowned at him. "How very Grinchy of you. I hope my decorations didn't bother you too much when you were at my house."

"I didn't really notice them."

"Well, that's a shame for you," she informed him smartly, "because they're lovely."

"If you like that sort of thing."

"Most people do."

"I'm not most people."

"That's for sure." She finished with a sarcastic tip of her head.

When he let out a deep sigh, she felt his presence even more completely for the sudden silence between them. It was a heaviness—the weight of her attraction to him. Ugh.

"Well, now that we've thoroughly gotten on each other's nerves, guess I'll see you around, Candy Cane."

"Hopefully not too soon," she said. Not that she meant to keep being catty. But she meant the words—he might be hot, but the farther away he stayed, the better off she'd be. And as for that look between them a few minutes ago . . . well, maybe *that* was why she was being catty. To make sure he didn't think that look meant anything. Because it *couldn't* mean anything— she wasn't going to let it.

"I second that," he informed her.

Fine, whatever.

Just then, Rachel appeared between them with a smile. "Hey, you two."

Crap. Now it would be awkward for either of them to walk away.

She looked to Candice. "I've already put some plans

in place to help you get rolling on the party. Mick and Logan are going to clear snow from Miss Ellie's garden for the outside part of the party, and clear paths to the door."

"And to the dock, too, please," Candice requested. "I'm thinking we'll have ice-skating."

Rachel's face brightened. "Oh that's nice!" Then she got back to business. "And Mike is going to loan Shane his truck—and Shane, you can bring the Santa chair and banquet tables to Miss Ellie's and help Candice get it all set up and in place." Then she looked back and forth between them with a smile. "Don't you love it when a plan comes together?"

"You're screwy, and you're driving me crazy, too."

George Bailey, *It's a Wonderful Life*

Eight

Candice blinked. Twice. "Wh—wh—wh—"

"I think what she's trying to say is something like over her dead body," Shane volunteered.

"No," Candice spat, finding her voice. Then looked to Rachel. "Just . . . I thought you said Mick would do it. And since he lives right up the road that makes more sense. Don't you think?"

"Not really," Rachel replied. "Mick has taken on an integral role in repairing the church. Since his bricklaying job slows in winter and is pretty much impossible anyway until after all this snow melts, he can be on-site full-time, coordinating work and making sure it moves forward. And most of the guys are juggling their help with their regular jobs—plus holiday and family stuff. So Shane is the perfect choice to help with something extra, so long as he's willing."

"I'm willing," he said, voice low. "Told Grampy I'd do whatever's needed while I'm here and I meant it."

Rachel smiled. "Then it's settled."

As Candice walked away, toward her car parked around the corner, she struggled with warring emotions.

One part of her wanted to be back at the tree-lighting, cold or not, singing carols and hanging out with the people she'd become friends with the last couple of years. But another part of her, like when she'd left the diner, wanted to just go home, put on some flannel pajamas, and hug her unaffectionate cat whether he liked it or not.

One part of her wanted to be as far away from Shane Dalton as possible. So that she would quit feeling all tingly and heavy and warm inside, so that her body would quit pulsing with old needs he'd somehow made new again. But another part of her wanted . . . more.

Dangerous things. Like kissing. And touching.

For her, getting physical with a man was real, true intimacy. She didn't do it lightly—and that part wasn't about Bobby; she'd *never* done it lightly, even before him.

She had to be comfortable with a guy, and she'd always been aware of certain risks in succumbing to desire: Would you like how it felt with that person once you were in it, moving forward with the touching and the kissing? Would *they* like how it felt to touch and kiss *you*? Would you kiss the same? What if it all felt more awkward than natural, or more like effort than passion?

But with Bobby, the chemistry had been so strong that it had brushed all those risks aside. The kissing and touching—and the sex; the sweet, hot sex—had come as naturally as breathing. The risks with him had turned out to be entirely different ones.

And already, she feared . . . suspected . . . *knew* . . . that it would be the same with Shane. Like breathing. No trying, just doing.

Getting into her car and starting the ignition, she turned the heat on high and felt . . . safe. Cocooned. She'd sought that feeling in her house, too, and even in her job. That safety of being alone, totally at her ease, wrapped in that solitary comfort.

But as she put the car in Drive and eased out onto the slushy street, heading away from the lights and energy of the square, she experienced a certain pull back in that direction—again, suffering the struggle to go two opposite ways—and knew the time really had come for her to make some changes.

She wasn't sure the change should be Shane Dalton, though.

In a couple of weeks, she'd never see him again. And passion, sex—it came with emotions for her. And why would she want to get involved—especially that way— with someone who would only be in her life such a short time?

He can't hurt you later.

She wasn't sure where the words had come from, but it was as if someone had whispered them in her ear.

And it hit her how true they were—if you know

something has limits and you go into it with eyes wide open, maybe that made the ending okay. After all, how much could someone hurt her in only a week or two or however long he'd be here?

But what are you thinking?

You aren't the sort of woman who has fly-by-night affairs. You aren't the sort of woman who has any *affairs. You don't know how to make a move on a guy— and even if you did, what if he rejected you?*

Okay, that settled it. As she turned onto Blue Valley Road, she decided once and for all—Shane Dalton was a bad idea for her, chemistry or not.

And as for the fact that Rachel was insisting on shoving them together, totally ruining her grand plan of avoidance . . . well, she'd take that as it came. He'd be in her space at Miss Ellie's for a day, maybe two. She'd live. And then he'd leave. And life—and Christmas— would go on in Destiny just fine without him.

A few nights later, Shane sat at Grampy Hoskins' old Formica kitchen table eating dinner—again. Tonight old-fashioned chicken and noodles from the Crock-Pot, good for a wintry night.

Grampy had invited him, so he'd accepted—a hungry man couldn't really afford to refuse, after all. But also turned out the old man was decent company—a damn sight better than sitting alone in the rooms above the store.

"You said Edna has you over for dinner sometimes," Shane remarked as he bit into a freshly buttered biscuit. "You ever invite *her* over *here*?"

Grampy's thick white brows knit. "Over here? No." He'd sounded like it was a preposterous idea.

"I'm just sayin'—for an old guy, you're a pretty damn good cook."

Grampy waved away the compliment. "It's the slow cooker does the work—not me."

Shane just shrugged. "Good eatin', no matter who's doin' the work," Shane told him, "and maybe Edna wouldn't mind a home-cooked meal she didn't have to make herself."

Now Grampy arched a brow. "What's got into you all the sudden?"

And Shane sat up a little straighter. "What do you mean?"

Grampy eyed him curiously. "Don't get me wrong, but you just ain't struck me as the sort to sit around thinkin' about what other people might like or not like."

Shane turned that over in his head. Maybe caring for his father had made him that way for a while, a little more considerate—but then he'd stopped. And Grampy's observation was on the money—it wasn't Shane's nature. Because he was a bad egg. So he said to Grampy, "You're right. All you damn nice people around here must be rubbing off on me. Forget I said anything."

Huh, why had that popped into his head—that he was a "bad egg"?

But, ah, he remembered now—his father had once confided to him that his mother had said that. On the long drive to Montana. *Your mama wanted you gone, Shaney, just like she wanted me gone. Thinks you're just a bad egg, no good in ya. But that don't matter none to me, Shaney, I still love ya. And I'm not all that much of a good egg myself, so me and you, we'll stick together. Me and you against the world, huh? We'll get us a new start, just the two of us.*

And that was how it had always been. As an adult, looking back, Shane could see his father hadn't instilled many values in him—truth was, his father had gotten them to Montana on money stolen from his employer at the time, a tire shop owner who'd trusted him too much with the till.

But Shane had been as glad as he was scared and hurt upon finding out he was such a burden that his mom didn't want him anymore. Glad *somebody* loved him. Even if his father had always been stealing something here or there to get them by. He'd taught Shane that it was okay to take from people who had more than you— "since they probably just took it from somebody else," his dad was fond of saying.

Shane understood now that wasn't true. Growing up had shown him that . . . and shown him, too, that maybe his *dad* never really *had* grown up in some ways. And so he'd tried to earn an honest living as much as possible, keep both him and his pop afloat as best as he was able.

They'd run with a crowd that made it easy to do the wrong thing, but he'd tried to find balance there—at least as well as a guy could who'd been deemed trouble before he was even ten years old.

And so maybe making that long return trip to Ohio from Montana had somehow brought back memories of the drive in the other direction, like the "bad egg" one.

"You do any cookin'?" Grampy asked.

Shane shook his head, then shoveled a forkful of chicken and noodles into his mouth. "Nope."

"Easier than you'd think with a Crock-Pot. You maybe oughta think o' gettin' yourself one when you get where you're goin'."

Shane considered the idea for a moment—but Miami was hot, and food like this wouldn't make much sense there. And he'd probably be too busy anyway. With the fast cars and fast women and all. Though . . . maybe all that had somehow started sounding a little less exciting since his last phone call from Donnie V.

After dinner, they opened up a holiday tin covered with polar bears and snowmen to have some of Edna's gingerbread for dessert, which she'd given Grampy at the tree-lighting gala. "Damn, this is good," Shane remarked. He'd never really eaten gingerbread before—gingerbread cookies, and houses, but not real gingerbread.

"Edna's a fine baker for sure," Grampy said.

And Shane tilted his head and asked Grampy something he'd been wondering. "About Edna—you, uh, ever think about trying to get you some of that?"

Grampy looked confused. "Some o' what? Her gingerbread? Already got some." He gave the slice in his hand a little shake.

After which Shane couldn't hold in a small laugh. "That's not what I meant. I meant . . ." He reached for a more old-fashioned way of saying it. "You ever think about dating her?"

At this, Grampy jerked to stiff attention, clearly even more shocked at this suggestion than the last one. "Why, no. I told ya, Edna's my dearest, oldest friend."

"Uh, maybe that's my point. You already know you get along with her. And she's an unattached woman and you're an unattached dude, so I'm just doing the math is all."

"But her late husband, Eddie, was my best friend. So it don't seem right."

"How long ago'd he die?" Shane asked.

"Reckon . . . twenty-five, maybe even thirty years now."

Shane just blinked. "Dude. I was a little kid then."

"So?"

"So it was a damn long time ago. I think it'd be okay for you two to hook up. If you wanted to, I mean."

Across the table, Grampy stayed silent for a moment, appearing to think that over.

Finally, Shane asked, "Are you telling me you've really never thought about this before? In all these years?"

Grampy nodded. "Can't say as I have."

Shane sighed. "Well then, maybe it's a bad idea. Seems like if you had those kinds of feelings for her, it would have crossed your mind by now."

So it surprised the hell out of him when Grampy lifted a hand and said, "Well now, just hold your horses there for a minute and let me ponder this."

Which made Shane laugh again and inform him, "I think you're into her and you don't even know it. Know why?"

"Why?"

"There's something in your face right now I haven't seen before—a little light in your eye. I think you're *way* into Edna, dude, and you're just now figuring it out."

This made the old man flatten out his lips between

his white mustache and beard. "Well now, you might be puttin' the cart ahead of the horse there, son—and maybe you best just stop lookin' at me tryin' to figure out what's goin' on inside me. But . . . like I said, just let me ruminate on this awhile."

And suddenly Grampy Hoskins seemed . . . a little nervous. Like a kid with his first crush. Shane wouldn't have believed it if he hadn't witnessed it himself—but hell, it was almost . . . cute or something. Even though Shane couldn't remember the last time he'd thought anything was cute.

Well, other than little miss Candy Cane. At moments anyway.

Mainly the ones where she wasn't acting like he was the scum of the earth.

"So while you're here," Grampy said then, "what say you help me get my sleigh in the yard?"

Shane squinted. "Your what?" Was he hearing things?

And Grampy just laughed, leaning back in his chair to pat his belly under the bib of his overalls. "My sleigh. Got a real nice one—out in the barn." He pointed over his shoulder—but Shane had only been to Grampy's house after dark, so he didn't know there *was* a barn. "I put it in the front yard as a Christmas decoration every year even since I quit puttin' up a tree, I still bring out the sleigh. Folks enjoy it—it's a Destiny tradition."

Together, the two men put on their coats, and Grampy grabbed a couple of flashlights from a drawer to help them make their way on a path already well beaten down in the snow. Once there, he undid a paddle lock, swung open a wooden door, and flipped a few switches until dim lights came on, inside and out.

Before Shane stood a shiny red sleigh worthy of Santa himself.

"Damn," he said. "Nice."

Coming from Montana, he'd seen a few sleighs hitched up here and there over the years, but he'd never had occasion to actually get this close to one, and it felt a little like he'd stepped into a Christmas card. "Does it work?" he asked. "I mean, do you ever use it? Take a sleigh ride like they talk about in songs?"

"Hell yeah," Grampy said, surprising him with the vigor of the answer. Then he slanted a look in Shane's direction. "Don't tell me you ain't never been on a sleigh ride before?"

"Um, nope."

Grampy just shook his head, like it was a shortcoming. "One o' life's simple pleasures, son."

"Sounds cold," Shane thought out loud.

"That's why the good Lord made blankets and hats," the old man told him. Then grinned. "Let's hook up the horse and take her for a spin out the ridge."

Shane just stared, nonplussed. "You have a horse? And a ridge?"

Grampy looked at him like he was slow. "Yes, I have a horse and a ridge."

Shane defended himself with widened eyes. "I've never been here in the daylight, so how would I know?"

A moment later, Grampy led Shane out along another well-trodden path in the snow to another barn—bigger, in fact—with a horse inside it. Along with horse *smell*. "This here's Charley. Get it? Charley Horse."

The horse was sizable and stout, sporting a thick brown winter coat—with a white star on his forehead.

Grampy showed Shane step by step how to harness the docile beast and get him attached to the sleigh. Shane didn't suspect it was a skill he'd need in Miami, but he could tell Grampy was enjoying the teaching of it, so he pretended to enjoy the learning.

Grampy explained to Shane that the back barn door opened into a meadow where Charley grazed in better weather and that other than being watered and fed, he mostly took care of himself. "But as you might expect, he's been spendin' the better part of his time inside since the storm hit."

Grampy soon climbed up onto the sleigh's black leather seat and motioned Shane to join him.

Shane wore a zip-up hoodie under his coat, and he pulled the hood up as Grampy gave a soft, "Get up," snapping the reins. Already he was pretty sure he was right—this was gonna be cold. He shoved his hands in his pockets.

But soon he realized he couldn't keep them there—he needed them to hold on for dear life because for being a staid, quiet type of old man, Grampy was driving this thing like a bat out of hell.

"Damn," Shane muttered under his breath as they picked up speed on a straight stretch. The moon shining on the snow was the only thing lighting the way on Grampy's ridge and this seemed dangerous as hell.

"Grab hold o' somethin' and don't be a wimp, boy," Grampy said. "I ain't no Sunday driver."

Shane did as he was told, cold hands or not. With one he gripped the seat and with the other a small rail in front of him. Cold air bit at his face as Grampy snapped the reins harder and yelled, "Hyah!" Like he was a damn barrel racer or something.

As Charley picked up speed, pressing through the snow, which seemed less deep here—maybe from wind on the ridge—the sleigh seemed to fly and even caught a little air a time or two. Shane wasn't sure whether to be invigorated or to fear for his life, but he eventually opted for the first, just continuing to hold on tight.

Soon enough he found himself laughing—at the whole damn thing. Who'd have thought he'd find himself soaring through the night on a sleigh with an old man at the reins in the middle of nowhere when he'd expected to be in Miami by now? And who'd have thought he'd actually be enjoying it? Next to him, Grampy wore a big smile, too, and Shane was glad to see the old guy having some fun.

After a brisk and wild few minutes, Grampy pulled up on the reins and eventually brought the horse to a stop. They'd gotten far enough from the house and barns that no lights could be seen at all but for the winter moon and stars overhead. Grampy turned to him with a sly look unlike anything Shane had witnessed on his face before. "Reckon you think I'm some ole stick-in-the-mud codger, but who's the stick-in-the-mud now, m'boy?"

Shane couldn't argue with that.

That was when Grampy looked like he'd just gotten a great idea. "Want to drive us back?"

"Not really."

To Shane's surprise, Grampy just laughed, then shoved the reins into his hands anyway. "Let me show ya how to drive."

"I'm not sure I want—"

"Shush, and listen," Grampy said. Then instructed

him on how to guide the sleigh, whether he wanted to learn or not.

So Shane listened, did what the old man told him, and soon had them and Charley starting gingerly back along the path they'd just carved on the ridge. "There ya go," Grampy said softly. "You got it. Now keep 'er goin'. And don't be afraid to pick up a little speed—this ain't a parkin' lot."

Shane just cast the old guy an amused look of warning, then refocused on the path before him as he got used to driving the sleigh.

"So . . . you and the Sheridan girl?" Grampy asked out of the blue, sounding hopeful.

This earned Grampy another sideways glance. "Nope, she still hates my guts."

"That's a shame," the old man said. "She's a perty one. Sweet, too."

"And tomorrow," Shane informed him, concentrating on his task as he spoke, "I'm supposed to help her set up for a town Christmas party."

"Biggest shindig in Destiny and most always a good one," Grampy said, then sounded pleased with himself as he added, "I'll be playin' Santa Claus."

Shane shot him a look from behind the reins. "I'm not sitting on your knee, old man."

Grampy let out a belly laugh at that. And they rode in silence another moment before he asked, "So if she didn't hate your guts, would you . . . wanna get you some o' that?"

Now it was Shane who laughed. Grampy was catching on.

Then he thought it over and conceded, "Maybe."

"I know what you're feeling. I won't ever tell a soul. Hope to die, I won't."

George Bailey, *It's a Wonderful Life*

Nine

Candice had a plan in place. She'd spent time at Miss Ellie's the past couple of days getting the party mapped out in her mind, letting the pieces come together. She'd made lists and diagrams. She'd called on Jenny to help organize refreshments, and as promised, Mike and Logan had spent yesterday clearing snow while she had instructed them on the task—even if Mike had groused a little, Logan had been his amiable self and told Mike to, "Shut up and do what the lady says."

Mike had once made her mother cry by giving her a speeding ticket. But in fairness, her mother was a terrible driver. And she'd decided to let the grousing go both because Mike, for all his hotness, could just be a bit of a hard-ass who probably only a woman with a personality as strong as Rachel's could live with, and because Candice knew all the guys were overworked right now, doing their normal jobs *plus* helping with repairs *plus* handling the extra activities and duties that Christmastime brought.

Being at the party site the last two days had also, of course, meant spending time with Miss Ellie, who was severely hard of hearing yet pleasant to be with otherwise. For a woman in her nineties, she was always of cheerful disposition and wearing a smile. And she seemed excited about having the party at her cottage. "We should have started this years ago!" the old woman exclaimed when Candice had first arrived. "Thank you for organizing it, dear!"

Today Shane was due to bring over party supplies from the church and community building. They wouldn't set up all the tables inside Miss Ellie's house just yet, but they could erect the ones in the garden, unload the space heaters the town council had bought for the event, and generally get everything ready that could be gotten that way in advance.

And she was going to be more polite to him this time. Because he was right—she treated him like a criminal for no reason. Or, well, she *had* a reason, but she supposed "he has the same bad-boy demeanor as my loser ex-boyfriend from a million years ago" was a silly one. So . . . potent as that might feel to her, she had to let it go now. That didn't mean she was going to take Tessa's advice and put the moves on the guy or anything, but she could be cordial to him. Normal.

Miss Ellie's Christmas tree had long since been up and decorated, along with the rest of the house, making the lovely old-fashioned Victorian cottage the perfect setting for a Christmas get-together. Now she and Shane had to do the rest.

She'd just heated some hot chocolate on Miss Ellie's stove for the two of them when she heard a vehicle pull into the driveway. She steeled herself as she handed Miss Ellie's mug to her and awaited the knock on the door. *You can do this. Just ignore that he's hot and scary. Even if the scary is for a different reason now—he's scary because a part of you* does *totally want to put the moves on him. Yes, just ignore that. For the good of the town, the good of the party. Be the normal woman you usually manage to be. Even if your heart is beating way too hard right now.*

When the knock came at the door, she nearly threw her own mug up in the air, somehow surprised even though she'd known it was coming. And her heart beat harder still. *This is ridiculous. Why does he make me so nervous?*

She set her cup aside on a doily and blinked once, twice, as she went to answer, somehow feeling as uneasy as she had the last time—up the road at her house during the blizzard. Maybe because now his hotness—something about sexy eyes and dark hair and quiet masculinity—was so obvious to her. How had it even been a question before?

Fear. And shock. Those changed things.

But now he just looked plain sexy. In a wintry, cuddly way. His dark hair touched the collar of his coat, a hood hanging out the back, and the dark stubble on his jaw gave her the unexpected urge to touch it. With her fingertips. The mere thought of which made her pull in her breath.

Say something. "Hi."

He appeared surprised. Maybe by her simple pleasantness. "Hi."

"Come in," she said, blinking some more—but then even going so far as to reach out the open door and tug on the sleeve of his coat. *What are you doing? Stop that.*

As his eyes dropped to her fingers on his sleeve, he looked as taken aback as she felt. "This is a far cry from the last time I knocked on a door you answered." Then he shook his head as if trying to clear it. "Am I dreaming? Did I miss something?"

He was being a smart-ass. But she supposed she deserved that. "I'm . . . over whatever my problem was. It was just jarring to have a stranger at my door in the middle of the night."

"Yep. Got that. Loud and clear."

"But everyone says you're an okay guy, so . . . I'm happy to have your help with this."

He just gave her a look from beneath guarded lids, along with a small smile. Which she somehow felt in her panties, but tried not to. "You're spoiling me. I'm waiting to wake up any second now."

"It's not a dream, I promise," she assured him as he finally stepped inside onto the braided oval rug in Miss Ellie's small foyer. "I can be a nice, normal person." *Even if I can't stop this darn blinking.* She blinked again.

In response, he gave a short nod—and even if he still looked a little suspect, he said, "I can, too."

"Good. That will make this a lot more pleasant." She glanced across the room to the cottage's owner. "Now come and meet Miss Ellie. And don't mind that she's hard of hearing—just roll with it." She realized then that her hand was on his sleeve again and she was pulling him by it. But she pursed her lips and looked away as she dragged him gently across the room, trying to roll with *that* as if it was normal, too.

"Miss Ellie," she said loudly, "this is Shane! He's come to help us prepare for the party!"

"Well, what's a shame about that? Sounds more like a blessing. And he's easy on the eyes, too!"

For some reason, the last part made Candice fear she was blushing. As if in agreement. Which made it so she couldn't look at Shane then, even though she kind of wanted to, to acknowledge Miss Ellie's hearing error. Instead, though, she tried again. "No, his *name* is Shane. Shane Dalton."

"Well, it's nice to meet you, Shame," she said. "That's a mighty unusual name, but welcome to Destiny!"

Candice started to try again, "No, Miss Ellie, it's—"

But now it was Shane who reached out, closing his hand around her wrist, to say softly, "It's fine." And then to Miss Ellie, "Nice to meet you, ma'am."

And Candice realized he had indeed rolled with it—better than her. And it made her resolve all the more to just roll with *this*. With him. Today. All of it. Better than she had so far.

"Hot chocolate?" she asked him, blinking again. The truth was, she was still trying to get used to looking at him. At all that handsomeness and hotness. And those blue, blue eyes with the little scar to one side. She was still trying to process the tingling sensation that had raced up her arm when he'd touched her just now.

"Sounds good," he said.

Still no gloves, she realized. His fingers had been cool on her skin, yet somehow made her feel too warm. She was glad to escape to the kitchen, glad when he stayed behind and she could hear him attempting polite conversation. "Nice place for a party."

"Well, aren't you the charmer?" she heard Miss Ellie reply. "I'm flattered, but my face is nothing special these days, for a party or anything else. Now when I was younger, I would have knocked your socks off, young man, believe you me."

"I do believe you, ma'am," Shane replied, and it warmed Candice's heart a little to hear him be so nice to the elderly woman.

She rescued him then, though, re-entering the room to pass him a steaming mug. He took a sip and said, "Got a truckload of stuff out there, Candy, so you just tell me where you want it all."

She nodded, and a few minutes later they got to work together. And her uneasiness finally faded, along with the nervous blinks, thank goodness.

Some tables they left folded on Miss Ellie's side porch to be put up in the kitchen and living room the day before the party. Others they set up in the garden—and wiped snow off the smaller ones that resided there permanently throughout the year.

"Nice garden," Shane commented as they worked.

Candice looked around, then said, "It *is* pretty in winter. But you should see it in summer when there are flowers, or in spring, when the trees are in bloom."

"How does she take care of it?" he asked.

"Her daughters do a lot of it," Candice explained. "But other people help out, too, from time to time. It's almost a community project."

"You seem like . . . a fixture here," he commented as he used a broom to clear a small wrought-iron café table of snow, along with the two matching chairs pulled up to it. "Like you know everybody and everybody knows you. I mean, for just moving here two years ago."

She supposed she hadn't been as clear with him on that topic as she'd intended. "Oh—I've lived in Destiny all my life. I'd meant that I'd only moved into my house a couple of years ago."

He tipped his head back and said, "Ah, that makes a lot more sense. Guess I wondered how you'd become . . . so much a part of things that fast."

Maybe the observation shouldn't have surprised her, but it did. Since, despite being born and raised here, she certainly didn't think of herself as being very active in the community—though she was glad that was changing. So she simply told him, "Destiny is like that. We embrace people. Some of the guys you're working with in town haven't been here all that long, in fact—or they left for a lot of years and came back."

"So does your whole family live here?"

She considered her answer as she used a second broom to sweep snow off the brick walkway that led to the gazebo. "It's just my mother and me. But Tessa, Lucky's wife, is my cousin, and so I have her and my aunt and uncle here as well."

He nodded. "Your dad die then or something?"

The question caught her off guard. No one ever asked

about her dad because no one had to. Everyone already knew about her dad. It was an old, old subject. And not one she was accustomed to talking about.

She shook her head, kept sweeping. "I didn't know him. He left us when I was little."

Though she peeked up just long enough to see something on his face that looked like . . . compassion. "Sorry," he said.

The simple word reminded her that he'd recently lost *his* father. Though he'd had him up until now, so it seemed a far different thing, a vastly different kind of loss. But it still prompted her to inquire, "How did *your* dad die?"

"Lung cancer."

Cancer deaths were hard. She'd known enough people who'd gone through them to understand that. "I'm sorry—that's rough."

He just shook his head. "It happens. Always kinda thought it might. Man had a lot of vices and smoking was one of 'em."

She wasn't quite sure how to take his matter-of-fact response. But then, they barely knew each other and it was a personal topic—maybe he was just putting on a brave face.

"So it was just the two of you then?"

He nodded, still working.

So she kept working, too.

And a long enough moment passed in silence that it surprised her when he volunteered more. "I know what it's like—being left that way, the way your dad did."

Her chest constricted. Because she thought she'd put on a pretty brave face, too—but maybe he'd seen . . . that she still felt it. The abandonment.

She still wondered about it—how a man could do that

and not look back. She thought she should be long past it now, but maybe she wasn't. She'd watched her mother struggle for too many years when she was little. She'd witnessed the hurt. And she'd felt her own.

It took a few seconds before she could respond, and even then it was only one quick word. "How?"

"Haven't seen my mom since I was little," he said. "She sent me away with my dad to Montana."

"Sent you away?" Maybe it was a horrible thing to ask for clarification on—but she was too dumbfounded to guard her words.

"Guess I was a pretty bad kid," he said. "She just . . . wanted me gone." He'd tried to make that part sound light, too—but it didn't work.

And Candice wasn't sure how to respond. She wasn't sure how she'd even ended up in such a personal conversation with him. This was supposed to be all business, after all, getting a job done.

But they'd suddenly catapulted into something deep, and what he'd just said—she felt that, too. Because of her own dad. She'd been younger when he'd left, a toddler—she had only the faintest memories of him. But the feelings were the same. That she'd done something wrong, been unlovable in some way.

And so even if she wasn't wholly comfortable with this turn the conversation had taken, she had to say something sympathetic, had to let him know she got it. "It's an awful thing," she said softly, "to not be wanted by someone who's supposed to want you the most."

Of course, that was a maudlin, depressing thought. Her reply seemed to cast a deeper cold over the snowy garden. *Geez, Candice, merry freaking Christmas.*

Shane kept working for a moment, but then tossed a glance her way that came, oddly, with almost a hint of a smile. "Whoda thunk me and you would have anything in common, Candy?"

Ah, that's why the expression. Because it was true, and almost humorous in a way.

Though one thing still made her bristle. "Just so you know," she told him, "I'm liking you better, but you *have* to quit calling me Candy."

He challenged her with one arched brow. "What if I don't?"

And she couldn't think of a thing to say to that—other than, "No more hot chocolate."

He stayed completely straight-faced. "I'm shaking in my shoes with fear."

She raised her gaze to him, conceding earnestly, "Guess I don't have much to hold over your head."

"Nope," he agreed, looking back to his work. Though it caught her entirely off guard when, a moment later, he said, "I could give you something to bargain with, though."

And something in the very suggestion made her nervous as she stopped sweeping again to blink and ask, "What?"

Instead of giving her an answer, Shane looked toward the big red-upholstered Santa chair he'd unloaded earlier and set near the white picket garden gate. He wasn't sure what was happening here, like how the hell he'd ended up telling Miss Candy Cane about his mother. He didn't talk about that, not to anyone. And yet . . . he just had.

So now he was changing the subject—but it was

something he hadn't totally thought through yet. He motioned toward the oversized chair, ready to move it into the gazebo. And he stayed quiet until they had picked it up together, carrying it toward its appointed spot. "I was thinking . . . of taking Grampy Hoskins a Christmas tree."

When she just stared at him across the back of the chair like he'd grown reindeer antlers, he went on—albeit uncertainly. "You know, decorate it, surprise him with it."

Tilting her head as they continued carrying the chair, she said, "I thought you didn't like Christmas or Christmas stuff." As if she'd caught him at something.

"I don't," he assured her as they maneuvered the two steps up into the white gazebo. "But *he* does. And I'm thinking he'd like a tree is all."

"What makes you think he doesn't already have one?"

"Been to his house. He doesn't. Told me he missed having one but that it's hard, physically, for him to put one up."

Her expression softened, her eyes going a little sad, until finally she said, "That's nice of you." Even if she sounded almost pained to admit it.

Yet Shane wasn't doing it to be nice—not exactly. He just figured the old man had done him a good turn—a big one—and that he could return the favor. So he only shrugged.

As they set the big chair in place, however, she went back to looking skeptical. "But what does that have to do with me?"

He always felt like she was accusing him of something, even now. "Don't worry, Candy—I'm still not into the raping and pillaging thing. Just figured I could use a little help with it is all. Since I'm not a big fan of that stuff, not sure I really know how to go about it."

And when she didn't answer right away, he decided to let her off the hook. "I'm sure I can figure it out on my own, though."

"I didn't say I wouldn't help," she quickly replied. "I was just still . . . digesting it. And also wondering what the bargaining chip is."

"If I keep calling you Candy, you can withdraw the help."

"Sold," she told him without missing a beat. "I'm happy to do it."

She didn't smile, but she almost *sounded* happy. Which almost might have made him think she was beginning to like him, like she'd said a few minutes ago, except that she still kept acting so damn wary of him all the time. What the hell was that about?

"You free tomorrow? Thought maybe we could take care of it while he's working at the store."

"Yeah, I could do it tomorrow," she agreed. Even if she already sounded a little reticent again.

But whatever. He took the high road. "Thanks."

"You're welcome," she said softly. And he noticed the color in her cheeks from the cold, and it made him want to keep her warm in a way. But he didn't know how to make a woman like her warm.

"You, uh, need a break, inside?" he asked. "You look . . . chilled."

She shook her head. "Me? I'm fine. You don't even have any gloves on. What kind of guy doesn't wear gloves working out in the snow?"

"The kind who lost his. And thought he was headed to Miami anyway," he reminded her. And yeah, his hands were damn cold, as usual. Both Mick Brody and Grampy had offered him a pair of gloves at different points, but he'd refused—acted like he didn't need them, because . . . he wasn't sure why. Maybe he just didn't want any more charity than he absolutely had to take. Shelter. Food. That was enough. His hands would be fine.

"Aren't they freezing?" she asked—just as he shoved them in his coat pockets to warm them up a little.

"They're okay," he claimed. He could take it. He could take a lot. And he'd already known that before he'd shown up in Destiny—but being this down on his luck . . . well, he was trying to see it as just one more rough patch of life to get through before Miami. Before fun and sun. And money. Finally some good money. Doing good work. He wasn't sure if it would be *honest* work, but it would still be *good* work—the best he could make it.

"If you say so," she said. Skeptical as ever. And then, "That's it."

He didn't understand. "What's it?"

She looked around the garden. "That's everything I needed you to do. So you're done—free to go."

He gave a short nod. "Oh. Okay." And felt weirdly disappointed given that it was cold outside and his hands *were* freezing and he should be more than happy to get in the truck he'd driven here and turn up the heat.

Then he pointed toward some boxes of white lights, not yet opened, on the cottage's side porch. "Those for out here?"

She nodded. "Yes—I thought it would be pretty to put them in the trees, and maybe around the roof of the gazebo."

"Then I'm not done."

And he didn't give her a chance to contradict him before he started toward the porch and began unboxing lights, plugging them in, end to end, and stringing them through the trees.

The truth was, he'd never actually put Christmas lights in trees or shrubs before. Not in his whole damn life. And the further truth was, he almost enjoyed it. He couldn't put his finger on why—it was just one more job to be completed—but there was no denying that the garden looked a little more like a winter wonderland with each strand that went up.

Candy—which he could still call her in his head even if not to her face—had bought clips that held them in place around the roof and along the posts of the gazebo, and others that stuck in the ground, allowing them to create a lighted path from the garden gate to the Santa chair.

Shane had only scant memories of any visits to Santa as a kid—and they must have been before Montana because his father just hadn't been that kind of dad, which suited him fine. But as he stood there admiring their handiwork, he couldn't help thinking that it would probably feel pretty freaking magical for a little kid to come trotting up this path to see the big guy.

And he said without weighing it, "Grampy should show up in his sleigh."

"Huh?" Candy asked, fiddling with some last lights in a bush next to where he stood.

He looked over at her. "Grampy should show up here at the party in his Santa suit in his red sleigh."

And that was when Little Miss Candy Cane lifted her gaze to his and let out the softest, prettiest gasp he'd ever heard, covering her mouth with one mitten.

"What's wrong?" he asked.

And she said, "That's amazing," her eyes sparkling like the lights in the trees all around them. "Perfect. I love it."

And he found himself studying her lips, redder than usual from the chill, and looking soft and feminine and like something to be kissed. And he felt a little frozen in time, and not as cold all the sudden, as he started deciding what he was gonna do about that.

"You can put the star up. Way up at the top."

Mary Bailey, *It's a Wonderful Life*

Ten

*T*heir eyes met, and he could have sworn he saw the same impulse in hers.

Until she lowered them, blinked, and took a step back. "Well, Operation Grampy Tree tomorrow?"

He took a step back, too. Instinct of some sort kicking in. Someone backs away from you—you back away from them as well. "Yeah," he said. And then he felt . . . his newfound poverty once again. "I'd, uh, offer to pick you up, but . . ."

She smiled gently. And he realized he hadn't seen her smile as much as he'd like. It made her prettier than she already was. "*I'll* pick *you* up. How's one o'clock?"

"Good." He gave a succinct nod. And considered

telling her he'd be at the church working, but maybe Miss Candy Cane wouldn't want the whole town to think she was hanging out with a guy like him. Since she seemed to think he was so scary and all. "I'll meet you at the Mercantile. Or . . . better yet, how about I walk up to the corner of town square—so Grampy won't see and wonder what's up."

Though keeping the old man from getting suspicious was only part of his reasoning. He also didn't need Grampy's interrogation about what was happening between him and Candy anymore, either. Especially since . . . he suddenly wasn't a hundred percent sure himself.

Shane stood waiting for her on the corner, hands stuffed in his pockets, when she pulled up in a late-model sedan.

From there, they drove to Becker's Landscaping, which he'd already learned became a Christmas tree lot this time of year, and they walked along snowy aisles of trees perusing the choices. Shane and his dad had put up a tree a few times when he was younger, but never a live one, so it was a new experience for him. Whereas Candy seemed like a Christmas tree expert, pointing out pros and cons about pine needles and branches and size.

After she selected one and he'd agreed to it since it seemed like a nice-enough-looking tree, he dragged it to her car, where Adam Becker helped him tie it to the roof. When Candy explained to Adam who the tree was for, he said, "Really? Then it's on me. And in fact . . ." He held up one finger. "Wait right here." Then he returned a minute later with a tree stand built for watering, which he tossed in for free as well.

"That's really nice, man," Shane said, a little astonished. Where he came from, nobody gave you anything for free. Everything came with a price—of one kind or another. "Thanks." And he meant that wholeheartedly, because when he'd come up with this grand plan, he'd kind of forgotten that the tree would cost money. So Adam's generosity meant more than he knew.

"Anything for Grampy," Adam said. Then added with a wink, "We look out for one another around here."

When Shane and Candy got back in the car, she smiled over at him and announced, "Next stop—Edna's."

Which made him tilt a confused look in her direction. "Why?"

"She's Grampy's best friend, so I called her to ask for advice on how to decorate his tree."

Shane just blinked, still a little confused. *"How?"*

"What style of decoration," she explained. "I mean, there are a million different ways to decorate a tree, and we want him to like it. I suspected his taste would run toward the old-fashioned and traditional, and I was right. But better yet, Edna said she has more ornaments and lights than she can fit on her own tree, so she offered to put together a box of them that should suit his taste."

The fact that there were *a million different ways to decorate a tree* was news to Shane, and he was honest with her, saying, "Good thing I asked for your help. This is more involved than I thought."

After they crossed the pretty stone bridge that led into Edna's orchard, she greeted them at the front door with cups of hot chocolate. Damn, people drank a lot of hot chocolate around here. But the tree lot had left them pretty cold, so he was more than happy to accept.

"Nice what you're doin' for Willie, son," she said to him as they moved fully into the small farmhouse.

But Shane just shrugged it off. "He's been good to me."

"I didn't know the dang fool man hadn't been puttin' a tree up. If he'd told anybody, I'm sure the whole town would be over there lendin' a hand. But seein's as he didn't, real good o' you to step in and do it."

From there, Edna opened up a cardboard box on her dining room table and showed them a few of the ornaments she was sending along. One was a wooden rocking horse, another a snowman made from a pine-cone painted white. "From my grandkids when they was little," she explained. "Pains me not to be able to use 'em all, but over a lifetime, meaningful ornaments build up. So I swap 'em out as best I can. This," she said, unwrapping an old-looking one made of glass that reminded Shane—unexpectedly—of his own grandparents' Christmas tree, a very long time ago, "was on my family tree when I was a girl down in Kentucky. It's a special one, so you tell Willie to be careful with it."

All of this was yet another revelation to Shane—he had no idea people were collecting Christmas ornaments over a lifetime or placing such value on them. "*I* better be careful with it, too. In fact—" he lifted his gaze to hers "—you sure you want to send this one with us? Maybe you should just hold on to it."

It surprised him when Edna laughed and even patted his shoulder. "Nah, I trust ya. And as I say, I'll be happy for someone to enjoy it—Willie in particular."

Shane lifted his gaze back to the older woman's then, trying to read her eyes. Wondering why Willie in particular. Wondering if it was possible she harbored any romantic feelings for him she'd never expressed.

Not that he knew why he was so hot to fix up two old folks who seemed to have their lives in better order than he did.

Maybe because it just made sense to him. Like it was easy to make that mental leap, so why hadn't they? Nothing in his own life had been particularly easy, so maybe when he saw something this obvious, it just felt like something he could maybe . . . fix, make right, without . . . say, having to go all the way to Miami to do it.

"Now, do ya got everything else ya need?" Edna asked them, wrapping the ornaments back up in tissue paper. "What are ya gonna do for garland?"

Shane just looked to Candy, since he, of course, had no idea. Unfortunately, this was the first time she'd looked stumped, too. "I didn't think about that," she admitted. "But I guess we can just pick some up at the store."

Yet Edna appeared displeased.

"What's wrong?" Shane asked.

The older woman scrunched up her nose and made a face. "Don't know as I like the idea of my vintage ornaments goin' on a tree with plain ol' store-bought garland."

And then Candy was scrunching *her* nose, too. "I'm not sure we have any other choice."

"Sure ya do," Edna said with a succinct nod. "How about we string us up some cranberries and popcorn?"

As Candy's eyes brightened, Shane suffered a twinge in his groin at the inexplicable excitement in her gaze, and a little more astonishment that people actually did these things. He'd heard of people stringing popcorn in olden times, after all, but he had no idea anyone still actually did that.

He stayed quiet, though, and hoped none of his reactions were showing.

"Tell ya what," Edna said. "I've got me some microwavable popcorn and some cranberries left over from Thanksgiving. I don't have Farris today, so if y'all don't mind me goin' over to Willie's with ya, we can work on all this together at his place. Get the tree up, get the lights on, get this garland goin', and it'll be done in no time."

"Of course," Candy answered. "We could use the help."

And in one way, it made perfect sense to Shane—especially when it came to his little quest to fix up Edna and Grampy. But in another, he couldn't help feeling kind of disappointed. Maybe he'd been looking forward to spending the afternoon with little Miss Candy Cane, just the two of them. He hadn't quite known that until now, but damn—there it was, plain as the cute little nose on her cute little face.

So as he carried a box of ornaments to Candy's car, it was with slightly less enthusiasm than he'd felt half an hour earlier.

Yet as they made their way out onto the highway, Edna following behind them in a small pickup, he snapped out of it. After all, what was he thinking? He was only here temporarily. And Candy wasn't the sort of girl who'd be into a no-strings fling. She'd never told him that, but she didn't have to—it was written all over her. Hell, he should probably just count himself lucky that she'd consented to be cordial to him.

And turned out it actually helped having Edna in on the project. Despite Grampy not inviting her over, she seemed comfortable getting into drawers and cabinets as needed, finding extension cords for lights and bowls for the popcorn and cranberries. She even put a stack of old Christmas albums on an old console stereo, another visceral and unexpected reminder for Shane of times at his grandparents'—his mother's parents, he was pretty sure—very early in life.

He'd thought he didn't remember much about those early years, but he supposed every now and then he found himself transported there when he least expected it—by a song on the radio, a smell of some sort, or . . . a glass Christmas ornament or console stereo.

He built a fire in Grampy's hearth, then he and Candy got the tree erected in the stand and worked on the lights while Edna started stringing the garland with sewing equipment brought from her place.

Crisscrossing strands of lights had them laughing more than once, had Candy teasing him with a grin as she said, "I'm starting to believe you about not knowing how to do this." He heard Nat King Cole telling him to have a merry little Christmas as snow began to fall outside the big picture window where they'd put the tree, and once the lights were in place, he reached for the mug of hot chocolate that Edna had of course immediately whipped up for them as soon as they'd walked in the door. And as he peered out into the snow drifting gently downward and the red sleigh now adorning the front yard of the old farmhouse, something inside him felt . . . warm.

It was almost a hard feeling to recognize, put his finger on—warmth. It was the kind that was more than physical, more than a pair of gloves could ever provide. It was . . . well, maybe it was just nice to know that places and people like this existed. At least outside old movies or storybooks. And maybe—to his utter surprise—it was nice to have somehow actually become a part of that.

This—standing in an old house putting up a Christmas tree with two women he barely knew in order to please an old man whom he knew only a little bit better—was nothing Shane could have envisioned for himself in any stretch of the imagination. But the even more surprising thing was that . . . it felt like such a good, easy place to be.

Easy. Not a lot of that in his life. But this . . . this was pretty easy. Crisscrossed light strands and all.

"We're makin' good progress," Edna said, drawing his gaze to where she sat on the couch methodically sliding cranberries onto a needle. "But stringin' garland does take some time, so I expect the best way to proceed is for y'all to work on the popcorn. I've done threaded ya up a couple needles and there's bowls o' popcorn on the kitchen counter."

And so Shane soon found himself doing the absolute last thing he could have expected when he'd suggested this tree idea—holding a sewing needle between his fingers. And having no freaking idea what to do with it.

Damn, he'd much rather do something . . . manly,

something he knew how to do. Go chop some firewood, or work on a car or something. But instead he found himself watching Candy, who sat next to him on a love seat, as she delicately pushed the needle held in one hand through a fluffy kernel of popcorn in the other.

When Edna announced she was going to go make some more hot chocolate and left the room, Shane tried to copy Candy's move—and broke the piece of popcorn.

Dropping the bits of it back into the bowl, he picked up another—and got the same result. "Shit," he whispered.

And Candy looked over. "What's wrong?"

He felt . . . clumsy, awkward. "I don't know how to do this," he confessed.

It shocked the hell out of him when she reached over and plucked two small pieces of broken popcorn off his jeans, his thigh. She didn't touch him exactly, but just having her hand there, that *close* to touching, sent another hot twinge upward. "No worries—you can just eat your mistakes," she said with an easy smile.

Easy. Again. And who would have expected easy to ever come from the once cold Miss Candy Cane?

"But so far they're *all* mistakes," he told her in a low voice, slanting a small half grin back at her.

"It takes a gentle touch when you insert the needle into the popcorn," she explained, briefly meeting his gaze. Then she reached across his lap into the bowl on the other side of him, grabbing onto a piece. "And you want to put the needle into a soft area." Her voice went low for that part as she closed her hand delicately over his on the needle, her fingers bracketing his own, and sending a ribbon of sensation up his arm. Then she pushed the needle into a tender white part of the kernel she held. And he felt what she meant—the gentle way the needle entered the popcorn, not breaking it.

And when he switched his gaze from their hands to her eyes, her face was closer to his than he'd realized. And she had him thinking about soft spots. Pressing into them. And heat that was about more than warmth from the fire or his surroundings. He dropped his eyes to her lips then—a soft, rich color not unlike cranberries. And he suffered that hot, familiar pull—that urge to connect, to kiss.

That was when Edna re-entered the room, fresh mugs in both hands. He and Candy both sat up straighter and Candy refocused on the popcorn and said, "Now *you* try it." Attempting to sound normal. But she didn't quite. And that made what lay between his legs a little firmer, because he knew she had been right there with him, ready, wanting, feeling the same thing.

Shane could barely concentrate on stringing popcorn at the moment, but he tried. Took it slow, thought of soft spots, some more appealing than others. Gently pressed the needle to the white part of the kernel and managed to get it all the way smoothly through.

And listened as Candy said in little more than a whisper, "There, you did it." Though she didn't quite smile. Because she was still caught up in their near-kiss, something that had been so close he could almost taste it on his lips—but not well enough, of course.

"Funny about this tree," Edna said, oblivious to the sexual tension across the room. "All of us know Willie so well, but it took somebody new to think of a way to make his Christmas special."

Shane still just blew it off, though, shaking his head. "It's not that big of a thing."

"Might be bigger than you think," she said smartly, lowering two steaming mugs to the coffee table in front of them. "I do believe our Grampy has taken a shine to you. You sure you don't want to stick around here a little longer?"

And Shane leaped to his usual reply. "Aw, no, I can't. I'm just passing through. On my way to Miami."

"That's a shame," Edna said.

And Shane didn't know how to answer that because, other than his father, and maybe a few women along the way, he couldn't recall many people who'd seemed to care much about having him around. So he said nothing and looked back to his popcorn.

The music played on and the garlands were strung. Shane's was a lot shorter than the rest, but it didn't much matter when it came time to drape them all around the tree and add the ornaments.

They'd just finished, the three of them standing back to admire their handiwork, and Edna saying, "Well, we done us a good job here, kids," when Shane heard the door and realized Grampy was home from his day at the General Mercantile.

He walked in, clearly relieved to see familiar faces. "Dang, I saw the cars and the lights on and almost wondered if I had the right place—"

And that was when he stopped, caught sight of the tree. It twinkled with white lights and was topped by a shiny golden star. The rest of it was simple—the home-made garland and old-fashioned ornaments—but Shane couldn't deny that it had turned out nice.

"What on earth . . . ?" Grampy looked stymied.

"It was Shane's idea," Candy informed him. Even though he didn't know why everybody kept making such a big thing out of that.

Grampy looked over at him. "Why, son, what a mighty nice gesture. I'm beside myself here." Then he turned back to the tree. "And what a perty one. What a nice job y'all did." He shook his head, looking as if he was still trying to fathom it. "I can't thank y'all enough. This is sure gonna make my Christmas season brighter, I'll tell ya that much. Gotta count m'self lucky to have such kind folks in my life."

"All the ornaments are Edna's," Shane volunteered. "As soon as she found out about this, she jumped in to help." Hoping Grampy would take his point. About him and Edna.

Grampy shifted his gaze to Edna and said, "Why, thank ya, my dear friend."

And Shane wanted to roll his eyes. *Not friend. Quit calling her your friend.*

Soon enough, they were eating some of Edna's delicious gingerbread around the tree, which Shane complimented, followed by Grampy. "Mmm mmm, Edna, I can't ever get me enough o' your gingerbread."

Edna just laughed. "That's what you say about my apple pie in the summer and fall."

"You got somethin' good in every season, woman."

And in case Grampy was missing the point—and Shane was pretty sure he was—as he passed by him a few minutes later, he said, under his breath, "I still think you should be gettin' you some of that."

Grampy's face just turned red, and Shane shook his

head, deciding maybe there was no hope for the old guy. You could lead a horse to water, after all . . .

And hell, maybe Shane was being arrogant to think he'd come up with this great idea—maybe if it was meant to be, it would've *been* already.

But on the other hand, it took me to think of putting up a tree for the old man, didn't it?

"Grampy," Candy said as Shane re-entered the room after taking some empty plates in to the kitchen sink, "Shane came up with another great idea, too."

Grampy cast Shane a slightly more cautious look this time. "What's that?"

"He suggested you show up to the party at Miss Ellie's in your sleigh." She smiled. "I think it's perfect! The kids will see Santa pull up in his bright red sleigh, just like they've always heard about! We'll just tell them the reindeer are resting and that the horse takes their place sometime." She winked—and despite himself, Shane thought it was cute as hell.

"Why, that's plumb genius," Edna said. "Ain't it, Willie?"

Grampy Hoskins moved his gaze among the three of them, and admitted, "It's perty dang good. Perty dang good indeed." Then he pointed at Shane. "You got a good head on your shoulders, son."

And now it was Shane who winked. "Then maybe you oughta listen to my other suggestions, too."

"What's he talkin' about?" Edna asked.

And Grampy was quick to say, "Nothin' in particular—he just has a bunch o' ideas on how I oughta . . . run things, that's all." Then he gave Shane another pointed look. "Which I'm considerin'." Though it felt more like he was saying, *Shut the hell up.*

Shane just arched an eyebrow smugly in his direction.

"Speakin' o' the sleigh," Grampy said then, "what say we hook it up and then you take Candice here out for a ride. Little celebration for all your hard work today."

Shane slanted him a glance, thinking maybe he wasn't the only one trying to fix somebody up here. And the fact was—Shane was tired. It was long since past dark and he'd put in a morning of cleanup at the church before all this tree business this afternoon. But it still didn't sound like a bad idea to him, all things considered.

Especially when Candy said, "I've never ridden in your sleigh before."

"Say it ain't so!" Grampy exclaimed. "Well, then, by all means, that settles it. We're hitchin' up Charley and sendin' you two out for a ride on the ridge."

Candice thought she probably should have refused. Probably should have pointed out that it was late and that she should take Shane home, or maybe even just ask Edna to drop him off since the Mercantile was more on her way than it was on Candice's.

And yet she hadn't.

Even despite the heat she'd felt moving between them earlier.

Maybe *because* of the heat she'd felt moving between them.

More than heat—it had bordered on fire.

And it had been a long time since Candice had been stupid enough to play with fire.

Now she was out in the dark in a red sleigh with

Shane—her scary-in-more-than-one-way stranger—and the night was cold but she still felt plenty warm inside.

A plaid blanket lay across their laps, and Edna had insisted on fixing up a thermos of hot chocolate, which for some reason had made Shane laugh.

Their takeoff had felt a little rocky and Charley hadn't been totally cooperative, but the ride had since grown smoother. The moon shone down on a fresh blanket of white, lighting their way now that the earlier snowfall had stopped after dropping a new inch or so atop what was already there.

"Have you driven a lot of sleighs?" she asked, curious.

"Just this one," he said, eyes on the task. "Grampy insisted on teaching me."

They made a little small talk then, about the day, about Grampy's gratitude, about Edna's baking, about this afternoon's snow and being thankful the damaged roofs in town were covered—the church's now officially undergoing its temporary repair. And after just a short moment of comfortable silence between them, Shane said, "What about sleigh rides?"

She looked at him, confused. "What about them?"

"At the party," Shane said. "After Grampy shows up in his Santa suit, somebody—more experienced at this than me—could give people sleigh rides."

And Candice couldn't help smiling. "I love that idea!" she said. She was already planning ice-skating, and adding sleigh rides would be another quaint winter activity. She tilted her head and had to admit, even if she almost didn't want to, "Grampy was right—you've got a good head on your shoulders."

And a handsome one, too. But she kept that part to herself. And wondered a little more about him. What made him tick? What were his secrets? What had his life been like in Montana? What was this job in Miami he was headed for but never talked about?

Yet she supposed all her questions mostly boiled down to wondering one core thing: Underneath it all, was Shane Dalton naughty or nice?

Far back on Grampy's ridge, Shane pulled up on the reins, bringing horse and sleigh to a halt. And as Candice took in the stillness of the night now that *they'd* gone still, too, she said to Shane, "Listen to that."

"I don't hear anything," he told her.

"That's what I mean. Pure silence." Winter brought silence. In the summer, even if you were out in the country like this, there were sounds. Crickets in the grass, a breeze wafting through leaves on trees, the distant bark of a dog or moo of a cow or call of a bird. But snow cover like this seemed to wrap a still silence around the landscape that nothing else ever did or ever could.

"It's quiet like this in Montana sometimes," he told her. "Wide-open spaces. Not much filling them."

"There was a time when this kind of silence would make me feel . . . lonely," she confessed—wondering why on earth she was sharing something so personal and which perhaps left her more . . . vulnerable in front of him.

"And now?" he asked.

She cast him a quick sideways glance, but then raised her gaze back to the moon above. "Now I think it's . . . nice. Well, nice when you have someone to share it with anyway," she added on a soft laugh.

At which point she realized with some horror that she'd sounded . . . almost romantic. Like she thought they were on a date. So, blinking nervously a few times, she busied herself with pouring the hot chocolate into the cups Edna had sent along.

As she passed him one, she thought—as always—how cold his hands must be. And when she saw him warming them around the cup, she said without forethought, "Give me one of your hands."

His look was questioning, a little surprised—maybe even intrigued. But he slowly withdrew one from the cup and held it out to her.

She took it between her own hands, between the red mittens she wore, and said, "To warm it up."

And despite herself, she liked how it felt, even through the mittens, to touch him that way, to hold his hand in hers. Enough that she realized she might have just unwittingly started something here, something that made her lower her eyes and blink once, twice more.

"What about the other one?" he asked, his voice holding just a hint of flirtation.

She said, "If you put your cup down, I'll warm them *both* up."

He did, and she held one of his hands in each of hers. And it made *her* feel warmer too, somehow, despite the temperatures.

"It's almost like you don't hate me anymore," he teased her.

Though it made her feel bad. She'd been pretty rotten to him, she supposed, even after the night of the snowstorm. And she'd had her reasons, of course, but he couldn't know that and they weren't his fault.

"I never . . . hated you," she tried to explain. "I just thought . . ."

"Thought what?"

She blinked. And was honest. "That you . . . seemed like trouble."

He responded by freeing his fingers from her mittened grip, changing the connection so that he held her hands in his now. And he leaned closer, something a little wicked in his gaze as he said, "You got that part right then, Candy."

She pulled in her breath.

"Because the truth is, I'm more trouble than you can handle."

And then he kissed her.

"Want me to kiss her, huh?"

George Bailey, *It's a Wonderful Life*

Eleven

*H*is mouth came down firm and hot on hers. For a man who'd been out in the cold a long while, everything about him felt like solid heat right now and the touch of his lips on hers flooded her body with warmth.

She felt awkward at first, kissing him back—it had been so long since she'd been kissed. But the unbidden pull she'd suffered toward him since they'd met was strong enough to quickly override that, quickly make her forget to think about the act of kissing and just kiss. Just *be* kissed. Once she stopped thinking and simply let herself feel, her mouth moved against and melded to his effortlessly, instinctually, as the kiss moved all through her.

Her heart beat harder and she almost couldn't believe she was letting this happen—letting herself succumb to a guy who'd just confirmed her fears about him.

And yet it felt too good to stop. And hadn't she been slowly lowering her guard anyway? Not because she had suddenly decided he was a good guy but . . . because it was time. To quit hiding. To quit running. Because Tessa was right and life was short, and here was a hot, sexy man who seemed equally drawn to her for some reason, and maybe she should just try to put her worries aside. At least for this one moment.

At some point, his hands left hers, one sliding up under her parka to her hip, the other looping around her shoulder, pulling her closer. One of her own hands rose unplanned to his chest between the open zipper of his coat, and even through her mitten and his shirt, she could feel the very maleness of him. That stark masculinity that had emanated from him since the very first moment they'd met, she now got to touch.

One kiss turned into another, and another—and what had started out feeling hot, urgent, over the course of a few minutes relaxed into something still firm but slower, sweeter. Kisses that were more comfortable, like their mouths had gotten to know each other.

Candice's heart still beat madly in her chest, from the thrill of it, the mere energy of connecting with a man this way after so long, but it had become easier now and she kissed him without thought.

When it ended and he pulled back, his eyes were filled with . . . perhaps it was mischief. Or . . . the satisfaction of knowing they'd both liked what had just happened and that there wasn't a thing in the world she could say to convince him otherwise.

The silence made her feel awkward again, urged her to fill the void. "Well—*that* was unexpected." It came out sounding nervous—ugh. And she felt herself blinking.

His reply, however, didn't sound nervous at all. More challenging, in fact. "Was it?"

She opened her mouth to answer, but nothing came out. Her heart continued to pound.

So he kept going. "Because seems to me like this has been coming for a while." He even had the nerve to arch one brow and add, "You weren't really afraid of me—were you, Candy? You were just afraid of *this*." He wagged a finger back and forth between them.

And she didn't like it—not at all—that he was suggesting she feared passion, or kissing, or whatever he was referring to exactly. But she supposed it was, all too sadly, the truth.

Still, she said, "It's like I told you—you seemed . . . like someone to be wary of." She hated that she kept saying that, though, kept accusing him of that. And mostly, she didn't want to hear him tell her again that she was right—because she didn't *want* to be right. So she rushed ahead to something else. "And you called me Candy again, by the way."

"Well, we're done with Grampy's tree," he told her with a sly wink. "You don't have anything else to hold over me."

"I could quit keeping your hands warm." *What are you doing? Flirting with him? Now?*

"You *already* quit."

"I didn't quit—you moved them."

"To better places."

Something in the words warmed her all over again. Even if she was still pretty warm already from making out with him. She just shrugged. "Your choice, your fault."

And he laughed. Then grabbed her mittened hands in both of his. "All right, *Candice*. I kinda like having my hands kept warm, so I'm taking you up on it again. Even if Candy suits you more." He stopped, met her gaze, his eyes twinkling blue even in the wintry moonlight. "I just think of you that way now. In my head."

"You think of me?" The words came out before she could stop them, too soft, too girlish.

But if he noticed, it didn't show. "Yep."

She cast him a sideways glance. "A lot?"

"Pretty damn much if you want to know the truth."

She sucked in her breath. Excited by that. And still a little uneasy. About him. All of it. "I *do* want to know the truth."

"The truth is that I'd like to do more than kiss you."

He'd just said it. That plain. Like it was nothing.

"But you're trouble?" she asked. Maybe she was hoping he'd answer differently this time, tell her what she wanted to hear.

Instead, though, he only said, "Been on Santa's naughty list my whole life." And ended with another wink.

And somehow the confirmation sobered her. Reminded her. Of practical life matters. "Trouble is the last thing I need."

"And yet here you are sitting right beside it."

Yep, here she was. Feeling ripped down the middle, torn between desire and what seemed to her a healthy, sensible trepidation. The sheer masculinity he gave off emanated down through his hands and up into her, into her very core, almost irresistibly. Almost.

She let go of his hands.

Looked back ahead, out into the clear, snow-covered night.

"This has been nice, but we should probably get back to Grampy and Edna."

To her surprise, his expression held almost a sense of amusement. Maybe because it was another confession— even if a silent one this time—that he was just too much for her to handle, like he'd said. "Okay, Candy Cane," he told her.

At hearing the name, she darted a reprimanding look in his direction.

But he defended himself. "Hey, you aren't keeping my hands warm anymore. All bets are off."

"I guess they are," she murmured.

And the whole ride back, she wondered if . . . she'd blown something, some chance she should have taken.

Tessa would think so. And maybe she'd even be right. And yet . . . a girl had to protect herself, didn't she? A girl had to protect her heart. And the rest of herself, too.

As they returned to the house, things felt more normal—they made normal conversation, Shane explaining he was going to park the sleigh back in the yard as a decoration again, and that he'd help Grampy unhitch the horse and get it put away.

"Put away a lot of horses, have you?" she asked matter-of-factly.

"Only this one," he said. "Grampy—"

"Insisted," she finished for him. And they shared a light smile.

Goodbyes and more thank yous were said. Edna had brought several tins of holiday snacks along and insisted Shane take the rest of the peppermint bark. "Since I know you're partial to it," she added.

The drive back to town held more conversation. Candice worked to keep it going, in fact, because it felt so much less awkward that way. And the longer Shane was here, the more topics there were, in fact, to discuss. He was a part of things now.

They talked more about the repairs happening in town. They talked more about the party. It was almost easy—same as it had gotten with him over the last couple of days.

Except for when she remembered that they'd made out for a few minutes a little while ago and that she still felt his touch on her lips . . . and her hands . . . and her hips.

As they approached the Mercantile on the quiet Destiny thoroughfare not far from town square, empty on a cold winter's night, he said, "Thanks for the help today." He sounded sincere, serious.

"You're welcome, and I was happy to," she replied. "It was . . . a good thing to do."

And as she pulled into the drive that led to the parking area in back and brought the car to a halt, he looked over at her in the dim light from surrounding buildings and said, "You want to come in with me, Candy Cane?"

Oh boy. She hadn't seen *that* coming. Not at all.

And her body—her body wanted her to. It veritably hummed with longing.

But the rest of her . . . couldn't.

She shook her head, blinked once quickly, didn't quite meet his eyes. "Oh—no, I can't."

He gave a short nod, expression softening. "Okay. Just thought I'd ask, just in case—and . . . I get it. This was just . . . a few kisses. And warm hands for a few minutes. But they were nice ones, Candy Cane. Goodnight."

And as he got out of the car and walked around it, away from her, starting toward the stairs that led up to the rooms above the store—Candice was inexplicably struck with the unexpected urge to stop him. From walking away. Entirely. She lowered her window.

He heard it and looked back.

"Would you like to go with me to the snowcat contest Thursday night at Creekside Park?"

He squinted, appearing utterly perplexed. "The what cat contest?"

"Snowcat."

"What the hell's a snowcat?"

"A cat made of snow." Wasn't that obvious? But when he just looked at her, still clearly confused, she explained, "It's become a thing here over the last few years. Sometimes people make snowcats instead of snowmen. So my friend, Amy—you've probably met her, she's Logan's wife—has organized it as a new holiday event."

"That's kind of wacky," he said, expression back to being amused again. "If I come, do I have to build one?"

She shook her head. "No. It can be a spectator sport. We can just walk around and drink hot chocolate."

He laughed. "Hot chocolate—of course."

She narrowed her gaze. "What's so funny about hot chocolate?"

"Nothing," he claimed, still grinning slightly. Then he took a few steps back toward the car, approaching the window, and lowered his chin to meet her eyes. "Are you asking me on a date, Candy?"

She was honest. "I don't know. Maybe." Another blink she hoped he didn't see.

And he said, "Okay, sure. I'll go to the snowcat contest with you." Then bent toward the window, cupping her cheek in one palm, and gave her a small but intensely lingering kiss on the mouth. The sensation rippled straight down into her panties.

Then he stood back up and said, "Maybe you'll keep my hands warm again." And tossed her a wink before turning to walk away.

A couple of days later, Candice found herself in Under the Covers, pulling off one of the same mittens in which she'd held Shane's hands to dangle it in front of the stray kitty, Holly, where she sat on a shelf in the romance section. The small grayish cat—sort of a teenager in the cat world, she thought—batted gently at it as Candice smiled down at her. Then she heard Amy, around the corner at the register, offering Jenny and Mick's son, Dustin, a candy cane.

And she sighed, visions of Shane Dalton dancing in her head.

What had she been thinking the other night? Inviting him to the snowcat contest? Was she insane? She'd been smart enough to stop the madness out on the sleigh ride, smart enough not to let passion get the best of her—but that quickly she'd found a way to see him again?

Are you asking me on a date, Candy? She could still hear his deep voice wrapping around the words. And she still wasn't certain. But it sure *seemed* like a date. Just one she was both worried and a little excited to go on.

Around the corner, Amy said to Jenny, "See you guys tonight! I can't wait! From what I hear, the whole town is coming!"

And that was when it hit Candice. Not only had she asked her scary, sexy stranger on a date—she'd asked him on a date the entire town of Destiny would be attending. Oh God. Letting her eyes go wide, she whispered to the cat, "What have I done?"

The cat didn't answer, just swiped her paw at the mitten again.

When Candice emerged from the shelves a few minutes later, having selected a couple of books to give as gifts, Jenny was gone, but now Amy stood with Tessa and Rachel. "Hey," Tessa said to her, "want to hang with Rachel and me tonight at the park?"

Candice tilted her head. "Did Mike and Lucky talk their way out of going?"

"The opposite," Rachel said. "The brothers Romo insisted that if they had to go—and they do—that they were teaming up to build what Mike claims will be the snowcat to end all snowcats. So Tessa and I decided to go together."

It was funny to picture one of Destiny's finest and one of Destiny's toughest building a snowcat, and Candice squinted slightly. "I assumed this was mostly a kid's contest. No?" She looked back and forth between the other women.

And Amy shook her head. "We have a kid's division, a youth division, and an adult division."

"This sounds complex," Candice mused. She'd had no idea.

Amy just shrugged. "If I'm gonna organize a snowcat contest, I'm gonna do it up right."

"So are you in?" Tessa asked.

And Candice blinked. Twice. "Thanks, but I . . . made plans with someone else."

The others just looked at her, waiting for her to go on. Because they pretty much comprised her entire social circle and they knew it. "Are you bringing Aunt Alice?" Tessa asked.

"No—Mom's going with some of the ladies from the church."

They all widened their gazes on her expectantly then, still awaiting more—so she finally faced the music. "I'm coming with Shane Dalton."

"Really?" Amy asked, eyes sparkling. She had a long history of matchmaking in Destiny and was always delighted by the notion of romance. "Wow!"

And Tessa said, "Hallelujah!" just as Rachel chimed in with, "Well, that's a switch from your attitude the other day. The party setup must have gone *really* well."

She tried to play it off cool, like it was normal, no big thing—like she went on dates with strangers all the time. "Yeah, I guess he isn't so bad when you get to know him." *If you don't count him even* admitting *that he's someone to be wary of.*

"I'm thrilled you decided to take my advice," Tessa said, looking smugly pleased.

And Amy put her hands on her hips. "Hey, who's the matchmaker around here anyway?"

Tessa just shrugged, still wearing the same proud, aloof look.

But Rachel moved straight onto, "Well, I'm just glad someone around here is taking advantage of this opportunity, because hc's totally hot. He looks like a guy who could be a lot of fun to cozy up to on a winter's night. Like, say, naked."

The other women just laughed—while Candice proceeded to blink a few more times. "Let's not get ahead of ourselves," she said. "This is just a friendly date, nothing more."

"Just sayin'," Rachel added with a wink, "if I were you, I'd *make* it something more."

"Well . . ." Blinking yet again, Candice tried to think of how to respond. And tried to stop blinking, too. "He's only here temporarily, you know."

Yet Rachel only shrugged. "No muss, no fuss. No messy breakup or complicated emotions."

Okay, Candice was trying to play it cool—well, as cool as a woman who hadn't been on a date in five years could, which wasn't very—but at this she had to be honest. "If I made it something more, I'd have complicated emotions. That's just how I'm wired."

"Oh, don't mind Rachel," Amy said, swiping a hand down through the air. "We all have complicated emotions. Even her. When she met Mike—oh my gosh, the drama."

"But that's once in a lifetime," Rachel insisted, fluffing it off. "If you go into it knowing the deal, knowing that it can't really go anywhere serious, then it can just be . . . a little holiday cheer. Nothing more, nothing less." She ended with a grin.

A little holiday cheer.

The words stayed in Candice's head the whole drive

home. They stayed in her head as she wrapped the books she'd bought and added them to the gifts already under the tree. They stayed in her head as she worked on the vacuum cleaner manual next to the fire with a white cat draped across her ankles like a blanket.

Some women could look at sex like that—and maybe at this moment in time, Candice wished she were one of them. But she just wasn't. And so if she let this thing with Shane go any further than it already had, she would go into it *knowing*. That she'd end up attached. And hurt.

"So I can't," she told Frosty.

He let out a small mew. If she was reading that correctly, he was saying: *Who cares? Pet me.*

She supposed it didn't matter much what she wore to the snowcat contest given that they'd have coats on the whole time, but when she was getting ready, she still chose a pretty pink sweater with shimmery white embroidered snowflakes. And though she commonly pulled her hair back into a ponytail, tonight she left it down. With the thought of being girlish and maybe a little bit pretty. If she was going to go on a date— even if she didn't plan on letting it lead to any holiday cheer—she may as well try to look pretty.

She had Shane's number and they'd arranged by text for her to pick him up at the General Mercantile at five while the snowcat building portion of the event was still taking place—with judging at seven. And as she drove toward town, she gave herself a pep talk.

It's just a friendly date, like you told the girls. People will be happy to see you out and about, but no one will make a big thing of it. It's two people walking around a snowcat contest together, nothing more.

Maybe you'll keep his hands warm again, but that's all.

Or . . . maybe you'll even let him kiss you goodnight. But that's certainly where things will stop.

Because you know yourself too well. And you don't want to get hurt. She would certainly never let herself spend another five years pining over a guy, but . . . why even take the chance? *And if you ever get close to someone again, it should be someone who makes sense. Not a guy who seems to have a sketchy past and, in fact, a sketchy future. Not a guy who's only going to be in your life for a couple of weeks, tops. Nope, it's just a friendly date.*

She felt good about that—solid about it—as she pulled into the drive next to the Mercantile. It would be an easy, pleasant evening, with maybe a little hand-warming—if even that. He had pockets, after all—maybe he should just use them.

That was when Shane appeared from the back of the Mercantile and her heart made a leap that caught her off guard. When he opened the car door and got inside, he smelled of soap and masculinity, and he still hadn't shaven, the dark stubble on his jaw starting to transition into a light beard. "Hi, Candy Cane," he said in that deep voice of his.

And she felt it in her panties.

And despite herself, thought of holiday cheer.

"Why, she lights up like a firefly whenever you're around."

Mrs. Bailey, *It's a Wonderful Life*

Twelve

*D*amn—just getting in the car with Candy set off some kind of electric reaction inside Shane. And just seeing her took him back to the other night, to kissing her in the sleigh. It had built up all day between them, so when he'd finally been alone with her, kissing had come naturally, like the obvious thing to do. And it had felt even better than he'd imagined.

"Hi," she said, sounding a little more timid than you'd expect from a woman who'd asked him out.

She'd kissed a little timidly, too—but maybe it turned out that he'd liked that. The last time he'd connected with a timid woman was . . . never. And maybe that bit of hesitation in the kiss had turned him on. Because she'd kissed him anyway, hesitant or not. And then she'd let go of the shyness altogether—at least for a few hot, sweet minutes. And it had felt like a . . . reward. A prize. Like something she didn't do with just anybody.

"How are the repairs going?"

"Okay as far as I can tell," he told her. "Mick seems to think we're on target to get done by the wedding that's supposed to happen on Christmas Eve."

She nodded, smiled. "That's great. From what I hear, Anita is counting on it—doesn't want to make alternate plans." She was turning the car around, pulling back out onto the street, but glanced over at him to ask, "Have you met Anita or Chief Tolliver?"

"No," he said, shaking his head.

And just the quick flash of eye contact, even in the low, late-day light of winter, rekindled some of that electricity. Made him remember thinking her gasp when he'd suggested Grampy arrive at the party in his sleigh was the prettiest he'd ever heard. But when he'd first kissed her—no, turned out *that* was the prettiest gasp he'd ever heard.

"You should come to the wedding," she suggested. "Since you're helping to get the church ready and all."

But he shook his head. "I don't even know them. And it's not like I expect an invitation."

"Weddings are pretty all-inclusive around here and you'd be welcome. They're both very grateful to everyone who's pitching in to make this happen."

But besides the fact that it sounded strange to him to go to a wedding of someone he didn't know, he had a bigger reason to decline. "Can't anyway. I need to be headed south by Christmas Eve or I won't have a job."

As they approached town square, the brightly lit tree coming into view, she asked, "What kind of job *is* it?" But she sounded tentative, like maybe she somehow knew, sensed, that it might not be your normal, everyday kind of employment.

"I do parts and body work on cars," he said. "It's a parts job." And he left it at that. Since he didn't know much more. Since he was still hoping the situation would turn out okay. Even if the truth was . . . well, the job had sounded good when he was back in Montana making plans, but that last phone call with Donnie V. had left him with some niggling doubts. And he didn't really want to encourage more questions about it.

A few days ago, he wouldn't have given a shit if she or anyone else here thought poorly of him, but now, he realized, he didn't want that. For some reason he couldn't quite grasp, people here seemed to like him. And he guessed he couldn't see any reason to spoil their delusions.

She stayed quiet as they drove on, maybe not quite buying his answer. Maybe he hadn't sounded very convincing.

Which took him back to those kisses—how she'd suddenly gotten nervous and pulled back, big-time. And when he'd taken a shot and invited her in, he'd understood—yeah, she *really* didn't do this, kiss or anything else, with just anybody.

And that was a letdown—he thought it could be really good between them if she'd just relax and let it happen. But it had also reminded him who he was dealing with: the woman who'd acted like he was an ax murderer for most of the time they'd known each other.

So it had shocked the hell out of him when she'd called over to him, invited him to this snow thing—or cat thing; whatever the hell it was. And it made him wonder . . . if maybe deep down inside, she *wanted* to relax, wanted him to *help her* relax. And that idea turned him on, too.

He didn't normally get turned on by mere ideas. Or prim women. But there was something about Candy that made him keep noticing her. Maybe it was her perky little ponytails—though he liked that tonight she'd let her hair down. Or maybe it was the way she blushed and blinked when she was nervous. Or . . . maybe it was the way he'd caught her looking at him on more than one occasion when she thought he didn't see. And those sleigh ride kisses had confirmed that she was just as into him as he was into her.

Even if they might not seem to fit together.

Hell, maybe that was the fun part, the part that had him getting a little hard right now even just riding next to her in the car.

"So this thing we're going to," he asked. "I know you explained it to me, but . . . what is it again?" He squinted slightly.

"*A snowcat-building contest,*" she said slowly, as if he might be a little thickheaded. "People are building snowcats right now, and then they'll be judged, and prizes awarded."

"Snowcats," he repeated. "Got it." As if that was normal.

When they arrived at Creekside Park near Edna's orchard, though, the parking lot was packed, and Shane realized that apparently in Destiny, Ohio snowcats *were* normal. Or they at least drew a crowd anyway.

According to the signs, the event was sponsored by the Under the Covers bookstore. And as they got out and walked into the event on paths cleared in the snow, he took in numerous teams of two building . . . yep, cats made of snow.

There were big cats and small cats, standing cats and sleeping cats, cartoon cats, and very serious-looking cats. In addition to the cats, there was the requisite hot chocolate stand, as well as a booth to buy funnel cakes and a table filled with baked goods for sale, run by the Destiny Bulldogs cheerleaders. Small pine trees in the park had been strung with colored lights and strands of bigger white bulbs draped from temporary light poles overhead along the path.

"Shane, buddy, what's up?" Logan Whitaker asked as they passed by him. Then he addressed Candy. "You keepin' this guy in line or what?"

Next to him, Candy blinked. "Um—or what," she said uncertainly, and easygoing Logan laughed.

"Heard what you did for Grampy—taking him a tree. Good man," he said, slapping Shane on the back.

Shane bit back the urge to remind Logan it might take more than that to make a good man, and next thing he knew, he caught sight of Duke Dawson up the way, who'd spotted him, too. "Hey, there's Shane." He was with a beautiful, dark-haired woman with Christmas red lips, to whom he said, "Honey, have you met Shane Dalton? He's been helping out in town."

They exchanged pleasantries, Candy joining in on the conversation as Duke introduced his girlfriend, Anna—and then Amy Whitaker joined them, looking bright-eyed and excited. "Isn't this great, you guys?

Can you believe this turnout? And have you seen the cats people are making? They're all adorable!"

Soon enough, though, the small crowd dispersed, and Shane and Candice headed for the hot chocolate stand—where Shane made a point of paying—after which they started taking in the snowcat construction. And he couldn't deny that Amy was right, some of the cats were damn impressive. Adam Becker and a young girl Shane learned was his girlfriend's daughter were creating a cat as tall as him. Candy pointed out another being built by Adam's twin sons. At least two dozen cats were being carved and shaped from the snow, with even Mike and Lucky Romo constructing one that looked like it would give Adam's a run for his money.

As they walked along, more people he'd met—and some he hadn't—greeted them, including him like he was a lifelong resident of Destiny. Sometimes this place—or the people here, more particularly—threw him. Why were they so nice? So damn trusting? For all they knew, he'd rob them blind while they slept. For all they knew, he was what Candy had worried he was that night in the blizzard—someone to be wary of. But no one treated him that way.

Once they'd thrown away their empty hot chocolate cups, he found himself jamming his cold hands in his pockets—which urged him to ask the woman next to him, "Gonna keep my hands warm again, Candy Cane?"

She cast him a sideways glance that appeared unsettled at best—then drew her gaze away and blinked. "People would talk," she told him.

He cocked a grin her way. "What would they say?"

"They'd think . . . we're on a date. That we're, like, a couple."

He shrugged. The truth was, as tight knit as this community seemed, he understood why she might not want that. So he said, "Fair enough. But who knows—maybe later I'll get lucky with those mittens of yours. Pink tonight, I see." He raised his eyes back to hers. "How many pairs of mittens do you own?"

She shrugged. "I don't know. Pretty many. I like mittens."

"They're cute on you," he told her. He thought pretty much anything was cute on his Candy Cane.

"Well, howdy there, son," Grampy greeted him from behind then, and he turned to see the old man standing next to Edna and wearing a big smile. "If it ain't my Christmas tree delivery crew, all in one place again."

He let out a laugh and the group of four chatted a little about the tree and the snowcats—until Edna and Candy started talking about the big party at Miss Ellie's, which was coming up in a couple of days. He took the opportunity to draw Grampy a few steps away and ask, "You make a move on Edna yet?"

"Shush, boy—keep it down," Grampy said, though Shane thought he'd been pretty quiet about it.

"Well, have you?"

"If ya must know—no," Grampy replied, sounding a little put out with him. "And why are you so all-fired determined about this anyway? Don't take this the wrong way, son, but I ain't seen you *this* gung-ho on anything since you come to town."

"Maybe when my dad died," Shane told the old man, "it just made me see that life is short and all that. And seems like you've already wasted a hell of a lot of time here."

"Have I?" Grampy asked. "'Cause I'm not sure I see it that way. What I mean is . . . I've always enjoyed Edna's company and companionship just the way it is. So don't know as I wanna go messin' with a perfectly good situation when I don't even know if . . . if . . ."

"If what?"

Grampy lowered his voice yet still a little more. "If I got them kinda feelin's for her."

Shane thought this through. To him, it was still either something you felt or something you didn't—pretty cut and dried. But maybe for Grampy, in a long-standing relationship, it was harder to figure out. So he said, "Would you like to kiss her? Does that idea do anything for you?"

Grampy's brow knit. "Kiss her?"

"Yes, kiss her. Surely you aren't so old that you forgot what a kiss is? Or what it feels like to want one from somebody."

Grampy looked uneasy as he glanced over at Edna, who now chattered away to Candy, something about a gingerbread house.

"Well?" Shane prodded.

"Well . . . maybe you just let me think on that awhile," Grampy said, giving a decisive nod about being totally indecisive.

Shane just sighed, since thinking seemed to be Grampy's answer to this every single time they discussed it. "Yeah, you just take your time and let a few more years pass while you puzzle it through."

Just then, Amy's voice sounded over a microphone.

"Attention everyone! First, thank you all so much for coming to the inaugural Destiny Snowcat Competition. I think we can agree that all the entries are magnificent—real works of snow art!" She paused and let people applaud.

After announcing winners in the kids and youth categories, she moved on to the adult category. "Third place, and a $25 gift card good toward purchases at the Farris-Romo Family Apple Orchard, goes to Dan and Caroline Lindley, for their adorable cat and mouse creation. Second place, with six movie tickets to the Ambassador Theater, goes to Mike and Lucky Romo for their exquisite cat on a motorcycle—which, for what it lacked in artistry it made up for in originality."

"Hey!" Mike groused from somewhere nearby, eliciting light laughter from the crowd.

"And first place, along with a very generous $50 gift card from Dolly's Main Street Café, goes to Adam Becker and Sophie Simpkins! How about that, folks? A twelve-year-old bold enough to compete with the adults and she takes the first place prize!"

"Comes as no surprise to me," Candy informed Shane matter-of-factly. "Adam and Sophie have made a tradition of building a snowcat in her front yard every year since she was little. It would have been *more* shocking if they hadn't won."

Of course, Shane still thought the only *really* shocking thing about this was that everyone acted like building snowcats was completely commonplace—but he kept his mouth shut. He was learning to do that around here, at least in some respects. This little town was unique in a lot of ways and this was just one more.

When people started moving to their cars, ready to warm up, Shane was more than a little surprised to realize he was actually sorry the event was over. He was in a holding pattern in Destiny, just biding his time and waiting to leave—he'd never expected to actually start liking it here. And he wasn't sure if it was the event itself or the people there or the woman next to him wearing sparkly pink mittens, but he wasn't yet ready for the evening to end.

So when Candy tentatively suggested, "Um . . . if you wanted . . . we could get some pie or something at Dolly's," he was quick to say, "That sounds good, Candy Cane."

Normally at any Destiny event, Grampy was caught up in conversation. He knew everyone in town, after all, and many since they'd been born. Events like the Christmas tree lighting and this snowcat celebration— odd an event as that seemed like to him—were a high-light of his life, and truthfully, had been for a long time. Maybe too long.

Now, though, he found himself standing quietly alone near the funnel cake stand that was shutting down for the night, a little melancholy that soon he'd be heading to the quiet solitude of home.

Which, no doubt about it, had been made a lot more cheerful by that Christmas tree Shane and the ladies had brought him. A gesture that had touched him, and shown him he hadn't been wrong in seeing something good in the younger fella.

But the house would nonetheless be quiet and still. Maybe it was a feeling that came on harder in winter, when the ground was covered in snow. He loved Christmastime, but a winter's night could have a bleak feel about it.

As Sue Ann and Adam walked by, their kids in tow, he lifted a hand in a silent wave as Adam held up his and Sophie's first place trophy with a grin. He imagined they would go back to Sue Ann's house on Holly Lane, not far from the General Mercantile, to celebrate with some of her cookies and eggnog around the fireplace. And it brought back a warmth from a long time ago—memories of Christmases with his wife, Dory, and their boy when he was young.

"Don't let this go to your head, Mike, or I'll have to knock some sense into it."

The familiar voice drew his glance to the right, where Edna stood talking and laughing with Mike and Rachel Romo about *his* win tonight. Mike and Rachel shared ownership of the orchard with Edna and helped her run it, so they were a tight-knit group, right down to their pretty little girl, who Mike toted on his hip at the moment. Farris held the second place trophy while Mike said teasingly, "We better hide that from Great-Grandma Edna or she might steal it. I think she's jealous."

As he added a wink, Edna said, "Yep, done gone to your head."

"Doesn't take much with him," Rachel added good-naturedly.

"You wouldn't like me if I weren't a self-assured man," he replied.

"It's known far and wide," Edna said with great authority, "that Rachel is the only woman on the planet who could handle you and all your self-assurance, Michael Romo. You're dang lucky she came along when she did."

"Don't worry, Edna—I'm clear on that. She never lets me forget it." He ended by leaning over to kiss Rachel on the cheek.

And Grampy let himself imagine . . . kissing Edna on the cheek. Or the mouth. Like Shane had suggested.

That was when a chill ran through him. Dag nab—must be getting even colder out here. Then he gave his head a little shake to clear it. Of confusion. Since he supposed that was what he felt at the idea of kissing his dear old friend.

And it was at just that moment that Edna saw him in the shadows and headed toward him. She wore the same practical blue down parka he'd seen her in for years and on her head a fuzzy hat with a ball on top. Her gray hair curled around the edges of it and familiar faded blue eyes smiled up at him. "Whatcha hidin' over here for? Nearly mistook ya for a stranger."

He gave his head another shake. "Just tired, I reckon. Too much snowcat excitement for me."

She chuckled. "The kids are bringin' Farris back to my house to warm up with some hot chocolate. Me and Farris have been workin' on a gingerbread house and we might finish that up while we're at it—and of course I got a fresh batch of gingerbread for eatin', too. Seein's as you generally never met a piece of gingerbread you didn't like, thought you might want to join us."

For some reason, Grampy felt a little frozen in place by the invitation.

Not that invitations from Edna were unusual—he'd

enjoyed many such gatherings with her and her family over the years. He was at ease with about anyone.

And hadn't he just been quietly lamenting his loneliness, almost wishing he had something like this to do tonight?

So it made no cotton-pickin' sense at all when he heard himself say, "Sweet of ya to ask, Edna, but I'm pert tuckered out, so I'm gonna head on home and enjoy that Christmas tree." He even smiled.

And of course his old friend smiled back. "Well then, you get on home and get rested up—and reckon I'll see ya at the party on Saturday."

And with that, he turned and walked his weary old body toward the parking lot. His joints were stiff, bones aching from the cold. As he climbed into his truck and turned the key, then cranked the heat on high, it felt good to know he'd soon be warm again.

But there was more than one kinda warm in this world, and he'd just passed up one of them—for no good reason at all. And as he turned out of Creekside Park onto the road that led home, he thought maybe he *deserved* to be lonely.

Candice and Shane parked on the far side of the square in order to walk past the tall, lit tree on the way to the café. Just like the last one, she wasn't sure where this invitation had come from, but it had simply popped out of her mouth when she'd realized . . . she wasn't ready to go home yet. She liked being with him too much now. When on earth had *that* happened?

Decorating Miss Ellie's yard? Stringing popcorn for Grampy's tree? On the sleigh ride when he'd given her those kisses that were more delicious than any holiday treat Edna could ever whip up? She wasn't sure—she only knew that the feeling was growing, becoming a pervasive thing, a thing she didn't want to let go of.

Now would be a good time to run. Just end this. Take back the pie invitation—pretend you're tired or sick or something.

Because something had shifted in the last day or so. She'd crossed a certain line. The line of desire. No turning back. A wanting that couldn't be undone or taken away or turned off. She knew herself too well—and this was exactly the feeling she'd been trying to protect herself from all this time. But now here it was.

She could blame Tessa for pushing her toward this. She could blame Rachel for sending him to Miss Ellie's the other day. She could really blame *all* the girls for their reckless encouragement. But of course she knew deep inside that she was the only one responsible for it. Because she knew better. She knew that once you let yourself go there, into desire, there was no getting back out. It was like a bottomless well—once you climb in, you're in.

And of course, she saw softer sides of him now—whether or not he meant to let them show. He'd wanted to give Grampy a Christmas tree, after all. And watching a tough guy like him learn to string popcorn had warmed her heart—and other parts of her at the same time. He'd opened up to her a little about his father, and about his mom's abandonment when he was little; he'd let her know he felt things. He didn't seem like a man who knew a lot about giving and receiving love, except possibly with his dad, but . . . maybe that made him seem all the more in *need* of some love.

Not that she was in love with him—she was thinking of love in the broader sense. But she'd seen something in him now that drew her to him—more and more with each passing hour, it seemed.

"My hands are cold," he told her as they walked past the tree, and she looked over to see him slanting a slightly sly, playful look her way.

"Last I checked, you still have perfectly good pockets," she teased.

"But keeping them warm between your mittens is more fun."

"Fine," she said, then reached out her mittened hand and took his. And they walked the rest of the way holding hands.

Just before reaching Dolly's, though, Candice pulled up short as they passed the jewelry store next door, glancing in the display window to see if a locket she'd noticed a few weeks ago was still there. It was.

She started to move on, her hand still in Shane's, when he asked, "Whatcha got your eye on there, Candy?"

She used her free hand to motion to the old-fashioned, oval-shaped locket. "It's a lot like one I used to have," she explained. "It was a gift to my mom from my father when they were young and it had a picture of him in it. She kept it and gave it to me to remember him by."

Of course, this drew a questioning look from her companion—so she said, "I know, I know. I told you he was a jerk, and yet I valued this piece of jewelry from him." She shook her head. "I can't explain that really, except . . . that maybe it felt like just one tiny little piece of him to hold on to." After which she shrugged. "But when I lost it one summer, I figured it was meant to be gone. And I haven't really missed it. Except . . . ever since this showed up in the window here, I keep checking back on it, wondering if I should replace it. I did really love the locket."

What she didn't tell him was that she hadn't actually lost it. It had been among the jewelry Bobby had stolen from her. Having the sentimental piece taken had only added insult to injury.

When they walked into the diner, a few tables were taken and Candice led him to a booth as far from the other diners as possible. They ordered two slices of pumpkin pie as Johnny Mathis informed them over the loudspeakers that it was the most wonderful time of the year.

"So, how's your truck?" she asked as they both dug into the pie.

He shoveled the first bite in his mouth and told her, "At the body shop as of yesterday. Engine and grille repairs all done—the parts they were waiting on came in. So it's looking good to get to Miami by Christmas."

Christmas. It was just over a week away now. But when she thought of Shane leaving, she feared hers wouldn't be very merry. She hoped that didn't show on her face as she tried to cover it with, "Great."

"Good pie," he said.

And she nodded. "Dolly's makes great pie. So this job," she went on without bothering to segue, "what's so special about it that you'd go all the way to Miami for it?"

"Pays good," he said simply, still eating.

She attempted not to sound overly concerned with his business as she mused aloud, "A lot of jobs pay good.

Just seems like there must be something pretty out-standing about it to take you so far."

"Maybe I wanted a new start—someplace different than I've ever been before. So maybe it's not just about money. I don't know about you, but I could live without all this snow." He wiped a napkin across his mouth.

And she tilted her head, thinking. "I guess I like having all four seasons. And snow is nice at Christmas."

He shrugged. "If you're a Christmas person, I guess."

He resumed eating, and she studied him, suspecting he could like Christmas more than he thought if he'd only let himself. "For a guy who doesn't like Christmas, you sure have been throwing yourself into it. Decorating gardens and trees, stringing popcorn. You even drove a one-horse open sleigh, for heaven's sake. I mean, you can't get much more jingle-all-the-way than that."

He laughed. "I've just been helping out is all. But I do like that movie."

"What movie?"

"*Jingle All the Way.*"

Candice just stared at him, nonplussed. "As a Christmas movie aficionado, I'm going to call that Arnold Schwarzenegger's worst acting job ever."

Shane raised his eyebrows. "Ever? Come on? The man's a pretty bad actor, so that's an awful bold state-ment. And there's a lot of funny stuff in it. Sinbad as the crazy postman? The runaway reindeer? The wooden wise man whose head ends up on fire and gets kicked through a window at carolers? It's a great movie."

Candice just gave him a look. As drawn to him as she'd become, and as . . . well, as let down as she felt about his unwavering determination to go to Miami as soon as possible, she was kind of disappointed to hear this was his taste in film.

And clearly her look said it all, because he replied to it with, "Okay, if you're such a Christmas movie authority, what's *your* favorite?"

"Easy. *It's a Wonderful Life*."

"Never seen it."

Her eyes flew wide, and her fork paused midair. "What? You've never seen *It's a Wonderful Life*? How is that even possible?"

He laid down his own fork and held up his hands. "Because it just is. Everybody can't see every movie."

"Well, you need to see *that* one. It's amazing. It never gets old. I watch it every year."

His eyebrows shot up again. "Every year?"

"Without fail. My Christmas isn't complete without it."

The way he looked at her then implied that maybe she needed to get a more exciting life. So she sort of wished she'd shut up already. But on the other hand, she couldn't help thinking that if he only saw it, he'd understand. "I own it," she told him.

"I'm not surprised."

"And you seriously need to watch it."

He leaned slightly forward over the table. "Are you inviting me over, Candy?"

"Yes," she said.

"When?"

"Right now."

"I think I'll go out and find a girl and do a little passionate necking."

George Bailey, *It's a Wonderful Life*

Thirteen

Just like the invitation to the snowcat competition, Candice hadn't thought this through. She'd just heard herself saying it before she could even consider the words. And as they drove to her house, she felt the weight of what she'd put into play here.

She'd just invited a man over to her house. After dark. A man who'd recently kissed her and she'd more or less pushed him away. But now she kept issuing invitations. Snowcat contest, pie, movie—each one drawing him a little deeper into her space, into her world. So if he thought she was inviting him over for sex—well, she didn't think that was an unreasonable assumption.

"It's just for the movie," she heard herself say in the darkness of the car.

He didn't pretend not to understand what she meant. "It can be for whatever you want it to be, Candy."

"Well, it's just for the movie," she reiterated.

And he laughed.

Of course, she knew she had the option of making it *not* just for the movie.

Tessa and Rachel and the rest of the girls would surely approve of that.

But . . . he was leaving. Soon. Really soon. And she deserved more than some fly-by-night affair. So as they turned into her driveway, even as she felt that certain invisible pull of desire, she resolved that it would still be just for the movie. Because it made sense to protect her heart. Didn't it?

The fact that he'd been there before made having him there again more comfortable than it would have been otherwise. Especially when her silly cat greeted him like an old friend, hopping right up into his lap when he sat down on the couch. "Hey there, Frosty," he said. "Staying out of the snow these days?"

"Yes," Candice answered for the cat. "As you already saw, snow and Frosty don't mix. Or . . . they mix too well, I guess." She went around the room turning on lights, then told Shane she was heading to the kitchen for some snacks.

When she came back, he was on his feet, stooped down, building a fire in the hearth.

"Thanks," she told him softly, watching his butt. He'd had his coat on all night, but now it was off, and the way he was shifting and moving and bending made it hard not to see how his jeans curved over that part of him. She had unwittingly noticed his butt more than once while trimming Grampy's tree, too. *If he takes off his shoes and is wearing thick, cozy socks again, I'm a goner.*

Once the fire was going, crackling and blazing, he came back to the couch. She'd put the DVD in and had it queued up, ready to go. A tray of Christmas cookies and candies rested on the coffee table alongside two steaming mugs.

"Let me guess," he said, sitting back down next to her. "Hot chocolate."

"Of course."

He laughed.

"Seriously—what's funny about hot chocolate?"

"Nothing," he said. "But I've drunk more hot chocolate since coming to Destiny than I have in my whole life."

She just shrugged. "It's winter. And we like hot chocolate. So what?" Then she motioned toward the tray. "You should try some of Sue Ann's cookies." They were cutout and decorated, in shapes of stars, trees, bells, and reindeer. "They're delicious, from an old family recipe. Amy's buckeyes are yummy, too." The regional treat consisted of a peanut butter mixture dipped in chocolate. "And I made these." They were drop cookies with crushed candy cane crumbs mixed in.

He went straight for those, picking one up, and took a big bite. "Mmm mmm," he said in approval, then gave her a look that was downright smoldering. "I told you candy canes are my weakness."

The look moved all through her body, and she

decided it was a good thing to just . . . ignore. "Ready to start the movie?" she asked, glancing toward the TV as she reached for the remote.

"Can we turn out some of these lights?" he asked.

"Um . . . sure," she said, even though she thought that was a positively horrible idea and had, of course, turned them *on* for a very good reason. Fortunately, though, even after she went around the room flicking off a couple of lamps and an overhead dome, the fire and Christmas tree kept the room at least somewhat illuminated—in a warm way. Even if the dim lighting nearly made her trip over the cat, now curled up on a rug next to the fireplace.

Though when she returned to the couch, Shane had—uh-oh—removed his shoes. And wore cozy, gray, snuggly socks underneath. Her gaze rose to his sexy eyes to find him casting her a warm, seductive sort of glance, so she dropped her own gaze—back to the socks. Hell, no place seemed safe to look at the moment. *And what is it with you and socks suddenly? Since when do you find socks of all things such a turn-on? You're being ridiculous.*

Yet as she sat back down and started the movie, she realized—the problem was that when you really started being into someone . . . *everything* about them was sexy. Even their socks.

"Here we go," she told him as the movie began, two blinking stars in the cosmos having a discussion about George Bailey, saying tonight was his crucial night. And as the story got underway, she couldn't help wondering if tonight might be *her* crucial night. Albeit in a far different way. And she was pretty sure no one was

going to send an angel down to save her from herself—
what happened here was entirely up to her, for better
or worse.

At first, she sensed Shane quietly scoffing at the whole
scenario, at Clarence the angel, at the old-fashioned
feel of the black-and-white movie. But just like when
she watched it every year, she could tell he was soon
sucked in to the story, seeing George's life unfold, the
joys and disappointments alike.

She nibbled on a couple of Sue Ann's cookies out
of nervousness—just at having him here, being on the
same couch with him. But *he* didn't seem nervous at
all, stretching out and making himself right at home.
The move put him farther away from her, at one end,
but when he extended his legs and crossed his feet at
the ankles, it placed *them* perilously close to her own
feet, which she'd drawn up next to her.

And by the time Mary said, "Welcome home,
Mr. Bailey," on her wedding night with George, Shane's
feet were touching hers. Just a little.

She felt herself blinking at the TV screen, hoping he
wouldn't notice. Then she reached for another cookie.

She considered resituating herself, moving her feet
away from the cozy warmth of his—which, simple as
it was, somehow rippled up through her legs and into
her abdomen. And to stay like they were was to . . .
welcome it. That was the message it sent. Which also
would probably imply wanting to touch more of him
than just his feet. And maybe not every guy would
make that leap—but she had a feeling *this* guy would.

So she knew she should move *her* feet. She should
scoot a little farther away.

And yet . . . what if you let this happen? All of it?

What if you just let go completely and let your lust and desire take over here?

You'll probably get hurt, that's what.

This was so different than with Bobby. *The difference being—you know now. You get it. You understand what you're in for.*

And yet you're still considering it?

Yes. You are.

Because maybe Tessa was right. And Rachel, and all of them.

She would never personally minimize something as intimate as sex into holiday cheer—but . . . was it possible that maybe even just a night—or two, or three, depending on how things went—would somehow . . . give her something that would make the imminent pain worth it?

Even if this wasn't how she operated. Not what she wanted. Not what worked for her.

Maybe it was time to consider making something *else* work for her.

Doing what Tessa said and taking a chance.

Deciding that maybe the hurt she'd feel later *would* be worth it for the joy she'd feel now.

Believing that the joy would be greater than the pain.

As George hid the petals from Zuzu's flower, Candice stole a glance over at Shane. She took in the line of his heavily stubbled jaw, the broadness of his shoulders, the way his dark hair touched the collar of his shirt.

It was hard to explain to herself, but already, this quickly, she felt a certain comfort with him, with all those little things about him, and it all added up to what made the idea of sleeping with him this soon even feasible.

Chemistry. It was a curious thing. It could make an

otherwise normal, even prim woman suddenly feel at ease with the idea of touching someone she barely knew. Someone she'd never touched before.

Candice had always been . . . selective about touching. Some women were comfortable with casual sex, and that meant being comfortable sharing your body, and someone else's body, in the most open, raw, intimate way. But she'd never understood the ease with which so many people accomplished this. Maybe that was why she was more comfortable hiding herself away in her great big house and putting her focus on instructions. Manuals. Guides. How-tos. Maybe she thought the things she wrote manuals for were all ultimately simpler than the act of touching someone else in an intimate way.

Bobby had been the one anomaly to that way of feeling in her whole life. Of course, she'd dated *before* him. She'd kissed guys before him, made out with guys before him. But they'd been guys she'd known awhile. Or guys she'd dated some first. Bobby had been her only lover. And it had happened fast. Magically. Perfectly. He'd wounded her over and over again *out* of bed, but *in* bed, they'd been perfect together.

And she'd always felt sure that something so perfect could only happen once. That two people so sexually in sync, two people so connected in the ways of touching and loving, could only come together once in a lifetime. She'd had her magic and it hadn't lasted. She wouldn't get another turn at it. That didn't happen. *Couldn't* happen.

Only . . . that was the thing about chemistry. Chemistry could change what you think might happen, what you *want* to happen. Chemistry could wipe away certain fears even as it created new ones. Chemistry could . . . almost make her believe in magic again.

And so . . . she didn't shift her feet away.

Simple move—so simple that it was actually a non-move. And yet, something in the gesture felt . . . unaccountably bold.

Maybe asking him out had seemed bold. Maybe inviting him here, to her house, had felt bold. But the greater courage came, for Candice, in accepting—and silently, quietly returning—this small, warm touch, even if just between their sock-covered feet.

And that small, warm connection . . . felt good. It was like holding his hand, but somehow more personal.

And they stayed that way through the rest of the movie. Right up until that perfect ending, that moment when Clarence gets his wings. And then *The End* flashed across the screen—and that same little burst of joy and satisfaction she always got from the story rushed through her, and she felt it more for having shared it with someone.

So she cast a shy glance in Shane's direction—to find him looking back. "Well?" she asked cautiously.

Relief struck when he said, "Loved it." And she knew he meant it. Not because he sounded particularly emotional about it, but because Shane was straightforward, up front.

"I'm glad," she said, sorry when the words came out more whispery than intended. But the way he was looking at her right now, with their feet still all cozied up together, had, in fact, stolen a little of her breath.

"I'm glad, too," he said. "Glad you invited me over." There was sex in his eyes.

And she felt it squarely between her legs.

It still amazed her to feel that again—she hadn't in so long. No one had come into her life to make her want to. Until now.

It surprised her a little when he pulled *his* feet away then, got up, walked to the fire. She immediately missed the physical connection. She'd had no idea feet were such erogenous zones for her. But maybe they were only that way with Shane.

She used the remote to turn off the movie, then shifted her gaze to where he stood jabbing lightly at the flames with the poker before setting it aside and putting another log on. Sparks flew and she followed the urge to stand up herself, walk to where he stood.

"Is it warm?" she asked. "At the Mercantile? Where you're sleeping?" Funny, ever since she'd started softening toward him, she'd been concerned about his keeping warm.

He kept his gaze on the fire. "There's a space heater."

"A space heater doesn't always give off much heat."

He shrugged. "It's okay. I've got plenty of blankets."

"I worry about your hands being cold," she said. Though she immediately regretted the confession the moment it left her.

And when he slanted her a sexy grin, she realized just how close they stood. Their faces were mere inches apart. She could smell him—some simple, masculine sort of scent she couldn't put her finger on.

"I know you do," he said, embarrassing her a little. "But they're fine."

"I don't believe you," she whispered. "They felt cold through my mittens on the sleigh. And earlier tonight."

That was when he reached up both hands to touch her face. "Do they feel cold now?"

"No," she murmured. "Warm. Hot." From the fire, she realized. But the heat spread all through her. Along with the look in his eyes as they grew shaded, his gaze falling on her lips.

Chemistry. It ran thick and hot through her veins as their mouths moved toward one another, slowly but certainly, like magnets being drawn together.

When his met hers, liquid heat saturated her body. Her eyes shut of their own volition as if to feel the kiss even more. And feel it she did. It was as intoxicating as the most potent wine—one taste and she was lost to the sensation, her soft body sinking into the hard maleness of his.

He kept his hands on her face as his mouth moved over hers, the kisses starting slow but growing deeper now. When his tongue pressed between her lips, a bolt of pleasure shot to the tender spot between her thighs.

And with that came full surrender. Inside her. She could run from this if she wanted to. She could push it away. It wasn't that she didn't have the strength to fight her desire. It was that she . . . wanted this.

He wasn't the perfect guy, for many reasons. It wasn't the perfect situation. But she wanted this enough to take the risk—to risk not knowing how she'd feel when it was over and he was long gone. To risk not knowing how she'd feel when she was alone again, maybe aching for his touch or his kiss or his mere presence.

And so when his hands left her face, wrapping around her to pull her to him, chest to chest, hip to hip, she kissed him with all the pent-up passion inside her and thought of nothing but how ready she was to let this happen.

Soon his kisses trailed from her mouth down onto her neck, the pleasure from them expanding outward through her arms, breasts. She leaned her head back to give him better access as the sensation rippled deliciously through her.

She found herself touching him, too, then—her fingers threading through his thick, dark hair, her hands exploring his broad shoulders, arms.

When his kisses rose back up onto her cheek, his voice rasped deeply in her ear. "Why aren't you scared of me anymore?"

She sucked in her breath at the question—then told him the truth. "I am."

He pulled back slightly, looked at her. "Then why . . . ?"

More honesty spilled from her. "I guess . . . I want this more than I fear you."

Shane tilted his head, narrowed his gaze on her eyes. "Just what is it you're so afraid of, Candy Cane?" She almost didn't hear the silly name anymore, and she thought he didn't, either, because he asked the question in complete seriousness.

And as for the answer—she wasn't sure what to say, how to explain. So she kept it vague. "Just . . . bad things."

"What happened to you bad, honey? Is this about your dad?"

"No."

"What then?"

Candice bit her lip. She should probably just make something up. She should end this conversation by claiming she wasn't afraid of anything at all. And yet . . . even as little time as they'd spent together, she sensed that he'd see through it. She'd been her genuine self with him up to now, after all, at least once she'd gotten past being mean to him. And it seemed hard—or maybe even felt wrong—to change that now.

"It's just that . . . the last guy I was with turned out to be a jerk, and I got hurt. And I know that has nothing to do with you, or with now . . ." She'd lowered her eyes, a little embarrassed—and almost regretted the decision to be so open. She definitely wasn't going to tell him the guy was years ago and the only one she'd ever slept with. The very notion suddenly made her feel . . . backward, immature. And maybe . . . sad. That it had taken so long to feel this again, want this again. Sad to have pushed aside all those normal, human, womanly emotions somewhere along the way.

She forced herself to raise her eyes to his and try to make him understand. "And . . . you said yourself that you were trouble. I guess all of it just made me cautious."

He met her gaze and told her, "I *am* trouble, but . . . you won't have to worry about that. Because I can't make you any promises, Candy, trouble or not. I have to leave when my truck is ready. It's not even a choice—I need the job."

"I know that," she said. "But you asked what I was afraid of, so I told you."

"You know that," he said, eyes narrowed slightly, "and you still . . . want this to happen?"

More honesty, this time the full-on kind. "I want it so much I can barely breathe."

At this, his eyebrows rose. "You said no pretty fast the other night. A couple of times. This seems like a big switch."

"Well, maybe I did some thinking since then. And maybe I decided . . . you could give me the perfect Christmas present."

"You look a little older without your clothes on."

George Bailey, *It's a Wonderful Life*

Fourteen

Their bodies had separated slightly in the last few moments, but now Shane lowered a hand to her hip and drew her demandingly back to him, pelvis to pelvis. A small whimper left Candice's throat at the feel of him there—at the hardness that connected with the soft, needy place between her legs.

Chemistry. Again, it was chemistry that made this okay. Normally, the idea of being crushed so intimately against a guy she didn't know very well would totally turn her off—but this didn't. This only felt good, and right, and like something she wanted more of. Now.

So she was glad when he didn't say any more, question her any further. She was glad when he resumed kissing her. Glad when his mouth took hers, glad when his tongue pressed its way back inside. She was glad when the physical sensations instantly consumed her again, taking away all this thinking and talking, and leaving room for only feeling and doing. She didn't *want* to think. She didn't want to examine this too closely. She wanted to give herself over to it completely.

And that's what she did.

Her breasts ached for his touch, so when he eased a hand upward from her waist to stroke his thumb across one nipple through her sweater and bra, she gasped even amid their kiss. And then he began to shape and mold, massage the soft flesh in his hand, his every caress sending shock waves through her and straight to her panties.

Oh Lord, she shouldn't have waited so long—she felt this almost too much. Every touch was like fire on her skin, a fire that set off tumultuous earthquakes inside her.

She never even thought about hiding her responses. She'd never been good at pretending, and she'd pretended nothing with Shane so far, so why change that now? She didn't think she could even if she wanted to. So when his kisses dropped to her neck again and she heard herself panting, sighing feverishly, it never occurred to her to hold that in, to hold back on expressing the pleasure he delivered to her.

And by the time his hands dropped to the bottom hem of her sweater, sliding underneath, his palms gliding up her sides and onto the cups of her bra, she'd almost ceased thinking altogether. Once she'd made this grand decision to have sex with him, she'd been in it all the way, no doubts or regrets or worries, and now she just wanted to bask in every aspect of the experience.

Both his hands closed fully over her breasts and a low moan left her throat. And the bra she'd chosen tonight was a thin, lacy one, and when his thumbs began to stroke across her taut nipples, the tips of his thumbs lingering, playing with them, she had to bite her lip to keep from crying out. She'd forgotten how this felt— how consuming such touches could be.

Soon enough, he was reaching to pull her sweater off over her head and she raised her arms, helping him remove it with ease. And up until now, she had, in ways, felt timid and almost childish around him—letting so many kinds of fear get in the way of their attraction—but in this moment, standing before him in the firelight in her bra, taking in the movement of his eyes as they danced across her skin, she felt like a fully sexual woman.

"Damn, Candy," he murmured. "I knew you were a pretty little thing, but . . ."

"But what?" she breathed.

"But I didn't know you were so fucking *hot*."

Her breath hitched on another little gasp as the words traveled through her, saturating her being. They made her *feel* hot. Made her *become* hot.

"I'm even hotter," she began tentatively—but then pushed back the very urge to be tentative and continued, "with the rest of my clothes off."

And for the first time, a low groan echoed from his throat. And she could feel the full measure of *his* desire, too—in the dark, shaded look in his eyes, the way his jaw hung slack. And in the way he said, "Then what are we waiting for, honey?"

She bit her lip. Asked the only necessary question. "Do you have . . . ?" A condom.

But she didn't need to voice that part, because he quickly said, "Never leave home without it."

The statement brought a grim reminder. *He's had a lot of sex. With a lot of women.*

But don't think about that; don't let that intimidate you.

So she just gave a short nod and said, "Good."

Then he looked toward the foyer, the big Victorian house's staircase. "You wanna go upstairs?"

And she softly said, "No—it's too far away. Here."

In response, he stepped up close again, reached for the button on her blue jeans, flicking it open.

After which she pushed the unbuttoned shirt from his shoulders, watching him shrug free of it, then reached for the bottom edge of the dark T-shirt he wore. She lifted it up, dropped her eyes to take in the lean muscles of his stomach, and tried not to shudder even though the muscles in her *own* stomach rippled at the sight.

And maybe with a tinge more fear. Fear now of what this would be like. Would she measure up? Would any old hints of nervousness show through?

Push it down, push it down.

She did. Then raised her gaze back to him as she thrust the T-shirt up over a broad, muscular chest that made her heart quiver, and watched as he ripped it off over his head.

And talk about hot. Of its own volition, her tongue came out to touch her upper lip. Seeing him shirtless took her breath away.

And then she experienced something she never had before—even with Bobby. Abject urgency.

Her heart suddenly beat faster. Molten lava seemed to shoot through her veins. And she could barely speak—but when she managed to, she said one little word. "Hurry."

And then things moved fast, which was what she wanted now—badly. She didn't hesitate to reach for the button on his jeans, then the zipper. She pushed the denim from his hips to reveal snug, sexy, black boxer briefs underneath, and he shoved her jeans to her thighs, uncovering white panties printed with pink snowflakes.

"God, that's cute," he murmured low.

But she wasn't in a cute mood, so she just said, "Take them off me."

They both hurried the rest of the way out of their jeans before Shane placed his hands back on her hips, guiding her backward toward the couch.

She reclined on it, more ready for this than she'd been for anything in a long time, and just as he was lowering himself atop her—he pulled back, stood up. "Shit," he murmured. Then rushed to grab up his jeans and dig out a well-worn brown leather wallet, plucking a square foil packet from inside.

Meeting her gaze again, he cast a grin that confirmed he'd *definitely* made Santa's naughty list. "You got me so excited I forgot, that fast."

She bit her lip, her back arching involuntarily, like a cat. "Don't make me wait any longer, Shane."

And he didn't. Kneeling next to her, he smoothly drew her snowflake panties down and off. Then shrugged free of his own underwear, lingering just long enough to let her study him there for a scintillating moment before he rolled on the condom.

And then he was between her parted thighs, positioning himself, pressing into her, making her hold her breath with anticipation—until he pushed, driving gently, gently but oh so firmly, until he sank into her. A high sigh of pleasure left her as her eyes fell shut.

Oh Lord, it felt good, right. To be filled with him.

It created a sensation like no other.

And she wanted to stay connected to him like this forever.

Above her, his breath caught. From excitement, arousal. She liked it. "So tight," he rasped.

It made her own breath thready and a little jagged. "It's . . . been a while," she admitted.

He spoke low and sexy in her ear. "So you're a good girl. That's what I thought. On Santa's nice list," he added with a chuckle.

"Not tonight," she promised him.

And at this, he cast a wicked grin and said, "Remember when you were teaching me to string popcorn, what you said about pushing the needle in to the soft spot?"

"Mmm hmm," she affirmed.

"I was thinking about *this* then, wondering how it would feel."

She sucked in her breath. "And?"

"A hell of a lot better than stringing popcorn."

And then he began to move in her. And she met his thrusts, their bodies taking on that primal rhythm, old as time, in the glow of the Christmas tree.

Part of Candice couldn't believe this was happening—it felt almost surreal. But the rest of her simply basked in it. *It feels surreal because you waited so long to give yourself to a guy again.* And she was glad she hadn't waited even one more night. This was indeed the perfect Christmas present.

Shane cupped Candy's ass as he rained kisses across her neck, chest, breasts—even though they hadn't gotten around to taking her bra off yet, an oversight he needed to fix.

So he eased his hands behind her back and smoothly undid the hook, rife with anticipation as the bra loosened around her and she freed her arms from his neck long enough to let him pull the delicate lace away.

A low sound left his throat at the sight of her pert breasts and puckered pink nipples. She looked like some sort of perfect creamy Christmas fantasy lying beneath him, her usually sweet face now etched with passion, her body a perfect holiday treat he couldn't even have imagined she was hiding under those sweaters of hers.

He wasted no time lowering his mouth to taste her there—kissing, licking, then suckling first one hardened peak and then the other. She emitted shaky breaths above him that made him a little crazy, made him want to come.

Damn, he usually had more control than this. Though it had actually been a while for him, too. Not as long as for her, he suspected, but given his father's death and the illness leading up to it, he hadn't exactly been out on the prowl for that kind of fun in a while.

Even so, he didn't honestly think his response was about that. He thought it was about *her*. She wasn't his usual type. Santa's nice list wasn't generally where he went shopping for girls. And to have ended up with her like this—considering that she'd treated him like a criminal until recently—made him feel . . . what?

Powerful?

Special in some way?

He wasn't sure what it was, but he just wanted to make Candy feel good.

And so he wasn't *about* to come yet—much as he might want to just let go and let it happen. But that required pulling back, away from her.

She gasped slightly at the withdrawal, her eyes filling with alarm. "Wh-wh-why?"

Damn, she looked so sad. And he couldn't have that. So he rushed to reassure her. "Don't worry, honey—I'm not going anywhere."

"But I want . . . I want . . ."

His grin probably bordered on wicked—because he *knew* what she wanted. Him back inside her. But he also knew she'd like what she got instead. So he just said, "Shhh . . ." and then bent to mold and kiss her sweet, round breasts some more—and then he descended, letting his mouth drop to her pale, trim stomach.

She gasped then, maybe not so much at the tummy kisses as because they hinted at what was coming. And he had to amend his thoughts once more—because no, *that* was the prettiest gasp he'd ever heard.

As he kissed his way downward, he let his eyes connect with hers, let her see the hunger inside him, what she did to him.

Then he used his hands to part her legs a little wider and kiss her where she was warm and wet for him.

"Oh!" she called out. And something about the response—strong and uncontrolled—urged him to make her climax hard and fast. Later they could take their time—he could tease her, bring her to the brink and back again—but right now, he just needed to take her there.

So he raked his tongue over the hot nub of flesh between her legs and listened to the sweet, jagged moan it wrenched from her pretty lips. He licked her there again, again, until she was digging her fingers into the couch cushions at either side of her, clearly maddened.

He didn't stop, so ready to make her come that he could taste it—until her flesh shuddered around him and she was thrusting at his mouth, crying out, screaming her orgasm, filling him with the heat of satisfaction as it rocked her.

Her pretty sighs filled the air as he pulled back, sat up, giving her a moment to come down from that peak—and as he gazed down on her lovely nakedness, the lights on the tree reflecting shadows of blue, red, green, across her skin, he couldn't resist one more naughty grin as he said, "Damn, Candy Cane—you make Christmas a lot more fun."

She smiled up at him, her satisfaction visible in the twinkle of her eyes. "So do you," she said. "Now come back inside me."

His chest constricted as he told her, "My pleasure." And he angled his body over hers once more, pushing his way back into that snug heat until they both let out hot sighs.

And as he began to move in her, he thought he could gladly stay like this with her for a very long time—but it was in that very moment that his drives into her sweet softness pushed him over the edge he'd already been hovering too near before. And he willingly let himself drop over it this time—let himself explode inside her hard, hard, hard, as she again cried out her pleasure.

And as he collapsed gently atop her, spent, she whispered, "Now this is what I call a merry Christmas."

Hours later, Candice lay naked beneath the covers of her bed, curled in Shane Dalton's muscular arms. She wasn't sure how this had happened. She only knew that he smelled good, some combination of hot musky guy and cool peppermint, and that she'd forgotten how this felt. To be held this way. To have her skin pressed up against a man's hard, lean body. To have her palm resting on a firm, bare male chest, her fingertips nestled in the dusting of dark hair drizzled so deliciously across it. Like sprinkles on a cupcake. A scrumptious man cupcake.

Lord, she'd clearly been hanging out with Rachel and the other girls too much if she was having thoughts like that.

Or maybe it was some natural result of the way she'd let herself be deprived for so long.

But you didn't really have much of a choice. Shallow dating pool and all.

And even as much as her body was loving this, soaking up every touch and kiss like they were filled with water and she were a dry sponge, maybe for her heart, her mind, the deprivation had been wise in a way. Maybe, deep down, she'd known exactly what she was doing when she'd chosen not to let herself even begin going down that road for such a long while.

Because his body was so warm against hers beneath the sheets, their legs tangled so comfortably yet intimately. Because she never wanted to move, never wanted either of them to leave this bed. She wanted to hold on to this, wanted much, much more of this. She wanted to stay connected to him like this . . . forever.

Which was a crazy long time, and an even crazier thought. But what woman hadn't felt this? And this . . . this was perhaps what she'd been unwittingly protecting herself from. That uncontrollable rush of emotion, chemistry gone wild and deep, and feeling dangerously like an attachment she wouldn't be able to break free of.

But don't think about that now. You took the risk, you decided it was worth it. You can hurt over this later, when he's long gone, but for now, enjoy what you have with him. Make the most of it. Because it's temporary. This is all you'll ever have, as good as it gets, so make it count.

"Jesus," Shane muttered then.

The morning sun creeping in her bedroom's tall windows must have woken him. "What?" she whispered, worried—and at the same time, she lifted her head and followed his eyes to an old mantel across the room from the foot of the bed.

"Your cat's staring at us."

True enough, Frosty sat on the mantelpiece like another item of bric-a-brac, glaring a hole through them. "Sorry about that." The truth was, she hadn't seen Frosty since before they'd had sex last night and for the moment had practically forgotten she even *had* a cat.

"No problem," Shane said. "Just a freaky thing to wake up to."

She giggled lightly—then found herself playfully stroking little arcs back and forth on his chest with her fingertips. It surprised her to be this comfortable with him this way this fast—but maybe it was like riding a bike.

In response, he ran the tip of one index finger down her hand and up her arm, his other arm still wrapped tight and cozy around her. Then he met her gaze. "Any regrets, Candy?"

"Nope." It was true. Even if she knew she'd struggle with his departure now; even if she knew she'd just made her emotions, her life—because what was life if not your emotions?—a lot more complicated.

"Good," he said. Then arched one brow, his look one that only a guy who was pure trouble could deliver. "Wanna do it again?"

She bit her lip as fresh desire flared between her thighs and said, "Oh yeah."

"He's making violent love to me."

Mary Hatch, *It's a Wonderful Life*

Fifteen

*H*ands on her hips, Shane pushed his way inside her. And mmm, yeah, wait—no, *that* was the prettiest gasp he'd ever heard.

Part of him couldn't believe they'd ended up like this, him and Little Miss Candy Cane. Turned out she had a hot, naughty side, too—one he hadn't anticipated. And that made him all the more into her.

And she was . . . honest. She didn't hold back, attempt to hide or mask things. She didn't try to act like she had everything completely under control. He hadn't met many people like that and he wasn't sure what to make of it—but maybe he liked that about her, too. Maybe he thought anyone willing to be that real all the time possibly . . . did actually have things under control.

But it was a whole different kind of control he thought about as he moved in her, thrusting firm and deep, watching pleasure and passion etch themselves onto her face. Right now, he wanted to control her every response and fulfill her every desire. She wasn't very experienced—he could tell. But he didn't mind. Because she mostly let him *take* control, let him lead, guide, show, give.

Gripping her ass tight, he said, "Put your arms around my neck," then rolled to his back until she was on top. She let out a breath at the different way that obviously felt to her—and he liked that, too. Then gave her one more instruction. "Now ride me, honey."

And she did. Taking back just a little of that control, and looking so damn beautiful doing it. As she sat upright astride him, he lifted his hands to cup the softness of her breasts, molding and massaging in rhythm with her movements. He tweaked their hard, puckered tips, noting their rosy color in the morning light. He still didn't know why his father had sent him to Destiny and had long since given up trying to figure it out, but at the moment, he was damn glad fate or God or whoever else had brought him here.

He didn't know her well—*wouldn't* know her well. And as he'd told her, this was only sex—all it *could* be. But he knew his life was richer for this moment. *All* these moments. With her. In bed and out.

He watched her, prodded her. He thrust up into her; he caressed and explored. Their eyes met, blotting out everything else in the room—in the world—in that moment, and she came sobbing, whimpering, eyes falling shut, head dropping back.

And as he took all that in, let his gaze drop from

her flushed cheeks to her pale breasts to the spot where their bodies were joined, a whole other kind of control entered the picture—the kind he lost just then, his own climax rushing over him like a tidal wave out of nowhere, forcing him to drive high and hard up into her, emptying himself there.

He heard, saw, nothing for a few seconds—was just gone to that place where the ecstasy owns you. And when he came back down to find himself holding this sweet, sexy, naked redhead in his arms in a strange bed, in a strange town, in a strange existence, one thought permeated his brain. *I never lose control that way. Ever.*

But it had been a while since he'd gone to bed with a woman.

And hell, life hadn't exactly been normal or easy lately.

So it doesn't mean anything.

Other than that you clearly needed that release.

She peered timidly up at him then, green eyes shining on him like crystals. Her voice came as soft as her expression. "That was nice."

"Yeah—it was."

He kissed her then without really planning it. Maybe because her lips were like the color of the cranberries they'd strung together. Maybe because she looked like she *wanted* to be kissed—as a reassurance that he'd liked what they'd just done, too. Or maybe because all this touching and kissing with her had just . . . come easy somehow, felt natural.

Just then, her white cat came pouncing up onto the bed next to them—and made his way straight for Shane, settling warmly against his other side.

The woman he held rolled her eyes. "And the bromance continues."

He slanted her an amused glance. "You jealous?"

"Of you or of him?"

He just laughed. And told her with a wink, "Well, you're better off with *him*. You should stay away from guys like *me*."

She met his gaze, looking a little bolder now—almost challenging. "Because you're such a big bundle of trouble?"

He kept his expression light, easy. "Yes ma'am."

And she gave her head a pretty tilt, a curving lock of pale auburn hair falling across her cheek. "You don't *seem* like such a bad guy."

He tossed her another wicked grin. "You don't know me that well yet."

"Where'd you get that scar, mister?" she asked then, reaching a fingertip to gently touch the mark beside his eye. A little thing he barely noticed about himself anymore. "Bar fight? Or something worse?"

And for the first time ever, given the nature of the conversation, Shane almost wished he *had* gotten it in a bar fight. "Actually," he said, "it happened in a bike accident."

"You have a motorcycle?" she asked.

He only sighed. Then laughed at himself a little. "No—I meant a bicycle. I was thrown over the handlebars when I was twelve."

Which drew a gentle trill of laughter from her, too. "Yeah, you're *so* tough and bad. Here I'd been thinking that scar had come from some of that trouble you claim to be. Hate to tell you this, but I'm starting not to believe you very much about that."

Though in response, he just shrugged. Got a little more somber. "Doesn't take fighting in bars to make a guy trouble. Surely you know that, Candy."

"Yeah," she said softly, almost wistfully. "I do." Then she gave her head a thoughtful tilt. "Mind if I ask you something?"

"Probably." He chuckled again—but this sounded like it would be a little more serious than the last question. "I mean, if you have to ask first, it's something I might not want to tell you—right?"

Instead of answering that, however, she moved straight on to the question. "Remember when you told me your mother wanted you gone, and that she thought you were bad? I was wondering how you know that. I mean . . . if she actually told you that."

Shit. He hadn't seen *this* coming. And suddenly regretted that strange moment of openness in the garden at Miss Ellie's. That was what Candy did to him—she put him at ease, maybe too much.

There was no keeping his light expression in place at the mention of his mother, so he didn't even try. And didn't particularly want to discuss this. "What does it matter?"

"I just wondered. I mean—you keep telling me what a bad guy you are, and I'm curious what you have to back that up. Or . . . where it came from."

He just looked at her. Was she wanting to absolve him somehow? Wanting to find out he was a better person than he'd painted himself to her? So he'd be a safer bet? So it would make more sense for her to be in bed with him right now?

He could do that. After all, he was leaving soon—in

less than a week if he was going to make it to Miami by the twenty-fifth. And he'd gotten a call from the A1 Body Shop saying the body work on his truck was done and they were ready to paint, so it wouldn't be long now. He could leave her with better ideas about him and it wouldn't hurt a damn thing.

But . . . he *was* who he *was*. And since she was so open and honest with him about who *she* was , , , hell—he just didn't see the good in not keeping it real here.

"Look, honey," he said, "no matter how you slice it, I'm no Prince Charming. I could tell you a lifetime of stories about running with the wrong crowd and getting into bad shit. Doesn't mean I'm the devil—but don't be expecting me to get my wings anytime soon, either." He winked. "I'm no angel second class, or even third or fourth."

He couldn't read her expression—couldn't tell if she was disappointed, convinced, anything—as she said, "Are you going to answer the part about your mom? Did she tell you she wanted you gone?"

And at this, Shane thought back. The answer didn't matter in the big picture, but maybe it was a question he'd never really thought about before. And even if it felt like a lifetime ago, a whole other world, now images flashed in his mind. Times he'd gotten in trouble at school and she'd been called in to talk to the teacher. Times he hadn't done his chores or had bullied a neighbor kid, a time he carelessly dropped a glass figurine she'd valued and that he shouldn't have had his hands on in the first place. The fact was—his mother hadn't needed to *tell* him he was bad. Looking back, he could see he'd been a handful—he'd been angry at his parents' divorce. And he'd blamed *her*, though he wasn't sure why now.

"No, I don't think she ever actually told me. But I got in trouble a lot."

"Plenty of kids get in trouble a lot. That doesn't mean their mother wants them gone."

The words, which he'd shared with her and were seared into his brain from a long time ago, made him flash back again to when they'd been said. On that car ride to Montana with his dad. They'd been passing over flat, barren land that seemed to stretch forever in all directions, land that had made Shane feel like they must be traveling to the ends of the earth. And his dad had been reassuring him that things would be better. Better than barren land. And better than at home.

"My dad told me," he said to Candice.

"Your dad told you your mother said you were bad and that she wanted you gone?"

He gave a short nod.

And she looked unexpectedly outraged, her brow knitting. "I'm sorry, but why would he do that? Why would *any* parent tell their child that? Even if it was true—why would you burden your kid with something so hurtful?"

Huh. He'd never thought about it before, but maybe he could see her point. Though it didn't change anything, so he only shrugged. "Okay, my dad might not have been the best judge of what to say to a little kid. But that doesn't mean she didn't say it."

"It also doesn't mean she did."

Shane sighed—taken back to a time and a place he'd rather forget. And he thought Candy was making a pretty big assumption here. He flicked a pointed glance in her direction. "And again, what the hell does this matter? And why the hell are we talking about it?"

"Well, it just seems to me like the kind of thing one parent would say about the other after a bad divorce or something—you know?"

He took that in, turned it over in his head. She was suggesting that his dad would hurt him in order to get back at his mother. And she didn't even know either one of them, so besides being awful damn presumptuous, it was also on the verge of pissing him off. "My dad was no saint, but he was the best dad to me he could be—he loved me."

As she tensed slightly next to him, he knew he'd spoken a little harshly. And he hoped she'd let this drop now. But instead she quietly, almost cautiously said, "Maybe he loved you too much. Maybe he wanted you all to himself."

"Damn, girl," he muttered. Trying to bite his lip. Trying not to tell her to mind her own business, that she didn't know what she was talking about, that his dad was the one parent who had given a shit about him so to shut the hell up about this.

But he knew deep down she meant well. He knew deep down she just didn't like the idea of a parent abandoning a kid—because she'd been there, too. "Candy, honey, are you sure you aren't trying to fix for me what you can't fix for yourself?"

She looked confused. "What do you mean?"

"Remember, you filled me in on *your* past, too."

Her eyes changed then, telling him maybe she'd forgotten. But she shook her head and said, "No, this isn't about that. This is about . . . facts, that's all. The facts, for me, are that my dad went out to the store one night and never came back. Cut and dried. Simple as can be. The facts for you don't seem as clear—you have this idea about yourself and I just wondered how it got there, where it came from. And it sounds to me like it came more from your dad than your mom." Her voice went quiet then, as maybe she, too, heard for the first time that the accusation was . . . big. She whispered the last part. "That's all."

"Well, here's a fact for ya—and the only one that really matters in the end," he said. "She let him take me. Never called, never wrote, never heard from her again." Then he pushed back the covers, jarring both her and the cat slightly, but he didn't care at the moment. "Now if it's all right with you, I'm gonna go take a shower."

Candice lay in bed with Frosty, watching Shane stalk naked toward the bathroom down the hall. Two thoughts warred in her head. That he had a great butt. And oh Lord—why had she interrogated him that way?

But as soon as he disappeared behind a closed door and she heard the water running, the second thought weighed down on her.

She hadn't meant to be so pushy about something so personal. *This is what you get by being too isolated— you become socially awkward in sensitive moments.* Ugh.

Maybe he was right in a way; maybe this *was* about her own issues. She knew what it was like to be left by a parent. But when hers had left, it hadn't formed her core opinion about herself. Her mom had worked hard, even amid her own heartbreak—one more bad boy; they were always leaving—to be both mother and father to her. And she'd had this warm, loving community to make her feel normal and loved and whole.

And yeah, sure, it had still left a scar. Deep down, any kid in this situation had to wonder how a parent could do that and if it was about *them*? But again, it hadn't ruled her life. And so maybe she didn't want it ruling Shane's, either.

Although maybe it was too late for that.

And none of her concern.

And God—what if she'd taken the nicest thing to happen to her in a very long time and blown it to bits with her careless analysis?

She lay shaking her head at her insensitivity.

"I need to fix this," she said softly to Frosty, who lay stretched out near her feet.

He flicked his tail as if to say, *Whatever.*

"Thanks for your concern," she told him—then rolled her eyes. "You probably just want him all to yourself."

And it hit her then—how much *she* wanted him. Not necessarily to herself. But in her bed. For at least the next few days until he left Destiny. One night hadn't been enough. And she knew that once you formed that emotional attachment—that thing she'd been so wary of—two nights, or three nights, or ten nights wouldn't be enough, either. But she at least wanted him for as long as she could have him. Trouble or not.

So she bounded out of bed and threw on some clothes, trying to make herself look as pretty as she could without the aid of a shower or bathroom supplies. And she dashed downstairs and decided to make a more romantic breakfast for him than the first awkward one they'd shared together in her kitchen.

When he entered the room twenty minutes later—Frosty faithfully on his heels, of course—she turned from the stove to face him with the plate of pancakes she'd just scooped off the griddle.

"Consider these apology pancakes," she told him. "Is there any chance we can forget that last conversation and get back to the fun stuff?"

He didn't smile. Instead he simply arched one brow and said, "Fun stuff?"

She walked over and rose on her tiptoes to kiss him on his stubble-covered cheek, then held up the plate once more. "Kissing? Flirting? Pancakes?"

He met her gaze. "Throw in some more hot sex and you've got a deal, Candy Cane."

"Sort of a fallen angel, aren't you? What happened to your wings?"

Sixteen

The Destiny town Christmas party was tomorrow, and that meant a morning of phone calls and emails, and an afternoon of final decorating and setup at Miss Ellie's house. Shane watched TV and played with the cat—though he claimed he didn't enjoy that part—while Candice took care of the morning tasks, after which he helped with the afternoon ones.

Candice made sure to again thank Miss Ellie for letting them use her house. "It's really the perfect place for the party," she said, then glanced toward Shane, who was carrying some empty boxes down to the basement. "And with a little help from Shane, I think we're all set."

"Oh, I don't think it'll rain, honey, or that you'll get wet," Miss Ellie said, as usual not quite hearing what Candice said. "But if it does, you get that Shame fella to keep you warm—he's a looker, that one."

It surprised Candice to feel her cheeks heat, but she instantly realized it was more about remembering ways Shane had indeed ended up keeping her warm last night than being embarrassed in front of Miss Ellie.

As the two prepared to leave, the old woman gazed out the window on her front yard and said, "A snowman."

Candice and Shane just looked at each other, and Candice said gently, "There isn't a snowman in your yard, Miss Ellie." Was the old woman imagining things? Miss Ellie had long been hard of hearing, but even at her advanced age, she'd never been senile.

That was when Miss Ellie looked over at her and said sensibly, "Of course there isn't. You and Shame should build one. That'd be a nice extra touch." She ended with a succinct nod, clearly feeling adamant on it.

Again, Candice and Shane exchanged glances, and this time he said, "Up for it, Candy Cane?"

Yet no matter how warm he'd kept her last night, her eyes dropped to his hands. "You don't have gloves."

He winked. "Good thing I'm a tough guy."

"I bet if I go into Miss Ellie's hall closet, I can find a pair." She looked back toward the old woman in her easy chair by the front window. "Miss Ellie, do you have any gloves? For a man?"

Miss Ellie looked a little surprised, then thoughtful. "Well, I had a great deal of love for my Harvey before he passed. He was a wonderful husband." Then she, too, looked at Shane's hands. "You're gonna need some gloves if you're going to build us a snowman, Shane. Check the hall closet."

Shane just smiled at the old woman, then returned a few minutes later with an old pair of brown gloves that must have once belonged to Harvey. "Thank you, Miss Ellie," he told her, holding up one glove-covered hand.

"Good that they get some use," she said. "Things get old sitting around not being used. Getting used makes things . . . matter more, I think."

Candice found herself pondering the elderly lady's words as she and Shane bundled up and went outside. They somehow made her think of . . . herself. Romantically, sexually. Something in her had stagnated over the years, maybe almost atrophied. It made her feel alive in some fresh, new way to have all these feelings she'd forgotten about flowing through her veins again.

Together, they built a snowman as tall as Shane. It was hard work, but still fun. Candice couldn't remember the last time she'd built one.

As they worked together on the lower part of the body, Shane leaned over to kiss her, and despite the cold, the sensation tingled all through her. He stopped to kiss her again—longer this time—as they carved and smoothed out the shape. After he placed a pair of earmuffs on the snowman's head, courtesy of Miss Ellie's closet as well, he kissed her once more. And he kissed her yet again as she tied a navy blue scarf around the snowman's neck.

She couldn't help smiling at him—her nose was cold and her fingers nearly frozen beneath her mittens, but those kisses did help warm her up from the inside out.

"Do you still hate Christmas?" she asked teasingly.

He gave her a sexy, flirty grin. "Guess maybe it has its high points, after all."

A few minutes later, as they finally left Miss Ellie's, Candice wasn't sure what would happen next—between them. So she said, "Well . . . guess we're done getting ready. All that's left now is the party."

He nodded next to her in the car. "If you don't mind driving me to town, I should probably stop by the church. Mick texted me a few minutes ago to say they could use some manpower this afternoon—they're working 'til dark, trying to beat that Christmas Eve deadline."

Okay, that wasn't what Candice had been hoping for—but she certainly understood. "Of course," she said, steering the car past her own house toward town. "Do you think they'll make it? In time for the wedding?"

Shane nodded. "It'll be tight, but according to Mick, all systems are still go. And since we focused completely on the church instead of the community building, they plan to have the reception in the church basement—since it should be empty of pews and stuff from upstairs by then."

Candice nodded as they rounded a bend on Blue Valley Road. "Good—that's great. I'm so glad it's all going to work out."

Driving through town a few minutes later, they passed the General Mercantile and the big tree on the square, soon after pulling up in front of the church. She watched as Shane reached for the door handle—and realized his hands were bare again. "You're not wearing the gloves."

He gave a shrug. "They were Harvey's. I couldn't just take 'em. Left 'em inside before we took off."

She flashed him a look in reply. "Yeah, you're a really bad guy—returning gloves no one would ever miss if you used them for a day or two. Downright villainous."

It made him let out a small laugh. "Don't go giving me those wings just yet, Candy." Then he opened the door—looking back at her to say, "So . . . guess I'll see you tomorrow? At the party."

Oh. Tomorrow. Not tonight.

Candice just nodded. Feeling a little sad, empty, to be saying goodbye. She'd hoped this would stretch on, after all. And her chest tightened at the idea that this was already over, that she'd gotten exactly what she hadn't wanted—a one-night stand. What about the more sex he'd bargained for when they'd been making up this morning?

And it was the memory of that conversation that made her go out on a limb here and hope she wouldn't end up feeling silly, or rejected. "Unless . . . well, after being out in the cold, I was thinking of putting a pot of chili on the stove for later. If . . . you wanted some."

He grinned at her across the car. "I want some."

And suddenly, she was pretty sure he wasn't just talking about chili, so she smiled back.

"I'll get Mick to drop me off later."

"See you then," she said, trying not to smile too much, or look too elated. Even though she was.

And as she started back toward Blue Valley Lake, she realized something. *People will know now. Whoever's around when he asks Mick to drive him. And Mick will tell Jenny. And by tomorrow all of Destiny will know I'm officially having a hot fling with the stranger in town.*

And she didn't care one little bit. She'd just completely thrown caution to the wind. Jumped into the fire with both feet. Fire had never been so appealing before.

Well, Bobby had been fire. Appealing fire.

But quit comparing him to Bobby.

He's not Bobby. They're not the same guy.

Wings or not, Shane was exactly what she wanted and needed right now and she didn't care who knew or how it felt later. "Merry Christmas to *me*," she said out loud to no one, wearing a big grin as she drove.

And as she approached the Mercantile, she made a sudden, unplanned right turn into the parking lot. Now that she was in the fire, all the way, there was something she needed to pick up before heading home—one more Christmas gift.

Shane had never been with a woman like Candy before. And as he laid her back on her couch, then proceeded to pull down her blue jeans, along with her panties, his erection tightened to a degree that almost hurt. She excited him that much.

Maybe because of that whole thing about them being on opposite sides of Santa's list. He'd never been with a woman so . . . wholly good, and kind, and pure. And yet he was getting to see a side of her that was equally as naughty as it was nice, a side he knew no one else in Destiny probably even imagined she could possess. It was hard not to be turned on by that.

But maybe there was more to it. Maybe it was about the fact that she'd let him in. Into her life. Into her bed. That something in him had won her over, made her desires greater than her fears. It was hard not to be turned on by that, too.

Funny thing was, as he stripped her sweater off over her head, then licked a trail between her lush breasts, using his hands over the cups of her bra to push them together, he never would have dreamed he could like this so much.

A nice girl. In an old-fashioned house. In a quaint little town. Not his usual style by a long shot. And God knows, if anyone had told him a few weeks ago that being with this kind of woman would have him so excited, he'd have thought they were crazy. But here he was, hard as a brick, rolling on a condom, his groin aching with the need to plunge himself inside her.

Like last night, the Christmas tree lit the room and a low fire crackled and hissed in the hearth. Her clingy white cat lay sleeping next to it. And he liked every damn thing about the moment, for reasons he sure as hell couldn't understand.

Of course, the part he liked best of all was when she opened her legs for him, eager and wanting, and he pushed his way snugly inside her warmth. A low groan erupted from his throat as the muscles of his lower abdomen spasmed with pleasure at the entry. And her hot, sexy, feminine little gasp told him she was right there with him, that they were in perfect sync, both soaking up every bit of heat and lust and pleasure that the connection delivered.

As he began to move in her, she cried out at each thrust—drives that started out slow and deep, reaching for that total, fullest immersion in her, but then turned harder, faster, more powerful. He wanted to make her feel it, feel it, feel it.

Her cries and whimpers escalated with the hot rhythm he set—until he realized that if they kept up like this, he'd come. And he wasn't ready for that, not even close. And not just for him—but for her, too. He didn't want to rush this—he wanted to make her feel *everything*.

When he drew out of her, she released a disappointed sigh—but he quickly assured her, "It's okay, honey—I just want to make you feel good."

"You were," she said emphatically.

"Well, even better," he promised—and then he dropped to his knees next to the couch, angling her toward him, hands on her bare, pale hips, and bent to rake his tongue through her moist folds.

The way her body shuddered echoed the shivery, ragged breath that escaped her. She tasted at once sweet and salty, and he could have sworn he felt her surge with more moisture against his mouth.

He kissed and tongued that soft, most sensitive spot on her, his mouth soon closing over the delicate but swollen nub he knew lay at the heart of her excitement. She sucked in her breath, panting and moaning beneath his ministrations, and when he slid two fingers up into her wetness, she thrust against them, and against his mouth—her moves heated and rhythmic.

As her heat grew, he could almost feel it himself—flowing down over him like some invisible liquid warmth that permeated his skin, his flesh, making him hot from the inside out. *Come, baby. Come for me.* He wanted to see that, wanted to make it happen.

And then it did. She climaxed against his mouth, sobbing, her face wrenched in what looked like agony but he knew was pure release. He loved feeling her let go like that, loved her utter abandon with him.

When it had passed and she relaxed back into the

couch cushions, he rose up over her again and rasped with a wink, "Guess it pays to be on Santa's nice list, Candy."

She giggled—and then her eyes went darker, sexier. Knowing almost no one else had ever witnessed this part of Little Miss Candy Cane made him feel downright . . . privileged. Especially when she whispered, "Come back inside me, Shane."

Mmm, he was more than happy to, so he wasted no time—except to change things up a little by instructing her, "Turn over, honey."

"Huh?"

"On your hands and knees." And then he helped her, guided her, using his hands to position her until she was facing away from him, her palms planted on the arm of the couch.

Then he pushed his way back inside her. God, yes. It was snug and hot there. A place he never wanted to leave. And the next thing he knew, his body had taken over and he was driving into her—hard, hard, hard— making her cry out again.

The moment he came was one of replete bliss. So replete that . . . hell, why was this so different? Different than with any other woman. But as he collapsed gently atop her afterward, he supposed it came back to her Candy Cane sweetness, her goodness, her openness. He supposed it came back to everything she was—from this house and her silly cat to the cookies she baked and the movies she loved and the heart she put into throwing a party for her beloved little town.

And it was only as he was drifting off to sleep a few minutes later, the two of them under a soft throw, naked on her couch, her warm curves cuddled against him and the Christmas tree still throwing a colorful glow through the darkness, that it hit him. This felt safe. Everything about it. Everything about *her*.

It was a safe place. An easy place. And maybe he hadn't had much safe and easy in his life up until now. There were vague memories of it from a long, long time ago, sometime before his parents broke up, sometime before Montana—but he'd nearly forgotten that, that sense of safety all around him. And Candy—and Destiny—were giving him that.

Too bad it couldn't last.

"**Y**ou never really did tell me about this job you're going to in Miami," Candice mused aloud. Now that she'd gotten to know him better, she was all the more curious.

But when she tried to meet Shane's gaze, peering up from his embrace on the couch in the dimly lit living room, he didn't quite look at her, keeping his eyes shaded. And she almost thought he wasn't going to answer her at all—when he finally said, "Truth is—I don't know the exact details of it. Hoping it's just a high-end parts supplier."

She raised her eyebrows. "Hoping?"

Again, he couldn't directly meet her gaze. "Well . . . possible it's a chop shop."

"Chop shop?" She wasn't entirely sure what that meant.

And a hint of regret colored his expression as he said, "They take stolen cars and dismantle them to sell the parts."

She just blinked, a flutter of dismay passing through her stomach. "You're going to steal cars?"

"No," he said quickly, emphatically. "I'll just be . . . the shop manager. I'll oversee the work. I won't do anything but make sure the cars get taken apart the right way, keeping all the pieces in good shape. Because I'm good with cars."

She bit her lip, still trying to wrap her brain around it. "But it's . . . illegal. Right?"

He let out a sigh. "Well . . . not in a way that really hurts anybody."

She stiffened slightly in his grasp. "There's not really any such thing as a victimless crime. I mean, the people who own the cars—"

"Will have good insurance policies to take care of them."

"And the insurance companies will have to pay out a lot of money. And raise people's rates. Or lower employee salaries. Who knows the ways it might trickle down."

He stayed quiet for a moment, finally saying, "Look, I might be wrong. I *hope* I'm wrong. Like I said, it might be a perfectly legit parts shop." Then he stopped, sighed. And started sounding a little more self-righteous. "See? I told you I was trouble."

She wasn't sure why, but something in his tone . . . softened her judgment, that fast. Even if maybe that was foolish. Because she'd come to care for him. "Well, I suppose I've known worse."

Still holding her against him, he tipped his head back against a throw pillow. "Really?"

And she thought about the truth in those words, and decided that if he'd admitted something to her, maybe she could admit something to him, too. "I had a boyfriend once who . . . well, the upshot is that I loved him and he paid me back by stealing some money and jewelry from me—that locket, in fact; the one I told you about—and running off with my best friend."

Lord, she hadn't said that out loud—maybe ever. She'd never had to, because everyone in town had known what happened due to the Destiny grapevine. It was a hard thing to give voice to, even now.

"Seriously?" Shane asked, squinting. "Wow. Damn, honey. That's . . . pretty fucking awful. And that guy must have been an idiot."

And she had no idea why, but for some reason the *rest* of her truth popped out of her mouth then, as well. "It really hurt me, really made me . . . withdraw a lot. I mean . . ." She stopped, shook her head. "I just haven't really dated anyone since it happened. Until . . . well . . . you."

Oh God. Only as the words left her did she realize the size and impact of her confession.

And as their eyes met in the room's shadows, she knew he understood what a big thing it was for her to have had sex with him.

He stayed quiet for a moment—and then he whispered, his voice coming out a little throaty, "What makes *me* so special, Candy?"

She shook her head against his broad chest, at a loss for an answer. Then just tried to keep being honest. "You . . . excited me. And so . . . I guess it was time— that's all." *Yeah, that's good—make it sound like it's not* quite *as huge a thing as it really is.*

But she wasn't sure it had worked when he gently asked, "You gonna be okay when I leave, Candy Cane?"

"I'm a big girl," she promised, her heart pumping

too hard. She wondered if he felt it, too, since they lay chest-to-chest at the moment.

"That doesn't answer my question," he said.

So she took a deep breath. "Look, it's been a couple of days, and I knew it was temporary. And I'm glad it'll be at least a couple *more* days. And I'll be sorry when you're gone." She slowed down then, quit barreling ahead, the emotion hitting her. "*Really* sorry. But . . ."

"But . . . ?"

"But you seem pretty dead set on leaving . . . even when I think you know plenty of people around here would be happy if you stayed."

His brows rose slightly as he met her gaze. "People?"

"Grampy, Edna," she said. "And you seem to have made friends with Mick and some of the other guys in town."

He hesitated only slightly before asking, "Would *you* be happy if I stayed?"

"Of course."

"But you're not going to ask me to?"

"No. That decision would have to be yours." With Bobby she'd been . . . needy. She never wanted to be that again.

"I've never had much," he said softly.

"And . . . ?" she asked, wondering what he was getting at.

"The kind of money that comes with this job, Candy—it's . . . too much to pass up. And if it turns out not to be honest work, well . . . I'll at least make it as honest as I can. And I won't do it forever. But it's . . . a new start, a way to build a better future for myself."

There for a second, she'd almost thought he would

tell her he'd consider staying. But now she realized she was wrong. And that was okay. Even if her heart dropped a little.

She'd once wanted more from Bobby than he could give her. And maybe she wanted that from Shane, too. The difference this time was that she wouldn't ask him for it, wouldn't try to pull from him something that wasn't freely given. The difference was that she'd grown up enough to know that the whole thing about letting something go and seeing if it came back to you was true.

And she was willing to let Shane go. And he wasn't coming back. But she was still able to love him.

Oh God. It happened again. I love him. That fast. Already. I love him.

Yet . . . even if this broke her heart again, even if it broke it badly . . . well, it was okay. Strange way to feel, but it was true. Because the love part was worth it.

And maybe what she was learning this Christmas was—love you give away, without trying to get something back, *that* was real love.

"Remember, no man is a failure who has friends."

Clarence Odbody, Angel 2nd Class, *It's a Wonderful Life*

Seventeen

Candice stood outside Miss Ellie's front door, looking out over the Destiny Christmas party. In the distance, past the snowman she and Shane had built, people ice-skated on frozen, picturesque Blue Valley Lake, the few bare trees along the shoreline strung with white lights.

Children ran and played in the garden at the side of the house, waiting for Santa to appear, and each new arrival hung an ornament they'd brought from home on a small pine tree just inside the garden gate—an activity her cousin Tessa had helped organize. A bright sun shone down over it all, from a clear blue sky, making the cold temperatures bearable.

Behind her, from inside, she could hear Caroline playing carols on Miss Ellie's piano—a number of voices could be heard harmonizing on "Up on the Roof Top." And a peek in the front window revealed that Miss Ellie herself seemed to be having a grand afternoon, clapping her hands in time with the music.

Later, her daughters would help her outside so that she could enjoy some of the outdoor activities. While most people might, by now, be feeling the imposition of hosting such an elaborate party and having so much action going on in and around their home, Miss Ellie looked to be truly enjoying it all, giving Candice the idea that maybe the party should *always* be held here, even after the church was fully repaired.

She smiled upon seeing the Brodys make their way up the front walk along the path Mike and Logan had cleared. All were bundled up, and Mick carried little Dustin on one hip while Jenny toted ice skates and a plastic container of cookies.

As Candice stepped up to take the container and say hello, Jenny beamed at her. "Candice, this was such a wonderful idea! It's a winter wonderland!"

She didn't bother hiding her own smile. "Thanks— I'm pleased with how it's turned out."

"Daddy, where's Santa?"

Mick looked to his toddler son, then glanced around. "We probably beat him here. But we'll have some of Mommy's cookies while we're waiting—and you brought your ornament to hang, right?"

The little boy dutifully nodded, then held up the ornament Candice hadn't noticed in his little mittened hand until now. It was tiny reindeer fashioned from clothespins painted brown and glued together to form both antlers and legs, with some other details added, as well. Though the paint was worn off the edges and it looked like it had seen better days. "Grandma 'Nita let me pick one off her tree," Dustin announced with pride to Candice.

"Well, you picked a very nice one," she assured him.

Then he informed her, "It's a reindeer."

She feigned surprise as she looked closer. "Well, how about that—it sure is!"

"Big fan of reindeer, this one," Mick said. "Can't get enough of 'em all the sudden."

Then Jenny spoke under her breath to Candice. "But Anita acted a little funny about him taking that particular ornament, so we plan to guard it with our lives." She shook her head. "She said it had a special meaning for her—and I suggested Dustin pick another, but then Anita insisted he take it. Still, we're going to be super careful with it and be sure to take it back with us later when we leave."

Candice nodded—and Dustin asked again, "Where's Santa? Is he here? When is he coming?"

They all laughed at his impatience and Candice told him, "He should be pulling up in his sleigh anytime now."

Both Jenny and Mick looked at her, wide-eyed. "In his sleigh?" Mick asked. "That's new."

She nodded, shrugged. "What can I say—I take my party-planning duties seriously. I pulled some strings with the big guy."

"Impressive," Mick mused.

In reply, Candice tilted her head and quietly added

a small confession. "Actually, I can't take all—or even any—of the credit. It was Shane's idea." Then she glanced back to Mick. "So speaking of Anita, how are things looking at the church?"

He tipped his head back slightly. "Good. So long as we keep moving at the current pace, we'll be set for the wedding. New carpet comes tomorrow, and the damaged front pews have been refinished and are ready to be put back where they belong. The ceiling might not look so great, with only short-term roof repairs in place, but as long as nobody looks up, we're good." He finished with a wink—then, at Dustin's prodding, headed toward the garden, the boy still in his arms.

"Well, what a relief for Anita," Candice said to Jenny.

Jenny nodded, smiled. "You can say that again. Anita and Dad are so grateful for all the help, and they're looking forward to getting to thank everyone today."

Hearing that made Candice's heart expand a little. "Oh, I'm glad they're coming. I know she's been pretty overwhelmed lately, but a party will be good for her."

Just then, Tessa and Rachel exited the garden and joined them near the front stoop. "The ornament tree seems to be a big hit with the kids," Tessa said, then glanced to Jenny. "Dustin just hung his—he was so excited to pick exactly the right spot."

"Mike helped Farris hang hers a little while ago," Rachel added with an easy smile.

"I think after a quick warm-up inside, Lucky and I are going to try ice-skating," Tessa announced. "Amy and Logan are already on the ice." She pointed vaguely in the direction of the lake. "And again, Candice—great job on the party! It's amazing."

It was from the corner of her eye that Candice saw

Shane approaching up the front walk. He wore a hoodie under his coat, with the hood pulled up, and had his hands stuffed in his pockets. The mere sight of him heated her up inside and made her skin tingle beneath her winter apparel.

"I think all the hot chocolate machines are finally set up," he told her—then added a playful wink. Implying there had been a million of them or something.

"There are only three," she pointed out, returning his teasing smile.

He let out a light laugh. "Three. At one party. I think you just made my point for me."

"Which is?" she asked, eyebrows arched in playful challenge.

"This place has a serious hot chocolate obsession," he said. "Hot chocolate and cats." Then he shook his head lightly. "Does anyone even own a dog in this town?"

"I do."

They all looked up to see Adam and Sue Ann exiting Miss Ellie's house, skates draped over their arms. "But I'm lucky he stays," Adam added with a grim shake of his head, "with all the preferential treatment given to cats around here."

"It's more like *he's* lucky the cats *let* him stay," Sue Ann pointed out.

Shane chuckled—then motioned toward the house. "Need to grab some more cups from inside for the hot chocolate stand on the dock."

And Candice watched him go, aware of how much she simply liked being near him now. Or maybe she always had. But now she no longer had to fight the intense attraction, the sheer magnetism.

Adam and Sue Ann had proceeded down the walk

toward the lake, Tessa and Rachel promising to join them soon—but before they headed inside, Candice realized Rachel was giving her a look.

"What?" she asked. "Do I have icing on my face?" She'd been eating a gingerbread man with white icing piped around the edges a few minutes earlier.

"Things have changed," Rachel speculated, tone suspicious, eyes narrowed in what looked almost like accusation.

Candice tried to play dumb. "What are you talking about?"

"You and Shane." Rachel pointed one finger—her hand covered by a stylish leopard-print glove—in the general direction in which he'd just disappeared. "Something's happened between you two. You're not all snippy with him anymore. And he winked at you."

"So what?" Candice replied, realizing it wasn't exactly the strongest defensive stance in the world, especially since she felt her cheeks warming, even in the freezing temps.

And Rachel smiled—as Jenny let out a soft little gasp. The two of them and Tessa looked as if they'd just discovered a huge secret. Even though it was purely conjecture on their parts. "So what's *up* is the better question," Rachel said slyly.

Then Jenny pointed at her, clearly having a revelation. "Mick said Shane asked to be dropped at your house last night. That he made some claim of helping you with some last-minute party stuff. But it wasn't party stuff at all, was it?"

Candice appreciated that Shane had been polite enough to try to cover up what was taking place between them—and apparently it had even worked until Rachel had figured it out anyway, with way less to go on. And now she added, "I think it was a *private* party. Of the sexy kind."

"Okay, okay, fine—but keep it down," Candice said, trying to shush them.

After which Tessa's eyebrows shot up—since apparently she'd been holding out for the confirmation Candice had just delivered. "Really?" she asked. "You took my advice?"

"I guess I kinda did," Candice admitted.

"And?" Tessa asked.

All three ladies leaned closer in anticipation.

So Candice tried to keep it real, but also light. "It was great," she said softly. "As in . . . amazing and miraculous and the perfect holiday fling. He'll only be here a few more days, after all. But for now . . . it's fun. *Really* fun."

Her cousin and the other two smiled. "Holiday cheer," Rachel said smugly.

And Candice simply replied, "Something like that."

And sure, she already knew her holiday cheer would also be her New Year's heartache—but she still had no regrets. How could she? She'd fallen hard for him. And she was living in the moment, enjoying the time she had with him for all it was worth. She'd worry about the fallout later. When she had no other choice.

"I'm so happy for you," Tessa said, reaching out to give her a hug.

Then Rachel did, too.

"It's not like we've gotten engaged or anything," Candice said, trying to play it off. But she appreciated her friends' support, and she knew that *they* knew this was about more than having a fling—that it was about . . . really living again. Really being open again. To possibilities. To romance. To love.

What they *didn't* need to know was that she was more than just *open* to love—she was already in it.

As Rachel and Tessa headed inside to get warm, leaving her with Jenny, she again took in the winter splendor of it all. People kept arriving and more kids—and even a few adults—now stood in line near the tree by the gate, waiting to hang their ornaments. She could hear children laughing—and more singing, too. Now a rousing rendition of "Jingle Bells." She spotted Adam's adolescent twin sons building a snowman of their own near hers and Shane's just as Lettie Hart and LeeAnn Turner stopped, Lettie placing a hand on Candice's arm, to tell her what a great party it was.

She smiled, accepting the compliment, and feeling like she was in a dream. Not only had normally reserved, keep-to-herself Candice thrown a great party—she had a hot, mysterious lover, too.

And yeah, some of the mysteries around Shane were . . . troubling. What he'd told her about his job in Miami had been more than a little disillusioning. She didn't like to think of him doing something illegal for a living. Maybe it was true that the guy she'd come to know wasn't an angel—but he also didn't seem like a criminal, either.

And of course, it had reminded her that maybe she'd been right to be wary. That she didn't really know him—that no one here did.

And maybe what he'd told her should have made her afraid. Like she used to be.

But somehow it hadn't.

He'd wanted to give Grampy a Christmas tree. He'd made sure to return Harvey's gloves. He'd rescued her cat in a blizzard. And he'd helped repair the church.

No matter how she looked at it, he just wasn't a bad guy. No matter how much he kept telling her he was.

That job in Miami notwithstanding.

Just then, the door opened behind them and Shane came out, a sleeve of cups and some red party napkins in hand. He whisked past them, giving Candice a sexy grin on the way.

"You know," Jenny said to her then, "I would never suggest that it was a good thing the roof caved in on the church, especially with the wedding about to happen there. But . . . maybe this party is one good thing that came out of the blizzard." Her neighbor squeezed her mitten-covered hand, then went off in the direction of her husband and child.

And, of course, Candice could think of *another* good thing that had come out of the blizzard. He was crossing Blue Valley Road toward the lake right now.

She stood there a few moments longer, watching. As he delivered the cups and napkins to the hot chocolate table, handing one of each to Ed Fisher, she noticed how different he seemed than when they'd first met. A moment later, she could see him talking, laughing, with Tyler Fleet, home from college on Christmas break, and then helping Old Mrs. Lampton add some tiny marshmallows and whipped cream to her cup.

So perhaps all that had happened—the blizzard, wrecking his truck—hadn't been good only for her, but for Shane, too.

Even if he wasn't a forever kind of guy.

* * *

Shane wrapped both palms around a paper cup of hot chocolate as he stood on the dock looking out over the ice-skaters on the lake. Sure, he liked to give the whole town a hard time about their hot chocolate consumption, but at the moment, he was damn glad to have it, both to warm his hands and the rest of him, too, as he drank it.

Despite the cold, though, it was a nice day. The sun was shining, and the people here were nice. He supposed Destiny—complete with its sense of community—had grown on him a little.

"You plan on staying in town?"

The question had come from Raybourne Fleet, a local cop he'd been chatting with after also meeting the guy's son, who was home from college between semesters.

Shane shook his head. "No—headed to Florida." Then he answered the next question before it was asked. "Have a job waiting for me—need to get there by Christmas."

"Why now, that's a dang cryin' shame."

He turned to see that Edna had approached. She wore a powder blue parka with matching fluffy earmuffs. "I knew you'd be leavin', but didn't know it'd be before the holiday. Was expectin' you'd be at the big Christmas dinner at my house. I bake a big ole turkey and Willie whips up some mean mashed potatoes."

Hmm, Shane couldn't deny it sounded nice. And he almost suffered a small pang of regret that he couldn't be there. It sounded . . . easy. Like an easy place to be. And, well, if he was completely honest with himself, like a better kind of Christmas than he'd anticipated the first year without his dad. And better than he'd have in Miami.

But hadn't he decided he didn't really *want* or *need* Christmas? So he tried to make light of it. "Will there be gingerbread?" he asked Edna.

"Of course."

Having grown fond of the older woman, he gave her a teasing grin. "You could almost tempt me with that, Edna."

"In my experience," she said, "I've found that almost is a lot like maybe—it usually turns out to mean no." Then she dropped her gaze to his hands. "But what else should I expect from a dang fool boy who don't even have the sense to wear gloves?"

He just laughed and told her, "I'm fine."

"Lucky your fingers ain't froze off."

Edna was maybe the one person on the planet he didn't mind giving him a hard time. Well, okay, her and little miss Candy Cane. And it was damn shocking, actually, that he'd put up with that from *anybody*. So it struck him odd that he'd found two such people in the same little town.

Must be losing my edge. Maybe this town was making him soft. So it was probably good his time here was almost over. Even if he wasn't as sure about the job with Donnie V. as he used to be. And even if . . . maybe, just maybe, he might miss a few things about this place when he was gone.

He looked up to see one of those things walking down the snowy path to the dock. And he met Candy's bright gaze and gave her a smile without even thinking about it. Damn girl seemed to have that effect on him lately—making him smile for no good reason whatsoever.

Then again, maybe there *were* reasons. Hot sex was a

reason. Her pretty face was a reason. Seeing how happy it made her to have thrown this party was a decent reason, too. He was glad he'd been part of putting it together and making her proud.

She hadn't told him she was proud, but he could tell. And she deserved to be. Everybody was having a great time and Santa hadn't even arrived yet.

Upon reaching them, she smiled at Edna as she curled one mittened hand around his wrist. "Mind if I steal him away for a minute?"

"Not at all," Edna said. "I come down here to sit on one o' these here benches and watch some folks skate, so that's what I aim to do." The wooden benches were among things Shane had helped deliver from the church basement.

"You're not skating?" Shane teased her.

"On these knees?" She glanced down. "Nope, I'll leave that craziness to you younger folk. But if I was your age, I'd be skatin' circles around ya—figure eights to be exact." She winked.

"I don't doubt it. Probably still could now," he added on a laugh.

Edna laughed, too. "I'm spry, boy, but not *that* spry."

"Wouldn't take much," he assured her.

Her eyebrows lifted. "Why's that?"

"I've never done it before."

"Never ice-skated?" The older woman gave a succinct nod in Candy's direction. "You best fix that, Candice. This fella is headed south soon—can't let him leave the last taste o' winter he might ever have without gettin' him out on that ice."

At this, though, he drew back slightly as he set down

his near-empty cup. "O-ho-ho no—I don't think so," he said, holding his hands up in defense.

"Scaredy-cat," Edna accused dryly, then ended the conversation by heading toward the benches where a few people sat putting on skates.

Shane just gave his head a good-natured shake as he turned back to Candy, remembering she'd wanted to steal him away. "Whatcha need, Candy Cane?"

In reply, she grabbed his hand and pulled him to the far side of the dock, where they had more privacy, no one else around. Then she flashed a smile that warmed him from the inside out—even more than the hot chocolate had. "I just wanted to give you something." She held up a small package—wrapped in Santa paper with a white ribbon tied around it.

It threw him, made his gut clench slightly. Damn, he hadn't seen this coming. "Honey, I'm sorry," he said. "I didn't get you anything. I didn't know you were . . ." He trailed off then, feeling awkward.

But she sounded completely relaxed when she replied, "I don't care about that, Shane. It's a gift from the heart. Nothing big, promise. Just something I want you to have."

And as Shane took the package from her, he somehow felt all her sweetness wrapped up inside it along with whatever else was there. Confusing emotions warred within him, at once both liking and *not* liking that she'd done this.

He tore the paper off, and when he saw what was inside realized he should have known. Of course. A pair of men's winter gloves. Dark red with a surprisingly masculine-looking white snowflake design on top.

She was right—a small gift. And simple and obvious as hell. And yet it touched him more than he could easily understand.

He hadn't been given many gifts in his life—even less since reaching adulthood.

But he chose not to let it show. Not much anyway.

He gave her a smile. "Gloves."

She smiled back. "I know you won't get much use out of them once you leave, but they should make the next few days easier anyway."

"They will," he agreed, putting them on to find they fit perfectly. He couldn't deny it felt good to suddenly no longer have his hands exposed to the cold. "Thank you."

Then he lifted his newly gloved hands to her face, cupping her cheeks, and gave her a firm yet gentle kiss on the lips. Not caring if anyone saw. And she didn't seem to care, either. She simply kept her eyes on his afterward and he soaked up the warmth of that connection. A different kind of warmth than gloves or hot chocolate could provide. And he knew he'd miss it when it was gone.

"The only problem is that now you won't need me to keep your hands warm," she teased.

"Don't worry, Candy," he said. "You can keep other parts of me warm." He winked, and she laughed.

Then she whispered up to him, "That will definitely be my pleasure."

He raised his eyebrows suggestively. "You're making me want to blow off this party and head straight to your house."

But another trill of her soft laughter filled the air as she said, "No way, mister. I'm the hostess of this soiree and I'll be here 'til the last person is done skating or caroling. Now come on—let's teach you how to ice-skate."

At this, he cocked his head. "Uh, no thanks. Not my thing, honey."

Yet she just shrugged. "Neither was Christmas. Neither were Christmas trees. But look at you now. Things change, and it's time for this to change, too."

"I don't have any skates," he told her triumphantly, knowing that would solve the problem.

Which was when Logan Whitaker stepped up, two worn brown leather ice skates dangling from his fingertips. "Here, buddy, borrow mine. I'm all done and ready to head inside and warm up."

Shit. "We're probably not the same size," Shane told him. "I'm a ten and a half."

A smile spread across Logan's face. "Me too."

"It's a Christmas miracle," Candy announced.

"They're all around," Logan's wife, Amy, said from behind him then.

Shane still didn't make a move to accept the offered skates—but he didn't have to, because Candy reached out and took them anyway, thanking Logan for the loan. And Shane realized that he could put up a fight about this and look like a jerk to a woman—and a whole town—who'd been pretty damn good to him. Or he could just roll with it. The way he'd ended up rolling with everything else since he'd gotten here. And which, much as he hated to admit it, even to himself, had turned out . . . pretty okay. Pretty *damn* okay.

Ten minutes later, he and Candy were all laced into the skates, and everything was fine—until they stood up, both teetering on thin blades that seemed impossible to balance upon. He glanced over at her, a little confused. "Um, why don't you look any better at this than I do?"

"I was never exactly very good at it," she said with a shrug. "And it's been a while."

He scrunched his nose lightly, a little perplexed. "Then why are we doing this?"

"Because it's fun," she informed him, clearly trying to sound convincing.

As they moved clumsily from the dock down onto the ice, hanging on to each other for dear life, he grumbled under his breath, "I can think of a lot of better ways to have fun with you." And as they started out onto the frozen lake with the other skaters, Shane felt like a baby calf on brand new, wobbly legs. Candy truly wasn't any more skilled at this than he was and he thought they must look ridiculous, since it was like the blind leading the blind.

And he'd just begun to wonder, again, why on earth they were doing it—when he *understood* why. When he realized they were laughing together. When he realized they were holding hands—or grabbing on to each other's coats, arms, waists, to try to keep from falling. When he realized that they hadn't ever actually fallen, though—and were in fact still on their teetering feet.

And soon enough, they were side by side, holding hands and beginning to glide slightly forward, pushing one skate gingerly in front of the other, and Shane said, "Hey, we're kind of doing it. We're skating."

"See?" she said, giggling. "I told you—it's fun!"

And that was when he heard the faint jingle of sleigh bells somewhere in the distance, growing louder, closer—and they both looked up to see a magical sight: Santa Claus had just rounded the bend on Blue Valley Road in a horse-drawn sleigh.

"Isn't It wonderful? Merry Christmas!"

George Bailey, *It's a Wonderful Life*

Eighteen

Gasps filled the wintry air, but no one said a word as Grampy Hoskins, in full Santa regalia, drew nearer. The bells on the horse and sleigh continued jingle-jangling as Grampy called out a hearty, "Ho-ho-ho! Merry Christmas! Merry Christmas!"

As Shane had told Candy, he'd never been a big fan of this holiday, and he could scarcely remember a time when he believed in something as simple and pure as a red-suited old man who delivered toys and joy to children on Christmas Eve for no good reason. But for a few brief seconds, some childlike part of him almost had faith in that kind of magic, somehow feeling it all around them in the crisp, cold breeze.

Across the road, adults and children alike came out from the house and the garden to stare in awe at the approaching sleigh.

"It's Santa! He's here! He's here!" a little boy could be heard saying from the yard.

He and Candy had come to a silent stop on the ice, and now he looked down to see the woman at his side beaming up at him. "You did this," she said softly.

"What?" he asked. *"Me?"*

She nodded. "Yes, of course *you*. It was all your idea for Santa to arrive in the sleigh."

Oh. Yeah. He'd almost forgotten that somehow.

"And it's amazing."

And with that, she looped her arms around his neck and pulled him down into a long, hot kiss. Maybe the best kiss of his life. Even while wobbling on a pair of thin metal blades on an ice-covered lake. Because her mouth was warm. Her whole body was hot. And because he'd never been kissed for thinking of something amazing before.

To his utter surprise, Shane was almost sorry the ice-skating had to end—but there was business to be done, as in orchestrating the whole visit from Santa. There were little kids to line up, and small gifts to hand out from a big red drawstring sack on the sleigh pre-packed with them. So they hurried to get their shoes back on and reached the road in time to watch Grampy make a grand entrance with more ho-ho-ho-ing and, "Heard there was some little children gathered here today a wantin' to meet me and tell me what they want in their stockin's—am I in the right place?"

As he disembarked from the sleigh carrying the red bag, Shane and Candy joined him, escorting him toward the house as he told the kids gathering around, "Santa needs to head inside for just a minute, but I'll be out in the garden real soon."

The plan was for Shane to stick with Grampy while he rested inside briefly, making sure his beard and the rest of his costume was still in place before he started officially greeting a long line of children. Candy would get the kids lined up and act as a sort of non-costumed elf for the duration.

Grampy seemed in fine spirits—and when he passed Edna near the cookie table, Shane noticed they exchanged smiles.

"Good to see ya, Santa," she told him with a wink.

"Have you been good this year, Edna?" he asked in his deeper-than-usual Santa voice.

She just laughed. "'Bout as good as any year, I reckon."

"Well, that might put you on my naughty list, young lady," he said, moving on through the house—and Shane tossed him a look. What had gotten into the old guy? Something good maybe, seemed like.

As they stepped into a bedroom and closed the door, Shane gave Grampy the requisite cup of hot chocolate and asked how his ride over had been.

"Dang fun, that's how. Had to stick to the sides of the road and choose my path careful-like since most of the snow's been cleared off 'em now—but felt like the real man in red ever' time I passed by a car and got a wave or a honk. Doggone magical is what it was."

Magical. That word kept coming up the last little

while. And Shane had no idea why, but that was the moment it hit him—there was something he'd never asked Grampy before. And why the hell hadn't it occurred to him until this moment?

Maybe because you weren't meant to think of it until now. Maybe it'll be a real *Christmas miracle, the kind people around here could almost make a guy believe in*. "Hey Grampy," he said. "You ever know a man named Gary Dalton?"

The timing of it made Shane almost sure Grampy would say yes, and that the connection would somehow reveal the reason Shane's dad had sent him here.

So it was a bit of a blow when the old man shook his head and said, "Nope. Why ya ask?"

But just as quickly as the anticipation had built in him, he let it go. It didn't matter. His father hadn't sent him here for any reason whatsoever—it had all been a mistake. Maybe a mistake that had . . . well, not been all bad, by a long shot, and a mistake that had led him on a path he never would have traveled otherwise. But still, it had been a mistake.

So now he just shook his head. "Well, never thought to mention it before, but I'm not here entirely by chance." Then he explained to Grampy what had brought him to Destiny, and the various dead ends he'd found after arriving.

"That, son," Grampy said when he was done, "is a perplexment."

Shane just shrugged. "Figured it was worth a shot to ask."

And then, still behind his Santa beard, Grampy tilted his head and said, "Well, there's worse places in the world to be stuck. But seems to me you probably know that by now."

Shane gave a short nod. "I do."

"Son, I know you're dead-set on Miami and all—but way I see it is, no matter how ya slice it, ya musta been meant to come here. I'm *glad* your dad sent ya this way. Havin' ya around has made my life . . . well, a little better than it was before ya showed up—that's all."

Shane wasn't sure what to say to that. Just like the gloves from Candy, it touched him, but he just wasn't good at letting that show, at knowing how to. Finally he said, "Well, feeling's mutual, Grampy." Even if it came out sounding a little stiff. "You've been good to me. The whole town has. And I won't forget that." But then he moved straight on to, "Anything else you need before you do the Santa gig in the garden?"

"Don't believe so," Grampy replied.

"Well then, break a leg," Shane said. "Or whatever fake Santas do." Then he patted Grampy on the red-clad shoulder and left the room.

He walked out onto Miss Ellie's recessed side porch, taking in the big line of kids now amassed in the garden. Candy and a couple of the other ladies, Jenny Brody and Amy Whitaker, were trying to keep them entertained with cookies and other treats—and it made him smile to himself when he saw that his Candy Cane was handing out candy canes.

Walking down into the winter wonderland, draped in snow and twinkling lights, he sidestepped the line of kids, trying to stay out of the way. And when he found himself next to the tree hung with ornaments from the partygoers, he started taking in the decorations—

until his eye was drawn to one ornament in particular: a reindeer made from clothespins glued together, then decorated with little pieces of felt and black bead eyes.

Strange. Something about it took him back in time, back to a memory he couldn't quite grasp. Was it another vague recollection from a grandparent's house? School? Somewhere else? He reached out, gently cupping it in his palm, holding it slightly away from the branches to see it better.

That was when Candy approached, smiling, then teasing him. "See what a Christmas guy you are now? Even appreciating homemade ornaments."

He drew his hand down, letting the reindeer hang suspended again. "That one seems familiar to me." But he still had no idea why. "I must have seen one like it somewhere or something." It was clever, with the clothespins. So maybe that made it memorable from wherever he'd seen a similar one.

"It belongs to Anita, the lady getting married on Christmas Eve. She let Jenny's little boy bring it today. And she and Walter are supposed to be here somewhere—so I'll have to introduce you."

He nodded—to be nice—but was only vaguely interested. He liked the people here and all, but he'd already met plenty of new ones today. And he was happy to have pitched in on the work at the church, and glad it would be done in time for this big wedding—but it didn't particularly matter to him whether he met the bride and groom.

"Is Grampy ready to make his big entrance?" she asked.

"As far as I know," Shane said. "Surprised he isn't out here yet."

And just then, Edna peeked around the corner of the porch. "Shane," she called. "Willie says he needs your help with somethin'."

Grampy stood before the mirror in Miss Ellie's frilly bedroom holding a broken black Santa belt in his hand. He'd gone to tighten it a little and the dang thing had just snapped in two like an old rubberband. But then, it was an old belt. Made of cheap plastic. So he reckoned it was bound to happen sooner or later—he'd been wearing this same costume a lotta years now.

Hopefully Shane could figure a way to hold it together for the rest of the day. And he guessed he could have gotten anybody to come to his aid, but most folks were partying it up with their families, and Shane never minded helping when he was asked. Grampy liked that about him.

'Course, he could have asked Edna, too. But somehow he felt antsy about that right now. He'd been thinking a lot about her lately, about what Shane had suggested. And the truth—the truth he was just finally starting to admit to himself—was that maybe he did have them kinda feelings for her. But now he didn't know what the heck he wanted to do about it. They'd been friends for so long, after all. And he didn't want to lose that. It was hard when big things like that changed. And maybe not worth the risk.

So when he'd opened the bedroom door and peeked out and seen Edna standing there talking to a few other folks, he'd followed his gut and asked her to go fetch Shane.

Just then, Shane entered the bedroom. "What's up?" he asked, dark brows knit.

"This," Grampy said, holding up the broken belt.

Shane scrunched up his mouth, silently taking in the problem.

"Can't very well be a proper Santa without the belt."

Shane shifted his weight from one foot to the other. "Actually, you probably could. They're little kids. They're not gonna notice."

But Grampy was having none of that. "Nope, nope, nope. Santa wears a big black belt, and without it, somethin's just missin'. Folks are takin' pictures for their mantels and all, and the costume's gotta be right."

Now Shane pursed his lips and Grampy couldn't tell if he was annoyed or trying to think of a solution—or both. Finally he said, "Gimme a sec." Then disappeared right back out the door, closing it behind him.

A few minutes later, he came back in, a roll of silver duct tape in one fist, a black Magic Marker in the other.

And Grampy smiled. "I had me a feelin' you'd come up with somethin'."

"One thing my dad taught me—duct tape fixes anything."

Grampy watched as Shane took the broken belt from him, laid the two pieces out on the bed, and began neatly duct taping them together.

"Heard you was seen kissin' sweet little Candice down by the lake," Grampy ventured. Edna had dropped that nugget of gossip in the short time it had taken him to ask her to find Shane.

"Guilty as charged," Shane said without looking up from his task.

"So is it just kissin'? Or more than kissin'?"

At this Shane stopped and gave him a pointed look.

"Last I heard, a guy's not supposed to more-than-kiss and tell."

That made Grampy smile bigger. Seemed to him that Candice could use a little romance and excitement in her life. And it was hard not to feel good when two folks found that sort of thing together.

"Well, glad to hear all that makin' eyes at each other finally led someplace better than just eyes." He finished with a laugh.

Now Shane had taken the freshly taped belt up in one hand and begun coloring the tape black with the thick marker. "Since you've been so hot on getting us together, you'll be happy to know the kissing started when we took that sleigh ride at your place."

"S'that right?" Grampy asked, letting his chest puff out with a bit of pride.

Shane continued converting the duct tape from silver to black. "Turns out," he said, eyes focused on the belt, "a sleigh ride is a good place for getting cold, and then wanting to get warm, and then kissing." Then he looked up at Grampy. "You given any thought to my suggestion about getting with Edna?"

The way Shane put it—"getting with"—would have made Grampy laugh . . . if it didn't make him so nervous. And the hardest part was that he couldn't remember a time in a great many years when he'd *been* nervous. He'd thought he was long past anything that could bring that kind of emotion rising up. But sometimes life had a way of surprising you.

"Reckon I have, son. And the truth is," he managed to say around a thickness that had grown in his throat, "maybe I . . . do have them kinda feelin's for her. Think they've just been too mixed in with everything else for me to really recognize 'em until now. But thing is, after so long . . ." He stopped, shook his head beneath the Santa hat. "I plumb don't know how to go about it."

Like before, Shane stayed quiet a minute, screwing up his mouth a little, but also stopping his work on the belt to peer out the light blue sheers covering the nearest window. So Grampy peeked out on the front yard, too. The view was filled with snow, and people, and a couple of snowmen, and a whole frozen lake in the distance. But he had a feeling Shane was looking at the red sleigh, still hitched to Charley, sitting near the mailbox.

After a minute, he drew his gaze back in and planted it on Grampy. "Maybe you get cold together," he suggested, "and let it lead to getting warm."

Grampy took that in. The vision of him and Edna out in the sleigh, a brisk wind on their faces, far away from anyone else—except each other. The cold, a blanket crossing both their laps, the closeness it could easily, naturally bring.

It was a dang good idea.

So dang good that it made him feel bold, almost brave.

So dang good that . . . he wanted to make it happen right now, right this minute.

Because when you got right down to it, all we really had was this moment in life. And this brand new desire came with the burning knowledge that he'd waited too long already—he'd let so dang much time pass them by. Shane was right about that. And if he waited—if he waited even one more day, one more hour, all the courage coming over him right now might dwindle away.

And he didn't want that to happen. He wanted to live. He wanted to make the most of his life. He didn't want to be an old man just sitting around waiting to die when there was so much more living to do.

"You're right," Grampy said decisively. "I'm doin' it. We ain't a gettin' no younger, and Lordy Lord, it's hittin' me how dang much time I've wasted already." Then he unzipped his red, fur-trimmed Santa jacket, took it off, and shoved it at Shane.

"What are you doing?" Shane asked, Santa coat in one hand, finished belt in the other.

"I'm takin' Edna on a sleigh ride, that's what."

Shane blinked. "Now?"

"Yep, now." Grampy had never felt any compulsion more strongly in his life.

"But, um, what about this whole Santa gig?" Shane looked a little dumbstruck. "What about all the kids waiting outside?"

Grampy had just dropped his Santa pants, revealing overalls underneath, yet this halted him in place. Made him realize he was being irresponsible. Making rash decisions.

But he'd never done that before, not ever—and he didn't want to stop now that he'd started. Because maybe just every once in a while, rash was good. Rash was decisive. Rash got the job done. "This sleigh ride can't wait, son," he told Shane. "I might lose my nerve. Needs to happen now."

Shane let out a sigh. "Well, I'm glad you suddenly get the point here, Grampy, but again . . . kids? Santa?"

Grampy thought the dilemma over for a minute—and the perfect, easy solution hit him. "You do it."

"What?"

"You do it," he said again.

"Me?"

"Yep." This seemed way simpler than Shane was making it.

"Uh, I'm not the right guy for that," his young friend claimed. "I mean . . . don't take this the wrong way, but . . . you're a little bigger in the belly region than me."

At this, Grampy just swiped a dismissive hand down through the air. "Why, I'm sure Miss Ellie has a throw pillow you can shove up under the coat. Tighten up the belt you just fixed and that oughta hold it in place."

"I never should have fixed the damn belt," Shane muttered. "And trust me—no one's gonna believe I'm freaking Santa Claus."

" 'Course you shoulda." Grampy dropped his red hat on the bed. "And it's the outfit and attitude that makes a fella Santa—not whether he's fat or skinny."

"Well, I have a *bad* attitude," he said—yet that only made Grampy laugh.

"Adam Becker filled in for me a few years back and nobody was the wiser." He finished with a brisk nod.

"Yeah, well, Adam Becker is a dad. I'm not. And I'm bad with kids."

Grampy refused to let Shane's naysaying wear him down, though. "No time like the present to change that," he insisted. And with that, he removed the last piece of the costume over his head—the fluffy white beard. He laid it over Shane's forearm, suffering only a tiny hint of guilt—and feeling more exuberant about life than he could remember in a long time. Edna and the sleigh awaited him.

He slapped Shane on the back, saying, "Wish me luck, son!" and headed out the door—to his future.

Shane just stood there, staring at the pieces of Santa costume that littered the bedroom. It looked like Santa Claus had exploded.

Just then, the door reopened—and he lifted his gaze, hoping to see Grampy had come to his senses. But instead it was only Candy.

"What the hell happened in here?" she asked, taking in the strewn costume. "And where's Grampy? The natives are getting restless out there."

"He left," Shane said dejectedly.

Her expression went grave. "*Left*? What do you mean *left*?"

"He's gone to try to romance Edna."

"Romance Edna?" Candy leaned slightly forward now. "Since when does Grampy romance Edna? And he had to do this *now*?"

"Maybe since I suggested it," Shane admitted. Then he met her look with his own. "But trust me, the now part was all *his* idea."

Candy sighed, plopping down on a frilly quilted bed-spread. "Well, what on earth are we going to do? Especially after that grand entrance he made. The kids are expecting Santa Claus."

"The old man had the crazy idea *I* could do it," Shane told her, shaking his head. "He totally didn't get how insane that is."

At this, however, Candy gazed up at him, tilting her head first one way, then the other.

And he felt the sudden need to go on. "I mean, Santa's old and white-haired. I'm not. Santa's a jolly old soul. I'm not. Santa has a belly like a bowl full of jelly. I don't. You're seeing my point here, right?"

When she stayed quiet, though, he knew he was in trouble. Especially when she scrunched up her cute little nose and said, "Really, it kind of makes sense."

Shane glared at her. "Makes sense? In what crazy-ass world does it make sense?"

"Well, *someone* has to do it. And none of the kids know you—any of the other men in town they might recognize."

Shane thought about other arguments he could make. That apparently they hadn't recognized Adam Becker a few years ago, so really, anyone could do it. That he had no fucking idea how to talk to kids. That he would look ridiculous and never be able to pull this off. But he could already feel it was a lost cause.

So instead he just said, "This is a nightmare." Then pointed a finger at her. "And if anybody was trying to get me to stay, this isn't the way."

And for some reason, it surprised him when she merely shrugged and said, "You're not staying anyway, remember? You're just passing through on your way to Miami. Now come on—let's get you in this suit and out in that gazebo before the little kids start rioting."

"It's a miracle!"

Mary Bailey, *It's a Wonderful Life*

Nineteen

$\mathcal{S}$hane felt like a stranger in a strange land—not to mention a colossal idiot—as he meandered out into the snow-covered garden. How the hell had this happened?

There were a lot of things about Destiny he'd admittedly come to like: Candy, Grampy, Edna, the guys he'd gotten to know through repairing the church, the whole sense of community—and despite himself, he even kind of liked how into Christmas they were. But how had getting stranded here in a blizzard led to this surreal moment: him in a baggy Santa suit, a pillow strapped to his stomach, and an itchy fake beard on his face, saying a pretty weak-sounding, "Ho-ho-ho," as he made his way to the gazebo?

But then the strangest damn thing happened. All the little kids in the garden, all wrapped up in their little coats and hats, looked up at him—at his entry—like he was the coolest thing they'd ever seen. Okay, maybe a few of them—on closer inspection—appeared slightly terrified. But mostly, they were in awe. And he swallowed nervously, realizing what this meant. *Oh shit, I have to really do this. I have to do a good job. I have to make them believe and not ruin their Christmas.* What the hell had Grampy been thinking, handing off such an important task to him?

Yet then he understood. *He thinks I'm a better guy than I really am. I've maybe . . .* seemed *like a better guy than I really am. Because something about this place, these people, have* made *me a better guy than I really am.* But maybe something in that was . . . real, or at least . . . changing. Because he was pretty sure a month ago he wouldn't have given a shit about letting down a bunch of little kids, especially in a situation he'd been dragged into kicking and screaming—and now, for some reason, he did.

And when he made eye contact with Candy, standing near the big Santa chair in the gazebo, he knew it was because of her. He didn't want to let her down. He didn't want her to think he was a bad guy anymore. Whether or not it was really true.

"Come on over and take a seat here, Santa," Candy said in a loud voice, clearly designed more for the kids to hear than for him. "Santa is super excited to be here today—aren't you, Santa?"

He silently thanked her for feeding him a line, even a simple one—because he *so* didn't know how to do this. But as he entered the gazebo and sat down on the big red Santa throne, he tried to project his voice and speak deeper as he said to the children waiting in line, "Yes, yes, Candy—I sure am!"

He saw Rachel Farris, standing with her husband and little girl, look to Tessa Romo next to her and silently mouth, *Candy*? Because, crap, no one here called her that but him. But he didn't care—he kept going. "I can't wait to meet all these little . . . whippersnappers." That seemed like what Grampy would say. "And hear what they want me to bring them on Christmas Eve."

"I wonder if they've all been good little girls and boys," Candy said loudly, shifting her smile from him out into the crowd,

"I sure hope so!" he said. Then looked out at the sea of kids to ask, "Have you all been good this year?"

A chorus of yeses sang out, but he actually heard one little boy say, "No," another say, "Not really," and a third announce sadly, "I tried, but I probably wasn't very good." It made him laugh softly behind the fake white beard, and decide that when those particular kids reached him, he'd have to say something to boost their confidence and let them know it was okay and that they really probably weren't so bad after all.

"Well, we'd better get things started here," he said, dropping his gaze to the first child in line, a little girl of six or seven, wearing a hot pink parka and furry snow boots. "Come on up and sit on Santa's lap, little girl."

She did so, situating herself on his knee like an old pro at it—and they both looked at her mother as she snapped a few pictures.

Then he said, "Tell me what you'd like for Christmas." And so it began . . .

* * *

Candice watched as Shane played each child like a violin. He'd had a shaky start, but the transformation into an effective Santa had happened quickly, leaving her completely amazed. She saw a side of Shane she'd never have imagined as he welcomed each child up into the gazebo—and as it continued, she suspected maybe it was a side he'd never even seen himself.

He asked each kid if they'd been good this year, and when little tow-headed Caleb Johnson said he kept getting in trouble at school, Shane actually fell into counseling him a little. "Santa knows what that's like, Caleb, and the important thing is that you just try your best. If you're trying your best, then you're on Santa's nice list."

"Really?" Caleb asked, wide-eyed.

"Really," Santa Shane assured him.

"So you'll still bring me a baseball bat and mitt?"

A quick glance from Shane toward Caleb's mom earned a subtle nod that allowed him to say, "Why, of course I'll bring you a bat and mitt. Just be careful not to play ball too close to any houses."

"I will—I promise!" Caleb answered excitedly.

By the time he left, Candice could tell Caleb's mother was pleased, as were many other parents. Most of them didn't know who the heck this Santa was—since it was pretty easy to see it wasn't Grampy—but no one really cared so long as their kid left Santa's lap happy.

After a while, Tessa took over elf duties, allowing Candice to go grab a cup of hot chocolate and stand near one the outdoor space heaters set up in the garden.

"Is that your new boyfriend up there?" Sue Ann stepped up to ask as Candice situated herself next to a few snow-covered holly bushes to watch the continuing Santa show from a distance.

She was glad the cold air probably already had her cheeks pink as she replied, "Well, boyfriend might be a strong term, given that he's leaving soon—but . . . yeah."

Sue Ann smiled. "He's doing a great job."

"I know," Candice agreed. "Especially without having any warning. Grampy just dropped his costume at Shane's feet and asked him to fill in—no notice."

Sue Ann lifted a cup of hot chocolate to her lips, took a sip, then gestured vaguely toward the road. "Yeah, I saw him and Edna take off in the sleigh a little while ago. What's *that* about?"

Candice had no idea if this was supposed to be a secret—but she hadn't been asked not to say anything, so she assumed it was okay to share. "Well," she said, "seems like there might be romance in the winter air for more than just me and Shane."

Sue Ann's eyes bolted open wide. "Grampy and Edna?"

"That seems to be the hope. On Grampy's side anyway."

"Wow. That never even occurred to me. But . . ." She tilted her head. "Makes sense in a way."

Candice hadn't really had a chance to think about it yet, but she couldn't refute Sue Ann's words. "I suppose it does. But I guess the big question is—will Edna feel the same way?"

Sue Ann gave her head a thoughtful tilt. "It would probably be hard at that age. To change things like that. To take those kinds of emotional risks. I mean, relationships are complicated."

"I think it can be hard at *any* age," Candice said. "For some people anyway." She knew some women at least appeared to drift breezily in and out of relationships with total ease—but for her, it had always been harder. And part of that had been Bobby's fault, but part of it was simply the way she was put together. When she connected with someone, it was a strong bond, not easily severed.

And even without having said any of that, Sue Ann seemed to read her thoughts loud and clear. "So this thing with Shane—are you gonna be okay when he leaves?"

She didn't know Sue Ann as well as she knew some of the girls, but she'd always liked her matter-of-fact way and independent spirit. So she decided to be her usual honest self and said, "Probably not. But I went into it with my eyes wide open and won't have any regrets."

Sue Ann let those words settle in the cold air around them for a moment before saying, "Well, maybe some-one else will come along. Maybe Shane is just . . . getting you warmed up for the next big thing."

Candice smiled. It was a nice idea. A fun idea, an idea that made this sound easy, like the simple little fling all her girlfriends had suggested. But inside she knew . . . this *was* the big thing, and Shane had her more than a little warmed up.

What she felt for him was the real deal. She knew this was fast, but she also knew sometimes things like this just happened that way, like a lightning bolt—which could apparently strike even in winter.

And her attachment to him had only grown with each passing minute this afternoon. Laughing with him on the ice, the way he'd kissed her in thanks for the gloves, and now watching him play Santa Claus for every little kid in Destiny.

Time and experience had shown her that a good man was hard to find. And no matter what Shane thought, she knew in her heart that he *was* a good man, and she'd found him. And the only problem at all was knowing he was leaving.

She'd accepted that all along. Even if she'd suggested a time or two that he stay, she'd known his departure was part of the package.

And then today as he'd unwillingly put on the Santa suit, he'd said something about staying, something that had almost sounded like he was thinking about it.

But don't even go there. Start thinking he might and it'll only hurt worse when he doesn't. He was Miami-bound for a job she suspected was beneath him and there was nothing she could do about it.

Just then, she looked up to see a welcome sight— Anita Garey and Walter Tolliver entered the garden gate only steps away. Both women instantly went to greet them and Candice said, "It's so good to see you two. Welcome to the party!"

They exchanged pleasantries, Anita saying what a nice job Candice had done with it, and Candice and Sue Ann commenting how wonderful it was that the wedding could take place as scheduled. Anita smiled and talked about her relief, and what a happy day it would be for her to finally make Walter her husband.

And yet, to her surprise, Candice thought Anita didn't seem as happy as she wanted them to think.

Anita rose on her tiptoes to check out the line of kids

still waiting to see Santa. "Looks like we're in time to watch Dustin sit on the big guy's lap," she told Walter, a heavyset, gray-mustached man. But then she squinted, adding, "Though that guy doesn't look so big."

"An understudy," Candice explained.

Then Sue Ann told them Grampy had had to step out unexpectedly and someone else had filled in.

Anita took Walter's gloved hand in hers and said, "Let's go up and see our little man."

When they were gone, Candice said to Sue Ann, "Is it just me, or . . . ?"

And Sue Ann shook her head. "No, it's not just you."

"I thought she'd be so happy."

In response, Sue Ann pursed her lips. Then confided, "Well, this is kind of a secret, but . . . Jenny told me that even as relieved as Anita is about the wedding that she's also bummed out because . . . apparently she has a son she hasn't seen in over twenty years or something."

Candice nodded. "Oh—yeah, I heard about that from Jenny once, too."

"Jenny said that just has her a little down, that it's been on her mind, along with everything else, as the wedding got closer."

"Well, at least she has Dustin now," Candice said. "Not the same, I know—but you can tell how much he means to her, that maybe he fills that void a little."

They both looked toward the gazebo then to see Jenny walking little Dustin up to sit on Shane's lap.

"Well, who's this handsome little whippersnapper?" she heard Shane ask.

Sue Ann looked at her. "Did he just say whippersnapper?"

"I think he's channeling Grampy," Candice said.

* * *

Grampy gently snapped the reins against Charley's back as the sleigh traversed a meadow near Sugar Creek. Edna's orchard lay in the distance, the apple trees still covered with a blanket of snow, some of which had melted and refrozen over time, leaving it to glisten in the sun. Though the weather seemed to be changing—clouds rolling in. Just a few at first, but soon they turned the blue sky to a pale wintry white.

"Now this is fun, Willie," Edna said, wearing a smile that lit him up inside. "Cold, but fun."

Indeed, now that the sun had gone behind the veil of clouds, the breeze was brisker and more biting. But Grampy took advantage of the situation. "Grab that blanket there on the seat beside ya and put it over our laps."

And as Edna spread the blanket over them, he was so bold as to scoot a little closer, wondering if she noticed.

She did. "You tryin' to snuggle up with me or somethin', old man?"

He knew Edna well, but he couldn't read her tone just now. And this was probably a real good time to be nervous. But he held that at bay. He hadn't run out on the party just to blow things by chickening out here. "Maybe I am," he told her, keeping his eyes on the snowy landscape ahead of them.

He felt her cast an uncertain look his way and couldn't read that, either.

So finally he said, "That okay with you?"

She took her sweet time answering. And despite the cold, Grampy feared he'd break out in a sweat any second now.

Until she finally said, "Reckon it's all right."

And relief barreled through him like a freight train.

But it still seemed like . . . time to say more. Time to

really go for this. The way he'd intended to when he'd grabbed Edna and insisted on this unplanned sleigh ride. She'd been understandably surprised at first, and he'd told her he was feeling spontaneous and getting too old not to act on it. She'd seemed to embrace that, happy to come along for the ride. And now here they were. And it was the moment of truth.

So he pulled back on the reins, giving a low, "Whoa," and brought both horse and sleigh to a standstill right in the middle of the snow-covered orchard. "Thing is, Edna, I'm sweet on you."

Lord, he hadn't meant to just blurt it out like that— but it was out there now, and there was nothing left to do but wait and see how she took it.

She looked at him, looked right into his eyes, clearly surprised. "Well, when did *this* start?"

He swallowed nervously. Felt the cold seeping into his bones even as the back of his neck began to perspire beneath the winter scarf he wore. "Just recently," he told her. "And if you don't feel the same way—why, we can just forget I ever opened that door. We can be the way we've always been. You're my dearest friend in the world and I'd never want to damage that.

"But it seemed to me the sensible thing to do was tell ya. In case ya might feel the same way. Because . . . well, me and you, we ain't spring chickens, and I just got to thinkin' that life's too short to let opportunities pass by.

"But again, if the idea don't appeal, if it's too late for old dogs to learn new tricks, if ya just want to keep things the way they are, you just say the word."

"That's the real reason behind this here spontaneous sleigh ride," she acknowledged.

He nodded. "Yes ma'am. Though the idea *was* spontaneous."

The woman he'd known longer than anyone in his life still looked uncertain, and uncharacteristically shy. He hadn't known Edna had a shy bone in her body, but maybe he'd just uncovered a part of her he'd never encountered before.

And he waited anxiously, every chilled nerve ending inside him standing at attention, until she said, cautiously, "Iffen a couple o' old dogs was to learn such a new trick, how do you propose they'd go about startin'?"

And his heart warmed. And, almost to his surprise, a few other parts of him, too.

"Well, I'm told that if you're cold, it can be nice to . . . warm each other up. And I'm cold."

"Me too," she said. And then she scooted just a little closer to him than she already was.

She wore gloves, but he reached for one of her hands with his own gloved hand and held it. And felt her holding his hand back. The sweet sensation was different than anything he could have expected or predicted. Safe. And indeed warm. It spread a low, saturating, new sort of warmth all through his body.

They sat silently that way, both of them just soaking up the newness of it, getting used to it, until finally he said, "This is nice."

And then she gave him the same smile he'd seen on so many occasions over the years—only this time it was different. It held so much more. It was only for him. But in a whole new way. "I'm glad you told me how you felt, Willie."

"We keep this up," he said to her, "and we might end up not feelin' like such old dogs after all."

They laughed softly together and she echoed his earlier thought by saying, "Funny the surprises life brings
along sometimes when you least expect 'em."

And the smile she gave him *then*—well, he felt it in
his chest, like something bursting open wide, something
being set free, like she'd just given him the best Christmas present he'd ever gotten. So then he did something
else spontaneous. He leaned over and kissed her.

It wasn't a long kiss; it wasn't a deep one. It was just
a peck really. But the nicest dang peck he could have
imagined.

And he was pretty sure she'd liked it, too, when she
gasped a little and said, "My, my—you're just full o'
surprises today."

Grampy wouldn't have minded if that moment had
never ended.

And then something curious happened—it started to
snow, white flakes wafting gently down over them.

"Was it supposed to snow?" Edna wondered aloud,
leaning her head back to peek toward the sky.

"Don't believe so," Grampy replied. "Reckon it's just
some Christmas angels lettin' us know they approve."

"Or . . . maybe they're wantin' me to keep you warm
some more, old man," she suggested.

Hmm, could be that Edna had some surprises of
her own.

He gave her a grin. "What say we take this old sleigh
back to my place and build us a fire and get all cozylike?"

Now she pulled back a little. "Been a dern long time
since I been cozylike with anybody."

But he understood. Change was hard. A little scary.
Though he suddenly felt easy about this, like they

were in it together and it would all be just fine. Better than fine. "Likewise," he told her. "But we'll take it slow. Ain't no need to rush things now. I feel like . . . we're right where we're supposed to be."

And as Grampy picked back up the reins and turned Charley and the sleigh toward home, he thought of Shane and looked forward to thanking him. The boy had brought a lot of good into his life in a short time. Sometimes younger folks didn't realize how much even small things could mean when you were older and a little lonely—but he had a feeling that this was going to be the best thing of all about meeting the younger man. A new beginning, new romance, that he'd never have had if Shane hadn't come along and pointed out what was right in front of his face all along.

By the time the last child left the gazebo, people were starting to disperse and the party drawing to a close. It had started to snow and people wanted to get home in case the roads got bad.

Shane heard Amy Whitaker across the way saying, "It's almost Christmas—a fresh coating of snow might be nice."

"Bite your tongue, Amy," Mike Romo replied as he picked up his little girl, preparing to depart. "The first foot and a half wasn't enough for you?"

"Come on, Mike, it's Christmas—get in the spirit," she said, taking Logan's hand and starting to move toward the garden gate as well.

The truth was, Shane felt invigorated. He never would have believed he could enjoy playing Santa so much. He'd been nervous at first, but somehow that had fallen away as he'd looked into the kids' faces and realized it was actually pretty damn easy to make them happy. And that had felt good.

Sure, he'd had a couple of cryers, and a few who were clearly scared shitless of a dude with a bad beard who they didn't know—and that had thrown him a little, each time. But Candy had usually been nearby, saying calming things and helping *him* come up with the right things to say, too.

So while part of him still wanted to pummel Grampy for putting him on the spot this way—and he certainly wasn't going to admit to the old guy that he'd ultimately enjoyed it—he felt . . . what was the right word? Uplifted? Fulfilled?

Hell, what did the right word matter? And no wonder he didn't know—he hadn't exactly spent a lot of time in uplifted or fulfilled territory. So he let it go and when he realized Candy and a few others were starting to clean up, he pitched in, too, collecting some strewn napkins and cups people had left lying on tables and a couple on the ground.

Candy walked over to say, "You were amazing, Shane."

Yet he tried to play if off as nothing. "Just glad it's over." Which was true but also partly a fib.

She just shook her head. "You seriously stunned me. I mean, I thought you'd do okay, but you completely nailed it. You made so many kids so happy today. You should be proud of yourself."

The words added to that good feeling inside him, but old habits died hard, so he still only shrugged inside the red suit. "Well, just glad I pulled it off. And glad I was here to pull Grampy's ass out of the fire on this." He gave her a wink. Then remembered he was still in the Santa suit and beard and decided maybe it was time to change back into himself. He pointed toward the house. "I'm gonna head in and get out of this thing. I'll be back in a minute to help out."

She smiled. "There's not much to do. Tidy things up, bring the hot chocolate machines inside, stuff like that. We can come back tomorrow for the big stuff."

He nodded, then started toward the cottage, passing by the decorated tree near the gate though most people had already removed their ornaments to take back home with them and it was barer now. A woman he didn't know stood next to it, looking at the same little wooden reindeer that had caught his eye earlier.

Although Shane wasn't normally outgoing, something about the coincidence—maybe combined with the fact that he'd been *forced* to be outgoing for the last couple of hours—drew him nearer.

"That one caught my eye, too," he said.

"My son made it," the woman told him. "Many years ago." She sounded too wistful for his taste, though, leaving him instantly sorry he'd come over.

"You did a nice job up there," she went on. She still looked sad, but like she was trying to turn it around. And despite himself, he appreciated the compliment. Especially from a stranger who had no reason to sugarcoat it.

And he wasn't sure why, but it made him want to cheer her up. He'd made all those little kids happy today, after all—maybe it would be just as easy to make this woman happy as well. So he tossed her a grin from behind the beard and said, "What would *you* like for Christmas?"

Her caustic laugh caught him off guard. "Oh, no one can bring me what *I* want. I'm getting married on Christmas Eve and—"

"Oh, you're her," he said. "The lady having the wedding at the church."

She nodded. "And that should be enough, right? Having the wedding of my dreams to the most wonderful man in the world. A real, true second shot at happiness I never thought I'd have." She sighed. "But much as I try to keep my chin up through thick and thin, there's . . . well, something missing from my Christmas every year, and the same thing'll be missing from my wedding. Guess I just never really accepted it." She gave her head a sad little shake.

Shane felt torn between still wishing he hadn't started this conversation and wondering what the big thing was that made this woman so downcast even when she should be happy. "What is it?" he asked cautiously. "What's missing?"

She looked embarrassed then, lowered her eyes, shook her head once more. "I'm sorry—I don't even know you and here I am dumping my troubles on you. That's not my usual way." Then she lifted her gaze to him again, trying for a smile. "Must be the Santa outfit. Always heard he was in the business of delivering miracles."

Shane wasn't sure what to say, but for Grampy's sake found himself trying to live up to the suit. Something in the moment—or maybe it was something in this woman's up-front way and sad eyes—pushed him to it. "Can't say I know much about miracles, but you can still tell me. If you want."

And so she said, "It's my son. I haven't seen him since he was nine."

Whoa. He had no idea how to respond, absorbing the emotion behind it but not really wanting to, and he was saved when Candy came up then, oblivious to the heavy moment, smiling and introducing them.

"Oh, I've been wanting you two to meet," she said cheerfully. "Anita, this is Shane. He's only in town temporarily, but he's been helping with the repairs at the church."

And the woman blinked, her eyes meeting his. Eyes that felt . . . suddenly familiar somehow. Her voice came out hushed, her expression changing as she said, "That's so funny—Shane was my boy's name."

And her words stole Shane's breath away.

Anita. His mother had been named Anita. And yeah, he'd heard this woman referred to as Anita a hundred times in the last few weeks, but it wasn't an unusual name; there were a million women named Anita; there'd been no reason to think . . . until now.

No wonder he'd almost recognized—remembered— that damn reindeer ornament.

No wonder her eyes felt familiar.

No wonder . . . his father had sent him to Destiny.

Still being in the Santa suit, his face partially hidden, helped him feel at least a little protected as he soaked in the startling realization. He took in more of her—her face, her clothes, her hair, everything about her. The things that were different, but also the things that had stayed the same.

This was his mother.

His mother.

Who had abandoned him all those years ago.

"Show me the way. I'm at the end of my rope. Show me the way, God."

George Bailey, *It's a Wonderful Life*

Twenty

Inside, though, he felt shaky, protected or not. Protection, of some kinds anyway, was really just an illusion. A stupid Santa costume couldn't protect him from the gaping hole inside him that had almost closed up over time but right now felt like it was opening, expanding, swallowing him.

He didn't understand. Any of this. How had his father known she was here? Why had he wanted Shane to find her? Why now? And the look on her face, the palpable pain coursing through her. That had made a hell of a lot more sense when he'd thought she was someone else, when he hadn't known her son was *him*.

After all, she'd sent him away, wanted him gone—so why was she mourning the loss this way? Mourning *him* this way? *I'm not dead—I was here, alive and kicking, the whole time, and where were you?* The very idea of being valued that way felt so foreign to him, the opposite of what he'd felt his whole life when it came to his mother—was it real? He couldn't make head nor tail of it.

How the fuck had this happened? How had he ended up standing here face-to-face with the mother who had rejected him over twenty long years ago? Memories of his childhood with her were vague, like a dream, full of snippets of recollections he didn't quite know the full truth behind.

He felt like he was about to explode. And he was on the verge of starting to shake on the outside now, too. He couldn't be here anymore. He couldn't.

So he murmured, "I have to go," and made a sudden turn to rush away.

He nearly ran over Candy—damn, that fast he'd somehow forgotten she was even there. The whole world had narrowed to him and the stranger who had given birth to him.

Candy's eyes widened with the shock of him plowing toward her. "You look like you've seen a ghost!"

"Maybe I did," he muttered, then went to move around her, get the hell out of here.

But that was when a hand closed on his shoulder, spun him around, and he found himself face-to-face with the woman named Anita, his mother, again. God, he couldn't believe that all this time it had been her wedding he'd been working to save.

And then her gaze bore into his. And he knew that she'd figured it out, too.

She looked nervous, shaky, her eyes wide and her lips trembling. "Can I see your face?" The words left her in a raspy whisper.

But he didn't make a move, didn't reply. He didn't *want* to show her his face.

That didn't stop her, though. She reached up, pulled down the beard. And he felt exposed, more on display than if he'd been naked. It had been a long time, but she would know. She would be able to tell. He knew it to the marrow of his bones.

"Are you . . . my Shane? Shane Dalton?"

He heard Candy let out a gasp somewhere behind him. Felt the whole garden go still, the few people still there now tuned in to the tense scene by the gate. He wanted to just sink down into the snow and disappear, end this, not face it.

And yet he couldn't. He couldn't run from this because this woman, his mother, hadn't let him. Once upon a time she'd pushed him away in the worst way possible—but now she wouldn't let him go, damn it.

"How could you?" He'd never planned to say the words, but heard them fall out in a rasp. *"How could you?"*

She shook her head helplessly, looking as stunned as he felt. "How could I what?"

His mouth began to tremble, his chest going hollow. He felt as if he'd walked into someone else's nightmare. "You sent me away with Dad. You never saw me again. Never even a phone call. Never even a fucking birthday card." He wanted to shut up now—he didn't want to be letting any of this out, letting her see that it mattered, that he gave a shit, that it had hurt him in any way. But one more sentence left him—though at least it came out a little more quietly. "You're my mother and I don't even know you."

The woman before him appeared shocked, wounded. But he wasn't sure why. After all, what did she expect?

And then she began to shake her head, looking forsaken and confused. "Shane, I never . . . that's not . . . that's not what happened. At all."

Something in his chest pinched. Tight. But he didn't say anything. He didn't move a muscle. Part of him didn't want to hear what she meant by that, what she had to say about it. But he stayed, kept standing there—another part of him waiting, wondering . . . fearing. Did the truth lie someplace different than where he'd always believed?

"Honey, I never sent you away." She pressed her hands to her chest through her coat. "I would *never, ever, ever* have done that. You were *my world, my life.* Losing you . . ." She stopped, shook her head again. "It destroyed me. It changed me, turned me hard inside. You were my everything."

Now Shane was the one shaking his head. Because this just didn't add up. They were pretty words, what every mother should claim—but this didn't make any sense. "Then what happened? Why didn't I ever hear from you again?"

"Baby, your father . . ." She looked so damn pained, like she was about to collapse in a heap, but he couldn't let that affect him. Even if it surprised him to discover that there remained some invisible tiny thread, something that connected to his heart and pulled on it to see her suffering. There was some tiny bond that hadn't quite been completely severed, even after all these horrible years apart.

"Your father . . . took you. He kidnapped you."

Shane's chest went as tight as a stretched rubber band. "What?" That was ridiculous. Kidnapped? Who kidnapped their own kid?

"He took you for the weekend and never brought you back. Just disappeared with you. And it was a long time ago. Things like Amber alerts weren't common yet and there just weren't easy ways to track people down."

A memory shot into Shane's mind like a bullet. A stop in Illinois to trade in his dad's car for a different one. *I've always been more of a Ford man, Shaney. So what am I doing driving this old Dodge? What do you think about this one? What say you and me give this Taurus a nice drive and if we like it, we'll take it—huh? A new car for a new start together—how about that?*

And Shane had thought it was . . . like a gift for him or something. A way to make him feel better about his mom sending him away, a way to distract him. The Taurus had been newer, nicer, than the cars they usually drove, and Shane had pointed it out on the lot, thinking the teal color made it look sharper than the other boring sedans. But now . . . had it been like . . . a getaway car? A way to keep them from being as easily trackable?

"The local cops weren't helpful," she went on. "They thought I was blowing it out of proportion when I reported that he hadn't brought you home on Sunday, made me feel like I was being irrational, emotional, like there had to be some logical explanation. And so I waited. But by the time they took me seriously, it was too late."

And he was acutely aware that Candy had suggested this very thing, that his father hadn't been honest with him—but how could he believe that? Because she was making this sound too simple. Even if in the back of his mind he knew good and well that people kidnapped their own kids all the time—this couldn't be that. That couldn't have happened to *him*. His heart beat too hard and he gave in to the urge to argue with her. "You wanted to be rid of me. I was too much of a handful, just a burden to you. Dad said you weren't ready to have a kid when you did and that you just didn't want the responsibility."

His mother's eyes flew wide in anger. "He told you that? Why, that son of a bitch!"

And an even bigger anger flared in Shane's chest now. "Shut the hell up! He loved me. He was good to me. As good as he knew how to be anyway."

Now the woman before him—his mother, a stranger—appeared weakened, almost breathless, and her voice came out weaker, too, as she asked, "Oh Shane—Shane, has . . . has your life been good? Where have you been all this time?"

"Montana," he told her. "And it's been . . . fine. Until Dad died last month. Cancer."

And he knew fine was . . . almost an exaggeration. If his life had been so fine, he'd have something more to hang on to right now, and he wouldn't be crossing the whole damn country looking for something new and better. But he couldn't let her know that. He couldn't let her think his dad had failed him. Or that he needed anything. Or anyone.

And that was when she did the last thing he expected in that moment—she threw her arms around his neck and clung to him, strong and tight and desperate. He felt that in her embrace—desperation. Longing. An ache. A mother's love. As much as he didn't *want* to feel that, he did, practically permeating his flesh, coursing through his veins.

And he tried like hell not to feel *any* of it, tried to shut it out, put up some sort of wall against it, keep every ounce of anger in place no matter what the truth might or might not be. But then . . . something inside him gave way—until he was hugging her back, letting his arms close around this woman who'd given birth to him but whom he barely knew.

The winter sun sank early behind the trees and hills of eastern Ohio, and the freshly falling snow had added a bite to the cold air—but an emotion Shane had never known flooded his body. And for that moment in time, he let himself just succumb to it, succumb to what it was to be hugged by his mother.

Until it hit him that this was fucking insane, and too much to take, and he pulled away from her, saying, "I can't do this."

Then he turned and stalked aimlessly from the garden in the silly Santa suit he still wore, feeling like some surreal Christmas monstrosity.

He didn't know where he was going—hell, he didn't even have a car of his own to drive away in—but he didn't care. He just needed to be gone, anywhere else.

He barreled forward, dropping his gaze to his feet as

he trudged down the cottage's front path and onto the road, mostly empty of cars now. And he started toward Candy's house since, like once before, he simply had nowhere else to go.

Candy watched in horror as Shane left the garden. She wanted to go after him, but her feet felt frozen in place. And Anita apparently felt the same compulsion, starting toward the gate—yet that was when, for the first time since all this had started, Walter stepped up, blocking his fiancée's path, and saying in his calm, knowing way, "Let him go for now, honey. It's a shock to him, a shock to all of us—give him some time."

And despite herself, Candice thought maybe he was right. She herself was still trying to wrap her head around what she'd just seen unfold, so she couldn't imagine the jolt the rest of them were suffering. Even as much as it pained her to let him walk away alone, he probably wouldn't welcome any of them chasing after him at the moment.

Now Anita stood before her shaking, clearly a big ball of jumbled emotions. "I can't believe he's here," she said, "and—and, Lord, I'm so thankful he's well. Walter, did you see him? Did you see what a fine, handsome man he grew up to be?" She smiled at her intended, clearly filled with joy and relief—just before bursting into tears. "But to think he thought all this time that I didn't want him . . ." And then she collapsed into Walter's arms.

Candice wasn't sure what to do, but decided to retreat, especially since the last few party guests had left the garden now, too. Though when she heard Anita say, "It's nothing short of a miracle that he ended up here. How could that be?" she decided she should probably stay.

"I can tell you that part," she volunteered, stepping cautiously back toward Anita. "He arrived on the night of the blizzard. He wrecked his truck in a snowbank and walked to my house in the middle of the night." She went on to explain how he'd been on his way to Miami but had made a pitstop in Destiny because his father had told him to on his deathbed.

When she was done, Anita said, "It sounds like you've come to know him."

Candice nodded. "We're . . . seeing each other." The simple version of *I'm in love with him even though he's leaving any day now.*

Anita left Walter's lingering embrace, reaching out to take Candice's mittened hand, and asked gently, "Tell me about him. What's my boy like?"

As the snow continued falling around them, gathering on the shoulders of Anita's coat now and sprinkling her hair, Candice considered what a big, complicated question that was, one she could have answered in a hundred different ways. Finally she said, "He's . . . smarter than he probably gives himself credit for. And kinder than he thinks. Sweet when he wants to be. A tough guy . . . until he's not. He pays attention to what's going on around him—and he sees humor in little things. And today I learned that he has a soft spot for children that he probably never knew about until they were sitting on his lap.

"I think he had a rough upbringing. He sees himself as trouble. But what I see is . . . a good man who's just been a little lost." Now Candice squeezed Anita's hand in return, trying to console her, reassure her. "I'll . . . talk to him, Anita. I'll try to make him understand, come around."

Just then, Adam Becker, who'd been helping with cleanup down at the dock, stuck his head through the arched garden gate. "Did I just see a haggard Santa Claus walking down the road in the snow or did someone spike the eggnog?"

"Both," Candice informed him.

That was when Adam seemed to take in the vibe that something heavy was going on—or maybe he noticed Anita's tear-streaked face.

And while Candice had thought it wise to let Shane be for a while, now she wondered where he was headed—and if he'd have sense enough to come in out of the snow. Normally, yes—but right now wasn't normal, and she worried about his state of mind.

She approached Adam and touched his arm through his coat sleeve. "Can I ask a huge favor? I hate to run out on Miss Ellie, but I really have to go. Would you mind making sure anything that needs to be cleaned up today is, and promise her I'll be back tomorrow to do the rest?"

Adam must have seen the gravity of the situation in her eyes since he said, "Don't worry about coming back tomorrow, Candice. I'll make sure everything's taken care of. You did a great job with the party—Sue Ann is still here, and so are Mick and Jenny, and we'll take care of getting everything back in place for Miss Ellie. Go do whatever you need to do."

Her heart warmed and she made a mental note to tell

Sue Ann what a keeper Adam was. "Thank you," she replied, hoping he could feel the depth of her gratitude.

And as she started to leave, Anita called to her, "Tell him I love him. Tell him I love him more than anything and I always have."

Shane reached up under the Santa suit and into the pocket of the coat he wore underneath, pulling out the gloves Candy had given him. His hands were damn cold. Probably had been for a while, but it was just now hitting him. Hell, his hands had been cold since he'd shown up in this town—and maybe it had taken this fucking long to admit to himself that he wasn't impervious to everything.

In fact, maybe he wasn't impervious to *anything*. At the moment, he felt beat up. A little calmer than he had five minutes ago, leaving the garden, but just . . . tired—so damn tired. He was cold, wet, and shocked as hell.

And he didn't know what to think about anything his mother had said. Shit, his *mother*—who could have known he'd be having a conversation with his *mother* today? But maybe none of it mattered. He'd been headed for a new life somewhere else anyway, so maybe this changed nothing. Whether or not she'd loved him, whether or not his father had lied to him—that changed nothing, either. No one could go back and fix the past— his childhood, his upbringing. So what difference did it make where the truth lay?

He walked up Candice's driveway, now covered with fresh, still-falling snow, and made his way in the back door. He'd learned that she kept it unlocked. And he thought it was nice that places still existed where you could do that, but at the same time, he reminded himself to scold her for it—because no one was really safe anywhere, no matter what they thought.

He'd almost felt like *he* was safe *here*. In Destiny. He'd almost let his guard down. He'd started to relax. He'd started to grow fond of people, trust them. And then—boom—turned out he wasn't safe here at all. And it wasn't anyone's fault—it just was.

He pushed through the back door into the kitchen and smelled something good, then remembered Candy putting together a beef stew in the Crock-Pot this morning. Then he walked into the living room, thankful for the warmth of the house, annoyed by the needy white cat instantly at his feet. "Get away," he said to Frosty.

That's the problem with forming connections. You start spending time with people—or cats, for that matter—and they start caring about you. And then they want things from you. They want you to play Santa for them. Or help them repair a church. Or go ice-skating with them. Or pet them. He glared down at the cat still rubbing up against his ankles even as he tried to shed the Santa costume and his coat.

And none of that had actually been so bad. Some of it had been—hell, it had been downright nice or he wouldn't have gone along with it. But now suddenly here was his mother—Anita of the Christmas Eve wedding at the damaged church, which still blew his mind— wanting . . . what? Forgiveness? Absolution? Love? For him to act like they were some sort of normal mother and son after twenty-five years apart during which he'd thought she hated him? When he didn't even know for sure . . . what to believe. Or again, if it even mattered. After all, the damage was done. It wasn't fixable now.

It made him feel calmer to go through the routine of just getting back to normal. The steps of building a fire in the hearth calmed him. Setting the wet Santa suit out to dry nearby calmed him. Taking off his coat and his shoes calmed him. And hell, much as he hated to admit it, when he sat down on the couch to just rest finally, and Frosty hopped up next to him, curling up at his hip—that calmed him, too.

The truth was, when he'd left the party, he'd wished like hell he could go back to his place above the Mercantile and just be alone. Or maybe blow some of the last precious cash in his pocket on a bottle of something at a liquor store and get good and drunk and just forget about this for a little while.

But . . . this was better. Being at Candy's. With her silly cat. And her warm fireplace and her friendly Christmas tree. And knowing that in a while she'd come home.

It wasn't that he wanted to have to talk to her about all this. It was just that . . . she'd be there. And that it felt . . . better than choosing to be alone.

The front door opened sooner than he expected. And he suffered the brief fear that she'd have Anita with her—but thankfully she was by herself.

He looked up from his place on the couch. "Sorry I ruined your party."

"You didn't ruin it," she assured him. "It was wonderful, in fact. And it was pretty much over when . . . well, by the time . . ."

"By the time I ran into my mother for the first time

since I was a little kid?" He raised his eyebrows sardonically. The whole thing sounded absolutely, fucking surreal.

She let out a soft breath. And as their eyes met, saying more in silence than they could with words, he took in how damn pretty she looked even after a day of being out in the cold. She smelled like snow and cold air—it hung about her. But he'd never liked that fresh, odd scent of cold so much as he did in this moment.

"I can't imagine what you're feeling," she said softly.

"Is it still snowing?" he asked. And absently stroked the cat's side. Distractions. Because he wasn't quite ready to go there yet.

She nodded. "Coming down heavy now."

He nodded, too. "I started a fire."

"Thank you. It's nice to come home to." She walked over to it, took off her mittens and set them on the fireplace screen, held her fingers out to soak up the warmth.

They stayed quiet for a few minutes, so quiet that he wished he'd clicked on the TV before she came in or turned on some music or something.

Finally, she said, "Are you hungry for some stew?"

He gave another nod. "It smells great. Perfect on a cold night." And indeed it had gotten dark out quickly, early, from the snow plus being one of the shortest days of the year.

She took off her coat, walked to the coat tree near the front door, and hung it near where he'd hung his own a few minutes earlier. "I'll go dish some up and we can eat in here by the fire where it's cozy. Sound good?"

More stroking of the cat. And nodding. "Sounds perfect."

Only, as she walked behind the couch toward the doorway that led to the kitchen, he heard himself ask, "How do you think he knew? That she was here?"

His heart beat harder in the very asking. He'd been pretty happy Candy was willing to let it drop, so why had he opened this door of conversation?

She stopped, walked back to the couch, peering down at him. "Maybe he somehow kept up with where she was through common old acquaintances or something. Or maybe he Googled her. She owns a bar—"

"She does?" That surprised him.

"Yeah, the Dew Drop Inn outside town. So she's probably searchable on the Internet, even if only just a little. Or . . . you know there are those places you can pay online to get someone's address. So I guess there are a lot of ways he could have known."

Shane took a deep breath, let it back out. Tried not to feel this. He'd done good at that for a few minutes, and again wondered why the hell he'd returned to the subject.

"Well, however he knew, she's obviously the reason he told me to come here. But . . . the thing is, why? Why bother? Whether she sent me away or he took me, why send me back to her?"

Candy sat down on the arm of the couch next to him, reached out, touched his shoulder. "I think maybe it was . . . a classic deathbed confession, the kind you hear about. Maybe that's why he couldn't even get it all out—maybe he hadn't planned to say it at all, but it just started coming out in those last moments."

Shane squinted at her, thinking it through. He'd never seen his dad express much regret about anything in his life. "If he wanted me to know, would have made a lot more sense to tell me sooner. Like when he could at least think straight and make himself clear."

In reply, though, Candice just offered a slight shrug. "That's why it's called a deathbed confession—it's a thing a person realizes in the last few minutes of life that they can't die without telling you. Maybe he suddenly realized he wanted you to have a parent when he was gone. And . . . maybe he knew he'd done wrong by you all those years ago and didn't have the guts to fix it while he was alive, but then realized he didn't want you to be alone, that he wanted you to find out the truth in the end."

Something about that part hit him in the gut. Because he still didn't *know* the truth, and maybe he never really would, but . . . something in finding out his father had wanted him to reconnect with her made him feel . . . vulnerable. To think his dad had worried about him.

But also mad as hell if that *was* the truth. If his father had lied to him, stolen him, was that really love? How the hell could someone do that? Who thought that made any sense in the world?

And so he didn't know who to be angry with anymore, didn't know who'd been the one to handle a little kid's heart so recklessly. The fruitless anger began welling back up inside him anyway, though, like a monster that wanted to get out, rip things apart, go on some kind of rampage.

Candice must have seen it in his eyes because she whispered, "It's okay, Shane."

But as it stretched through his chest, his torso, his soul, he instantly said, "It's not. I shouldn't be around you right now." And then he pushed up off the couch and stormed out onto the front porch where he'd first met her, on a snowy night just like this. And he pulled back his fist and punched one of the thick, wooden columns that held up the roof overhead. "God damn it!" he yelled at the top of his lungs out into the otherwise silent, dark, snowy night.

He knew she stood somewhere behind him, watching. But it was okay—or as okay as it could be. He trusted her enough to let her see him at his worst, to let her see him drop all the walls and spew that anger out in some way that wouldn't hurt anybody. He trusted her enough to let her see him crumble a little then—his knees gave out and he sank to them on the wet, snowy porch. And then he leaned back his head and released some kind of primal yell that had pushed up and burst loose from somewhere deep inside.

He trusted her—but he didn't *like* letting her see him this way. So he crushed his eyes shut when tears gathered behind them—he kept them closed until it passed, until they were gone.

And then she was out on the porch with him, stooping down behind him, kneeling there, wrapping her arms around him from the back.

And he felt so damn . . . foolish. Talk about vulnerable. "I'm sorry, honey. Sorry you have to be involved in my drama, sorry you have to put up with me right now. Shit, you can't even drive me home, because look at the damn roads."

They were covered in deepening snow that continued to fall at a heavy rate, blotting out the moonlight and illuminated only by the house's exterior lights and a streetlamp.

"You don't have to be sorry," she promised him softly. "It's okay."

But he just shook his head. Covered one of her hands with his. "Why on earth are you so damn nice to me? Especially—" he stopped, actually laughed a little "—considering how mean you used to be."

He turned his head to see her sweet smile near his face. "Because I love you, Shane."

He blinked softly, taken aback. He sure as hell didn't feel very lovable. Shit, maybe he never had. And now he wasn't sure which of his parents had started that inside him, but he said to her, "You shouldn't love me, honey. I'm not worth it."

"Yes, you are." She sounded so sure. So sure that he almost believed it.

Only now he had to remind her. "You shouldn't love me because . . . in a couple days I'm gonna leave, gonna walk right out of your life and never look back. Because . . . thing is, there's a part of me that does think about staying. A part of me that wants to. But now . . . I can't. I just fucking can't. So you shouldn't love me, Candy. It's a losing proposition."

Behind him, with her chest pressed into his back and her face still beautifully close, she whispered, "I do anyway. And I know you're leaving. And I wish you wouldn't. There's so much to stay for—even more now. But no matter what happens, I forgive you for it."

Her words took his breath away. "You forgive me even before I've done it?"

She nodded. "It seems to me that . . . sometimes love is about . . . forgiving."

He said nothing more. She was too good for him.

It broke his heart in a way. And made him love her back.

Though it seemed useless to say it. Useless if he wasn't staying. So he kept it to himself—and realized how damn cold he'd gotten again, out there on the porch, snow blowing all around them. And he squeezed both of her hands in his.

Then he looked down at them, their hands, his fingers overtop hers, and said, "I finally get to keep *your* hands warm."

And she let out a sweet sigh near his ear, then kissed him on the cheek and said, "We should go inside."

"You're right."

And together they stood in their now wet-socked feet and wet clothes and stepped back through the door into the warmth and dryness. "Ready for that beef stew?" she asked.

"Yep," he said. And then, "Nope."

She looked up at him. "Nope?"

Because he needed to kiss her. And so that was what he did. He grabbed her and kissed her with every ounce of passion and fire and fear and anger and love inside him. "Food isn't what I need right now, Candy," he rasped in her ear.

And she murmured back, breathless, "What do you need?"

"To be inside you, making you melt, making you come, making you scream."

"I'll love you 'til the day I die."

Mary Hatch, *It's a Wonderful Life*

Twenty-one

*W*ell, Candice couldn't argue with that. In fact, the very suggestion, along with the hot rasp in his voice, made her heart beat faster and set the crux of her thighs tingling wildly. She bit her lower lip as she peered up at his darkly handsome face. "I want that, too."

His eyes fell half-shut in response, and his gaze dropped to her mouth as he lifted one hand to cup her jaw, rake his thumb over her lower lip. And Candice felt all the pain and passion inside him.

He'd spilled some of that pain just now on her front porch, and she'd been happy to be here for him, happy to try to comfort him or at least support him however she could. It was still hard to believe Anita Garey was

Shane's mother, hard to wrap her head around it—and if it was this hard for *her*, she could only imagine how difficult it was for *him*.

Now he was ready to spill some of that passion, slake some of it away inside her body. And she was happy to be here for him in that way, too.

And as for the knowledge that this was temporary— well, she'd already surrendered to that fact. It didn't change anything here. She didn't expect anything, wasn't holding him to anything—as from the moment she'd first allowed herself to go to bed with him, it was freely given, and maybe the closest thing she'd experienced to unconditional love.

"I want to make you forget everything bad, Shane," she said, a slight rasp in her own voice she'd never heard before. *He brings it out of me. He brings out pieces of me I never knew were there. He makes me . . . the woman I want to be.*

It hit her fully then. With Shane, she wasn't the stay-at-home technical writer keeping her head—and her heart—buried in the sand. With Shane, she wasn't frightened or even timid any longer. She'd come out of her shell—and not only with him but somehow in other parts of her life, too. With Shane, she was brave and vulnerable and . . . real.

It surprised her when the look in his eyes changed then—when the feral need softened just a little, and he murmured gently, "You do. You do that for me."

And it surprised her further when hearing that made her desire flare even more, connecting her to him so deeply that mere words could never express it; only her body could. "Take me," she said.

A low groan echoed from his throat. And Shane didn't want to go slow; in fact, he didn't think he could if he tried. He needed to fuse his flesh with hers, sink inside her, fill her up; let *her* fill *him* up in a whole different way.

When he crushed his mouth down onto her soft lips, it was with a stark hunger, a need to do as she'd just said—take her, take *from* her, take what she was offering. His hands instinctively clutched at her ass through her blue jeans, hauling her body up against his pelvis, needing to feel her there, needing to press his erection into her, make her feel it too.

Her gasp against his mouth told her she did, and it hardened him all the more.

And then he let her do the other thing she'd offered—take away the bad stuff. He focused wholly on her. Her curves, beneath his hands. Her lips, beneath his hungry mouth. The sweet, hot, sexy way she clung to him, her arms around his neck, letting him know her want burned just as strong as his.

His hands roamed her slender waist, then rose to her breasts, molding them, stroking his thumbs across their tips. He needed her naked, so he reached for the bottom of the red sweater she wore, soon yanking it off over her head. After unzipping his hoodie, she worked feverishly at the buttons on his shirt as he tugged at her zipper, yanking her jeans from her hips.

And then his mouth went dry. "Oh my God," he murmured, breath labored.

She'd paired a red bra with white panties decorated with . . . candy canes. He couldn't pull his eyes away.

"I . . . heard once that you have a thing for candy canes," she whispered, soft and sexy.

"I do," he assured her, his erection almost painful now. Then he reached down between them and stroked his middle finger up her center, over top a naughty-as-hell little candy cane that happened to be printed right there. "And I want to lick *this* one."

Another pretty gasp set him all the more on fire for her—and even as eager as he was to relieve his aching cock, he instead jerked her panties down with both hands and dropped to his knees.

"Lean back against the couch," he instructed her deeply. They stood behind it, and so she did as he'd instructed as he freed her from the panties completely, then used both hands to spread her legs.

It made her all the more beautiful and hot when he recalled how she'd been with him in the beginning—so worried and wary and fearful. And as he pressed his tongue to the cleft between her thighs, he loved who she'd become with him.

Her high whimpers of pleasure fueled him as he licked her, again, again. And part of him wanted to stretch this out, make it last for her, and for him too—but on the other hand, they had all night. So he followed the urge to just take her there, all the way, working his mouth at the crux of her pleasure until he could sense it rising, rising, reaching that hot, critical peak—and then she was coming against his mouth, crying out, eyes shut above him, letting him see her most private, intimate self.

When she came down from it, he sensed her knees beginning to give way, and he rose to catch her in his arms, whispering, "Lean on me, baby—lean on me."

She did, and he held her, kissing her head, her hair,

for just a few seconds before he couldn't hold back anymore—so he turned her body around to face away from him, bent her over the back of the couch. She let him guide her, and he sensed her urgency rising again, too, as he rushed to get his pants open.

His erection sprung free, impatiently seeking heat, and he wasted no time planting his hands on her hips, positioning himself, then thrusting his way inside her.

They both moaned deeply at the rough entry and—damn, it felt like coming home. Sweet, hot relief. The place he was supposed to be. So tight, so wet, so warm.

He drove into her, finding a rhythm, her body joining in, meeting his every plunge into her moisture. She cried out with each hot stroke, and low growls left his own throat as he got lost in the consuming bliss of it.

He took in her bare, pale, slender back, the red bra strap still stretching across it, and decided he needed to free her of that, so he flicked the hooks open and watched it fall over her outstretched arms in front of her. He moved his hands up, letting them glide over the two soft mounds of flesh, then gripped them tighter as he moved in her harder, harder.

It didn't take long to reach the point of no return. And just like when he'd been licking her sweet flesh, he could have held back, stretched it out, but instead, he just followed the powerful urge to come in her. He thrust, thrust, thrust, loving the way she called out as he spilled himself inside her.

And then *he* was the one collapsing a little, letting his body slump onto hers over the back of the couch.

"Damn, hon," he breathed. "That was . . . amazing."

And as he pulled out of her, he realized he'd forgotten

something—shit—and reached for some tissues on an end table to keep her tidy.

He tossed them in a wastebasket, then took her smoothly back into his arms and tumbled purposely over the back of the couch to land on the front side, drawing her there with him. He lay on his back, Candy nuzzled against his chest, her palms pressed there.

"About those tissues . . ." she began.

And he was quick to assure her. "I'm sorry, baby. But I promise you're fine, because I never forget."

"Until now," she added.

He nodded. "Until now."

"So *I'm* fine, but what about you?" she said playfully. "Could be I've been out carelessly having all kinds of wild sex with tons of different guys, so you could be in big trouble, mister."

A small chuckle left him as he met her pretty gaze. "Could be—but I don't think so."

She lowered her eyes, admitting, "Yeah, you never forget . . . and I never need to remember."

"Until now," he said.

"Until now."

"This is selfish, but I'm glad."

She raised her eyebrows. "Glad?"

"To be the only one for a while."

"Why's that?" she asked.

He supposed the answer was . . . well, something he'd normally never admit. But with Candy, it was easier. "Guess it makes me feel special."

"You *are* special," she promised him.

And he realized that he already knew she felt that way. And not just because she'd told him she loved him.

He'd known it before that, could feel it. Not too many people had ever made him feel that way before.

But he sure as hell wasn't one for getting all mushy and deep—and God knew there'd been enough of that today already, whether he'd meant for it to happen or not—so it seemed like a good time to change the subject. "I've worked up an appetite," he said. "Let's have some stew."

And that was when it hit him that for a blissful while she truly *had* taken away everything bad. He hadn't thought about what he'd found out earlier since they'd come inside. Only now it was coming back, bit by bit. Damn it.

Hadn't he had enough shit to deal with lately? His father's death. Wrecking his truck and getting stranded, while broke. And now this—his mother popping up at the Christmas party where he was playing Santa, when he hadn't seen her in twenty-five years.

But being here, with Candy, helped.

Hell, those adorable panties had helped.

Everything about her helped.

"**D**o you want to talk? About Anita?"

They lay in Candice's bed naked, the covers pulled to their waists. And she wasn't sure she should ask, but they'd eaten beef stew without discussing it, and they'd talked about the party without discussing it, and they'd watched *Jingle All the Way*—which Shane had been pleased to find on a cable channel—without discussing it. So maybe he'd be ready to talk about it now.

"Be nicer not to. Nicer to just lie here with you naked." Then he glanced toward the foot of the bed where a certain white feline sat. "And your cat. Though I'm not sure I like the way he's looking at me."

"The bromance getting a little heavy for you?" she teased him.

He laughed. Then his grin faded as he asked, "What's she like? Anita."

Candice thought back over Anita's history in their small town. "When she first came to Destiny and bought the Dew Drop Inn, people thought she was sort of . . . rough around the edges. Or maybe tough is a better word. She wasn't a typical Destiny resident.

"But then Chief Tolliver started dating her, and people got to know her, and . . . she's nice. I mean, I don't know her well, but I can tell you that she's a nice woman. People like her and are glad to see him find happiness again—his wife died a long time ago and Anita sort of . . . brought him back to life. And she dotes on Jenny and Mick's little boy. Maybe . . . maybe because she misses doting on *you*."

She was almost sorry to have added that last thought when his countenance darkened. And she wished she hadn't made him think about that—about all the years he'd lost with his mother.

"I still don't know what to believe," he said. "About the past. About what happened."

She understood that. No matter where the truth lay, one of his parents had failed him in the most awful way she could imagine. What if her own father came back right now? What if he somehow placed the blame on her mother, whom she loved dearly, who had been the one to take care of her and be there for her? It wouldn't be easy. It wouldn't be easy to see her whole life, her whole relationship with the parent who'd raised her, suddenly become one of deceit and lies. And Shane's dad wasn't even here to defend himself, meaning the answers would always remain a mystery.

So finally she said, "Maybe . . . It's not about figuring out what happened or who was to blame. Maybe it can be about . . . starting over."

Though Shane just looked at her like she was crazy. And maybe that was understandable. The news was so fresh, after all. "I can't think about that right now. I can't think about any of it." Then his face softened, harsh lines fading, and an undeniable need filled his eyes as he said, "Kiss me, Candy."

And she wanted him again, too. Wanted to slake his pain. And wanted to connect with him in that oh-so-intense and oh-so-pleasurable way.

And so she kissed him—she took his darkly stubbled face between her palms and kissed him warm and long and deep. And then she kissed him other places. She kissed his rough cheek. She kissed his soft neck. She kissed her way down his broad, muscled chest. And then she kissed a line down the center of his stomach, following the contours of the muscles there, until she arrived at his navel—and then lower.

Taking his firm erection in her hand, she kissed it, too. Softly. Tenderly. Then, loving the gentle moans it drew from him, she took him in her mouth.

She wanted to give him . . . all of her in that moment, all of herself that she could. And she hated that he was leaving. And she wondered if this news about Anita could possibly change anything, possibly make him stay, once he got used to the idea. And she almost hoped—but was afraid to. And so *she* ultimately chose to forget, too, about anything else but this moment, and his hot, virile body, and taking him to heaven.

They took each other there twice more before falling asleep in each other's arms.

"You need a hobby."

As the sound of his voice jarred her from slumber at some point in the night, she opened her eyes in the dark room, illuminated by moonlight that told her the snow had stopped falling outside. And she realized Shane was addressing Frosty, who was back at the foot of the bed, intently looking their way.

She simply let a soft giggle leave her, kissed his chest, rested her head there as she closed her eyes, and wished it could be this way always.

The trill of the phone by Candy's bed woke Shane from a sound sleep. Sound because of the woman next to him, he knew. He was surprised he'd slept so damn well, in fact, and the sun outside told him he'd slept long, too.

As she leaned over to answer, he glanced toward the clock to see it was past nine.

"Hello?" she said. Then, "No, I haven't." And her face went dark. "What? You're kidding. How can that be—how is it even possible?"

He waited quietly as she finished the call, her expression grim.

And when she hung up, she said, "That was Tessa. And I can't believe what she just told me."

"What?" he asked.

"The worst possible news. A fresh foot of snow fell last night, and there was a lot of wind, too, apparently."

She clearly hadn't gotten to the heart of the matter yet, so he prodded her. "And?"

"And the snow collapsed the church roof again."

He leaned slightly closer. "Really?"

She nodded.

And he said, "Well, I can tell you how it's possible. The repairs we did weren't meant to hold the weight of another big snowstorm. They were only supposed to be enough to get through the holidays and . . . the wedding." His mother's wedding. Not just some stranger's wedding anymore. But he went on. "It was just some tarps and plywood—nothing else."

Next to him, Candy sighed. "And who would have believed we'd get another big snow before Christmas. I mean, *one* that big is fairly unusual. But two . . ." She shook her head. "I don't ever remember anything like that happening here in my whole life."

"I'm sure nobody else expected it this soon, either," he agreed.

"Poor Anita," Candy said.

And Shane's chest tightened. Poor Anita. Everyone felt so damn sorry for Anita. And they'd probably feel even sorrier for her now—because her long-lost son had stormed away from her *and* her wedding was ruined, *again*.

Though he didn't say a word, Candy must have sensed his reaction because she told him, "I'm sorry. I just can't *not* feel bad for her about the wedding. And . . . about you. I feel bad for *both* of you. I know this whole situation is hard."

He just nodded because he didn't even know for sure how he felt.

Hell, he didn't like to think of the woman's wedding being ruined all over again, either. He didn't like to think of all the hard work people had gone to these past few weeks coming to this. Christmas Eve was only three days away—and if the roof had collapsed again, there would be no fixing the church in time to have a wedding there now.

But at the same time, he was still angry. Even if everything Anita said was true, had . . . had she just given up on finding him? Montana was long distance, sure—but he'd been there all this time, in one place more or less. And even if he didn't know the details or facts behind any of this, it was hard to believe that if she loved him so much she wouldn't have found a way, kept searching. To the ends of the fucking earth if that was what it took.

That was when Candice asked, her voice laced with caution, "Would . . . would you like me to take you to see Anita? Or maybe Walter? Both of them?"

"No," he answered quickly. Still mired in that fresh jolt of anger. Starting to consider, just a little, that maybe his father had been in the wrong—but somehow that just made him feel abandoned by *both* of them. Like they were both pieces of shit who didn't deserve his attention.

"You're sure?" she asked.

He nodded. "I'd rather just help you clean up at Miss Ellie's today." Lot less drama at Miss Ellie's, after all.

Yet Candy bit her pretty lower lip and informed him,

"Adam promised me that he, Sue Ann, Jenny, and Mick would take care of everything so that I didn't have to come back today. So we're kind of . . . off the hook." Though he could tell by her tone that she knew good and well this news didn't equal off the hook to him.

He let out a sigh. "How about we just start with breakfast, then?"

And in reply his pretty girl gave him a smile, and a good-morning kiss, and he thought she looked like a slightly naughty angel, naked next to him but wearing that sweet, innocent expression on her face. All she was missing was the halo and wings.

Kind of like Clarence in the movie. Well, if Clarence had been female and hot.

Shane felt in sort of a fog as he got up, took a shower, put back on yesterday's clothes, and joined Candy in the kitchen. He focused on her, his angelic Candy Cane, as she experimented with peppermint pancakes over the griddle. He focused on remembering all the ways they'd moved together last night. He focused on the silly cat who kept weaving figure eights around his ankles, even as he looked down and said, "Seriously. Hobby. Consider it."

Snowplows went by just as she was scooping the pancakes onto plates. And as they finished eating a little while later, Shane said, "You got a snow shovel, Candy? I should probably start trying to dig the car out."

"Yeah—in the toolshed."

That was when the doorbell rang, a surprise given the heavy snow accumulation.

They just looked at each other—before Candy silently rose to go answer.

And Shane pushed to his feet, too, but hung back, in the kitchen doorway, watching from a distance, because he already had a good idea who would be on the other side of that door.

A few seconds later he saw his mother again—just a sliver of her face actually, because Candy had only opened the door halfway. She stood next to her fiancé, and maybe he could sense more than see that she was tired and harried. "I made Walter bring me as soon as the plows went through," she said. "I'm so sorry to bother you, honey—but I had to. I had to see—is my boy with you? Is Shane here?"

Candy hadn't even answered yet, though, when Anita must have caught sight of him in her peripheral vision, because that was when she leaned past the door to look at him. The mother he hadn't seen since he was a little boy.

And now he was a man.

And she'd missed every damn thing in between.

And he realized even more than before that he had nothing to say to her—nothing at all.

"Don't you see what a mistake it would be to throw it all away?"

Clarence Odbody, Angel 2nd Class, *It's a Wonderful Life*

Twenty-two

When Shane made no response, not even moving a muscle, Walter said from behind Anita, "I told her maybe we oughtn't to come rushin' in, that maybe we should give you some time, son."

And it wasn't so much that Shane meant to keep standing there staring at them, not speaking, especially when Candy opened the door wider—but only that he couldn't think of a damn thing in the world he wanted to say. To either of them. He bore Walter no ill will—from everything he'd heard, the man was a pillar of the community and he seemed sensible, but Shane's mind just felt . . . empty. Too filled with emotion for anything as trivial as words to squeeze their way in.

When he still didn't reply, Candy hurried to fill the blank space. "I'm so sorry about the church. Is there any way they can fix it in time for the wedding?"

Anita had stepped through the door now, just over the threshold, and stood wringing her hands, her eyes flitting from Shane to Candy to the floor—and Shane knew he wasn't making this easy for her. But it wasn't out of cruelty. He just lacked any answers.

Still behind her, Walter let out a long sigh, and responded to Candy's question. "Don't seem likely, but folks are up there right now givin' it a look to see what they think."

"That doesn't matter," his mother interjected then. "I mean, it *does*. Of course it does. But . . ." She stopped, appearing torn, confused, yet then looked more directly at Shane. "Shane is what matters to me right now. And . . . maybe Walter was right, I should have waited, not pushed myself on you so fast. But Shaney, I've waited so long already. How could I stay away?"

And that was when Shane found his voice. "You've missed my whole life. I don't have any damn idea what to say. Or what to believe." He shook his head and was brutally honest. Honesty seemed like a good idea here. "And I guess this just seems . . . pointless to me. I mean, you don't even know me. And obviously, you didn't come looking for me."

At this, her eyes flew wide. "I did all I could, I swear. I didn't have any money, any resources. I tried to track your father down, but nobody would help me. And . . . and . . ." Her voice lost some of its steam then. "I can see how empty this must sound to you."

"Kinda, yeah." He hadn't planned to accuse her of anything, but maybe it needed to be said.

"Not a day has gone by," she told him, "that I haven't ached to know where you are, and to have you with me. Not a day, Shaney."

"I can attest to that, son," Walter added. "In the years I've known Anita—well, she told me about you on our very first date. And she talks about you all the time. She's never stopped looking for you—I've tried to help, too, but the trail had been too cold for too long and there just weren't any clues or leads to follow. She loves you dearly and always has."

Shane went silent again. And Anita took a step forward, her hands clasped together tight. The fact that she wore no gloves seemed almost ironic—though he guessed she'd just rushed out without them or something. "Is there anything I can say or do to make this better? Anything at all?"

And as Shane considered the question, he realized that was what it really all came down to. And he gave another honest answer. "That's the thing. I don't think there is. It's just . . . too much lost time. Too much lost . . . everything."

"I would do anything. *Anything.*" And that was when she rushed forward, toward him, collapsing on him in a fierce hug.

Hell. Like yesterday in the garden, he didn't want this, this closeness with her. This forced intimate moment with a mother he didn't know. And yet, there she was, clutching on to him so desperately—and even amid the cold and emotion that clung to her, he found . . . an old familiarity, something invisible and long-forgotten.

And it tore at his gut and made him hug her, too. Again, just like yesterday.

But shit—he wasn't the little boy she'd lost and he hadn't been anybody's little boy for a damn long time, so to hell with this. His heart beat too hard as he reached up to untwine her arms from around his shoulders, taking a step back away from her.

He didn't look at her eyes then—couldn't. Afraid of what he'd see. Her hurt. Memories. He wanted to fucking be done with this. So he just dropped his gaze to the floor and said, voice low, "I can't. Sorry—but I can't."

He then sensed Anita digging in the large purse that hung from a strap on her shoulder. His skin prickled with wishing she would just leave already—wishing *he* could leave. But he didn't have that luxury.

That was when she thrust a small wooden picture frame at him.

He didn't really want to take it, see what it held, but he felt he had no choice the way she was holding it out. And maybe if he did, it would hurry along her departure.

Accepting it, he glanced down at a picture of a red-haired woman holding a dark-headed little boy, maybe around seven. He only had a few pictures of himself that age or younger, but of course he knew it was him. He was smiling and so was she. A lit Christmas tree stood behind them, suddenly assaulting him with the memory, the knowledge that it was at his grandparents' house, that he remembered the little red sweater vest he wore, that he remembered his grandmother making the kind of star-shaped cookie he held in his hand. He remembered it all. Suddenly and too vividly. He remembered a whole other life that he'd thought he'd forgotten. His chest went hollow.

Because he also remembered . . . her love. Not just misbehaving and being yelled at and punished. But he remembered playing with her and opening presents she'd bought for him and being tucked in to bed at night—and a hundred other snippets of the past that were all . . . filled with love.

"I keep that next to my bed," she said of the picture. "Always have. But . . . but I want you to have it. Just to have some keepsake of me. It would . . . it would mean something to me."

Shane sucked in his breath, tried to find more words. "You . . . don't want it?"

Her reply came out quick, her breathing nervous and ragged. "It's my favorite picture of us together and I have copies—I can frame another. It's just . . . just . . . my way of showing you . . . how much I love you. I know it's not much. It's just . . . all I have."

"Okay," he murmured. Then lowered his eyes once more. He'd take the picture, but that was all.

And apparently she was reading him loud and clear because that was when she finally retreated—with the words, "I love you, Shane. And I'm so glad you're safe, and so proud of you."

And then she turned and walked out the door. Leaving him a little numb, and thinking about the pride she'd just proclaimed. Odd, given that she knew nothing about him at all, and yet somehow it warmed something inside him.

He slowly raised his gaze to see Walter still standing near the front door, still wide open—the room was getting cold. "I won't pretend to know what you're feeling right now," Walter told him, "but all I can say is—she has a lot of love to give you, son, if you'll accept it."

And then he turned and left, too, and relief flooded Shane.

Until he, for some reason, thought of Frosty—and that wide open door. He looked to Candy. "Where's the cat?"

Appearing surprised by the question, she pointed toward the hearth, where Frosty lay stretched out, warming beside the fire.

And Shane nodded, stepping up to finally shut the door. "I was just afraid . . ." He stopped, shook his head. "Just not in the mood to go chasing a white cat around in the snow."

"It's all right. He's still here." Her voice came out soft, comforting. Then she walked over to him, reaching up to touch his shoulder. "Are you okay? Do you want to talk about this?"

He met her pretty gaze only briefly, then let it drop. "Right now, I just want to shovel snow."

Her eyes widened slightly. "You want to shovel snow?"

"Yeah, I never thought I'd hear me say that, either. But it's just what I feel like doing right now." And with that, he set the framed picture his mother had given him facedown on a nearby table and went to find his shoes, which he'd left by the fireplace last night.

As he bundled up, finishing with the gloves Candy had given him, she said, "Lot of snow out there. Don't forget to take breaks and come in to warm up. And don't hurt your back. Or have a heart attack. Or anything else."

"I'm a big boy, honey," he said, eager to get out the door.

"I know. I just . . . care. That's all."

And it reminded him exactly how *much* she cared. She loved him. She'd told him so. And he'd had pretty damn much on his mind since then, so maybe that had gotten a little lost in it all—but now it was back. And hell, it felt nice. Even if maybe he wouldn't have thought that a few weeks ago.

Now he turned toward her, placed his gloved hand at the back of her neck, and leaned over to kiss her forehead. "Thank you, baby," he whispered. Then he walked to the door.

Though he stopped when he reached it, looking back. "Can I ask you something?"

"Anything," she said.

"What if your dad came back? What would you do?"

A certain darkness passed over her face, instantly telling him she didn't have an easy answer, which at least made him feel justified here. He'd asked the right question to really make her understand what he felt right now. She lowered her gaze, her expression somber, serious, until she met his eyes once more to quietly say, "Maybe I'd give him a chance. I'm not saying that would be easy—but I think I would. I think I'd have to."

Shane took that in, nodded, then walked out the door, heading toward the little shed at the rear of the driveway, painted the same color as the house. Hell, maybe he should have said more—and not about her dad. More about his feelings for her. But he wasn't sure exactly what his feelings *were*.

Or . . . maybe he knew but just wasn't sure it made

sense to say so. That he cared about her, too. Maybe even loved her. He wasn't entirely sure where that line lay.

And his head was so screwed up right now . . . and he wasn't the kind of guy who sat around thinking about his feelings—measuring them, labeling them. Even on the best of days, let alone the worst. So it was better he'd shut up.

Damn, the snow was deep. He followed the path Walter and Anita had left through the new foot of it that now covered the walk and nearly reached the top of the tires on Candy's sedan. He waded through the sea of thick, fluffy white, the cold biting at his cheeks and nose, until he'd gotten the shovel and started the job. And it was slow going. But it felt good to let the cold and hard work dissolve some of the heaviness inside him.

He'd just started making some headway when Mick Brody's truck pulled up and Mick started unloading a snowblower. "Figured you could use some help."

"Wouldn't turn it away," Shane said. Because, yeah, there were weird upsides to shoveling at the moment, but he'd already realized the sheer volume of snow here was going to make this a Herculean task.

Mick started at the foot of the lengthy driveway while Shane kept shoveling at the other end. And he thought they were going to work in companionable silence— until Mick said loudly over the noise of the blower, "None of my business, but heard you got some big news yesterday. You, uh, want to talk about it or anything?"

Hell. What was it with everyone talking about everything here? "No."

Mick chuckled. "No worries, dude, I get it. Not big on that kinda thing myself. Just felt like I should . . . say something, I guess. It's . . . a big thing."

Shane kept shoveling. "Thanks, but I'm good." Then he paused, shook his head. "Damn, news travels fast here."

"Well, Anita's marrying my father-in-law," Mick pointed out. And maybe the reminder was helpful, since sometimes it was hard to keep track of all the various ways people were linked and connected here. "But yeah, I know, it does. Took me a while to get used to that, everybody knowing everybody else's business." He gave his own head a short shake. "Believe me — never thought I'd want to be part of a place like this. But here I am."

And he sounded content enough about it. So Shane asked, "What changed?"

Mick stopped pushing the snowblower. "Everything." Then he pointed vaguely in the direction of his cottage up the road. "Jenny. She just changed the things I thought I wanted. Or . . . gave me more than I thought I could have. And for a guy who used to keep to myself, it's a switch for sure. But the people in this town—yeah, they might talk a lot and they might stick their nose in your business, but they're good people."

"Is *she* good people? Anita?"

Mick nodded. "She's pretty much been a grandma to my son since he was born. I wouldn't let just anybody do that. She's had a lot on her plate lately, but she's a strong woman—steady as a rock."

Shane sighed, taking all that in. Then he went back to shoveling. A signal to Mick that he was done talking.

Mick took it, and they finished the driveway and front walk in relative silence other than occasional small talk about less intense topics.

When the driveway was done and Shane had thanked him for the help, he said to Mick, "I bet you're the most popular guy in town today with that snowblower."

Mick just laughed. "Yeah—after I do Miss Ellie's, I'll head into town and see about the sidewalks in front of the Mercantile and Under the Covers—or if anybody else needs some help. And after that, guess I'll head to the church and find out what's happening there." He sounded doubtful about that last part already, though. Like it was probably a foregone conclusion that there wouldn't be a wedding there on Christmas Eve—even if, like Walter, he still held out a little hope.

Despite the cold, Shane puttered around a little more outside after Mick left. He found a bag of rock salt in the shed and sprinkled some on the walk to keep it from being slick. Then he cleared the snow off the car with a broom.

His muscles were good and sore by the time he finally slid the shed door shut. And he'd done some more thinking since Mick had left, too. There was a lot to piece together inside him right now. And yet . . . maybe he was beginning to feel some of those pieces slowly . . . falling into place.

The warmth of Candy's house wrapped around him the moment he stepped back inside. And when she greeted him with a big mug of hot chocolate, he tried not to laugh. As she took his gloves and coat, then tossed a cozy throw around his shoulders, he winked and said, "A guy could get used to this."

And he saw a flash of something in her eyes—like hope. But it disappeared just as fast. And he hated that. Hated disappointing her. Hated it in a way he felt in his gut. Because she deserved better. And she was . . . possibly the best person he'd ever known.

So he didn't hold back on what he was thinking now. Maybe the cold and hard work had muddied his head. Or . . . maybe it had cleared it. Either way, he said, "I'll think about it, Candy Cane."

"About what?" she asked.

"About . . . staying."

Her eyes lit—and something in his stomach tightened. Because he wasn't sure. He wasn't sure of anything.

It was simply that . . . maybe things were changing. Inside him. The same way they had for Mick. Maybe just hearing a guy like Mick—like *him*—acknowledge that, made it easier to acknowledge in himself.

"Not just for Anita, though," he told her.

"No?"

He shook his head, and was honest. With himself as much as with her. "For you. Because thing is . . . hell, I don't know much about love, Candy, but I'm thinking . . . I might just love you, too."

"Would you tell that guy I'm giving him the chance of a lifetime?"

Sam Wainwright, *It's a Wonderful Life*

Twenty-three

Candy looked understandably shocked, of course, her chest heaving slightly beneath the sweater she wore. He could feel her wanting to believe but also being afraid to. And with a guy like him, a guy who'd told her over and over that he was trouble and this was temporary, he couldn't blame her.

But the difference between her and pretty much every other woman he'd ever known was . . . she wasn't holding him to anything. She wasn't pushing him, or pulling him, or prodding him—she wasn't trying to make him do what she wanted. She'd let him just take his time and think about what *he* wanted.

"And I'm starting to think I'd be a fool to leave you," he told her. "That we should at least . . . see where things go. Between us."

Still, she appeared cautious as she asked softly, "What about the job?"

The job. God, it hardly seemed to matter at the moment. And the truth was, as hell-bent as he'd been on getting to Miami, he hadn't thought about the job much at all lately. It had fallen to the sidelines of his mind, behind Candy, behind Grampy and Edna, behind the Christmas party, behind the town of Destiny.

"It was . . . well, someplace to run to, if I'm honest. But what am I running from now?" He gave his head a slight shake. "I didn't have anything before, but now . . . I'm thinking maybe I do."

Candice had been trying to contain herself up to this point, but she felt herself starting to give in to . . . real hope for a future with him. She let herself begin to nod, meeting his gaze with her own. "You do, Shane," she promised him. "You do." Then she took the cup of hot chocolate from his hands, set it aside, lifted both palms to his stubbled, still-cold cheeks, and kissed him.

The warmth of his kiss poured through her, along with the joy of realizing dreams she'd been afraid to dream were actually maybe starting to come true. Part of her almost couldn't believe Shane had really just said he loved her, too, and that he might actually stay in Destiny, after all. But on the other hand, his staying made all the sense in the world. Now even more because his mother was here.

She got lost in the kisses as Shane's strong arms closed around her, wrapping her up in the cozy blanket with him, cocooning them together. She was so thankful she'd allowed him to . . . make her brave, with him, and with changing things in her life. Because look at them now.

When the kissing ended, she smiled up at him, her hands pressed to his chest, and said, "Maybe you should shovel snow more often if this is the effect it has on you."

They laughed together, and then snuggled on the couch near the lit Christmas tree. Frosty, predictably, jumped up and tried to wedge his way between them, but mostly ended up just sprawled across both their laps.

As Shane leaned his head back on the couch, she realized he was drifting to sleep, clearly tired from all the snow-shoveling, despite that it was early in the day. She was happy to just sit there, still cuddled with him, and soak in her new joy.

Of course, he'd only said he'd think about it—so maybe she shouldn't go assuming this was a done deal. But on the other hand, for a man like Shane, this felt . . . big. She was pretty sure he didn't go professing his love to a woman just every day. And up to now he'd sounded so determined to leave—Miami had seemed to represent such a new beginning to him that he'd refused to let go of that idea, to see that he could have a *better* new beginning someplace else. Until now. So it felt to Candice like . . . like he'd finally seen the light. And sometimes that really happened.

Other times it didn't. Wherever her father was, he'd never seen the light and come home. Bobby had never exactly seen the light, either. So maybe she'd lost faith in that somewhere along the way—faith in the notion that someone could suddenly just *get it,* change their mind, see what was good for them, what was right.

But now, suddenly, a future so much richer than anything she'd dreamed of was unfolding before her. She'd watched Tessa and so many other women find their unlikely Prince Charmings these past few years, and secretly she'd envied them, thinking she'd never get her own. And now Shane was changing that.

She soon gave in to the quiet, peaceful lull of the snow-covered day and let herself drift off to sleep against Shane's shoulder. Curled up against him and surrounded by warmth of so many kinds, it was the sweetest nap she'd ever taken.

She awoke an hour later to the gentle stirrings of Shane waking up, too. He seemed slightly surprised as he gave her a soft grin. "Whoa, I nodded off." Then he shifted his gaze toward the clock on the mantel. "What time is it?"

"Almost three," she replied, coming more fully awake.

That was when he got a faraway look in his eyes, something wistful she thought, and said, "If the roads are clear enough, would you mind driving me into town? To the church? Thinking I should see what's happening there and if I can help."

"Of course," she said. But she didn't make a big deal out of it. Out of the fact that he obviously cared enough about Anita's wedding to want to help make it happen.

She also didn't make a big deal out of it when he picked up the picture Anita had left with him before they walked out the door. Although it was framed, it was small enough to fit in his coat pocket, so he silently tucked it there.

Clearly he was dealing with this situation in his own

way. She knew he still had a lot of questions and confusion over what had happened to keep him and his mother apart all these years, but the very idea of his staying told her he was open to having her in his life. And Candice knew in her heart that was the best possible thing for both of them.

When they pulled up in front of the church, numerous cars and trucks populated the parking lot and the front doors stood wide open, making it clear people were inside assessing the situation.

"I'm having dinner at my mother's tonight at seven," she told him. "If you'd like to come." She felt a little sheepish just blurting that out, but honesty and openness seemed to work for her with Shane. "The truth is, word gets around in Destiny, and she's dying to meet you. But no pressure if you end up being here late or just want to hang out with Grampy or something. Whatever works for you."

"Tell you what," he said. "If you don't hear from me by six or so, assume I'm still helping out and I'll see you at your place later. Sound okay?"

She nodded, reminding him. "Back door's unlocked."

And he gave his head a short shake next to her in the car. "That's been driving me crazy, by the way."

But she just rolled her eyes. "This is Destiny, Shane. It's safe."

It surprised her a little when he laughed—until he said, "It's safe until some ax murderer type shows up at your door in a blizzard. You weren't so sure it was safe then—remember?"

She lowered her eyes sheepishly. "Well, turned out you weren't an ax murderer after all."

He gave her a sexy wink across the car. "Still trouble, Candy."

And as her whole body warmed, she cast him a small smile and said, "Well, if you're trouble, then it's the kind I'm looking for. And you can come to my door anytime."

And that was when he leaned over, placed his palm at the nape of her neck, and gave her a slow, steamy kiss goodbye. She watched him get out, thinking if he wasn't up for dinner with her mom tonight, it was no biggie—maybe he'd had enough of moms since yesterday. And on a lark, she lowered the passenger window and bent over to say, "Whether or not you come to dinner, afterward . . . you're going to be my dessert."

She watched his eyes widen for only a second before putting the window up and driving away, reveling in the new sense of confidence and sexuality Shane had given her. Or . . . given her *back*, after it had been stolen away so long ago.

Shane stood back watching and listening as Mick, Duke, Logan, and some of the other guys discussed the situation. Even as personally uninvolved in all this as he'd been up to now, it was a blow to see the newly replaced carpet and pews nearly as bad off as they'd been when the repairs had started a couple of weeks ago. Part of him couldn't believe his mother's bad luck.

The guys were, in turn, shaking their heads, mumbling things like, "Doesn't look good" and "I don't know about this, man."

And it was finally Mike Romo who spoke up to say, "In the interest of keeping it real, I'm gonna say what nobody else wants to. It can't be fixed in time. It's two days until Christmas Eve and it's physically impossible. Hell, we'd be hard put to have it back together by New Year's. I know nobody likes the idea of throwing in the towel on this, especially after all the hard work that's been put in, but the sad truth is—there's not going to be a wedding here on Christmas Eve."

The conversation continued, but Shane quietly slipped out, exiting through the front doors and back into the snow-covered Destiny day, and started making his way to the General Mercantile. He wasn't even sure why he was headed there at this point—he could easily call Candy and ask her to come back for him—but his mind was muddled by this news. Yeah, he'd heard Walter say the outlook was grim, but somehow he'd expected to get there and find a different conclusion. The people around here seemed pretty damn resourceful, and he supposed he'd just been waiting for some kind of Christmas miracle.

And now that there was no miracle . . . hell, maybe it brought him down a little from whatever cloud he'd been on the last few hours. Maybe it reminded him that nothing here was simple. Anita's wedding—or the cancellation of it—wouldn't be simple, and nothing about his relationship with her was simple.

And the cold hard truth was . . . he'd been suddenly acting like things with Candy were simple, but were they? Could any woman really be as giving and loving and undemanding as she seemed? Sure, she'd kind of blown his mind and hardened his cock with her promise of having him for dessert a little while ago, but realistically—how long would that last before it got more complicated?

Maybe it was a stupid worry just now, but somehow

the news that his mother's wedding wasn't going to come off as planned dropped a heavy dose of reality on him, thick as the blanket of snow that covered the ground and had collapsed the church roof again.

As he reached the Mercantile, he could see that Mick or someone else had cleared the snow away out front, and the parking lot had been plowed. He started toward the stairs in back that led to his rooms—when Grampy came out the front door, all bundled up in a parka and classic plaid hunting cap that covered his ears.

It was the first time he'd seen the old man since he'd gone rushing off in a sleigh, leaving Shane with a Santa suit and a job he didn't want—only about twenty-four hours ago, but it felt like much more time had passed given all that had happened between then and now.

Grampy cut right to the heart of things. "Heard ya got some shockin' news."

That was part of what had made him decide to leave the church—the sudden notion that once attention shifted from the repairs, it would turn to his *shockin' news*. So he'd run into exactly what he'd been trying to escape. "I don't really want to talk about it," he said, and kept on his path around the building.

It came as a relief when Grampy replied, "Fair enough. I'll leave ya alone then."

And normally Shane would have kept walking—but curiosity got the best of him when he remembered he wasn't the only one dealing with some drama. So he stopped, looked back. "How'd things go with Edna?"

Grampy broke into a big smile, maybe even bigger than when he'd seen his Christmas tree. "Real well. Real well indeed. And it's thanks to you."

This news did Shane's heart some good. "Well, I'm

glad it's working out for you." He nodded, cast the old guy a cursory smile, then went on his way again.

"Things could work out for you, too."

He stopped, sighed, and gave Grampy a look. "So much for not talking about it."

"I'll just say this one thing, then let ya be," Grampy told him. "Way I see it is . . . I know you've had your mind set on this job down in Florida. But seems to me things keep stackin' up here, things that are reasons to stay. There's nothin' waitin' for ya there, son. But here . . . there's a lot."

Shane knew that. He'd told Candy that very thing, more or less. And an hour ago, he'd started feeling pretty damned comfortable with the idea of staying, and with everything that it held—maybe even a future that included his mother. Now he guessed he just wanted some time alone to digest it all. So he said to Grampy, "I'm aware. Of the reasons."

"One of 'em is me," Grampy said then, catching him off guard.

And Shane squinted in his direction. "Huh?"

"I figured ya think I mean Candice and Anita. And I do. But I'm bein' selfish here, too. Maybe it seems like I got a hundred friends in this town, but . . . I like havin' you around is all. And I hope ya know I'm there for ya. If ya need anything."

Shane just nodded. "I do know. I've known it since you offered me a place to stay. Guess I just . . . need to do some thinking. Getting used to it all."

Grampy tipped his head back. "So you're sayin' ya might not leave, after all?"

Another short nod from Shane. "It's possible."

Then he turned and went on his way.

He was climbing the steps behind the Mercantile when his cell phone trilled from his pocket. "What now?" he muttered. Seemed the world had a way of bothering a guy at the moment when he most wanted to be left to himself.

But when he saw the call was from A1 Body Shop, he answered.

"Good news," said the voice on the other end. "Your truck's all ready to go."

Huh. "That *is* good news." It would be a relief to have his own wheels again. "I'll, uh, have to make arrangements to come get it."

"Mo told us your situation," the A1 guy said. "You're without transportation, right?"

"Right."

"We can send somebody to pick ya up if ya like."

Damn—sometimes he forgot how nice people were around here. And he doubted he'd get that same kind of offer in Miami, or most other places for that matter. "I'll take you up on that," he said.

An hour later, he was driving his newly painted pickup back to Destiny from Crestview.

It felt odd in a way—because the last time he'd been behind the wheel, driving this truck into Destiny, he'd wrecked and met Candy in the blizzard. He'd been passing through, just looking to solve a little mystery laid out by his father. Well, now he'd solved it—though part of him wished he hadn't. Part of him wished things had stayed the way they were—where he'd understood who he was and what his life was about, where he'd had all the answers.

So the same heaviness that had weighed him down earlier still hung about him as he parked behind the Mercantile and again climbed the steps to his sparsely appointed little room.

It was sure a hell of a lot more comfortable at Candy's—and he knew he could drive there right now and be greeted by her silly cat and a warm fire and her sweet embrace, and he could go have a nice home-cooked meal with her mother, who would probably be as kind and welcoming as everyone else in Destiny. And the General Mercantile was closed for the day now, but if he wanted a different kind of company, he could just as easily drive to Grampy's place. He could go to Dolly's Café for some pie or even stop by Edna's for some peppermint bark. He'd be welcome at all those places and more.

And yet . . . it was all suddenly making him uncomfortable.

It was a hell of a lot to deal with, all these people—especially now that one of them was his mother.

His mother.

Believe her and it made his entire relationship with his father a lie. Don't believe her and . . . well, if he didn't believe her, he couldn't stay here. Because if he stayed here, she'd be in his life. It was too small of a town to keep it from being that way. And maybe he wasn't ready for that.

Maybe, deep down, he wasn't sure he was ready for any of this. Promises. Commitments. Friends. Love.

After all, before making that fated turn toward this little town, he didn't have to worry about any of that. All he'd had to worry about was getting to Miami on time and doing a job he'd be good at and making big money.

Damn, that almost sounded nice again. Or, well, simple anyway. And it was the Christmas he'd planned on.

What are you really gonna do here anyway? Sponge off people some more? Get a low-paying gig at the A1 Body Shop? Tie yourself into a relationship with the mother who abandoned you? Commit to a woman who, in reality, barely knows you? She doesn't see the bad in you now, but she's bound to sooner or later.

And hell—already she was wanting to "take him home to Mom"?

Maybe things would feel different—better, like he had options—if his job in Miami didn't come with an expiration date. And yeah, it might not seem like the most aboveboard operation in the world, but another opportunity to make this kind of cash would be hard to come by. And this particular opportunity came without . . . weight. It sounded so damn easy right now compared to staying here.

And the fact was—he could still make it to Miami on time.

He could pack up his clothes, throw his duffels back in the pickup, and go. The same way he'd planned to all along.

And the more he thought about the simplicity of that plan, and about things like sun and sand and endless summer, the more it just . . . made sense.

Enough that he found himself doing just that—cramming clothes into the duffel bags he'd been traveling with, packing up stuff from the little bathroom.

Enough that his heart beat faster with the decision,

with the rightness of it. Or at least the ease of it. A few hours ago, staying in Destiny had started sounding good to him. But he'd just been . . . a little bit brainwashed or something. Because what sounded good now was leaving. And forgetting this place as fast as he could.

As darkness fell and he threw his stuff in the truck, though, he knew there were a few things he had to do before hitting the road. It required a couple of stops and spending a last chunk of what little money he had—but he methodically made those stops, his heart still pounding the whole time.

And on the way out of town, he stopped his truck on town square and got out. A few people sprinkled the sidewalks, coming and going at Dolly's or taking in the splendor of the big Christmas tree glowing in the night. And Shane took it in, too—all of it. The peaceful blanket of snow. Wreathes on lampposts. Frosted windowpanes on storefronts.

If you want to forget this place so bad, what are you doing?

But he cut himself a break. A lot had happened here, all of it completely unexpected. So maybe he was just taking a minute to . . . disconnect.

Soon enough, though, a brisk wind cut through him—and a few flakes of snow began to fall from the sky.

Time to get the hell out of Destiny before he didn't have the choice anymore.

As he climbed in the truck, he felt thankful to have warm gloves on his hands, and he thought of Candy, and something in his gut pinched.

But just ignore that. You're heading south, and by morning, you won't even need the damn gloves anymore.

"Strange, isn't it? Each man's life touches so many other lives, and when he isn't around he leaves an awful hole, doesn't he?"

Clarence Odbody, Angel 2nd Class, *It's a Wonderful Life*

Twenty-four

Candice walked up onto her front porch to see the glow of the Christmas tree in the window along with the silhouette of a certain cat on the windowsill. Her heart warmed as she pushed her way through the door, eager to find Shane inside and very ready for the earlier-promised dessert.

When she didn't see him in the living room, she called, "Shane? Are you here?"

She didn't get an answer. And nothing stirred. And her heart dropped a little.

A few lights were on, but they were the same she'd left illuminated for the cat when she'd left. And that was when it hit her that if Shane was here, he'd have probably built a fire—and the hearth was dark and cold and gray with ashes.

Well, it was disappointing that dessert would have to wait, but surely he'd arrive soon. And with that thought, she reached in her purse and pulled out her phone to check for messages. No calls, though, and no texts. Which seemed . . . off. It was after ten and she'd have thought if he wasn't going to be here by now, he'd have let her know.

She was just about to text him, hoping nothing was wrong, when Frosty came bounding down from the wide sill and trotted over to her. And as she sat down on the sofa and bent to pet him, she spotted something attached to his collar.

She narrowed her gaze to see . . . a tiny gift. A little box wrapped in silver paper and topped with a metallic blue bow. "What the heck . . . ?" she murmured, reaching for the cat, pulling him up beside her.

But then—oh, was this some sort of surprise from Shane? She smiled down at Frosty, because this was the cutest idea ever. And maybe . . . maybe she would soon find out Shane *was* here somewhere. Maybe waiting for her in bed? And maybe he hadn't answered because this was some fun, sexy plan—like a scavenger hunt that would lead her to him?

She bit her lip as she detached the little gift from Frosty's collar, thinking this was the perfect homecoming, and that if it led to Shane, he was definitely the perfect Christmas gift.

She tore off the silver wrapping, then lifted the lid from the little box—to find a locket. *The* locket. The one he'd seen her looking at in town on the night of the snowcat contest. Her heart flooded with even more love for him as she picked up the silver locket with one hand and pressed the other to her chest. Knowing he didn't have the money for this made her feel bad, but also told her how much he must have wanted to give it to her.

It had been cradled in the box by a piece of paper, folded up small, so she set the necklace carefully aside on the coffee table and pulled out the paper to discover a handwritten note.

I can't replace the picture inside, but I hope this helps you keep the memory of it anyway. And maybe this will help you remember me, too. I'm sorry, Candy, but I just can't stay.

Shane

Candice just sat there, staring at the words. They didn't seem real. Nothing *about* this seemed real.

Because . . . she'd known he still might not stay. Even if her heart had told her he would, she'd known that wasn't definite or final. But she'd never dreamed he would just . . . leave. Like this. Without even telling her. Without even giving her a chance to say goodbye. To kiss him, hold him, one last time. She'd never dreamed things could end so suddenly, without a shred of warning.

It made everything between them feel like . . . less. If he could just walk away so very easily—again, without even a goodbye, without even seeing her one last time—well, she must have been a lot less important to him than she'd begun to feel. Everything they'd done together, every moment they'd spent together, must have been . . . nothing.

Stop this. You went into this with your eyes wide open. You knew it was a fling. You knew it was temporary. You even knew he was trouble—because he told you, over and over. And you decided it would be worth it anyway.

You also knew it would hurt, but you decided that would be worth it, too.

You just never saw it ending . . . this way.

And . . . okay, after what he said this afternoon, you'd quit believing it would really end at all.

She shut her eyes, trying to crush back the tears gathering behind them. *Oh God, this really does hurt. I forgot. How much.* But now she remembered. Now she remembered why she'd kept to herself for so long, why she hadn't wanted to risk heartbreak again. Now she remembered that it felt like having your heart and soul ripped out.

But at least he hadn't done anything terrible to her. He hadn't betrayed her or taken anything from her.

All he'd done was . . . what he'd told her from the start. He'd left.

So she didn't even have the right to be mad—at least not technically speaking.

Even if the choice seemed cold.

Though he clearly thought a gift would smooth things over, make it better.

Apparently he did toss the word love around a lot more easily than she did. If there was a crime here, it was that he'd let her think he cared. He'd let her think he loved her, too. And even if he'd only told her that today, the way things were between them had, deep down, made her feel it before that.

Finally, she burst into tears. Great, heaping, buckled-over, sobbing tears. She lay down on the couch, hugging a throw pillow to her as she bawled, vaguely aware of Frosty sitting on the coffee table staring at her. One more man had walked out of her life.

"Well, it's just you and me again," she murmured to the cat through her tears.

"Meow," he said.

"But hey, that's not so bad," she went on, trying to stop crying. "We were just fine before him—we'll be fine after him."

Only as she said the words, she realized why they were a lie. They were fine before they had a taste of something really special, really grand, a richer life full of love and companionship and sex and . . . completeness.

And sure, like every modern woman, Candice wanted to feel complete without a man—hell, she *had* felt complete without a man. But something about having Shane in her life, in her home, falling in love with him . . . had made her world undeniably sweeter, better, fuller. And once you have that and then it's gone, are you really ever as fine as you were before?

She sighed, letting her eyes fall shut as this new sense of emptiness settled deep in her bones. Turned out Shane was trouble after all. Just a different kind than she'd ever feared. He was the kind of trouble that doesn't even say goodbye.

* * *

Grampy looked around the General Mercantile at everyone who had gathered when he'd spread the word to meet at the store at noon. One face was notably absent.

He'd found a note on the Mercantile's door this morning:

Thanks for all you did for me. I won't forget it, or you.

Shane

And the fact was, it hurt him. Losing the young man's company, his presence. And it hurt because he thought Shane had made the wrong decision and would likely lead a worse life for it. And it hurt that he'd gone so suddenly, without any sort of proper farewell.

Candice Sheridan stood near the doorway, near Tessa and Lucky Romo. Her cheeks were tear-stained and her eyes tired, and he thought it was mighty nice that she'd dragged herself out here in the cold when she'd probably rather huddle up in that big house of hers licking her wounds.

But Christmas Eve was tomorrow, and he couldn't stop the clock. And if Anita's boy had left . . . well, Grampy felt compelled to do *something* to try to make things better for the woman. Whether or not it would work was another matter.

According to Jenny Brody, word had already reached Anita that Shane had gone, and of course she wasn't taking it well. Jenny had told Grampy that between that and the church roof cave-in, she didn't think there was going to be a wedding tomorrow.

But Grampy hoped to change that. This town was good at banding together in times of trouble—and since this was just one more troubled time, he knew they could find a solution if they worked together.

"Here's what I'm thinkin'," Grampy said to everyone crowded into the store. "Our friends Anita and Walter have planned 'em a weddin' tomorrow. And just 'cause it can't take place at the church don't mean it can't happen someplace else. So I'm proposin' we figure out how to throw those two the perfect weddin' tomorrow night, a weddin' that'll make Anita forget all about that church—and about anything else sad. Now who's got any ideas?"

The crowd stayed quiet, until Jenny said, "I suggested having the whole thing at the Dew Drop, but Anita said no. And I guess I can understand that." And so could Grampy. Anita's bar was a fine enough place to meet up with friends, but the one-story cinderblock building didn't possess much ambience.

"I'm sure any of us would open up our homes for the wedding," Tessa said, "but most of them aren't large enough."

"And if it were any other season but winter, we could do it in Creekside Park," Amy volunteered, "or in someone's backyard."

"Yeah," Logan said on a sigh, "wintertime makes it tough. Really limits the options."

"Unless," Grampy said, giving his head a thoughtful tilt, "we just kinda . . . embrace the weather. It worked for the Christmas party at Miss Ellie's, after all."

"Just what are you brewin' up in that brain o' yours, old man?" Edna asked from his right.

He gave her a quick glance, complete with a grin, and

then said to everyone, "What about a weddin' on town square? Right next to the Christmas tree. Me myself, I can't think of a prettier sight in all o' Destiny."

He could see the idea percolating in folks' heads, could see them trying to get past the obvious draw-backs and wrap their minds around it.

Mike Romo said hopefully, "Walking paths have already been cleared there—we'd only have to remove enough snow to set up some chairs."

"And we can use the same outdoor heaters the town bought for the party at Miss Ellie's," Adam added.

"And God knows this town can provide hot chocolate to keep people warm, too," Candice chimed in with a small smile, and Grampy was happy to see a spark of light back in her eye.

Edna added to the idea then by saying, "Ya know, I got me a barn that fixes up real perty in every other season—don't see why it wouldn't fix up nice in winter, too. We just move them heaters over after the weddin' and it'd be a good place for a party after."

"Well then," Grampy concluded, "given that time ain't on our side, I'm thinkin' we need to get to work on this lickety split."

Mike Romo spoke up again. "I'll head up the barn preparations with Rachel and Logan and whoever else wants to join us." That made sense since he and Rachel ran the orchard along with Edna.

And Adam said, "I'll take on the town square prep with Mick—we'll both put our snowblowers to some more good use." He tossed a laugh in Mick's direction.

"Sounds good to me," Mick said. "Whatever it takes to make this happen."

"All right then, people," Grampy said, heartened by it all, "we got ourselves a plan."

Though as people started to disperse, eager to get to work on the two venues, Grampy's gaze landed on Candice, still clearly in the throes of heartbreak—and he started across the store toward her. He knew good and well he couldn't fix the situation, but he felt obliged to acknowledge her grief.

He spoke low. "I'm so sorry, darlin', about Shane leavin'."

Candice looked up, tried to smile at him but failed, so she just gave a short nod instead. "Me too."

"It's a disappointment for . . . well, quite a few of us, in different ways. I'm gonna miss the boy pretty dang bad myself. But . . . I'm grateful for the time he was here. And I know it's early days and a whole different type of emotion, but I hope you'll come to feel that way as well."

Before Candice could even formulate a reply, though, Jenny came over to them both and said, "Grampy, don't get me wrong, this whole idea is amazing—but . . . I'm not sure how we're going to convince Anita. Dad says she's completely despondent since hearing Shane left." She shook her head. "I still can't believe it. They find each other after twenty-five years—and he leaves after one day."

And without even weighing her words, Candice said, "I think he was just . . . scared of caring. Trusting. You know—like we all are once we've been hurt." And then she tilted her head, realizing that the more she thought about it, the more sense it made. "That's all it was. Being afraid to care."

Just like *she'd* been afraid to care about *him* at first. Some people could make that leap . . . and others couldn't. It didn't make him a bad person. It just meant . . . she wouldn't have him in her life to love. Which was still heartbreaking—but, well, she'd just love him from afar. And maybe always be sad for . . . not getting to explore that. But she wouldn't be angry with him for it.

"You knew Shane best," Jenny said to Candice. "Maybe you could shed some light on the situation for Anita, say something to help her feel better."

Candice didn't look forward to seeing the devastated woman, but she could hardly turn down the request. Especially when Grampy suggested to her, "Why don't you and me go see Anita together?"

When Anita answered the door—likely only because Grampy wouldn't stop knocking—Candice barely recognized her. In a bathrobe, with no makeup and her hair uncombed, she looked older than Candice had ever thought about her being. Maybe she hid it well in public, but suddenly Candice saw years of worry and strife in the lines beneath Anita's eyes and the paleness of her lips.

She didn't attempt a smile as she said, "What's so important that you keep banging on my door?"

Candice sensed that Grampy was taken aback, too—this wasn't Anita's usual way—but he asked, "Can we come in?"

"Not really in the mood for company," she said, her voice softer now, but her expression downright haggard.

"It's important," Grampy insisted, then pretty much stepped right past her into her living room—so Candice followed.

It was a modest home made even more so by the fact that, other than the furniture, everything had been packed into boxes for her move to Walter's house.

She turned from the door to face them. "Look, I know he's gone, and I know I'm the reason. If you came over to try to make me feel better, that's real nice, but this isn't the kind of thing a person gets over. Never did before—sure won't now."

The tension lay so thick across the room that Candice's first instinct was to retreat, leave, let Anita mourn in her own way. But Grampy persevered, taking a step toward her. "I'd never expect ya to get over it, but ya can't let it eat ya alive, either. You've been plannin' this weddin' a long time now, and I think you'd be a whole lot happier if you follow through with it and marry Walter tomorrow."

At the very mention of the wedding, Anita appeared all the more deflated. "Of course I want to marry Walter," she said. Then shook her head. "But I want it to be *right*, want it to be a *happy* wedding—because Walter deserves that."

"He does, and so do you," Grampy said. "And you can still have that tomorrow."

Her eyes opened wider on him, her look laced with uncharacteristic sarcasm. "Is that so? I'm sorry, but just where do you think we're going to have this happy wedding?"

"Town square," Grampy said simply. "Everybody's workin' on it right now." And as he went on, explaining in more detail, Candice saw Anita warring with her emotions.

She was clearly touched to hear the whole town was pulling together yet again on her behalf. "Took me a long time to feel like a real part of things here," she said, "and I guess this means I really am now. But . . ." She shook her head once more, dropped her gaze to the floor. "I just don't know if I can. So much has happened and I'm just so tired. My heart's broken into pieces right now."

And since Candice knew that part was about Shane, she took it as her cue to step up and take one of Anita's hands into hers. "Mine is, too," she assured the other woman. "But the thing is—he only left because he was afraid. Afraid of facing that his dad lied to him about you. Afraid of facing the past. Afraid of caring." Then the spot behind her eyes ached with a further truth that made her shut them tight for a second. "And it's possible I *pushed* him into leaving. I . . . I told him I loved him. And he acted okay with it, but I think, now, that maybe he just wasn't ready for that. Ready for *any* of this—me, you, everything. But . . . that doesn't mean he didn't care. About me. And about you, too."

Anita cautiously lifted her eyes and spoke quietly, somberly. "I don't have any reason to think he cared. In fact, I think he wishes he'd never laid eyes on me. That I was a complication he didn't need."

"I saw the way he hugged you," Candice said. "I saw the look on his face. And . . . he took the picture. The one you gave him. He took it with him. It's a small thing, maybe, but if he hadn't cared, he wouldn't have taken it. And what's between you two is complicated at best, I know—but I believe with my whole heart that he loves you. And that he knows *you* love *him*. And . . . that might just have to be enough. For you to know he's alive and well. To know you got to tell him you love him. To know he took that in and will always have it now." She stopped, shook her head. "But you can't let it steal the rest of the happiness in your life."

Anita drew in a breath, let it back out—and met Candice's gaze. "What about you?" she asked gently. "Are you going to let losing him steal *your* happiness?"

The loss still felt like an anchor on Candice's shoulders, chest. Every time she remembered he was gone, it got hard to breathe. She hadn't slept last night—mostly just cried on her pillow. But she said to Anita, "That's why I'm here right now. I'm trying to just . . . go on. Because even as much as this is killing me, I guess I think the best thing to do is try to go on."

"She's right, you know," Grampy said. "Everything else is just lost time. The more ya make yourself go on, the sooner ya get back to livin'. So what do you think, m'dear? You wanna put on a pretty dress tomorrow night and get married beneath the lights of that big Christmas tree? You wanna go on livin'?"

Anita appeared wholly uncertain about all of it, and Candice had no idea how the other woman was going to respond—until she looked at Grampy and said, "One condition. My parents died a long time ago, and so . . . would you do me the honor of givin' me away?"

Grampy's eyes lit at the request and Candice understood: This is what happens when you do go on living despite the bad things. You get that—to live. To love. And to celebrate the joys when they come.

* * *

Ohio and Kentucky had been snow-covered, along with the mountains of northern Tennessee. But by the time he crossed over the Georgia state line, the snowy weather was nothing but a memory. Like the rest of it would be soon. *Just gotta get to Miami and everything else will fade.*

As Shane pumped gas into his truck just off I-75 in Adairsville, Georgia, The Kinks singing "Father Christmas" over gas station loudspeakers, he reached into his coat pocket in search of his wallet—and instead pulled out the picture of him and his mother.

He hadn't taken the coat off since leaving Destiny— he'd driven most of the night, then slept for a while in his truck at a rest stop in Tennessee after reaching warm enough temperatures for that—or the picture wouldn't still be there. He didn't want to look at it and tried not to see it, but it was too late.

He peered first at the woman next to him in the frame. Remembered that woman. Her smile brought back . . . warmer memories than most of the ones he'd spent his life focusing on. He'd always recalled her being angry with him, disappointed—but this picture . . . it forced him to remember times long forgotten. It forced him to remember . . . laughter, playgrounds, picnics, holidays. It forced him to remember . . . she *had* loved him.

But when the pump shut off, he shoved the picture back in his pocket. He didn't want to think any more about that, or about what it meant regarding his father's version of things. Because like he'd told Anita, none of it mattered anyway. Maybe all that mattered was leaving this shit behind and getting back to the business of his new life. It was going to be a hell of a lot simpler, that was for sure.

Simpler than dealing with his mother.

Simpler than getting too serious too fast with Candy. She'd been . . . fun. Special, even. She was a great girl.

And something tightened in his chest when he allowed himself to wonder, just a little, if she would miss him now that he was gone. If it would change her life in any real way.

But probably not. People came and went in each other's lives all the time. And who was he to think he was important enough to change somebody's life? No matter what Clarence the Angel had said about people leaving a void.

His future was in Miami, and he was glad to finally be on his way to the existence he'd been aiming for when he'd left Montana, finally back on track. *Fast cars, fast women, fun in the sun—here I come, baby.* There was no looking back now.

"Every time you hear a bell ring, it means that some angel's just got his wings."

Clarence Odbody, Angel 2nd Class, *It's a Wonderful Life*

Twenty-five

As Candice stood across from town square, outside Amy's bookshop, just after dark on Christmas Eve, she couldn't believe it, but she felt . . . happy. Okay, not when Shane came to mind—she still ached at missing his touch and longing to look into his eyes and even just yearning to see his thick, cuddle-worthy socks because apparently he'd created in her some sort of bizarre man-sock fetish—but as people began to gather for Anita and Walter's wedding, the scene warmed her heart.

The square was aglow with thousands of twinkling colored lights on the big Christmas tree that Grampy loved so much, and Mick and Adam had strung white lights from poles and draped more in the smaller trees around the grouping of white chairs. Red velvet bows adorned the chairs along the center aisle.

The day had been bright and mild, leaving temps warmer than they'd been in weeks, and though it was still winter out, between the temperatures and the portable heaters, the air felt quite tolerable. Given the change in venue, the event had been declared casual, so many guests were arriving in blue jeans and parkas, but she still saw little girls dressed up in their Christmas best, a few men wearing suits and overcoats, and women in brightly colored coats and hats and scarves. The guitar player hired for the occasion had set up near one of the heaters and gently strummed pleasant acoustic versions of Christmas carols.

The bookstore served as Anita's dressing room, while Walter got ready in his office at the police station across the square. When Candice opened the shop door and peeked in, she saw Anita wearing a lovely long white gown, a white faux fur cape around her shoulders. She gasped and said, "The white fur is perfect! You look like a snow princess."

"It belongs to my mother," Amy said merrily, looking up from where she stood nearby. "She insisted Anita use it when she found out the wedding was outside."

As Candice stepped in and let the door shut behind her, Anita laughed and said, "I'm a little too old to be a princess, but maybe . . . a snow queen?"

"Absolutely," Jenny said, standing behind Anita in a long-sleeved red dress, adjusting the veil as they both peered into a standing oval mirror brought in for the occasion. Jenny and Mick were serving as the matron of honor and best man, and of course little Dustin would be the ring bearer. In the corner, Rachel was putting a sparkly white cardigan sweater onto her little girl, over her fluffy red flower girl dress.

"It's so good to hear you laugh," Candice told Anita.

Anita glanced up at her, her expression wistful. "I still wish Shane were here, of course, but you and Grampy were right—it's better to push on and keep living."

Candice stooped down beside where Anita sat and said to her privately, "For what it's worth, Shane wouldn't have wanted to mess up your wedding. Even as recently as the day before yesterday, he was up at the church seeing if he could help with anything."

Anita tilted her head, looking surprised, touched, and Candice realized why that mattered and that she probably should have mentioned it before. She squeezed Anita's hand and said, "I'll leave you to the rest of your preparations. Only fifteen minutes until wedding time."

Though as Candice stepped back out into the chill, again taking in the lovely scene, her heart wilted a little. Because the truth was . . . this wedding was a grand distraction. And maybe she'd wanted Anita to go through with it as much for Candice's sake as for her own. Candice had spent the day working with a large group in Edna's barn, getting it decorated for tonight. She'd run errands and helped set up portable fire pits and tables and chairs. She'd made table decorations involving sprigs of holly and candles and Mason jars.

And tomorrow it would be over.

Not for Anita. She and Walter were honeymooning in the Caribbean, taking a cruise. And she was moving in with Walter, and contemplating selling the Dew Drop Inn in order to spend more time with him, and with little Dustin. Anita had lots of big changes and a whole new existence on the horizon.

And even Grampy had a fun, new aspect of his life. He and Edna were suddenly . . . dating or something. Which everyone in town thought was adorable and that it was about time, Candice included.

But for Candice, after tomorrow, after Christmas, life would return to the same old boring routine as before Shane had come knocking on her door in the middle of the night. He'd blown into town with that blizzard—and then blown right back out again. And what she had to show for the whole thing was . . . a whole lot of snow. And some grand memories. And the locket she wore beneath her coat right now.

She reached up instinctively, pressed her mitten to it through the coat, and felt the hard metal against her chest.

That was when the bookshop's door opened to let Anita, Jenny, and the rest of the ladies—as well as little Farris—exit, ready for Anita's walk down the aisle. "You look beautiful, Anita," Candice told her—and she truly did.

A few minutes later, the crowd was all seated and Walter and Mick stood near the Christmas tree along with a minister. As the guitar player strummed "What Child Is This?", Jenny walked up the aisle, followed by adorable Dustin and Farris, who sprinkled poinsettia blossoms along the way. At one point, Farris started drifting toward her dad, Mike, in one of the white chairs, but Dustin took her hand and drew her the rest of the way up the aisle where his parents and grandpa waited, gently coaxing him forward.

Candice sat on the aisle in the back row, near where Grampy and Anita now stood. As Anita looped her arm through his, it gently began to snow—and even as much drama as snow had caused in Destiny this past month, something about the timing of *this* snow felt magical, and a few people even gasped in wonder.

"You ready to put bad times behind you, m'dear?" Candice heard Grampy whisper.

Anita's smile looked slightly strained yet sincere as she said, "Yes."

And that was when Candice saw . . . the strangest thing, a . . . a vision or something. She tilted her head, focusing, trying to make sense of it. The lighting was dim, but . . . a man who looked remarkably like Shane stood a few feet behind the bride and her escort.

Then he cautiously stepped up behind Grampy and Anita to ask, "Am I . . . too late?"

Candice gasped as her heart leaped to her throat, and even lifted her mittened hand to cover her mouth. Because he wasn't a vision at all—he was flesh and bone.

"N-no," Anita stammered, looking just as shocked as she had the other day in Miss Ellie's garden upon figuring out he was her son.

Now Shane switched his gaze back and forth between Grampy and Anita. "Can I . . . cut in?"

"Good Lord, of course," Grampy said, stepping aside. "This is where you belong, son."

Funny how quickly things could change. Candice had never been to a wedding filled with more joy. She could truly feel the love and elation just spilling from Anita as Shane walked her down the snowy aisle toward Walter. She could feel Walter's happiness, too, and everyone's actually—there was hardly a dry eye on the Destiny town square when the minister asked who gave this woman to be wed and Shane quietly said, "Her son." Even every snowflake that fell on lips and noses and shoulders felt infused with pure Christmas joy.

She could scarcely believe Shane had come back. And it only made her love him more that he'd done the right thing—for Anita. He was clearly ready to embark on a relationship with his mother and begin letting go of the past.

But when the wedding was over, she realized she was almost nervous about facing him herself. Because he'd come back here to walk his mother down the aisle, but that didn't change the fact that he'd left Candice behind.

So it was almost a relief when people swarmed him right after—Grampy and all the new friends he'd made in town. And it made it easy to slink quickly away toward her car by herself.

Walter and Anita headed to the reception at Edna's barn in grand fashion—driving Grampy's sleigh—and the wedding guests formed a caravan of cars behind it, following them down the road, across the stone bridge, and into the orchard.

Once there, Candice busied herself with greeting people and some final setup—she took charge of turning on the music to hear Elvis singing "I'll Be Home For Christmas" through speakers she'd helped put in place earlier. She had no idea where Shane was—or for that matter if he'd even attend the reception. Of course, it would only make sense given that he'd come back all this way for it, but who knew? Yes, he'd come home for Christmas, but maybe he was still heading to Miami and had to leave right away. Maybe he still didn't see Destiny as home for him at all, and in fact, perhaps it was even presumptuous to think he should. Her mind spun with questions and emotions as she straightened red napkins beside a tower of candy canes and white cupcakes.

And that was when a touch came on her arm and she looked up into Shane's captivating blue gaze.

"Hey," he said softly.

"Hey," she whispered, the one word coming out shaky. Like she felt inside.

"I'm . . . sorry for the way I left, Candy."

She nodded quickly. "It's . . . it's okay. I know you must have been feeling under a lot of pressure."

"It was still the wrong way to handle it," he told her. "Did, uh, Frosty deliver my present?"

It struck her again how adorable it was that he'd attached the gift to her kitty. "Yes," she said. "Thank you. I'm wearing it now." Though, crap, she hadn't exactly meant to say that part. It made the locket sound so special to her. Like she would cherish it always. Which was true. But at the moment she didn't need *him* knowing what a lovesick fool she was.

"Did you already put a picture of your father in it?" he asked, sounding a little surprised she had the necklace on.

She shook her head. And blurted out another truth. Because apparently she couldn't stop. Apparently she was a truth machine. "No, I put one of you in it. From my phone. The one I took next to the fire that time Frosty was climbing all over you and making me laugh. I printed it out." *And clearly intend to treasure the one picture I have of you.* Good Lord, shut up. "Because . . . you gave it to me. And my father never actually gave me much of anything. So I just . . . thought it made more sense." *Because I'm clearly in love with you and can't stop making that painfully obvious.* Then she shook her head. "I haven't had much sleep lately." *Oh God, stop it.* She'd meant to explain why she was babbling incoherently, but instead it pretty much only confirmed that she'd lost sleep over his departure. Truth machine.

And all of that embarrassing truth made her decide she might as well just put the rest of her thoughts on the table, too. "It's really great you came back for the wedding, Shane. I'm so glad you did. And it's . . . really wonderful to see you. And I love the locket. And I don't know what your plans are, but I realize I probably made more of things between us than you wanted." Her heart beat so hard just taking him in, feeling his presence, looking into those eyes, that she thought it might consume her. "So I know this doesn't change anything between us."

Just then, Anita came rushing up, and turning to the crowd at large she said, "Everyone! Everyone! If you haven't already met him, I want to introduce you all to my handsome son, Shane!" She looked into his eyes for the next part. "Having him here to give me away to Walter has made this truly the happiest day of my life."

Everyone applauded, the barn filled with warmth despite the cold outside, and the announcement seemed to open the door to another one, especially since Tessa was nudging her sister-in-law Anna, saying, "Tell them, tell them!"

Anna made a shushing face at Tessa and, looking a little embarrassed, said, "Oh—no, this is Anita and Walter's night. My news can wait for another time."

Anita, however, was quick to smile and say, "Anna, honey, this is a joyous night, and if there's more good news around here, I want to hear it!"

So Anna said, "Well, okay—if you're sure." Then she glanced toward her longtime boyfriend, Duke Dawson, and said with a smile, "Looks like we're next. Before coming to the wedding tonight, Duke made me peek in my stocking hanging from the mantel—and I found an engagement ring inside."

Duke and Anna had been together so long now that the crowd cheered, and Duke stepped up to say, "Guess seeing what Anita and Walter went through to get married made me realize it's time I make an honest woman outta this one," and he wrapped his arm around Anna's shoulder and kissed her.

And that was when Amy said, "Okay, I wasn't gonna do this here, but I guess I will." She glanced over at Anita then, who made approving, prodding motions for her to go on, then smiled back at the whole barn full of people. "I'm happy to tell you all that Logan and I will soon be adding another member to our family." However, given that they already had two cats and a dog, and that Amy was cat-crazy, everyone silently assumed she only meant another cat until she added, "We're having a baby next summer!"

Again, the crowd applauded and broke into even wider grins—but Amy interrupted to say, "And this seems like the perfect time to give Walter and Anita my present to them."

Despite it not being customary to force the bride and groom to open their gifts in the middle of the reception before even a toast had been made, people were used to humoring Amy in certain ways, so they did so now as she carried a box up to Anita, with Walter now standing at her side.

Walter took the box, holding it while Anita removed the lid—and looked utterly dumbstruck as she said, "A cat!" Holly from the bookstore, to be exact. Then she started looking around, appearing slightly panicked, her eyes finally landing on Amy. "This is sweet, Amy, really, but . . . I don't know about having a cat."

Yet Amy seemed undaunted. "You'll *love* having a cat! And this one really needs a home! And she's sweet as can be—ask anyone."

Anita's eyes resumed darting around, apparently seeking some other, more willing victim—the full measure of her desperation showing when her gaze stuck on Shane. "Wouldn't *you* like this nice cat?"

But he only threw up his hands. "Who, me? No, I already have a cat with Candice. Frosty is weird enough—we don't need another one."

And Candice spun her head to look at him, feeling a little confused—and like she might actually faint—as she tried to take in his words. "You already have a cat? With me?"

The crowd's attention was back on Anita and Walter now as Shane said to her, "If . . . you want things that way. If you don't, though, I understand."

She blinked. "I . . . thought you just came back for the wedding."

Yet Shane shook his head. "That was part of it, sure. But not all of it."

She remained a little breathless. "Well, maybe you could tell me the rest."

Next to her, he let out a sigh, looked into her eyes, and said, "As I was driving south, I guess I was thinking about George Bailey. And . . . well, before coming here, I wouldn't have believed much of anybody would miss me if I was gone, but you made me feel . . . important, like I mattered. And I realized I was leaving behind the best person to ever enter my life. And why the hell would I do that? I mean, I was going to Miami looking for a new beginning and looking for . . . some new kind of happy, you know? When I'd already found that—here, with you. If . . . if you're as into me as I am into you, that is."

Still struggling to breathe, she said, "Oh, I am. I totally am. I love you, Shane."

His brow knit and he almost looked surprised. "Really? Still? Even though I messed up?"

She nodded. "Love doesn't just stop when someone messes up."

He looked toward his mother, then back to her. "Yeah, I guess I'm starting to understand that." Then he eased his arms around her waist. "Damn, Candy Cane, I love you, too. And I'm gonna be a better man for you, I promise."

"You're already a good enough man for me, Shane."

And in response to that, Shane took her hand and drew her into the recesses of the barn, finding a shadowy corner—where he lifted both hands to her face and kissed her. Slow, sweet, deep, and in a way that trickled all the way to the tips of her fingers and toes, hitting a few particularly sensitive hot spots in between.

No moment had ever been more perfect for Candice, and after it ended, she said, "I thought I'd never get to kiss you again."

"Me too. And I'm so glad I came to my senses. Now I get to kiss you forever. And other stuff, too," he added with a wink. After which he looked around and said, "I know we should stay awhile, but all I can think about is getting you home."

"Impatient, are we?" she asked.

"Can't help it," he told her with his usual naughty grin. "Remember? Candy canes are my weakness."

Epilogue

One year later

'Twas the night before Christmas and all through the town

Cats were climbing onto dinner tables and being told to get down.

The stockings were all hung by the chimney with glee

With thanks that this year's Christmas was more drama-free.

Anita baked a ham and when Shane heard a clatter,

He and Walter ran to the kitchen to see what was the matter,

But alas, 'twas only Holly the cat causing a stir

And Candice said, "I hope the ham won't be covered with kitty fur."

Jenny, Mick, and Dustin were there, too, ready for dinner to be served,

And Anita finally had the family she deserved.

It had been a busy year with much to celebrate,

Shane had opened a body shop in Destiny and it was doing great!

He'd started the business after the Montana house sold,

And he'd begun to make peace about his dad and the things he'd been told.

Duke and Anna had gotten married up on Half Moon Hill

And Amy and Logan had a beautiful, healthy baby girl.

Candice had stopped writing manuals to take over the *Destiny Gazette*,

And her life was more fulfilling than she'd ever dreamed it could get.

But by the time dinner was over and the gift-giving through

Shane was more than ready to say goodnight and adieu.

He wanted Candice home and snug in their bed

As naughty visions of candy canes danced in his head.

When, after some hot chocolate, Shane suggested they say goodbye,

Candice said, "You're right—Grampy and Edna are expecting us for pie!"

The Christmas Eve festivities stretched on and on

And Shane began to give up on having naughty Christmas fun,

When what to his wandering eye did appear

But his Candy Cane wearing something red and sexy and sheer.

With a seductive grin, he said, "Finally, I get you
   alone.
"Well, except for the weird cat staring at us," he
   groaned.
But cats and delays aside, he wouldn't have traded
   this life
Where he'd learned about love and joy and what's
   right.
And he was heard to proclaim as he turned out the
   lights,
"A merry Destiny Christmas to all, and to all a good
   night."